XENOPHOBIA

Peter Cawdron
thinkingscifi.wordpress.com

Copyright Peter Cawdron 2013
All rights reserved.

The right of Peter Cawdron to be identified as the author of this work has been asserted by him in accordance with the Copyright, Designs and Patents Act 1988.

First published as an eBook by Peter Cawdron
US Edition

ISBN-13: 978-1490568232

ISBN-10: 1490568239

All the characters in this book are fictitious, and any resemblance to actual persons living or dead is purely coincidental.

Cover art by Jason Gurley. Used with permission.

""We can judge our progress by the courage of our questions and the depth of our answers, our willingness to embrace what is true rather than what feels good."

— Carl Sagan

CHAPTER 01: MALAWI

Dust kicks off the dry grassy field. Fine grains of sand blow outward with the downdraft from the twin rotor blades of the incoming Osprey.

Standing on the outskirts of a small African village, Dr. Elizabeth Bower shields her face from the sting of thousands of tiny dust particles, loose strips of grass, sand, dirt, and the occasional twig shooting across the ground as the Osprey touches down.

Liz doesn't like the Osprey. She loves flying in helicopters, and doesn't mind airplanes, even uncomfortable military flights, but a craft that's both a helicopter *and* a plane just doesn't sit right with her. Thoughts bounce around her head. If they were spoken aloud, she'd sound like a Luddite. Last year, on a flight from Kasungu, the Osprey she was on suffered an engine failure and that scared the hell out of her.

Goddamn flying coffin!

The pilot powers down the engine and the winds drop from those of a hurricane to a blustery summer storm.

Four soldiers run in as the tailgate on the Osprey lowers and the whine of the engines falls away. Dr. Liz follows them with one arm wrapped around her waist, preventing her white medical coat from flapping in the wind.

There isn't much point in wearing a clean white coat outside the village hospital, particularly on the rough stretch of ground that has been officially designated as LZ, the landing zone, but the military make such a big deal about their dress codes. Whether they're wearing fatigues, combat gear, or going for a run in their PT shorts, uniforms play an important part in their routine, and subconsciously, Liz feels she has to comply. For her, the knee-length jacket is a uniform of sorts, and she's noticed the soldiers respond to the white jacket, affording her respect on those few occasions when they interact.

For the most part, the soldiers stay out on patrol in the jungle, returning only once or twice a month. But when they return, the choppers come, bringing much-needed supplies. Liz has found that if she dresses in civvies, as they call her floral skirts and colorful T-shirts, there's a subtle, but perceptible, change in their demeanor. It's as though they're talking down to her. That some African villager is lying on a cot before her with abscessed sores or a broken leg seems incidental. With their military training, uniforms speak louder than either her words or actions. Apparently, eight years of medical school doesn't count for much if you don't dress properly.

Technically, *Médecins Sans Frontières* is an NGO, a non-governmental organization independent of the military and any particular country. Liz likes the autonomy that gives her. Her supplies normally come overland, but UN officials regularly turn a blind eye to packing a few crates on the military resupply runs, and that gives her more flexibility.

Médecins Sans Frontières means Doctors Without Borders, but as Liz understands all too well, it's impossible to be entirely apolitical. Even with field hospitals operating on both sides of the conflict, everyone sides with someone, and the US military, operating under the UN flag, has kept the rebels at bay for over two years, allowing her to run an effective vaccine program among the locals, something her companions to the north haven't been able to do. Tensions still simmer in the highlands, yet the civil war is all but over.

As she runs up to the open cargo hold of the Osprey, Liz expects to see her monthly resupply crate wrapped in the usual absurd amount of transparent plastic, full of boxes with medical markings. She's ordered more cots, mosquito nets, bandages, along with the standard complement of medicines and birthing packs for the pregnant women in the outlying villages.

The loadmaster walks down the steel ramp.

What the—

Troops line both sides of the Osprey, facing in toward each other. There are no crates.

Her heart sinks. There's no resupply coming. In that fraction of a second, Liz is already thinking about how she can stretch her existing supplies, and who she can scream at over the radio.

In the heat of the moment, Liz wants to rip into the quartermaster back at headquarters, but she knows it's all bluster. She's a lion roaring in the depths of her mind, but on the phone she'll be polite, realizing the admin team would've done everything possible to get those supplies to her. Resignation sets in, followed by the realization she needs to be resourceful and make do with what she has.

Sergeant Jameson seems as surprised as she is, which is a little bemusing. He stands there scratching his head. With his short, blonde hair shaved close to the scalp and his skin pink from the African sun, Jameson looks more British than American.

4

Liz could be mistaken for one of the natives. Her grandparents immigrated to England in the 1980s and she grew up hearing stories of the sun-soaked continent. Her dark skin allows her to blend in with the villagers. She keeps her curly hair shorter than most of the women in the village, giving her almost boyish looks, although the curves of her body dispel any doubt about her gender. The only thing that distinguishes Liz as a foreigner is her British accent and Western clothing.

"Where's the resupply?" Jameson yells over the whine of the idling engines, although Liz doubts he's talking about her medicine. Jameson's after more rations and ammunition.

They're a strange lot, the soldiers. Their uniform patches distinguish them as Rangers, but they keep to themselves, even when they're around the village.

Liz can't figure them out.

The Americans are all business. They play with the kids in the village from time to time, and talk warmly with the elders, but they're aloof, it's as though they're just passing through.

The soldiers never really talk to Liz in anything other than an official capacity, and she isn't sure if they're embarrassed by *Médecins,* or if they just aren't confident dealing with an NGO. Perhaps it's her. Maybe she's the prickly one.

Liz would like to follow that line of reasoning further, but now is not the time, and her confusion about the supply situation consumes her thoughts. One thing she knows—the Americans are good at their job. The rebels have stuck to the tablelands, rarely venturing in force into the valley for fear of the Rangers.

Jameson yells at the loadmaster, "We were supposed to get parts for the M107."

"Get your men on board," the loadmaster yells back, ignoring him. "We've got orders to pull you and your team out of here. We're headed to Dar es Salaam in Tanzania, and from there onto the USS William Lawrence."

"You were supposed to be dropping off supplies," Jameson shouts over the whine of the engines.

"Not anymore. Change of orders. Get your kit together. You too, Doc."

"I don't think you understand," Liz yells, struggling to be heard over the turboprops still fanning the air. "I'm with *Médecins Sans Frontières*, part of UNVASCO."

"They're pulling everyone out," the loadmaster yells. "UN, US, French, Australians, military and civilian, NGOs, the works. *Everyone's* leaving."

"What?" Liz yells, unable to accept this bombshell. "Do you realize what'll happen here if we leave? Do you understand the kind of bloodshed that'll be unleashed? Which dick-weed, pencil-pushing, brain-dead bureaucrat dreamed up this stupid idea?"

"The Secretary-General of the United Nations, Ma'am. At the request of the Security Council."

"And that's supposed to impress me?" Liz asks, furious.

The loadmaster ignores her, talking to Jameson, which pisses her off even more.

Typical bloody army! No consideration for anyone or anything other than their damn stupid orders. Never any thought about right or wrong—just, yes sir, three bags full, sir!

"Get your men to square away their kit and get on board."

Jameson leads Liz away from the Osprey. He must sense her rage as he takes her gently by the arm. His men follow close behind. Liz isn't happy about being patronized, but she can see Jameson's being considerate, and she's pleased to get away from what she considers to be a ridiculously expensive flying metal fortress.

What would the world be like if this kind of money was spent on helping, rather than hurting people? And yet even as these thoughts blaze across her mind, she knows she's being both irrationally angry and naive. Such thinking's an oversimplification. Not everyone chooses to play nice, and reality often forces a response of kill or be killed. If only reason could prevail over our brute nature, but it doesn't, and it won't. As much as it pains her to admit it, shepherds are needed to keep the wolves from their prey—only both sides think *they're* the ones holding the crook and staff.

"Listen, doc," Jameson says. "I need you to calm down."

Somehow, Liz finds the fortitude to bite her lip and not yell at him.

Jameson's a good man. Breathe, Liz. Deep breaths. Get through the moment. Push through the anger, or you won't be thinking clearly.

Liz doesn't know how anyone can think straight with the high-pitched whine of the engines and the wind constantly swirling around them. She can't.

The loadmaster follows a few paces behind them.

"Have the men stow their kit and meet back here in five," Jameson says to Private Bosco.

"You're going to leave?" Liz asks, her mind reeling at the prospect of being left alone in Africa. "You're just going to up and abandon the hospital?"

"You heard the loadmaster. We've got orders."

"Orders?" Liz says with disbelief. "You and your bloody orders. Why can't anyone ever be ordered to *think*? Why is it always 'Do this—do that?' Why is it never 'Do what's right,' huh?"

Dr. Kowalski comes up beside them, having seen her berating the sergeant. Kowalski's an older man of European descent with thick gray hair tossed carelessly to one side. He wears small round glasses like those immortalized by John Lennon, only they make his face look large by comparison. In any other context, he could be mistaken for a mad scientist, only his demeanor is such that Liz doubts he could hurt a fly.

"What's going on?"

"They're pulling us out, Mitch. Can you believe that? No explanation as to why, just some vague bullshit—Orders to evacuate."

"That doesn't make any sense. What about our patients? What about the staff?"

"I've got to call this in to Kasungu," Liz growls, turning back to the loadmaster. "I want to talk to someone in charge."

"There's no one in Kasungu," the loadmaster says. "They pulled them out two days ago."

"Why the hell hasn't anyone told us?"

Elizabeth Bower is fuming. Her hands sit defiantly on her hips. Her world's falling apart.

"I don't know. They were supposed to."

"Well, I'm not leaving," Liz replies stubbornly.

"You have to," the loadmaster says emphatically.

"I'll have you know, the military has no jurisdiction over an NGO medical mission. You're here for our security, nothing more. We're answerable to the UN High Commission in Lilongwe, not some idiot thousands of miles away in New York."

"You don't understand," the loadmaster replies, but Liz cuts him off before he can continue.

"I don't understand?" she yells, her finger just inches from his nose. "Oh, I understand exactly what this is. Some politician's losing votes over bodybags and decides another Bosnia or Rwanda's nothing compared to saving their sorry ass in the next election!

"You can't give me one good reason why you're pulling out, other than that you're following orders. I'm sorry, but that's just not good enough. As a doctor, I have a duty of care for my patients and my staff. I will not just up and leave. I cannot abandon them."

She's in full voice. Liz didn't get to be in charge of a field hospital in the middle of a smoldering civil war by being a wallflower. She has no problem raising her voice.

"You and I can run. It's easy for us. We just hop on some bloody flying contraption and disappear into the sunset. But what about them?"

Liz points at several of the nurses standing outside the hospital tent, watching the commotion from a distance.

"You and I might be able to wave a passport and hop on a flight to Europe or the US, but they can't. I've got a responsibility to support my African staff. I won't leave them to the rebels."

"We've an obligation to care for these people," Dr. Kowalski adds, adjusting his glasses as he speaks. His voice is calm. Liz can see he's trying to take the emotion out of the moment. "If we simply up and go, the militia will come riding in here and steal our supplies. God knows what they'll do to the villagers that have collaborated with us. You can't pull us out like this. Surely, there's been a mistake. There must be some other way."

Jameson's unusually quiet. Liz can see him weighing his options mentally.

"But they're Africans," the loadmaster protests, pointing at the nurses and the medical orderly. "They can blend in with the rest of the natives."

"It's not that simple," Dr. Kowalski explains. "If someone stumbles in here with a broken arm or a bullet wound, we'll treat them regardless of where they've come from. The rebels know that. They may not dare attack you openly, but don't think for a minute that they're not out there watching and waiting. They know about everything that goes on in this village. They'll stroll in with a bag of seed, or some other pretense to keep tabs on people. This is exactly what they've been holding out for. They haven't been trying to *beat* the UN, merely outlast it. You're playing right into their hands."

"It's not my problem," the loadmaster snaps. "You've got five minutes to get on that aircraft or I'm leaving without you." He looks for support from Jameson, but the sergeant remains silent.

Liz feels like screaming. The loadmaster's being completely unreasonable.

Kowalski mutters under his breath, "Typical bloody bureaucracy."

The loadmaster isn't going to waste any more time. He turns and jogs back over to the open bay of the Osprey. Soldiers mill around the back of the aircraft, taking the opportunity to stretch their legs, or to urinate in the bushes on the edge of the clearing, which infuriates the loadmaster. He starts yelling at them, corralling them back into the aircraft.

"Like herding cats," Kowalski says, laughing as he watches the loadmaster waving his arms and calling for the troops to re-board the Osprey. "So, what do we do, Liz?"

Liz looks at Jameson. His eyes seem to say something his lips can't.

"We'll be fine," she says. Her voice sounds convincing, but she knows her bravado's sorely misplaced.

Jameson's silent, his eyes focus straight ahead, looking into the middle distance. If she didn't know better, she'd think he was being berated by a general.

Liz feels guilty, as though she's put Jameson in a difficult position. She says, "Honestly. You should follow your orders. We'll make do."

Standing there in his camouflage gear, Jameson flips his regulation-issue army cap on his head. His eyes focus intently on her as his lips pull tight. Liz feels a little intimidated by him. She has to say something, to articulate some kind of plan. Her mind races, scrambling for options.

Best laid plans of mice and men—that's what the military do, right? They always have a plan. There's always maps, compasses, and hastily drawn lines. Liz needs a plan. She's determined to offer something to break the impasse.

"We'll bring in a couple of trucks from Mzimba—drive the staff and patients down to Ksaungu, where there'll be more treatment options.

"The rebels will leave the villagers alone, but if they catch anyone that worked in the hospital, they'll kill them for mingling with us foreign devils. We've got to get our staff out of here. We owe them that much."

"And from Ksaungu?" Jameson asks.

"From Ksaungu, they'll be able to make their way overland to Mozambique. Mitch and I will drive on to Lilongwe. There'll be someone there. The UN isn't going to abandon the capital. We'll be able to get a flight out to Kenya or South Africa."

Private Bosco comes up beside Sergeant Jameson. "We're ready."

"Bring the guys in," Jameson replies.

With a yell, Bosco calls the other soldiers over.

The loadmaster stands by the cockpit of the Osprey, talking with the pilots. Jameson jogs over to him.

Liz can't hear what's being said, but the exchange is heated, with arms flying as the two men go toe-to-toe, pointing, waving, yelling. Snippets float on the breeze, barely audible above the whine of the idling engines.

"She's a goddamn Brit. Let the SAS take care of her... You're disobeying a direct order... We've no idea if there'll even *be* any more evacuation flights!"

Alile runs over to talk to Liz and Kowalski.

Alile's the most senior nurse in the hospital. She's native to Malawi but received her formal medical training as a registered nurse in South Africa. Liz knows Alile's concerned about the young woman with the premature baby.

For her own part, Liz is in a tailspin. She's trying to gauge her own thinking, trying to detach herself from her emotional outrage and think clearly about the implications of the decision before her. Choosing between staying and going could be the difference between life and death for Kowalski and her. The easy thing to do would be to board the Osprey, but that would betray every principle she holds as a physician.

"Is everything okay?" Alile asks. Her dark skin glistens in the sunlight. Colorful beads twinkle on her scalp, woven into her tightly braided hair.

Most of the African women keep their hair in plaits, with braids running in cornrows woven hard against the skull. Alile's hair looks pretty. Liz has never had time for plaits and braids—they take hours to put in, and only last a couple of weeks before they have to be painstakingly unpicked and woven in again. She doesn't see the point.

Liz can't lie to Alile.

"We've been asked to leave, but don't worry, we're not going anywhere."

"Did we at least get the powdered milk?"

Liz gestures to the empty ground around her, saying, "I'm sorry."

They had ordered milk powder to help the premature baby gain some weight. Liz feels as though she's let Alile down. Caring for a premature baby is no easy task in a Western hospital, let alone in the middle of a scorching, flyblown African summer. Even with mosquito nets and fans, insects are a real problem, carrying bacteria and causing complications for newborns.

Jameson jogs over to his waiting troops.

Alile leaves Liz and Kowalski, and walks back to join the other nurses.

Liz wants to tell her she doesn't have to go, that this isn't some exclusive foreigners-only club, but Liz understands her mindset. For Alile, there's always a sense of *us* and *them;* having US soldiers around only accentuates that perception. Liz tries to treat Alile as an equal, but the very act of making that effort reinforces the inequality between them.

Sixteen soldiers crouch on the edge of the landing zone, half-sitting on their heels, their elbows resting on their knees as they squat in front of Jameson. The sergeant explains what little he knows, as the two civilian doctors stand to one side. He says they're being pulled out because of a significant security threat being made against the US homeland, but he doesn't have any more details. Thoughts of 9/11 and the quagmires of the various wars in Iraq and Afghanistan rumble through her mind.

"So I'm asking for volunteers," Jameson adds after walking the troops through her plan to evacuate by land to Ksaungu and then move on to the capital, Lilongwe. "You should know, the crew of the Osprey have radioed our intentions through to theater command. They're not happy with the decision, but they're deferring to our judgment on the ground. Command says the last flight out of Lilongwe is scheduled in two days. If we make that, we get a free ride. If we don't, we're on a forced march across the mountains."

Liz is stunned. She assumed they were on their own. She expected Jameson to blindly follow orders. Her admiration for his professionalism as a soldier grows in bounds.

"What kind of distance are we talking about, Sarge?"

"A hundred klicks to Mozambique. Another three hundred to the coast."

"Finally, a chance for a little sightseeing," Private Mathers says. "I like it."

The soldier next to him elbows him, saying, "You would."

"And a chance for a little action. I'm in," Bosco says.

Mathers says, "If we miss the flight, we get the scenic tour of Africa."

"Humping through a couple of hundred klicks. Lions. Leopards. Snakes. Thick jungle. Sounds idyllic," Smithy adds.

It's only on hearing Smithy's voice that Liz realizes Smithy's a woman. At first glance, Liz assumed Smithy was simply a shorter, less muscular male soldier, but now that she looks closely, there's no doubt about Smithy's gender. Strands of blonde hair protrude from beneath her helmet while her baggy camouflage shirt conceals the outline of her breasts. Her hands are petite.

Liz cannot imagine violence being unleashed by such slender hands. Without makeup, Smithy's face looks like that of a clean-shaven teen, but her thin lips speak with a distinctly feminine pitch.

"It's a walk in the park," Smithy continues. "An overgrown, bug-infested, leech-filled park. I love it! Hey, Elvis. Are you in for a romp in the swamp?"

"Hell, yes," Elvis says, giving Smithy a high five.

With his sideburns and diamond-rimmed sunglasses, Elvis looks out of place in army fatigues—and that's clearly the image he wants to portray. Liz has no idea whether his southern accent's genuine or put on for show, but he sounds like *The King*.

The Rangers all sport buzz cuts, all except Elvis who has a mop of hair growing above his short back and sides. How does he get away with that? There must be quite a story behind that mop!

Elvis is larger than life. He sounds and looks like his namesake, Elvis Presley, right down to his cheesy grin, complete with beautiful straight, pearly white teeth.

Elvis looks out of place in Africa. He should be on a movie set. Not her type. Too many theatrics for me, she thinks, but I'd watch the movie.

"I'm asking for two fire teams, a total of eight men," Jameson says.

Although all the hands go up, there are some that shoot up like a pheasant being flushed by a golden retriever. Jameson calls out those soldiers by name, and Liz sees their passion—their fearless sense of drive and determination, regardless of danger.

He's smart.

Liz understands precisely why Jameson wants these particular men with him, but why Smithy? Jameson selects her without hesitation, along with Elvis and Bosco.

How do you pick someone to die?

There's no way of knowing what'll happen, but the likelihood of being killed in action has easily doubled, in her rough estimation.

There are whoops and hoorays from the soldiers as names are called. Liz can't bring herself to share in their enthusiasm. Malawi is lawless. Civil wars are cruel. Death comes easy. Elvis and Bosco seem better suited to deal with this than Smithy. Smithy, though, grins, and Liz can see she relishes the opportunity for adventure.

Smithy slaps Elvis on the arm, saying, "Looks like you're stuck with me, big guy."

"Abso-damn-lutely!"

The rest of the team is dismissed and piles into the Osprey.

Jameson explains his decision to the loadmaster as Bosco scavenges a radio and extra munitions from the soldiers on the Osprey. Elvis and Smithy joke around with the other troops loading into the helicopter.

"It's your funeral, buddy," the loadmaster says to Jameson. He walks off and raises the tailgate.

Smithy jogs away from the Osprey, grinning like a little girl on Christmas Day as she rests a machine gun over her shoulder, the proud spoils of banter with several of the soldiers on board the aircraft. Elvis jokes around with her, carrying two ammunition cans for the gun.

"Goddamn it," he cries, pointing at Smithy and her newly acquired semi-automatic machine gun. "Look! It's Combat Barbie, complete with a lightweight plastic SAW."

Smithy cocks her head to one side, exaggerating her movements as she twists from her hips, looking very much like a living plastic doll. She poses for the remaining soldiers and waves with her hand, saying, "Look what's new from Mattel."

The soldiers laugh and whistle. Smithy hams up her act with a fake smile as she says, "Oh, Ken. You're an airhead... I want a divorce. Now, where did I leave my handbag?"

Even Liz can't help but smile at Smithy's routine.

Bosco jogs up behind them, grinning. He's conned someone out of a civilian band radio. He raises the radio high over his head, and the soldiers cheer as though he's holding up the Vince Lombardi Trophy.

As the turboprops on the Osprey wind up to speed, a hail of fine stones and grit again sprays out across the grassy plain. The remaining soldiers along with the two doctors move back, catching the death-defying sight of the Osprey lifting off and banking above the trees before the craft turns and flies low over the village, out across the lake toward Tanzania.

As silence falls, Liz feels a twinge of regret. Even with Jameson standing beside her in his seemingly invincible US Army uniform, she feels abandoned. And yet she knows she would've felt unbearable guilt if she had boarded that flight. Watching the Osprey disappear into the distance, she can't help but wonder if she's made a mistake, one she won't be able to take back, one that could cost them their lives.

Elvis puts on his finest Mississippi accent, waving at the troop carrier as he calls out, "Y'all come back now, ya hear?"

That brings a smile to her face.

Jameson, though, wastes no time.

"Bosco, get on the net and see if you can figure out what the hell's got everyone so spooked. Elvis, take Mathers, Jones and Smithy—Go and get those trucks from Mzimba. Beg, borrow, steal. Do whatever it takes, but make sure there's plenty of diesel.

"Davidson, Chalmers and Phelps—recon the area and start thinking about approaches, defensive positions, and fields of fire."

The soldiers disperse as Jameson escorts Liz and Kowalski to the makeshift hospital, a series of three tents on the edge of the village with its grass topped mud huts and low stone walls. He speaks as they walk, briefing the doctors in a formal tone.

"The rebels on the tableland are going to see our troops pulling out. The fox is going to assume the chicken coop's open. I doubt they'll waste any time. If we can, I'd like to move out before nightfall."

"We'll get everyone ready," Liz replies, flicking the dust out of her hair. "Mitch, if you work with the nurses, I'll pack up the medicine and burn our records."

Time crawls.

Jameson helps fold up cots as Liz packs vials of medicine into a wooden crate.

A couple of hours pass before Bosco comes running in with the CB radio.

"You've got to hear this. There's some serious shit going down."

The radio signal's weak, with static breaking up the words. Bosco turns up the volume. Jameson leans on a box, while Liz sits on the edge of a rickety desk.

"...impeachment proceedings have begun in earnest within the House of Representatives."

A British reporter with a soft, feminine voice speaks over the top of a heated exchange between several distinctly American voices. Liz recognizes the southern accent of the US President.

"You have no right to sit here in judgment of my decisions. I do not recognize the legitimacy of these proceedings and will continue to press both the Senate and the Supreme Court to continue to recognize me as Commander-in-Chief of the United States of America."

"Response from Senator Johansen," the reporter says rapidly, identifying the next speaker while trying not to talk over the swell of anger and emotion growing within the argument.

"Article Four of the Outer Space Treaty, a binding international agreement that has been in effect for over fifty years, outlaws the militarization of space and the deployment of nuclear weapons beyond Earth."

The senator slows his speech, deliberately emphasizing his point.

"Mr. President, your lawless, reckless arrogance has plunged the United States into the abyss… never before… condemnation… Russia, China and…"

The signal breaks up, cutting into static as Liz strains to pick out fragments of each sentence.

The President replies, "… will not be lectured… easy to sit there and criticize me without the weight of responsibility on your shoulders… We have squandered our only opportunity to gain a strategic advantage in the event of hostilities… There will be war, mark my words. History has shown time and again that war is the inevitable consequence of a clash of cultures."

Reception on the radio fades.

"What the fuck?" Jameson cries as it becomes clear they've lost the signal.

"Oh, it gets better," Bosco replies. "You think that's fucked up, wait until you hear the rest of this shit."

He fiddles with the radio, changing the station.

Another British voice breaks through the static, which surprises Liz as she assumes Bosco's hunting for local radio stations or broadcasts from South Africa. She isn't sure, but both channels seem to be part of the BBC World Service. Again, the reporter's accent lends an air of authenticity to the commentary, one Liz finds convincing.

"The revelation of a secret government project concealing the existence…"

Static tears the sentence in two. Liz strains to hear what's being said.

"… has shaken not only the US but the world at large. For seven months, the President and his cabinet presided over what can only be described as a conspiracy of silence.

"Rumors of intimidation, career assassination, physical assault, incarceration on false charges and even murder threaten to topple the administration.

"The evidence is damning. President Addison and his security detail caught in a midnight meeting with David Alexander Wilson, ex-CIA chief of station for the United Kingdom and alleged ringmaster of the clandestine project."

"I don't get it," Jameson says. "What the hell is all this about?"

"Wait for it," Bosco replies, his words are terse and abrupt. He clearly doesn't want to talk over the broadcast.

"NASA officials vetoed the launch of the Orion spacecraft two weeks ago, with NASA administrative director Philip Monroe citing technical concerns over the rocket booster fuel pump, but an inside source has leaked telemetry readouts from rocket tests revealing no faults in the system, raising questions as to why the launch was scrubbed.

"With the arrest of David Alexander Wilson in Texas two days ago for the murder of NASA director Monroe, the house of cards surrounding the President finally came tumbling down. FBI surveillance has linked Wilson with the President, as well as with Monroe, exposing the conspiracy."

"Jesus!" Jameson mutters under his breath.

"Yesterday, the veil of secrecy was lifted when Congress formally impeached the President as an accessory to murder, with a secondary charge relating to the unlawful deployment of nuclear weapons in space. Further charges are expected as the investigation continues.

"Ostensibly, the Orion was scheduled to explore Cruithne, an asteroid that has been erroneously referred to as Earth's second moon. In reality, the Orion was tasked to intercept the alien spacecraft before it reached Earth's orbit."

"What the—" Jameson says, catching himself and avoiding talking over the radio.

"NASA director Monroe had objected to the inclusion of a 15 megaton thermonuclear warhead onboard the Orion, and was about to go public with the revelation, when he was murdered by Wilson.

"Details are still emerging, but it seems the crew of the Orion were not aware of their deadly payload. President Addison has admitted to his involvement in authorizing the placement of the nuclear device on the Orion as a contingency in the event of hostilities with the alien spacecraft, saying the inclusion of the bomb is not an overtly hostile act in itself, but Congress disagrees.

"The executive branch of government has been paralyzed, awaiting the outcome of impeachment proceedings. Congress contends the President exceeded his executive authority by placing a nuclear weapon on a civilian spacecraft. The Special Legal Council, established by the Senate, further contends that such an act is tantamount to a declaration of war against an unknown alien race.

"Around the world, condemnation has been swift, with the British government saying such an act threatens the very existence of life on Earth. While French ambassador…"

The broadcast descends into static again. Words fade in and out. Fragments come through, but there's barely enough content to grasp any meaning.

"Beijing has lodged a formal complaint… following UN Security Council resolution 2992, intended to limit interaction with the alien spacecraft until such… President is defiant, insisting his actions were in the national… unilateral action voted down by Congress… ultimate decision may rest with the nine members of the Supreme Court, five of whom are Republican appointees…"

Bosco slaps the side of the radio, shaking it in an irrational effort to improve the reception.

"As protests within the US mount, Congress has authorized the withdrawal of American forces from hot spots around the globe, bolstering its forces in country… National Guard… mobilized in support of police… Russia has withdrawn… Pakistan…"

Bosco turns up the radio volume but that makes the static worse. Slowly, the broadcast signal fades to a hiss.

CHAPTER 02: NIGHTFALL

Liz is troubled.

Keeping a stiff upper lip is stupid—of all the dumb British stereotypes to cling to when there's a goddamn alien spacecraft approaching Earth, but one must not be seen to be rattled. Hah!

She busies herself, throwing excess supplies on a cot, and wondering if the rebels will torch the hospital, or simply raid supplies.

Such a waste.

Her mind drifts.

Oh, to sit down in front of a television and be glued to the screen watching this soap opera unfold! Oh, to be paralyzed into inaction for all but bladder and bowel movements, and the occasional snack or cup of tea! To be lulled into in a vegetative state, hanging on every word of some network specialist who was never as much of a specialist as today. Who the hell specializes in first contact with ET anyway? Liz ponders these ideas as she packs medicine in small wooden crates.

She smiles, realizing how stupid it is to bemoan being stuck in Africa at a time of international crisis. International? Interplanetary? Interstellar? The television pundits would already have some suave term for the panic gripping the planet. Not that the birds and bees would notice—or cats and dogs, or any other species beyond *Homo sapiens*.

As much as she tries not to care, Liz feels torn by her isolation from the civilized world. *Bloody radio! Too many questions. I can't ask a stupid radio questions.*

Her eyes cast toward the setting sun lighting up the sky with pink hues high in the stratosphere. The thought of a spaceship out there somewhere beyond the haze is both exciting and terrifying. For once, she wishes she was back in London, if only to be closer to the news.

Somehow, knowing something, anything, seems better than being stuck in the middle of the jungle knowing nothing about what's going on, but it isn't. How much does *anyone* really know about what's happening on board an alien spaceship with Earth in its sights? Who are they? Why have they come here? Does anyone know? NASA? ESA? All they can do is guess. There's probably not much more to know, and not knowing anything is torture.

Liz thought she was ready for anything. Ever since she was a child, she brimmed with confidence, but now uncertainty clouds her thinking. Having spent a couple of years in Malawi, she thought she'd seen the worst of the civil war. She has never actually been on the front line, but she's treated those who have. Deep down, she likes to believe nothing can shake her, yet now her world seems to be tilting sideways—like the deck of the Titanic slowly slipping beneath the waves—straighten those deckchairs, Liz, while the band plays *Nearer My God to Thee*.

Liz busies herself organizing patients, assessing who can flee with the villagers, and prioritizing those in need of specialized care. She moves between villagers, talking with the remaining few patients as they lie on mats stretched out on the grass, waiting for the evacuation to begin. Most of the able-bodied patients have hobbled off with the rest of the tribe, along with several patients she had expected to stay. One man recovering from tuberculosis shouldn't have gone anywhere, but he feels he's better off with his family, and Liz can't fault him for that.

Liz is helpless as the exodus unfolds before her.

The village chief walks up to her and says, "The rebels will be angry. They'll burn our huts. My people will wait in the bush. Like all storms, this will blow over, and we'll return. We will rebuild."

Liz nods, unable to speak, knowing words are meaningless. There's nothing she can say that'll change anything.

The chief rests his aged hand on her shoulder, patting her gently. He understands her silence. He must see the heartache in her eyes.

So strange to be comforted by a man who has nothing. His home is about to burn. All he has left in this world is what little he can carry with him, yet his frail malnourished frame is resolute. He's at peace.

Their eyes lock. Then he turns and walks away, joining the last of the villagers walking toward the distant grassy plains.

Long shadows stretch across the land as the sun sets beyond the mountains.

Physically, nothing's changed since this morning, and yet nothing's the same.

Her hope of packing up the hospital and relocating is futile. The UN won't be back—not any time soon.

Jameson walks up behind her, saying, "We should leave the hospital tents standing. Give the rebels plenty to burn. Better they focus on the village than the people."

For Liz, it's heartbreaking to realize all her work is about to be destroyed.

"The rebels will be lazy," he says. "If they have easy targets, they'll attack. If they have to work for their prey, they'll soon tire. With the villagers going into the bush for a week or so, I figure the tribe will be safe."

"Yes," Liz says, nodding as Jameson walks over to talk to Bosco.

"Where the hell is Elvis?" Jameson asks Bosco, but Liz is barely aware of his frustration. She's distracted by the setting sun. It's beautiful—which is incongruous with life in Malawi. Brilliant reds and purples stretch across the sky, fading into the dark blue and then the black of the night.

The village is all but empty.

Outside the hospital, three nurses, an orderly, and a dozen patients wait for the trucks. One of the patients has a broken leg, several are recovering from malaria, while another's recovering from a severe bout of dysentery and has lost a lot of strength. She's improving steadily. Once she regains her muscle mass she'll be fine.

The eleven AIDS cases in the hospital, all with advanced symptoms, have left with their families. They said if they're to die, they want to die where they were born, not hundreds of miles away.

One of her patients is a sixteen year old girl with a premature baby born at roughly thirty weeks.

The baby's doing well, but should be in an intensive care unit. His breathing's shallow. His tiny hands move in spasms, rather than in a coordinated motion, and Liz fears there's been some brain damage from oxygen starvation during the protracted delivery, but such a diagnosis is beyond the scope of her equipment. She hopes he will show signs of normalizing as he grows in size. For now, it's a case of waiting, keeping him on a drip feed, and keeping his environment clean. His young mother, still very much a child herself, rarely leaves his side.

Liz buries herself in the concerns of her patients, even though her nurses are quite capable of caring for the handful of patients. She's trying to distract herself from the implications of having been abandoned as the world turns its focus out into space.

She sits down with Alile, watching as Kowalski finishes packing medical supplies outside one of the tents. "The nurses are talking," Alile says. "They say there's a spaceship from another world."

"Apparently there is," Liz replies with a forced smile. "It's hard to imagine, isn't it?"

Alile nods, asking, "Do you think they'll be friendly?"

"I hope so, but I really don't know. We're in uncharted territory."

"In Africa, we have a saying," Alile says. "*To get lost is to learn the way.*"

"I like that. When it comes to dealing with creatures from another planet, we're certainly lost, so I guess you're right—we'll learn along the way." Liz likes Alile. She sees a lot of herself in the young woman—a desire for knowledge, a desire to help others, a desire to change the world, even if it's only one person at a time. "The funny thing is," she continues, "I've been in Africa for five years, mostly in Kenya, but in the almost two years I've been in Malawi, I've barely thought about home—not the place, not the people, not even my family. Oh, sure, I get letters from them, and the odd present comes through the mail, but all of a sudden some spaceship arrives from another planet and I can't stop thinking about home. How strange is that?"

"It's not strange," Alile replies. "*Water that runs slow runs deep.*"

Liz isn't sure what Alile means by that, and is about to ask her to elaborate when Elvis pulls up in the squad Hummer, pulling a truck with a tow rope.

"We've got problems," is all Liz overhears as the private speaks with Jameson.

Liz feels she needs to be involved even though there's nothing she can do, and she'll probably only get in the way. It seems as though this is all her fault. She desperately wants to fix things, only this is no broken leg she can set.

"There were three trucks, none of them in working order. We salvaged what we could, and dragged the best of them back here, an old Deuce. Smithy says the transmission's gone, and there's a crack in the engine block, but she says she can get her working again."

"How long?" Jameson asks.

Elvis turns to Smithy as the young private walks up beside them, saying, "Three, four hours, if everything goes well."

"Okay, so worst case, eight to ten hours. Looks like we're going to be here for the night. We're going to need to set up some defensive positions.

"Doc, you're going to want to get your people into the village, behind the low stone walls. If we get into a firefight, keep your head down."

"Understood."

Gratitude sweeps over her. It's reassuring to see how calmly the soldiers deal with the disruption to their plans and the sudden possibility of violence. Their confidence gives her comfort, and her mind boggles at the realization her headstrong stubbornness could have caused Kowalski and her to be stranded alone in the village.

In the distance, most of the villagers are making their way down the grassy slope with their meager possessions wrapped in bundles on their shoulders, or balanced on their heads. The men herd cattle before them, kicking up the dry dust as they slap the ground with sticks. The sound drives the cattle on.

Shadows give way to the night.

The odd villager moves between the huts, either hiding possessions, or packing up cooking equipment.

Elvis uses the Hummer to pull the truck onto a dusty patch of ground normally covered in market stalls. A diesel generator starts up. Lights push back the night, attracting swarms of insects. Elvis mounts three lights on poles around the truck.

Smithy and he work on the engine, lifting the hood and crawling underneath the old truck as they seek to fix what looks like a classic American army vehicle from World War II. The truck can't be that old, although in Africa, anything's possible. Certainly, Elvis doesn't look out of place standing next to the olive truck, with its knobby tires and high wheel arches.

Liz can hear Smithy and Elvis joking with each other as they work. "Pass me a wrench," Smithy says, her feet sticking out from beneath the vehicle. Elvis is too busy looking at himself in a cracked wing mirror. He runs his hands through his hair, slicking back his dark locks.

"What the hell are you putting in your hair?" Smithy asks, her dusty face appearing from beneath the truck.

"Brake fluid."

"You fucking idiot!" Smithy replies, half laughing. Such strong language sounds strange coming from her baby face. "We *need* brakes. Don't go bleeding them dry for your goddamn hair!"

She disappears beneath the truck again as Elvis replies, "I can't help it if I'm sexy and you're not."

Smithy calls out, "Did you say hot?"

"You heard what you wanted to hear, baby... You know you want some of the sugar man."

"Hand me that wrench, you loser," Smithy replies. They both laugh. Elvis hums a tune. Liz can't quite make out the song as she walks past, but she's sure she knows the artist, and he hasn't been alive for decades.

"Hey, baby."

Liz knows exactly what's going on. This is all an act. Elvis is fishing for a response, trying to bait her. He must've guessed she's not one to condone sexism, and ordinarily she'd jump down his throat. Tonight, however, the pressure of the moment elicits a different response, one tempered by her appreciation of how the soldiers are sticking their necks out for her and her team.

"I am *not*," she says with a deliberate but polite smile, "your baby." That final word resonates only as a reference to newborns in her mind.

"Sure thing," Elvis replies with a swagger in his motion. "Whatever you say, sweet lips!"

Liz pauses for a moment, looking down at her feet, trying to compose herself. She isn't sure whether to be angry, or to laugh. She points her finger at him, shaking it softly, and smiling as she turns and walks on. "You're outrageous!" It's the accent—his Southern drawl. Liz just can't take Elvis seriously.

"She's got your measure," Smithy adds, laughing. Elvis grins.

Jameson sits on a stone wall, his M4 rifle leaning beside him. Liz wanders over. "Mind if I join you?"

"Nope."

She sits down beside him, looking out across the valley toward the tableland. Dry grasslands give way to dense jungle, leading up to the mountain plateau. "This isn't a good idea, is it?"

"Nope."

Well, he's honest. What else could he say? It's only after she's asked that question she realizes how silly her comment must sound to a soldier that's just turned down a free ride out of a war zone. Jameson chews on the end of a long blade of grass. He seems lost in thought.

"Is that all you're going to say?"

"Nope," Jameson replies, grinning.

"Very funny."

He smiles. "You see the dirt track leading down through the jungle?"

"Yeah," Liz replies, struggling to make out sections of the road as it winds its way through the distant highlands.

"At least a dozen trucks have driven down there in the last hour. Our friends are on the move, spreading out in force."

"That's not good, is it?" As the words leave her lips, she knows what's coming.

"Nope."

"What do you think'll happen?"

"Oh," Jameson replies. "I think all hell's about to break loose. I'm just hoping we're far enough away that we don't get too much attention too soon."

Liz is silent. Jameson picks up on her concern. "Bosco got through to Af-Com. The task force is already heading north, but there's a destroyer bringing up the rear, just off the coast of Madagascar. If we miss the flight from Lilongwe, they'll dispatch a helicopter once they're in range. We'll get your people down to Ksaungu, and assess the situation from there."

"What about all this other stuff?"

"What? The aliens?"

"Yeah," Liz replies, leaning back on her arms, and enjoying the cool wind cutting through the stifling heat of the day.

"I hardly believe it myself. Seems surreal. I try not to think about it too much. I need to focus on here and now. Once we get out of here, there'll be time to think about that. For now, it's not a factor."

Liz nods in silent agreement.

"And you? What do you think?" Jameson asks. "Do you think they're anything like the movies?"

Liz laughs. "Oh, no. I'm not sure what to think, but I doubt they're anything like what we see in Hollywood. I just can't imagine an intelligent alien species traveling a bazillion miles through space to blow up the White House, draw crop circles, and conduct anal probes on rednecks!"

Jameson laughs. "Yeah, seems pretty silly doesn't it? I wonder what they'll make of our movies."

"They'll think we have an overactive imagination."

"We do," Jameson replies.

Jameson's surprisingly relaxed for a soldier stranded in the middle of a civil war. Sitting there beside him, Liz doesn't feel compelled to talk. She's sure she could sit there silently for the next ten minutes, and neither of them would feel out of place, although she's curious about his thinking. The tone of her voice drops to just above a whisper, allowing her voice to carry genuine concern.

"You and your men are very calm, given the circumstances."

"You learn not to stew in the Rangers." Jameson could be talking about gardening. "Most people think the army's about combat, but the truth is, firefights last five to ten minutes, maybe half an hour, rarely longer than that. Firefights are few and far between. More often than not, we're marching or hiking, scouting or tracking. The glamor's quickly replaced with boredom. Excitement's the rare exception to mundane routines, so we learn to take it all in our stride."

Smithy climbs over the front of the radiator on the old truck. She has her baggy shirt off. Her breasts are prominent beneath her grubby tank top, but Liz notes Elvis isn't distracted by the view. He shimmies underneath the truck, following her directions. The odd swear word drifts by. Liz catches Elvis saying, "A-huh, a-huh. I've got this bad boy. Y'all just leave this to The King."

Smithy says something in reply, but Liz doesn't catch it, something about king-ding-a-ling. They're quite the pair. Elvis is muscular and imposing, while Smithy seems fragile by comparison, but they're clearly the best of friends.

"Don't you think he's a little—" Liz pauses.

Jameson raises an eyebrow.

"—strange?" she says.

"What? Elvis?" Jameson replies softly, turning his head slightly to one side.

"Yeah."

"Oh, he's got his quirks, but he's a great soldier."

"But don't you think the whole Elvis routine is a bit, I don't know, maybe a bit immature?"

Jameson laughs. "We're all children at heart, doc."

Liz doesn't have an answer for that. She doesn't necessarily agree, but she doesn't want to say something that might offend him—this is his team.

"When did you grow up, doc?"

"What do you mean?"

"I mean, there's no line of demarcation. There's no border to cross. Yet here we are, all grown up, or at least we like to think we are.

"These guys are kids. Look at them. Most of them can't even go into a bar in the US, and yet they're old enough to die for their country.

"Take Smithy. She's barely nineteen and looks as if she'd blow over in a stiff wind, but she's as tough as nails. She'd never been outside Iowa before signing up, let alone seen waves on the ocean. Now here she is, on the other side of the world, surrounded by global political forces and tribal tensions that make no sense to the daughter of a garage mechanic, but she's got a job to do, so she gets on with it.

"As for Elvis, sure, he's a little silly at times and plays the whole rock god thing a bit too much, but in battle, there's no one else I'd rather have by my side. He's cool under fire." Jameson pauses, pulling the chewed blade of grass from his mouth and tossing it into the weeds.

Liz nods. He's asked her a good question. It's only polite to provide an answer, so she says, "For me, my childhood ended on my sixth Christmas. Girls are supposed to be quiet and subdued, but not me. I was a terror."

"I find that hard to believe, doc."

"Why? Because I'm a woman?"

"Because you seem sweet."

Liz laughs. "Oh, appearances are deceiving. I didn't end up in Africa by collecting Girl Guide patches."

"You've got me there," Jameson replies, and she can tell he's warming to her.

"Honestly, I don't know how my parents put up with me. They should've had me on Ritalin or something.

"I was a klutz, always breaking things. Never on purpose, of course, but I'd walk into a store with my school bag on my back, and my mother would cry, 'Watch out!' I'd turn, trying to avoid god-knows-what, and I'd miss whatever it was my mother feared I was about to destroy, only to have my backpack connect with a shelf on the other side of the isle, one lined with ornaments. Mom would yell at me, and I'd turn again, trying to see what had happened, only to take out the shelf I'd missed at first."

Jameson laughs as she continues. "I was oblivious. I had no idea what was going on around me."

Jameson says, "The phrase, '*a bull in a china shop,*' does spring to mind."

"Yep. That was me. But I remember that sixth Christmas as if it were yesterday. I was so excited about Santa Claus coming and dropping off presents—my presents. I'd sat on his knee at the mall. I'd told him everything I wanted. And when Christmas Eve came around, I was manic, in a good kind of way. I set out a glass of milk and a couple of cookies for Santa, just in case he got peckish on his rounds.

"My Mom sent me to bed quite late. I should've gone out like a light, but there I was, lying in bed staring wide-eyed at the ceiling. I don't know how long I lay there, but it felt like an eternity in the darkness, waiting for the sound of reindeer on the roof.

"I saw some movement in the hall outside my room, just the fleeting shadow of feet shuffling past in the soft light. Everyone was in bed, or at least I *thought* they were all in bed, so this had to be him—this had to be Santa sneaking into *my* house. My house! And I was going to catch him. I was going to go out and say hello. I was going to tell all my friends about it the next day. *I* had caught Santa!

"Well, it's no surprise of course, but when I crept out into the hallway I saw my Mom and Dad quietly stacking presents under the Christmas tree in the living room. The glass of milk was half empty, and one of the cookies had a bite out of it.

"I walked forward in a daze. Mom must've seen me out of the corner of her eye. She turned. My Dad turned. They didn't have to say anything. I knew. They'd lied to me. I ran back to my room sobbing, crying.

"My Mom tried to explain that Santa's just a story parents tell their kids to make them feel special. I asked her *why* she would lie to me like that. It was cruel. I felt terrible. She never really answered my question, not to my satisfaction. I cried myself to sleep that night. That was it, my childhood was over. Oh, I still played with other kids, but the dream had been shattered."

"So," Jameson says, "you think Elvis is still living in a childhood dream?"

"Something like that."

"Don't lose your childlike innocence, doc. Even us grownups need something to hold on to."

Liz smiles at the irony of hearing this from an Army Ranger. She starts to say something, but Bosco sits down next to them.

"Reception here is lousy," he says. "but there are patches where the signal leaks through. Do you want to hear what they're talking about?"

Liz would rather continue talking with Jameson, but curiosity washes over her like a wave at the beach.

A hiss and crackle breaks from the radio. A man is speaking, but his words sound hollow, as though he's talking from inside a cave.

"Home Secretary Morris Miles has reassured the British public there will be transparency when it comes to interactions with the alien spacecraft.

"We're crossing live to the United Nations where NASA scientists are addressing the UN General Assembly, explaining the events of the past few months as the craft approached Earth before settling in its current position beyond the moon... Dr. Stephen Dupree, Director of Advanced Research with NASA's Ames Research Center."

"...you, please be seated."

Liz wants to ask if the radio could be turned up louder, but the prospect of interrupting the signal keeps her quiet. Bosco fiddles with the antenna, twisting it slightly, trying to pick up the channel with more clarity.

"...will try to avoid too much technical detail, but there's a need for..."

The static gets worse, and Jameson bats at the air in front of Bosco, signaling for him to stop playing with the aerial. Bosco returns the antenna to its original position and the three of them lean forward, straining to catch each word.

"...officially designated as the 'Morrison comet' after the amateur astronomer Richard Morrison from Darwin, Australia, who first detected what we now believe is a vessel of interstellar origin. Morrison located what he thought was a comet beyond the orbit of

Sedna almost nine months ago, at a distance of three light days from Earth.

"The motion of the comet was slightly off the ecliptic, the plane on which the majority of the planets orbit the sun, but that's not unusual for an object originating in the Oort cloud. Comet Morrison approached us from the opposite side of the solar system, on the far side of the sun. The comet was moving considerably faster than Sedna, but at that distance it was impossible to tell the angle on which it was moving, making it impossible to determine anything other than its relative speed.

"Roughly seven months ago, the object changed course, aligning with the ecliptic, and it became clear Morrison was *not* a naturally-occurring object like a comet or an asteroid. There was some speculation that the comet might have collided with another celestial object, but as Morrison appeared to remain intact, this possibility was quickly discarded. Because the object's position lay within ten degrees of the sun, as viewed from Earth, ground-based observations were largely obscured by the glare of the sun."

A disembodied voice requests clarification. "Please explain further."

"The Morrison Comet approached the sun from outside our solar system, moving against the sun's direction of travel around the Milky Way. Morrison was observed traveling in a parabolic arc toward the sun. Its motion was obscured by the sun for most of its approach, with its relative motion against the backdrop of the stars opposing that of Earth's orbit. Observations by the Keck Observatory in Hawaii revealed that the object was emitting gamma radiation, something that got NASA's attention, initiating the blackout."

The formal voice requests more clarification. "Please explain the term *blackout*."

Dupree continues. "*Blackout* is a NASA protocol for containing speculation in the event of close contact with an extraterrestrial intelligence. The intent is to avoid panic and confusion. By limiting the dissemination of information, it is designed to ensure a coordinated, measured response, rather than a half-cocked reaction, and avoid unwarranted speculation."

"In hindsight, was a blackout appropriate?" the deeply resonant voice asks.

"No, sir," Dupree replies, his voice barely audible in the static. There's a pause for a second, and Liz wonders what's running through the mind of a man thousands of miles away in what seems like another world. "The intention was to provide us with some breathing space so as to formulate an appropriate response, but too many people got burned."

"Please continue," the voice directs.

"Notification of the blackout was provided by the National Security Council and the President, who initiated a lockdown of the physical facility at AMES, and the transfer of key personnel from Keck."

"What made you so sure?" asks the interrogator. "What made you think this was indeed an alien spacecraft?"

"Initially, there was no way of making out any detail on the craft directly. The craft appeared as little more than a blur in our telescopes, but the gamma rays told us all that we needed to know.

Gamma rays are highly energetic particles not associated with comets. Gamma rays are indicative of subatomic collisions occurring under immense pressure. They're normally associated with catastrophic celestial events, like a supernova, that is, an exploding star. To see gamma rays being emitted by something within our solar system was alarming. Spectrometer analysis revealed the presence of hydrogen and helium in the coma, or the head, of this supposed comet, while the Doppler shift of this light indicated the comet was approaching the solar system at a significant speed."

"What do you define as a significant speed?"

"Based on our observations," Dupree continues, "we estimated the craft's speed when first detected at 11% of the speed of light.

"This is what confirmed the alien hypothesis for us. The craft's motion relative to Earth seemed much slower than the Doppler effect originally suggested. What we were seeing was a craft rapidly approaching us, while only drifting slightly to one side as it approached. At first, we'd mistaken that sideways motion as its actual motion, but that was an illusion.

"You must remember, all speed is relative to your vantage point. If you're driving down the freeway at 55 miles per hour and another car overtakes you, it might drift past at a leisurely pace, at what appears like a walking pace, yet that car is traveling at, say, 57 miles per hour relative to the road. In this case, the alien vessel was entering our solar system at a blistering pace, but changes in the Doppler shift indicated the craft was slowing, that it was braking.

"By the time the craft reached the orbit of Sedna it was traveling at 5% of the speed of light. Two and a half months later, when it passed Pluto, the craft had slowed to less than 2% of the speed of light, and yet at that speed it could still cover the length of the United States in less than a second."

The interviewer speaks again with a hint of condescension in his voice. It seems he already knows the answer to the question he's asking.

"And what caused this gamma radiation? In your opinion, why is this craft giving off this spectacular radiation? Was this display in any way threatening or hostile?"

"Oh, no," Dupree says. "This wasn't an aggressive act on their part. Space isn't empty. Even a vacuum contains a few atoms per cubic meter, as well as waves of electromagnetic energy streaming out from the sun. The craft was moving so fast it was colliding with these particles, causing them to fuse. The effect was, we saw tremendous amounts of energy being radiated by the vessel as it fired its engines to brake on entering our system—only the craft was moving so fast it took considerable time to shed that speed. In effect, we saw the tires smoking as it skidded to a stop."

"And what did NASA make of this?"

"The alien spacecraft was, in effect, using collisions with dust particles, solar winds and wisps of hydrogen to assist in slowing itself, fusing hydrogen into helium in a superheated plasma out in front of its shield. Think of it as being like a space capsule returning to Earth with its heat shield glowing white hot from friction with the atmosphere. Essentially, that's what we were seeing, only at higher speeds than we've ever imagined."

Another voice speaks with almost electronic monotony.

"Question from the floor: Ambassador Hans Jugen, Germany."

"You described a leading shield on the alien vessel, but the images we now see show no sign of any such shielding. How do you explain that?"

"Good question," Dr. Dupree replies. "Initially, our view of the object was obscured by the sun, but orbiting telescopes could resolve the basic outline of the craft. The SOHO satellite observing the sun was able to resolve the shield, which appeared broad, but thin. As best we understand the physics, it seems the shield was more of a buffer, a temporary sail. We were able to observe the sail unfolding out to a distance of five thousand miles."

"Five thousand miles?" the ambassador asks. "That's the distance from Germany to China."

"Yes," Dupree says. "As a point of comparison, the sail was roughly the size of the Continental US."

"But that's huge!" the ambassador says. "Yet now there's no such shield."

"That's correct. We theorized that this was an ablative shield, slowly burning up as the craft approached our sun. By the time the craft passed the orbit of Mars, the sail was all but gone."

"And that didn't bother you?"

"No, we saw no cause for alarm."

"You saw no cause for alarm," the ambassador replies, a sense of indignity carrying in his voice. "We've seen rioting in Munich, Stuttgart and Bonn. The US embassy in London has been torched. In your own land, protests have erupted in Los Angeles, San Francisco, Salt Lake City, Chicago, New York, and Washington DC, and you say there's no cause for alarm? Can you understand that for the majority of humanity, whether this thing fuses hydrogen or looks pretty against the backdrop of the stars is irrelevant? What we need to know is whether there's a credible threat to Earth!"

"Mr. Ambassador," the radio crackles. "I will tell you the same message I told President Addison: To the best of our knowledge, the answer is, no, there's no immediate threat. This kind of hysteria is the very reason the blackout was imposed."

The anger in the ambassador's voice rises above the unrest in the room.

"You've no right to act on our behalf. Not without the consent of the United Nations. You Americans think you can act with impunity. You think you're best placed to make decisions for the rest of the planet. But you have no right to represent humanity as a whole. You do not represent me!"

An uproar breaks through the crowd.

Dupree yells, struggling to be heard.

"We thought we were doing what was right; we thought we were doing what was in the best interests of humanity."

More yelling erupts.

"What would *you* have done?" Dupree asks, his voice shaking. He tries to yell above the commotion. "What *could* you have done if you'd known? It's easy to criticize our actions in hindsight, but we did what we thought was best. We had to ensure stability; we wanted to prevent panic. You don't yell fire in the middle of a crowded theater. We wanted to avoid inducing fear in the general population; we wanted to avoid a global meltdown of confidence."

"What arrogance!" the ambassador cries. "You thought you could contain this forever? You thought no one else would discover the craft? The alien spaceship threatens *all* of humanity, not just the US."

"But it's not a threat," Dupree pleads. "Don't you see? They weren't using the sun to cover their approach, they were using the sun to slow down; they swung around the sun to shed their excess speed. They *always* intended to come to a rest beside us. They—"

A squawk on Jameson's handheld military radio snaps the three of them back to reality. They aren't sitting in the safety of the US heartland listening to this debate. Liz is reminded that they're in Africa, in a country smoldering, about to burst into civil war.

"Sarge? This is Mathers. I've got two vehicles approaching, maybe four klicks out. Looks like they've pulled off the road. Suspect they're conducting recon."

"Roger that," Jameson replies into his radio. Turning to Liz, he adds, "You need to get your staff and patients ready for possible hostile contact."

With that, Jameson grabs his M4 rifle and runs down to Elvis and Smithy, yelling at them to finish up and grab their weapons.

CHAPTER 03: TEARS

Darkness falls. Stars appear overhead. Nothing happens for several hours.

Sitting there with her back against the low stone wall, Liz struggles with the tension. Uncertainty gnaws at her mind. What's happening out there? Where the hell are the Rangers?

The night air is stuffy. A hot, humid breeze blows in from the west, negating the earlier, cooler breeze from the south. Dark clouds roll in over the horizon. Flashes of lightning ripple above the hills. The crash of thunder is a distant murmur, but it grows louder as time passes. Liz wants the clouds slowly drifting overhead to burst—to break through and bring relief from the sweltering heat. With no word from the soldiers, all she can do is sit tight and wait for the impending storm.

The moon rises, softening the night. Dark shadows stretch across the village. Huts and fences cast elongated shadows on the ground.

Occasionally, Liz catches a glimpse of movement, and her heart stops. The soft crackle of a radio assures her she's seen a soldier creeping around the desolate village, and not a rebel sneaking into camp. The stars are radiant, with the planets Mars and Jupiter glistening like diamonds next to the Moon, but Liz doesn't appreciate their beauty. Her eyes barely notice the fine pinpricks of celestial light as clouds smother the sky.

"What are they going to make of all this?" Kowalski asks, slumping down beside her with his back against the low wall.

They who?

Liz is distracted, thinking about the rebels approaching, and the patients who have fled. Nurses move around in the darkened hut across from them.

Liz and Kowalski have housed the remaining patients inside two of the empty huts, rigging mosquito nets over them.

The nurses and doctors wear long-sleeved shirts. Even with mosquito repellent on their hands, the little bastards still swarm around, trying to get past the fine netting draped over their broad-brimmed hats. It seems as though the mosquitos have come to savor the smell of her repellent.

Liz misses the gist of Kowalski's question. She's worked with him for the past six months, ever since he transferred from Sudan. Liz likes him both as a friend and a colleague, but at times she finds it hard to understand what he's saying. Kowalski's originally from Czechoslovakia. His English is technically correct, but his speech is clipped. The rhythm with which he speaks and his sharp accent requires concentration on her part, or she's in danger of missing his meaning entirely.

Kowalski points at the sky, "You think they'll think we're nuts?"

"They'd be right," she replies, casting her eyes up and recognizing the constellation of Orion through the wisps of cloud cover.

"It must be quite something," he adds, with his natural cadence slightly accentuating his words. "Do you think they'll help us?"

"Well, if Africa's any yardstick to go by, it's clear we can't help ourselves. We can do with all the help we can get."

"Their spaceship, what do you think it looks like?"

"I don't know. Big, I guess." Her mind casts back to the various radio broadcasts they've listened to, and although there's been some mention of telescopes being pointed at the alien spaceship, there hasn't been any description offered. Liz figures their little corner of the world is probably among the few places on Earth that hasn't seen any images of the alien spacecraft. In her mind's eye, she can imagine the hype and near panic that must be gripping the Western world with its 24/7 media frenzy. Overnight, such images would've become ubiquitous, with every television network pundit offering an opinion on the weird shapes. Liz can understand why NASA kept the alien presence secret for so long, as the media has a way of encouraging hysteria.

"I think they come in peace," she adds softly. "Maybe it's just me reading my own hopes into their intent, but they have to come in peace. They're intelligent, far more intelligent than us. Intelligent people value peace. Anything else just doesn't make sense."

"Really?" Kowalski asks. "I think perhaps there are more considerations. Technical achievements and intelligence are not synonymous. I mean, here we are, by far the most intelligent species on our planet, and we're forever waging war against ourselves.

"I don't know that intelligence counts for much. Look at the warring tribes of Africa, the tension between China and Japan, Israel and the Middle East… it seems we're all too keen to drive each other into the ground.

"They may be advanced enough to cross the vast expanse of space, but I don't know that makes them any brighter than we are, just as you and I can't be described as smarter than Galileo or Aristotle, even though we have computers and vaccines."

"Yeah, I guess not," Liz replies, surprised.

"If anything, technology allows us to be dumb without consequence."

Liz laughs, saying, "You think they're dumb?"

Kowalski laughs as well. "Not dumb, but there's a danger in reading too much into how technically advanced they are. Morals rarely keep pace with technology, and collective intelligence can drop away. As life becomes more abstract, more divorced from reality by technology, it's easy to lose sight of what's right and wrong."

"You think they're evil?" Liz asks, mulling over the possibility.

"I don't know what to think. I doubt anyone does. And I doubt it's as clear-cut as our black and white stereotypes portray.

"I mean, all we have to go on is Hollywood and their depiction of aliens with acid for blood, and massive armies bred to invade the planet. I guess my point is, any assumptions we come up with are probably going to be absurdly off-key. This morning, I doubt anyone expected E.T. to turn up on their doorstep, and yet here he is!"

Liz watches as Kowalski swats a mosquito trying to get under the netting bunched loosely on his shoulder.

"Think about our fairytales," he continues. "Whether it's Snow White or Star Wars, there's always pure evil raging against naive innocence—the black knight riding in against King Arthur, but life's never that clear cut. Reality's... complicated."

Liz lowers her voice, trying to sound masculine as she adds, "Sort of like '*Luke, I am your father,*' I guess."

Kowalski laughs. She knows precisely what he means. Africa's neither black nor white. Some days the continent seems like nothing but a murky indistinct gray. Joking around with Kowalski helps distract Liz from the tension of the night.

Sweat drips from her brow. Dark clouds swirl overhead, blocking the starlight. Humidity hangs in the air. At any moment, the storm is going to break.

Liz should head inside one of the huts, but the nurses are quite capable of caring for the remaining patients. Besides, the tension of waiting for the unknown keeps her outdoors. She has to know. Will the rebels attack? Will they pass them by? A field hospital and a couple of doctors are small fish in a big pond.

Suddenly, Liz is aware of someone beside her, a ghost resolving in the dark. Startled, she turns. Her heart leaps into her throat, and she's on the verge of screaming. White eyes pierce the darkness. Jameson crouches next to her. His face has been painted in a disruption pattern, with jagged shades of charcoal and black. His radio crackles with a soft hiss.

"You scared the hell out of me," Kowalski says, expressing what Liz feels.

Jameson grins. His teeth are a stark contrast to the night. He hands them a couple of flak jackets. "Here. Put these on."

Liz pulls her hat off and slips the Kevlar vest over her head as Kowalski asks, "No helmets?"

"No spares. Keep your head down and you won't need one."

"Thanks," Liz says, feeling clumsy as she straps the heavy vest in place. She's worn Kevlar before in training scenarios, but never under fire.

Jameson speaks into his radio, saying, "Recon Sit Rep."

Over the static, Liz hears, "I've got three parties in the scrub. Delta at 11, 3 and 7. Over."

"Roger that."

Kneeling down beside them, Jameson draws a large circle in the dust with his finger. "They know there's been an outpost here. They're feeling us out, looking to see whether anyone's home, probing our defenses."

"Where are they?" Kowalski asks.

"Imagine a clock, with high noon facing due north."

He draws three lines, pointing at where the hours 11, 3 and 7 would've been if his circle had been a clock face.

"We've got movement at these locations. They're spoiling for a fight."

"What do we do?" Liz asks as she puts her hat back on.

"Nothing."

"Nothing?" she replies, incredulous. "You scared me half to death, and now you're telling me you're not going to do anything about a bunch of murderous thugs creeping up on us in the dark?" Her words are low, almost as though she's uttering something blasphemous.

"Rules of engagement. They haven't demonstrated hostile intent. We have to wait for them to initiate contact."

"They have us surrounded," she says.

Jameson points at the bulky contraption strapped to the front of his helmet. "Night vision. They think they're moving in under the cover of darkness, but we hold the tactical advantage."

"Do you have a gun I could use?" Kowalski asks.

"Have you ever fired a gun before?" Jameson asks in reply.

Kowalski pauses slightly before answering. "My father took me hunting when I was a teenager."

"Well, no offense to you and your father, but combat's rather different from shooting furry little critters that can't fight back. You're more likely to shoot one of us than you are one of them."

"But we need to protect ourselves," Kowalski replies. "What if we're overrun?"

"You've got to trust us on this. Let us do our job."

Kowalski doesn't look impressed by that response.

Jameson says, "Listen, doc, if I come through this with a bullet in my ass, I promise I won't tell you how to do your job, okay? Right now, you've got to let me do mine."

"Sure," Kowalski replies.

"Have either of you been in a combat situation before?" Neither Liz nor Kowalski answer. They simply shake their heads.

"All right. You've got to prepare yourself for what could happen. You'll hear a lot of gunfire. Don't freak out. Keep your head down. Stay low. If you need to move around, crawl. Whatever you do, don't stand up.

"We're going to fire some illumination flares when contact commences, but that's not to light them up; it's to destroy their ability to see in the dark, make it harder for them to pick out silhouettes moving at night. It's a bluff, something to mislead them, to make them feel like it's a fair fight. When it comes to warfare, there's no such thing as a fair fight—there's kill or be killed."

Liz nods her head, realizing she's being given access to the battle plan the Rangers have formulated.

"Gunfire is loud. It's intimidating, overwhelming, but I want you to listen for something else. Try to ignore the gunfire—listen for the sound of any impacts near you."

She isn't sure what he means. Jameson must pick up on her confusion as he mimics two distinctly different sounds. "You'll hear something like *ppft BANG, ppft BANG*." Liz screws her face up.

"If you hear that, they're shooting at you. Remember, these guys are firing supersonic rounds, so you'll hear the round whiz past, and strike something near you, before you hear the gunshot itself, *ppft BANG*." Liz nods.

"There's going to be a lot of noise, a lot of confusion. You'll swear someone's shooting right at you, but don't freak out—listen for where the rounds are landing—listen for the impact, the *ppft*. That's your best guide. There'll be a lot of sound echoing off the mud huts and the jungle, and that can be confusing. Listen for impact. If there's no impact nearby, you're fine—they're not firing at you."

Kowalski nods, which reminds Liz to nod as well. She feels like a school kid taking instruction from a Phys-Ed teacher.

"If you see poofs of dust or chips of mud and rock flying one way, the bullets are coming from the opposite direction, from roughly 180 degrees the other way. Stay low.

"You're going to want to run, but don't. Don't try to get away. As tempting as it is, you don't want to run from gunfire as you'll make yourself an obvious target.

"If bullets start raining down around you, move closer to the shooter. I know it sounds strange, but it's all about angles. If you move away from the shooter, in the direction the bullets are traveling, you'll make yourself an easy target. You want to do the opposite. Move under cover *toward* the shooter, as that destroys their angle. By moving closer, you're moving up against an obstacle that hides you from sight. From there, crawl laterally, left or right, but stay out of sight.

"Remember, if you can hear gunfire, those bullets have already passed by. You'll flinch and duck, but if they were on target they'd have already hit you.

"If you hear a whiz, or a crack, but no impact, they're shooting high, and the bullets are flying past. Just stay low, and don't panic.

"If there's a lull in the fighting, stay put. You'll just draw attention to yourself if you move around. We'll come for you. We know where you are. We've aligned our fields of fire to cover this location, so don't leave here; if you do you could be hit by friendly fire as much as by the rebels."

Liz swallows the knot in her throat.

"Stay low. Don't panic," she repeats back to him, already feeling panicked. In her time in Africa, she's had a few close calls with some of the tribesmen, but never anything that had made her feel as if she were in a war zone. With the UN presence, the civil war in Malawi had largely ground to a halt, but now she feels some of the fear she saw in the villagers' eyes when she first arrived.

"I need you to communicate this to your staff. Okay?" Jameson looks into her eyes. His eyes dart between each of her eyes, looking to see if she understands. Liz is out of her depth.

"Okay."

Jameson squeezes her shoulder gently. "The rebels are undisciplined. They'll fire at shadows. They'll let off a long rat-a-tat-tat. If you listen, you'll hear us firing back, but our rounds are smaller and we're using muzzle suppression to avoid a flash that might give away our position. Our rounds will sound more high-pitched, like the crack of a whip. Plus you'll only ever hear the Rangers firing controlled bursts. Just one or two shots at a time, but don't worry about that. Firefights are about precision, not bluster. We'll only fire when we're on target, when we're sure of a hit. If you hear lots and lots of machine gun fire, don't be scared. Remind yourself that they're wasting ammo, and they're giving away their position. If anything, they're making our job easier."

The radio crackles.

"I've got movement on the road," a voice says over the radio. Liz recognizes Bosco's nasal twang. "Lone truck. One occupant. Headlights off. Moving slow."

"Looks like they're delivering my spare parts," Smithy's says over the radio.

"It's about time." That's Elvis. There's no mistaking his voice even with the static.

Jameson speaks into the radio. "Warning shot. Single burst. Tracers overhead. Let them know we're here. We'll give them the opportunity to pull back."

"Roger that."

Jameson peers over the low stone wall. He flips his night vision goggles down, making him look more machine than man. Liz can't help herself, turning and kneeling as she peers over the rock wall. Kowalski stays where he is.

Liz can see the landing zone to one side, on a flat expanse before the dark jungle canopy. The truck Smithy's been working on has been dragged into the village, hidden from the road by the crest of a small hill.

Liz struggles to make out any detail in the grainy, murky darkness. The noise of a diesel engine rumbles in the distance.

Suddenly, the night lights up. For a second, it's as though lightning's struck. Gunfire streams out away from the village into the darkness. Tracer rounds snap through the air, leaving reddish phosphorescent trails. Thunder rolls around them. It takes Liz a moment to realize the chesty thump is that of a machine gun, not the storm breaking. She's surprised to see the faint outline of one of the Rangers illuminated briefly by the outgoing tracer rounds. He's lying prone thirty yards away. She expected him to be hidden, rather than lying out in the open on the landing zone. No sooner has he fired than he's on the move.

"Spotting wide," comes the call over the radio. "Elvis, you're clear. Eleven is stationary. Looks like an observation post."

"I've got movement at three." Liz is able to pick out Smithy's voice again.

"I've got movement at seven," another voice adds over the radio.

"The truck's conducting a three-point turn, pulling back," Bosco says, his voice breaking up with static.

"Stand by," Jameson says into his radio.

Liz is impressed by his clinical detachment, reminding her of some of her senior lecturers at medical school, and how calmly they'd describe a complex procedure like a heart bypass. She'd like to think of herself as calm in the operating theatre, but if a patient deteriorates on her, her nerves spike. She hasn't lost anyone, but she's come close enough to walk out of theater with her hands shaking. In Africa, though, not losing patients is nothing to brag about—the serious cases rarely make it as far as a field hospital.

Out of nowhere, a rebel machine gun opens fire, raking the village.

Liz ducks, even though she knows it's too late. If she'd been the target, she would've already become a casualty, and that thought terrifies her. She's treated plenty of gunshot wounds, and understands the damage a small piece of lead can do when accelerated faster than the speed of sound. Liz doesn't fancy lying on a stretcher, undergoing surgery in the middle of Africa, and decides she'll take Jameson's advice and keep her head down. She feels an impulse to watch, but knows there's nothing to see beyond fleeting flashes in the darkness. Safety first.

Jameson holds up his finger. "No *zing*. No *ppft*. This is a bluff, a fake, intended to draw us out—to get us to expose our positions.

"They might be amateurs, but they're not dumb enough to mount a frontal assault across an open grassy field. Don't worry about this. It's a diversion while they conduct a flanking maneuver. They're trying to keep us preoccupied with a frontal attack while the real action comes from three and seven."

He points as he speaks.

"Three is on the move," crackles the radio.

"Eleven is open," another voice says.

"Take him," Jameson replies, talking into the radio with no emotion at all. He might as well be ordering pizza.

A single crack resounds through the night.

"Eleven down."

Liz struggles to swallow the knot in her throat. In those few seconds, she's listened to the death of a rebel over the radio. There were no theatrics, no drama. If anything, life seems cheap—a human life's been snuffed out with the same level of emotion as swatting a fly.

Liz finds herself wondering about *"eleven,"* wondering whether the shot was immediately fatal. She doubts the man is dead just yet. There are very few places in the human body that will kill someone in an instant, and she finds herself wondering about a rebel bleeding to death in the jungle foliage. She's trained to save life—it's hard to ignore her instincts. She's never really made the emotional connection that soldiers are trained to kill. Intellectually, yes, but reality strikes hard.

Jameson speaks into his radio. "I am en route to three."

Liz breathes deeply. Jameson rests his hand on her shoulder as he speaks, reassuring her in a soft voice. "You'll be fine. This'll be over before you know it. Trust me." Liz nods as Jameson slinks away, melting into the night.

One of the nurses appears, crouching in the doorway to the stone hut.

"I've got this," Kowalski says, staying low as he darts into the hut, and with that Liz is alone.

Sweat runs down her forehead, soaking her collar. Her fingers feel sticky. The ground is rough. She shifts her weight, trying to clear away some of the smaller stones to make sitting bearable.

Sporadic gunfire erupts around the outskirts of the village. Each shot feels as though it's directed at her. She winces, trying to curl up into a ball, wanting to disappear.

No *zings*, no *ppfts*. Wasting ammo. Just fireworks. Nothing more. Keep calm. Stay low.

A flash of lightning crackles through the dark clouds. Liz expects the crash of thunder to break a few seconds later, but the resounding boom is almost instantaneous, breaking directly over the jungle, shaking the village. Liz jumps.

Large drops of rain begin to fall. At first, just one or two, but they strike her broad hat with unusual force. Within seconds, torrential rain falls. The temperature plummets.

Another bolt arcs through the sky, followed by a crash that shakes her bones. The Heavens are at war with Earth, competing with the Rangers and the rebels—gunfire screams at the deafening downpour. An explosion erupts from the far end of the village, from the area Jameson labeled seven o'clock.

Stay calm. Deep breaths.

Liz wants to run. The safety of the hut holds no allure. She wants to run from the village, and struggles to control the compulsion.

"Just fireworks," she whispers. "They're wasting ammo."

Liz tries to calm her nerves by pulling off her hat, allowing the rain to wash over her face. Another crash of thunder breaks overhead as a neon flash illuminates the village, pasting the huts with a ghostly glow. Hold on. Stay where you are. Everything's going to be okay. She doesn't believe her own thoughts.

Tears roll down her cheeks. She isn't sure why, and she doubts anyone would notice in the rain, but still she cries. Perhaps it's the release of tension brought on by the storm. Liz feels silly, and that makes her cry even more. She feels helpless as the storm rages around her and bullets whiz overhead.

The rain eases, allowing the sound of the battle to reach her ears. She turns at the roar of an engine. The rebel truck bounces along the muddy track. Flashes of light burst from the back of the open flatbed. *Ppfts* and *zings* race past her, but in the confusion she's powerless to do anything other than watch. Her white knuckles grip the edge of the wall.

The truck lurches toward her, bouncing out of a rut and careening up the embankment towards the village. Dirt flies through the air, dislodged by the truck's bumper as it catches the soggy ground. Liz finds herself sprayed with mud as the truck slams into the wall, coming to a halt ten feet away.

The door to the cabin swings open. A rebel slumps to the ground, dead. His body lands in a puddle on the other side of the wall.

Liz flinches at the nightmare unfolding before her. She's repulsed by the shadow of death looming over the village. Terror seizes her.

A bloody arm hangs down off the back of the flatbed truck. The arm twitches. Slowly, a wounded rebel gets to his feet. He staggers against the cab of the truck, using it for support as he stands on the wooden deck, towering over her. Liz wants to run, but her legs are numb. As much as she wills herself to move, her body refuses. She's shaking, but not from the cold.

Through the sound of the rain, she can hear the rebel cursing some African god. Their eyes meet. Neither the darkness nor the rain can hide her from his gaze. He sees her crouching beside the wall, paralyzed with fear. His eyes widen.

Smiling, he grabs his AK-47 from where it lies on the deck of the truck. A flash of lightning illuminates the village, turning the night into day. Liz watches in horror as the rebel brings his rifle to bear, pulling back on the bolt to load a round.

A crack of thunder shakes the ground as the rebel's chest explodes. A bullet tears through his ribcage, coming from his right. The rebel falls into the darkness, disappearing from sight.

Liz can't stop shaking. Demons move around her. Ghosts sink back into the night. Her heart races. The hair on the back of her neck rises in terror.

As suddenly as it came, the violence is replaced with the soft patter of rain. Liz stands there in the drizzle, rain dripping from her waterlogged clothes.

She shouldn't be standing up. She isn't even sure when she stood, but somehow she's standing. Jameson told her to stay down, but her muscles refuse to let her crouch.

Someone screams—a woman. The pitch of the woman's voice is unearthly, piercing the night with anguish, a banshee howling. Liz feels a sense of dread sweep over her—she'll die here in Africa.

A hand grabs her shoulder and she jumps. "Hey, it's okay," Kowalski says. "It's me. Come with me." Kowalski leads her into the hut. It's only then Liz realizes she's the one screaming.

CHAPTER 04: LAS VEGAS

The sun is high in the sky. Bright light creeps across the mud floor of the hut. A damp blanket's been draped over her, while a rolled up jacket acts as a pillow. The ground beneath her is unforgiving, and she stirs, feeling stiff.

The hut's empty. Kowalski's outside talking with one of the patients. Her neck's sore. She sits up, stretching her aching muscles.

"The axle's fucked," one of the soldiers yells, crawling under the rebel truck. "Goddamn it, Bosco. Can't you do anything right? Those nice rebels deliver us a perfectly good truck, and you shoot it to shit! Are trying to bury us here?"

Several other soldiers laugh, but the tall, lanky soldier is quiet. They're ribbing him, but this isn't a joke to Bosco.

Liz steps out of the hut. Smithy examines the rebel truck. Several large stones have been dislodged from the wall. The left front wheel has ridden up over part of it, dropping the chassis down onto the rocks, breaking the front axle. Smithy and Elvis don't make fun of Bosco. Instead, they seem intent in salvaging what they can from the rebel truck.

"Knock it off," Jameson says to the others. He turns to Smithy as she crouches down beside the front wheel, "What do you think?"

Hydraulic fluid mixes with oil as it seeps out on the ground.

Smithy replies, "This baby's not going anywhere, but she's good for parts."

Already, the sun's dried the puddles of water, leaving damp patches. Cracks form in the hardening mud.

"Hey," Kowalski says, coming over to Liz, and offering to help her walk over to where Jameson's sitting on the remains of the wall.

"What the hell happened to me?"

"You were shaking, mumbling. Your eyes were dilated."

Liz is silent. She knows what he's thinking, *You panicked. You were in shock.*

Kowalski hands her a canteen.

"I gave you a sedative."

"You gave me a headache."

"That too. I thought it best to let you sleep."

"Good morning, sunshine," Jameson says as Liz wanders past. It must be between ten and eleven in the morning, judging from the angle of the sun and sweltering heat of the day. Liz is in no mood for small talk. She splashes water on her face, running her hands through her hair, feeling a matted tangle. *Must look a mess.* For someone that prides herself on not caring what others think, it's an unusual thought.

"Sleep well?" Jameson asks.

"My head feels as if someone's been pounding on it with a jackhammer, and I have a hangover without having touched a drop of wine. Is there any fate worse?"

She squints in the bright light. Her backpack sits on the grass beside the soldier's gear. Rummaging through her one of the side pockets, she finds sunglasses and a hat.

"Oh, that's soooo much better," she mumbles.

Stretching her back, she looks around at her patients resting in the shade of a nearby tree. One of the nurses has cooked some maize and is dishing out bowls to the patients. They're chatting merrily with each other. Kowalski examines the premature baby, listening to its heartbeat and respiration with a stethoscope.

"Did I miss something?" Liz asks, sitting beside Jameson.

The bodies are gone. There's no blood. If it weren't for the holes where bullets punctured the thin sheet metal on the side of the truck, she'd never know there'd been a firefight the night before. Villagers crash trucks all the time, normally not like this, but a wreck on the side of the track is a common sight. It could be any other day.

"We routed the enemy around oh-one-hundred." Jameson's clinical in his description of what happened the night before. "Twelve combatants neutralized. We estimate the rebel strength at no more than forty."

"Was anyone hurt?" As the words leave her lips, she realizes the underlying assumption in her question—only US troops count. With three simple words, a dozen deaths have been dismissed. It's as though the rebels feel no more pain than a cow being led to slaughter, and yet she doesn't correct herself. He must know what she means. He has to agree.

"We came through the fight with little more than scratches. Bosco's army radio, though, didn't fare as well. It took some shrapnel from a fragmentation grenade." Jameson has a map out. Using a compass and grease pencil, he marks a number of positions with crosses and circles. He's doing some kind of arithmetic on the margin, so Liz remains silent, not wanting to break his concentration.

Elvis rummages around under the hood of the rebel truck. He runs a series of wires back to the flatbed trailer. Liz assumes he's doing something to help Smithy, who has had several of the Rangers pushing the other truck over next to the wreckage. She's looking to salvage parts.

Elvis stands on the back of the damaged truck holding a microphone. A cable leads down to an old metal speaker, the kind used on military parade grounds.

"*Bright-lit city*," resounds from the speaker. Liz is surprised by the resonance in his voice. He sounds surprisingly good singing *a cappella*. His voice has a natural vibrato, wavering softly as he sings the Elvis Presley classic, "Viva Las Vegas."

"*Gonna light my soul, gonna burn my soul so bad!*"

Liz laughs. He's getting the lyrics horribly wrong. It can't be nerves, and she can't imagine he doesn't know the lyrics. He must have sung this song a thousand times in the shower.

Elvis poses as he sings, with one arm outstretched and his legs shaking in time to some unheard beat, swiveling back and forth, appealing to a nonexistent audience. Liz is perplexed. Maybe he's simply pulling a mental blank with everyone staring at him.

"*There's a hundred ugly women waiting somewhere out there, and they're all breathing, but why should I care?*"

"Goddamn it, Elvis," Jameson yells, ruffling his map. "If you're going to torture us, at least get *fucking* words right!"

It's only then Liz realizes Elvis knows the lyrics. He's teasing them, tormenting the squad with his ham-fisted acting.

Elvis continues, swinging slowly in a half circle with his arm reaching toward the jungle. His hips and legs shake with a fever—having a sense of vigor Liz has only ever associated with red ant bites.

"A-huh, huh, yeah, baby. A-huh, huh, somewhere out there. Hmmm, yeah, yeah, somewhere out over there."

Smithy sticks her head out from underneath the rebel truck, yelling, "Get your crazy ass down from there before someone shoots you."

"Before I shoot you!" Bosco adds.

"And a devil like me's got nothing to spare, so take meeeeeee to Las Vegas. All the waaaaaay to Las Vegas. I—"

Smithy crawls out from beneath the truck, and yanks the wires from the battery, killing the tinny speaker.

"Oh, not fair," Elvis complains, dropping the microphone to his side.

"You stupid, dumb, hick, fuck farmer," Smithy yells, her hands set firmly on her hips. "What the hell are you trying to do? Bring in every goddamn rebel for miles around?"

"Nah," Bosco replies. "He's trying to scare them off."

Elvis laughs, dropping down off the truck, landing with a thud in the mud. His combat boots crunch on the gravel as he steps away from the truck.

"Is he all right?" Kowalski asks softly, his head appearing between Jameson and Liz. "Post-traumatic stress?"

"Oh, no," Liz replies. "I'd say this is a baseline normal response from Elvis."

"Yeeeeeeee-haw," Elvis yells, grabbing his hat and sunglasses from the front of the truck. "Hurry up, Smithy. We gotta get this show on the road. There are tour dates to be kept—fans to please. When are you gonna get me mobile, baby?"

"You're an idiot," Smithy replies, laughing as she goes back to work. Elvis doesn't mind. He picks up his rifle, kicking stones across the ground, still singing quietly to himself. This time, though, he gets the lyrics right.

Kowalski heads back to tend to the patients. Jameson sits there grinning.

"I don't know how you guys do it," Liz says. "I mean, I was terrified last night, but you can just switch this on and off at will."

"You get used to it," Jameson replies. "As you can see, the team needs to blow off some steam from time to time. It's healthy."

"As healthy as it can be living in the midst of madness," Liz adds.

Jameson doesn't reply, and Liz knows she's struck a raw nerve. There's only so much bravado someone can hide behind. Hers was an outward meltdown. Soldiers have inward reactions every bit as crippling in the long term as post-traumatic stress, but in the present it's easier for them to wear a mask and walk away.

"We'll be ready in an hour," Smithy says, grabbing a part from the rebel truck and carrying it over to the old Deuce. Wires and fine tubes dangle from a rusting metal cylinder in her hand.

"So what do we do without a radio?" Liz asks.

"We stick to the plan," Jameson replies. "Ordinarily, we'd stay in the area, waiting forty-eight hours for a 'lost comms' protocol to kick in, but I doubt they'll send choppers into a hostile LZ. Besides, we should be able to get a message out from Ksaungu before then.

"Within a day, this place is going to be crawling with rebels. If we don't get on the move soon, we're not going to have to worry about forty rebels, we'll have four hundred to deal with. Command's going to assume we were overrun, or we've continued on in the dark. They'll hope it's the latter. There'd better be someone waiting for us in Lilongwe."

Bosco walks past with the shattered remains of the army radio slung over his shoulder. He's got the public radio in his hand.

"I'm getting a fresh signal on the commercial band," he says. He drops the damaged radio on the grass beside the other backpacks, and sits down with the small blue radio.

"It's the BBC," he says.

A familiar voice breaks through the static.

"Although we have no concrete information about the nature of our celestial visitors, we can infer some valuable information from what we've observed so far."

The reception's better than it was the night before.

"I have here a bullet, just the copper/lead projectile that shoots out of a gun, not the casing with its powder and detonation cap. As you can see, I can toss this bullet in the air and catch it without any concern for safety. Why? Bullets are dangerous, right? Well, no. Bullets are only dangerous when they're traveling at high velocities."

Liz would rather not have such vivid memories of *that*.

"Standing here, I can toss this bullet, catching it in my hand without any danger at all. But if I fire this same bullet from a gun, imparting kinetic energy into the slug, and accelerating it to a thousand feet per second, it would pass straight through my hand, probably straight through my body.

"This is why the alien craft had to slow as it entered our solar system. Just the tiniest speck of dust or rock would be damaging to it. Given the sheer amount of kinetic energy latent within the alien craft, if they meant us harm, they need only have continued on at high speed. Even a small craft, or an asteroid the size of this building, traveling at half the speed of light, would be enough to destroy all life on Earth. There's just so much energy involved. But they slowed to a stop relative to Earth. That act in itself tells us something of their intentions. They intend to come in contact with us, not to destroy us."

Liz is fascinated by the discussion. They've dropped into the middle of an ongoing technical discussion about the alien spacecraft. All her cares dissolve. The tension of the previous night dissipates like a dream.

"Question from the floor: Ambassador Philip Cohern, Canada."

"Where have they come from?"

"We don't know. As the craft passed Neptune, some four light hours from Earth, it conducted a course correction, aligning with the ecliptic within our solar system, allowing it to move on the same plane as the planets. As best we understand their current trajectory, this would have been one of a number of course corrections to orient with our solar system. We have a rough understanding of the vessel's origin in the southern hemisphere, in either Triangulum, or Telescopium."

"Are those real constellations?" the ambassador asks.

"They're real," the speaker confirms. "Triangulum may not be as familiar to the public as Scorpio or Ares, but it's a constellation first identified by the Greek astronomer Ptolemy."

"So this—this thing," the ambassador continues. "Tell us more about what NASA observed as it approached Earth."

"The craft did not approach Earth directly. It passed through the inner solar system on the opposite side of the sun to us, swinging around behind the sun, slowing before it approached Earth. At the phenomenal speed with which the craft initially approached our solar system, the spaceship could have arrived here within a few hours, perhaps a day or so, but it slowed its approach, shedding its kinetic energy, taking over six months to reach us. Covering this kind of distance in less than a decade is phenomenal, so although six months sounds like a long time it's actually astonishingly quick. The craft arrived at Lagrange point Five, trailing the Earth-Moon system just eight days ago, and has remained stationary since then."

"Could you expand upon what a Lagrange point is for the assembly?"

"Sure," the scientist replies. "We think of outer space as empty, but it's not. Gravity shapes space, molding it into what could be figuratively described as different forms, different shapes. Think of a street map. Maps show us how to get from one place to another, but they're flat—they don't reveal the hills and gullies that define the land, so we make topographical maps—maps with wavy lines to indicate contours. In the same way, we see space as flat, but the gravitational attraction of the Sun, Moon and Earth means we need a topographical view of space, something to show us the gravitational hills and gullies. A Lagrange point is an area that acts like a hilltop. From a Lagrange point, any which way you move is down as you're pulled by the influence of gravity."

"So this behavior was expected?"

"I don't know about expected, but it's smart. They're sitting a way off—in a place from which they can easily go anywhere. They can come to Earth, go to the Moon, or retreat into interplanetary space with a minimum of effort."

"So you'd say this is a defensive position, rather than an offensive one?"

"I... I don't know," the scientist replies. "I don't think it makes sense to draw military parallels with an alien species. It could be neither offensive or defensive, just practical."

"What do you think their next move will be?"

"Well, I doubt they came here to go sightseeing on the Moon. They didn't just happen to cruise into our solar system. They were always headed for Earth. They knew where they were going long before we ever saw them. I'm think it only makes sense to assume they'll make contact with us."

"How?"

"Mr. Ambassador, I'm a scientist, not a soothsayer. We'll have to wait and see."

"Humor me," the ambassador says. "What's the most likely scenario?"

"There's no likely scenario. We're in uncharted territory. We think they picked up on our electromagnetic radiation, our TV and radio signals as they've been beamed into space over the past century, but they've made no effort to communicate with us via radio waves, and have ignored our attempts at dialogue."

"How have you tried to open dialogue?"

"With communication akin to the semaphore used between naval vessels in World War I—flashes of light deliberately sweeping across their craft, following a pattern of prime numbers. We're looking for an acknowledgement on the same frequency, but there's been nothing. It's as though they're not listening, which is counterintuitive, given they've just flown dozens of light-years to get here."

"What do you make of that?"

"Their ways are not our ways; their mode of communication has nothing in common with ours. It's for this reason I supported the launch of the Orion, as our physical presence in space would be something they'd recognize."

"Oh," the ambassador replies, "But there's a danger they could interpret our launch as a hostile act."

"I don't think that's likely. They would have already observed that we have thousands of satellites in orbit, that we have a space station with a crew, that we have deep space telescopes like the James Webb, so they know we're capable of spaceflight. Even though we've developed nuclear weapons, it's not likely we could be a serious threat. Since their shielding can protect them from the fusion of interstellar hydrogen turning into helium, a nuclear bomb would be like a firecracker."

"So you disagree with the Addison initiative?"

"Absolutely. Nuclear weapons are devastatingly effective on Earth because there's stuff to push around, air that can be superheated and compressed, but in space, they're little more than pretty fireworks."

Another voice breaks in over the top of the discussion.

"We interrupt this special session at the United Nations to bring you news from Washington D.C., where NASA special liaison

Jonathan McKinsey has just announced that the alien craft is in motion toward Earth. If the initial course holds, NASA expects the craft to enter a stable orbit some eight hundred to one thousand miles above Earth's surface within a day."

Jameson and Liz lock eyes. There's an unspoken understanding between them. As bad as things are in Malawi, they're about to get worse.

The radio transmission is confused. Several voices talk over the top of each other. Liz can make out terms like perihelion and apogee from a female voice, but it's the drone of a monotonous male voice mumbling in different languages that spooks her.

"*Nous venons en paix—Veniamo in pace—Ons kom in vrede—Ni revenos en paco—Wij komen in vrede—Wir kommen in Frieden—*"

"As you can hear," the commentator continues, speaking over the top of the voice. "The craft has begun transmitting at 1420 MHz, a frequency known as the hydrogen line, the quietest part of the radio spectrum. The alien craft is speaking, in a multitude of languages, repeating one phrase over and over, sending an unmistakable message."

"*Vimos en paz—Erchomaste se eirini—Dumating kami sa kapayapaan—Nou vini nan lape—We come in peace—Rydym yn dod mewn heddwch—dolazimo u miru—*"

The commentator remains silent, allowing the gravity of the moment to be conveyed by the rhythmic repetition of this single concept conveyed in so many tongues. The words cast a spell over Liz, leaving her in a trance. In the background, she's vaguely aware of the sound of a diesel engine starting and soldiers hollering.

Jameson says something, but she's barely aware of his words. He taps her knee, saying, "We need to get the hell out of here before the rebels return in force."

Bosco switches the radio off, and Liz finds herself snapped back into the hot, humid African jungle.

"Time to get this show on the road!" Elvis yells. "We're going to Vegas, baby. Vegas!"

CHAPTER 05: HOTEL KSAUNGU

The road to Ksaungu is full of refugees fleeing the fighting in the rural areas. They march along the side of the rough dirt track, spilling into the single lane as they herd goats and cattle before them. Men, women and children call out, pleading to be taken on board the Rangers' Hummer and the old truck, but the soldiers are firm, shouting at the stragglers, peeling their hands away from the back of the truck and watching as they collapse to the ground, still appealing to the soldiers.

"Surely, we could take some of them," Liz says, sitting in the cab of the truck. Elvis is driving. Jameson rides shotgun.

Elvis is quiet.

Jameson looks at her with eyes that pierce her soul, and for a moment she isn't sure if he's going to say anything at all. It seems his silence speaks loudest, saying what she already knows, that it's a futile, hollow effort. Within minutes, they could be joining the refugees on foot if the engine in the truck gives out, and adding more people in the back would only hasten that moment.

Besides, who should they save? Those who shout loudest? Those who push and shove others out of the way? And why these people? What about others further down the road? Are they any less deserving? It's easy to drive on—these people aren't in any immediate danger, and yet Liz can't escape the feeling that somehow she's condemning them to death.

"We can fight a battle," Jameson finally says. "We cannot fight a war."

Liz is silent.

Jameson examines a map of Ksaungu, talking to Elvis about their approach to the city and possible exit routes if they come under rebel fire. He settles on the Hotel Ksaungu as somewhere they can rest and take stock of the situation. He says it's been used by the Press Corps and will have good connections.

Government forces push north against the human tide flowing south, waving at the US Rangers and calling out as they drive past. They don't seem too bothered by the US soldiers heading away from the battle. Government troops sit on tanks, in the back of trucks, and on top of armored personnel carriers, smoking and joking, yelling and laughing.

After an hour or so, as the Rangers travel further down the road, Liz notices the civilians becoming more subdued. They're no longer clamoring to get on board the truck. They shuffle along the road, numb to the exodus forced upon them. In some ways, their sullen demeanor is more alarming than the villagers further north. They've lost the will to fight. They're fleeing on instinct rather than with purpose.

"Hey, what about them freaking aliens," Elvis says, half leaning on the steering wheel as the truck crawls along at barely fifteen miles an hour, bouncing in and out of potholes.

Liz is seated between Elvis and Jameson. She turns to Elvis, surprised by how he's blurted this out. For the most part, their conversation so far has been subdued, but Elvis isn't one to stay sullen for long.

"I mean, what a load of horseshit. *We come in peace*—yeah, right. Like anyone's going to believe that!"

"But they do come in peace," Liz says, somewhat confused by how he could assume anything else. How can he assume the worst? Is she being naive? It's a thought that registers, but doesn't sink in, as she desperately wants to believe the alien spaceship has come in peace.

"Come on, doc. Don't tell me you believe that bullshit. No one comes in peace. Hell, look at us. We're goddamn peacekeepers, and we blow shit up all the time!"

Elvis laughs.

"They're not like us," Liz protests, although she knows her indignation is irrational, not based on anything other than her gut instinct.

Elvis is bullish. He's chewing gum with his mouth open.

"How do you know that? Maybe they're just like us, doc. I mean, think about it, what is peace? I'll tell you what peace is—peace is an illusion, a dream. We came in peace at Plymouth Rock, and look how that turned out for the natives. You wanna know what peace is, doc? Peace is conquest. Peace is submission."

Jameson's quiet. Liz looks over at him, looking to see if he's going to come to her defense. He raises an eyebrow as if to say, "You're on your own on this one."

"But peace is important," Liz protests, not sure quite what else to say to Elvis.

"Oh, I don't doubt that, doc. But whenever you get two parties together with differing viewpoints, differing opinions, differing backgrounds, there will *never* be peace. If there's peace, it's because one group's subdued the other by force of arms."

Liz is sullen.

Elvis continues.

"You think that's what they mean to do, doc? To subdue us? To force peace upon us? Just like we've brought peace to Africa down the barrel of a gun? How well do you think that's going to work in good old America?"

Elvis laughs. His teeth are pearly white. From this angle, he really does look like Elvis Presley, with his baby face, his full cheeks, sideburns and wavy hair.

"I tell you, doc. Anyone that thinks these guys come in peace is kidding themselves. No one comes in peace. They bring peace as they always have—with a sword.

"Seriously, what do you think civilization would be like without the police? Without someone to enforce peace?

"Nah, I reckon those big green bugs know exactly what they're doing. They'll come down here with their silver flying saucers and ray guns and leave us in pieces."

He laughs yet again. This is a joke to him. Although he's raised some genuine concerns, his interest is fleeting. Liz tries desperately not to become entangled in his illogic. To reply to him would be to validate his point of view.

"My pappy saw a UFO once," he says, spending more time looking at her than at the road ahead of them. "Damn thing took one of our cows. We found a shredded cow skin the next day. No meat, no bones, just the flayed, bloody skin hanging on a barbwire fence out in one of the back fields.

"You think it's the same ones? Like a scout ship or something? Sent ahead to find out our weaknesses? Or maybe there's more of them. You know, like on *Star Trek* and shit. Lots of different aliens from different places, and they're all coming here."

Liz doesn't know where to begin.

"Do you think they can read our minds?"

"If they can," Liz finally replies, seizing the opening, "they won't find much."

Elvis bursts out laughing, slapping the steering wheel. He smiles at her.

Liz is surprised. She expected him to be offended by her comment, but Elvis takes it in his stride.

"So what of it, doc? Why aren't they talking to us? You know, like you and me. Why not just come down here and say, '*Hi, I'm Marvin the Martian*,' or whatever, and talk properly with us?"

"It's not that simple," Liz replies. "Before going to med school, I studied to be a vet. I made it through my first year, but my heart wasn't in it. I realized I wanted to help people, not farm animals and pets."

Elvis nods his head thoughtfully.

Jameson's content to listen.

"My father's a microbiologist, always talking about organic chemistry and how molecules form proteins, sugars and acids, but that was too abstract for me. He wanted me to follow in his footsteps, but I like to work with things I can touch. Medical science seems more real when stitching up a wound on a patient. Anyway, one of my first year veterinary courses was on animal psychology. I got to work with cats, dogs, dolphins, cows, you name it."

Elvis laughs. "So you put a dolphin on a couch and ask it about its childhood?"

"Something like that," Liz replies, feeling the tension between them softening. She's taken Elvis the wrong way. There's nothing malicious about him. He's just a good old-Southern boy. Stereotypes be damned, he'd probably love grits with a side of bacon and eggs for breakfast every day of his life if given the chance.

"You see, we talk to animals all the time, thinking they understand us, but they don't. They see the world through a different lens. There's no doubt they're intelligent and that they think for themselves, but they don't see the world as we do. You'll never catch a cow admiring a beautiful flower, or a dog stopping to enjoy a radiant sunset.

"We project our own emotions and feelings onto animals, but it's one way traffic. You and I see a dog as part of our family—the dog sees itself as part of a tribe, an inter-species animal pack. And just like a wild pack, your dog will want to know where it sits in the hierarchal order. You may think of your dog as being on the bottom rung, but I doubt it does, especially if you've got young kids. You might think you've got your dog well trained, but he thinks he's domesticated you, and he'll get shitty with you when you tell him off for bringing a bone inside."

"Hah," Elvis cries. "My pappy's dog definitely thinks he rules the roost. He'll chew anything in sight. He sits up on the couch like King Tut."

"Dogs have emotions, though," Jameson counters, joining the conversation. "They genuinely care about us, right?"

"Oh, they do," Liz replies, "but through the lens of their nature, not ours. They show empathy when people are distressed, but emotionally they never really develop beyond that of a two or a three year old child."

"What about cats?" Jameson asks.

"Domestic cats are different. Apart from lions, there are no cats that move in packs, so they see their inclusion in a family as being part of a litter, and as such, there'll be parents and other kittens—your children. When your cat brings a live mouse into the house, it's trying to teach you and your kids how to hunt. They must think we're stupid when we never catch any mice of our own!"

"Damn," Elvis says, laughing as he chews on some gum. He's clearly enjoying the conversation.

Liz says, "A few years ago, a bunch of divers freed a sperm whale from shark nets off the east coast of Australia. From memory, there were five or six divers involved. Anyway, once the whale was free it swam up beside each of them individually and took a good long look at them. It drifted up to their boat, stuck its head out of the water and looked at the support crew on deck. It was, by all accounts, a moving experience. Those divers came away saying they felt the whale expressed a sense of gratitude and appreciation, but they simply projected their own emotional expectations onto the animal."

"How can you know for sure?" Elvis asks. "Sounds to me as if the whale was glad to be rescued."

Liz laughs, saying, "Because, if they'd rescued a polar bear from a similar predicament, the bear would've eaten them."

"I don't know about that, doc," Jameson replies. "I remember seeing a documentary on PBS about that whale, and the guy that cut the whale loose said it was nervous as hell at first, treating them as though they were sharks or something, but once he started cutting the whale loose, she calmed down. He said working with her was like soothing a rattled horse."

"Precisely," Liz replies. "Like working with a horse, not a human. There's no doubt whales are intelligent, but that whale's response could just as well have been one of astonished bewilderment, curiosity, or disbelief as much as gratitude.

"You see, the point is, these are our emotions, not theirs. If those divers had freed a hungry great white shark it would've probably attacked them, but if it wasn't hungry, or if it was in shock, or disoriented, it too could be described as grateful, just like the whale. The reality is, those divers freed a mostly docile aquatic mammal, one more akin to a cow than a lion, one that doesn't have *Homo sapiens* on the menu."

"Isn't it a matter of degrees?" Elvis asks. "I mean, a cricket's smarter than a rock. A lizard is smarter than a cricket. A dog is smarter than a lizard, and on a good day, I'm smarter than my dog."

Jameson laughs. "You wish!"

"Haw haw," Elvis laughs in his distinct southern accent.

"In some regards, it's a matter of degrees," Liz replies. "As there's no doubt a doe cares for a newborn fawn, but all too often we read too much into these behaviors. We share 98% of our DNA with sex-crazed Bonobos, but that doesn't make them 98% human.

"You see, we're not the benchmark other species are trying to attain in terms of their intelligence and emotions. They're quite happy being themselves.

"There's little in the way of common ground between us and other animals. Think about dolphins. Cute, cuddly, friendly dolphins. Everyone loves dolphins, right? They're the good guys of the ocean. Yet for all we think we know about them, we really don't understand them at all. Male dolphins will gang rape females for days on end. Rival males will kill a newborn dolphin to bring a female back into heat. As playful as they seem in a dolphin show, as intelligent as they are, they're not humans, and we shouldn't treat them as such. Our morals—our values simply do not apply to them."

"I can't believe you're picking on dolphins," Elvis says. "Don't they save swimmers by dragging them to shore?"

Jameson says, "Yeah, but remember, you never hear from those they drag out to sea."

Elvis laughs.

Liz continues, saying, "Try as we may, we can't imagine life as a bat, relying on sonar rather than sight. We can't imagine sensing electric fields like a shark, or being a spider that sees four primary colors rather than three. In the same way, animals cannot imagine being human. We can teach gorillas to use sign language, we can teach parrots to hold a conversation, but they're adopting human precepts, not inheriting them as a child would.

"Think about it. Does a dog care who's the President of the United States? Does a cat care how much you earn? Does a goldfish know if you're married or single?

"We surround ourselves with artificial constructs—stuff we think is real—and these things influence our sense of culture, they carry emotional weight, yet they're meaningless to other animals."

"And you think these aliens are going to be like animals?" Jameson asks.

"Oh, no, but if we can't communicate openly with species on our own planet without reading our own emotions into their responses, what chance do we have of talking to someone from another planet? What chance do they have of talking to us without there being some kind of misunderstanding?"

"None," Elvis replies, grinning. "If any UFOs touch down south of the Mason-Dixon line, they're gonna regret cashing in those frequent flyer miles."

"You've got to see this from their perspective," Liz adds. "Saying, '*We come in peace*,' is probably all they *could* say without someone, somewhere taking things the wrong way. And, even then, can you imagine the conspiracy theory nuts? Oh, they'll be swinging from the chandeliers by now."

"Oh yeah," Elvis says. "I could name most of them. Ha ha."

Liz is excited about the conversation. The two soldiers might have only a passing interest, but Liz is electrified to think about first contact in detail. She makes the point, "Plus we don't just speak with words. Some scientists estimate that words make up only about half of any conversation. Most of what we say is conveyed by our posture, our body language, our tone of voice, our eyes. More than that, most of what we say is an extension of what's been said before. Saying '*I love you*' to someone after screaming at them for an hour doesn't really mean anything, right?"

Jameson says, "And you think these aliens are going to have a hard time understanding us?"

"We have a hard time understanding each other," Liz replies. "Our alien friends simply won't understand the subtleties and nuances of any one culture, let alone all of them. It doesn't matter how intelligent they are, it'll take them time to figure out our quirks and idiosyncrasies. They know nothing of our culture and idioms.

"Someone from another world isn't going to understand how heavily laced our speech is with references to our senses. Can you see what I mean? Can you hear what I'm saying? Has someone touched a raw nerve? Do you smell a rat? Did you find something distasteful? These aliens may have none of these senses, so even the most basic concepts could be meaningless to them.

"Here on Earth, we have creatures with completely alien senses. Stingrays detect the electrical impulses of a heart beating beneath the sand. Bats build a picture of the world around them using sonar. Butterflies taste with their feet!"

"No way," Elvis says.

"Yes way," Liz replies. "Chameleons move their eyes independently of each other, giving themselves two views at once. Imagine how confusing any of these senses would be for us, and you get an idea of how confusing our perspective could be to visitors from another planet."

"So," Elvis says, "You think these aliens will be alien in more ways than one?"

"Absolutely. They're aliens, right?" Liz asks rhetorically. "They're not movie extras in cheap plastic suits.

"As for feelings, think about what feelings are. They're a figurative extension of what we feel physically through our sense of touch. What about concepts like art, music, or religion? There's so much groundwork that'll have to be covered before we can even start to talk to ET in any depth.

"No, I think our alien visitors have said just enough: *We come in peace*. It's not too little, it's not too much. It's just enough to let us know they're in the neighborhood."

"So how do we talk to them?" Jameson asks as the truck trundles along.

"Well, it's just a guess on my part, but I'd say through science. Regardless of which culture you're from, regardless of which planet you call home, two plus two equals four, hydrogen has only one proton, stuff like that. Science is universal, so it's the logical place to start. Oh, these are exciting days."

"Yeah," Elvis replies, with sarcasm dripping from his words as he stares out across the dry savannah. "Real exciting. But I still think they're about to go all *Independence Day* on us."

Liz laughs, but it's more of a polite, almost nervous laugh than laughter at a joke. The uncertainty of First Contact—the fear of the unknown looms over them.

Silence descends on the cab of the truck. Physically, the cabin still groans and creaks as the truck hits potholes. Occasionally, the tires flick gravel against the underside of the vehicle. The old diesel engine rattles with a steady rhythm. The springs in the seats wheeze, rocking with the motion of the truck. But no one speaks.

Although the skies are clear, Liz feels as though dark clouds are rolling overhead. Is she right? Or is pride obscuring her point of view? She's so passionate, so confident, but since when were those tools of scientific investigation?

In 1616, the pope was convinced Galileo was wrong, calling his theories foolish and absurd. Perhaps she's being just as bullheaded? She's genuinely perplexed by the possibility. Is she blinded by her own conviction? Maybe she's overthinking things and is afraid of being wrong? As much as she doesn't want to admit it, deep down she's afraid Elvis might be right.

Liz glances at Jameson. He's examining the map. He radios something through to the Hummer, but she's barely aware of the words leaving his lips.

The soldiers appear to be deferring to her judgment on the nature of these aliens overhead—and why wouldn't they? It's all hypothetical at the moment—intangible to a squad leader from Utah and a grunt from Mississippi. They're men of war, not science. But she's a medical doctor, not a scientist. She understands the principles, but she has no reason to be so confident in her position. Liz sighs, knowing passion has got the better of her, hoping she's right, but knowing hers is an opinion, nothing more.

Grasslands give way to pockets of rainforest. Mud coats the track, making the drive difficult as the wheels occasionally slip into worn grooves. Liz has visions of getting stuck, and spending hours trying to push the truck out of a ditch, but Elvis seems to know when to drop down a gear and gun the engine so as to avoid sliding sideways into a rut.

For a moment, Liz dares to consider she could be wrong, and not just about her academic understanding of animal emotions—about everything. Life seems as incorporeal as the mist in the early morning. Everything she knows about medicine, science, and the bitterness of life in Africa—all of it seems surreal. It's as though she's awoken from a dream. A wake-up call has sounded from the stars, and it scares her to realize everything she's ever known, every aspect of life she trusts, is as frail as a house of cards. Everything that seemed so important suddenly becomes trivial and insignificant. Her mind casts back to Carl Sagan's *Pale Blue Dot* and a photograph of Earth from beyond the orbit of Pluto, with the entire history of humanity being consigned to nothing more than a tiny point of reflected light floating in the darkness. As Sagan noted, Earth is but a mote of dust drifting in a sunbeam.

No one notices as she shakes her head gently, trying to clear her thoughts. Perhaps they do, but they don't say anything. For her, those few seconds were both terrifying and exhilarating—she lost her grounding. Is that such a bad thing?

Liz breathes deeply, suppressing the anxiety welling up within. She shuts down this train of thought, clenching her fists. Her nails bite into her palms. Her forearm flexes. Slowly, a sense of calm returns and she finds herself in Africa, not among the stars.

As the road dries out, Jameson and Elvis chat idly about getting back to their base in Fort Benning, Georgia. They speak with a sense of nostalgia, and yet Liz wonders if they're really as enamored with the base when they're actually there. She doubts it. Nostalgia—the grass is always greener on the other side of the fence. In some ways, she envies them. They've got a common bond, something they can bullshit about to unwind and relive the pressure of the moment, leaving her feeling like a spare wheel.

"So you think we're going to make it, doc?" Elvis asks after a couple of miles, coming up with his question out of nowhere. Liz isn't sure what he means initially, but she can tell the question's been gnawing away at the back of his mind.

"Out of Africa?" she asks, wondering why he'd ask her. She hopes so, but she certainly doesn't know so.

"No. I mean, are we going to make it through all this alien stuff?"

"I'm sure we'll be fine," she replies with the scholarly authority only a doctor can pull off with aplomb. She has no idea, but she isn't going to let him in on that. It's important to maintain the illusion, if only for herself.

Liz is disappointed in her reaction. She's thrown up a facade, a pretense of confidence. Is it fear or pride that governed her response? She isn't sure, but she feels she's got to stay upbeat. She rationalizes her position.

Positive expectations are important. All too often a medical emergency or a chronic disease looks hopeless, and yet she's learned she can always give hope. It isn't a case of lying, more of framing the truth in an optimistic manner.

Looking into the eyes of a patient and telling them they've a 50/50 chance at life is heartbreaking. It has to be done, of course. But knowing that your life has no better odds than the toss of a coin or a roll of the dice is earth shattering. Hope can tip the balance. Hope endures when the body falters.

Liz has seen hope pull patients through against the odds. But placebos only work if you believe in them. For Jameson and Elvis, her words are a placebo—for her they're a lie.

"The boys are taking bets on this being the end of the world," Elvis continues. "Three-to-one against the aliens being peaceful. The smart money says they'll attack."

"I'll take those odds," Liz says in a show of bluster. "Put me down for twenty bucks on a nice, friendly neighbor. If I lose, I doubt there'll be anyone to collect."

Jameson laughs. He starts to say something, then seems to think better of it.

"No, go on," Liz says, turning toward him, wanting to know what's so funny.

"There's another bet," he says. "that you'd side against an attack."

"The odds?" she asks, surprised to be at the center of a betting proposition.

"Lousy—two to one."

"Which side were you on?"

"Oh," Jameson replies, lifting his hands in mock surrender. "Neither Elvis nor I would bet against you. And, hey, you came through."

Elvis laughs.

"This isn't the end of the world," Liz says, trying to convince not only Jameson and Elvis but herself. "This is just the beginning. In the centuries to come, this time will be seen as the dividing line in history. There will be everything that happened before Contact, and all that follows after. The implications are vast. Our science textbooks have become obsolete overnight with all we stand to learn about the universe. The world's changed—and for the better."

Liz wants to believe that. She has to believe that—any other response would be to capitulate to fear.

Jameson leans forward, pointing at Elvis as if to say, *I told you so.*

Elvis laughs, adding, "Oh, the world looks just as shitty today as it did yesterday, Doc."

Liz goes to say something, but Elvis cuts her off, saying, "I hope you're right, I really do."

"Me too," she replies with a forced smile.

The drive to Ksaungu takes six hours.

As they approach the city they see smoke rising lazily in the air. Dark black plumes hang above the distant buildings. Traffic's congested. All semblance of order has broken down. Cars, trucks, and motorcycles clog the roads and footpaths. Drivers honk their horns, yelling at each other, frustrated in the stifling heat. The stench of sewage hangs in the air.

During a rest stop, Liz moves to the back of the truck, giving Alile the chance to sit up front with Jameson and Elvis. Alile's reluctant, but Liz insists. There's no elite *foreigners-only* club, just humanity trying to survive its own best efforts at self-destruction. Besides, Liz can use the distraction of caring for others to forget about little green men in flying saucers for a while.

Liz sits in the back of the old truck talking with Kowalski, the nurses, and the patients.

The rear of the truck is covered with a tarpaulin canvas. There's little to hold onto, and Elvis isn't the most considerate of drivers. A slight breeze leaks in beneath gaps in the canvas near the cab of the truck. At the back, a loose flap flutters in the breeze, but the tires kick up dust. Fine grit and fumes swirl behind the truck, preventing them from opening the canvas to get some fresh air.

For the most part, everyone's in high spirits, but the premature baby's unusually lethargic. He's on a drip, and Liz is worried about him. His mother sits there rocking with the motion of the truck, stroking the child's head gently in the sweltering heat.

"Hey, doc," Jameson yells, leaning out of the window and lifting the front flap of canvas. "There are signs for a Red Cross station up ahead. Looks as if they're as stubborn as you. We're going to take your folks there, okay?"

"Yes. Please," she calls back over the sound of the diesel engine roaring as Elvis pulls out into heavy traffic, crossing a main thoroughfare.

The roads in Ksaungu are paved with asphalt, allowing Liz to open the canvas back, and let air circulate within the rear of the truck.

Bullet holes scar the rough concrete walls of various rundown buildings—the unmistakable testimony of war. Large chunks of masonry lie strewn on the street, marking where tanks have once battled for control of the provincial capital.

Power lines run down one side of the street in absurd bundles of ten to fifteen wires drooping from lamppost to lamppost. Numerous other wires peel away from the posts in what looks suspiciously like illegal wiring. At the very least, it's probably unregulated, with no regard for safety, but in Africa that doesn't mean it's illegal. Amidst the cars and trucks, horse-drawn carts trundle along carrying vegetables and meats to the markets.

The impromptu Red Cross hospital's been set up in an abandoned train station. Several of the staff come out to greet the Rangers as they pull up.

"Americans," one of the Red Cross doctors says in a distinctly Australian voice. "Well, you're a sight for sore eyes. I thought you'd all done a runner."

"We have," Jameson replies in a matter-of-fact tone of voice as he leads the Australian around to the back of the truck. "but we had a bit of unfinished business. Had to get some civvies to safety."

"You think Ksaungu's safe?" the Red Cross official asks.

"We're trying to get these folks to Mozambique," Liz says as she helps a patient down from the truck.

Jameson adds, "We have in-country staff and patients we couldn't abandon out there in the field. From here, we're headed to Lilongwe for evacuation."

"Lilongwe?" the Red Cross doctor asks. "You might want to rethink your plans. Lilongwe's under siege by the rebels. Last I heard, several suburbs had fallen to the uprising, but the government isn't giving up without a fight."

"What about the Red Cross?" Jameson asks as Liz stands beside him. "Are you pulling out?"

"We've removed all non-essential staff. If the fighting gets close, we'll pull back across the border, but for now, there's too much work to do."

Liz shakes hands with the Australian doctor, as does Alile. Kowalski isn't bothered with pleasantries. He waves as he moves patients out of the sun and into the shade of an overhanging patio.

"We're going to hole up in the Hotel Ksaungu," Jameson adds, "and try to make contact with US forces at sea."

"Good luck with that," the doctor replies. "We haven't seen sight nor sound of US or UN forces since they announced that bloody alien spaceship had arrived."

"Do you have contact with anyone in Mozambique?" Liz asks.

"We've got a couple of old buses making daily runs to the border. We can get your people on one, so long as they're fit to travel."

"Wonderful," Liz replies, smiling. Alile smiles as well, but without the same measure of conviction.

Liz and Alile follow the doctor inside the Red Cross station.

When she comes outside an hour or so later, the sun's setting. The Rangers lounge around, playing cards on the hood of the truck, never straying more than an arm's length from their M4 rifles. The Hummer's gone, presumably to the hotel.

"So what's the plan, doc?" Jameson asks. "Are you and Kowalski hooking up with the Red Cross?"

Jameson understands. She's not one of them. She's part of an NGO—and not even from the same country as the Rangers. What's the next step? In that moment, she sees a glimpse of the valor with which the Rangers serve. They've never had any official responsibility for her and her team. They didn't have to escort her to Ksaungu, let alone hang around outside the makeshift hospital. Bands of thugs roam the streets in pickup trucks, brandishing automatic rifles, but the Rangers' presence has ensured that the Red Cross outpost has remained orderly.

In private, Liz has often been critical of the military intervention in Malawi, saying, what's needed are civil engineers and teachers, not more guns and bombs. Now, though, she sees things in a different light.

Jameson has posed a good question—what *are* they going to do? In essence, Jameson's asking if she wants to be released from his military care. That's a novel thought, one with potentially profound implications for her and Kowalski. Bower's been running on autopilot. The Rangers don't owe her anything, while she owes them a debt beyond mere gratitude.

"Thank you for all you've done," she says, somewhat absentmindedly. "Ah, I'm going to have to consult Mitch on that. Can you give me a minute?"

"Sure."

Liz turns and walks back into the rundown building.

Kowalski's working with Alile to clean out an infected wound on the leg of a young boy. Liz doesn't recognize the boy. He must be a local.

"Shrapnel wound. So bloody messy I can't tell if there's metal still in there. I need an x-ray, but that's not happening this side of the border."

"Mitch," Liz says, and the tone of her voice gets his attention. He seems to predict what's coming next. "The soldiers need to move on. What do you want to do?"

You—it's a word pregnant with meaning. She didn't say we. Liz already knows what she wants to do, but she wants to hear Kowalski's perspective. She'd like to think he could persuade her to continue providing medical assistance at the makeshift hospital, but deep down she already knows she's going to leave with the soldiers. She hopes he'll say something that'll make her decision easier, some justification she can cling to without feeling like a traitor.

"I can't say I've ever been too fond of men marching around with guns," Kowalski replies, "but they saved our ass up there in Chikangawa."

He pulls his gloves off and slowly, thoughtfully, takes his glasses off to rub the bridge of his nose. They're both lost in thought. Kowalski turns to Alile, saying, "Will you finish up?"

Alile nods, averting her eyes from them. Liz notices.

Liz takes a sip of water from her canteen.

"It's one of those moments, isn't it?" Kowalski says. "We're at a crossroad. We can go one way or another, but we can never revisit this moment again if we change our minds. The luxury of choice is fleeting."

Liz tries to smile, but that act feels forced. Kowalski's right. She notes that he used the pronoun '*we*' in his reply. He's more circumspect than her. She struggles to swallow the lump in her throat.

"What do you think?" Kowalski asks.

Liz looks around. The field hospital's already overflowing. Patients lie on metal gurneys in the hallways, quietly enduring until someone can treat them, although treating's a misnomer. Beyond basic surgery, cleaning, and bandaging a wound, there isn't a lot that can be done.

"I need a crystal ball," she says, exasperated. "I mean, we're trying to make a decision based on information we don't have, information that can only come in the future. Will the government of Malawi prevail? Will all this play out in a matter of days or weeks, or will this war go on for years? Will the UN ever return? If so, when? And perhaps most important, what difference will that bloody alien spaceship make?"

Liz looks at Alile working away quietly on Kowalski's patient. Alile doesn't have to say what she's thinking.

Neither Alile nor the boy can flee with the soldiers. The best they can hope for is to get across the border into Mozambique as refugees. They're trapped by the cruelest of circumstances beyond their control—the country in which they were born.

Liz feels sick.

What a stupid, fucked up world. There's no merit, no compassion, no understanding.

There's nothing any of them can do about nationalities—and yet it's an artificial distinction that may make the difference between life and death. That Alile's fate is arbitrary and whimsical is barbaric. Liz hates herself for being European, even if only in name and not by ethnicity. How do the Americans do it? How does anyone? It's too bloody easy to look the other way.

"You should go," Alile says in her distinct African accent. "You came here to help us with our mess. You have helped. You can do no more. You should leave while you still can."

'*Our*'—there's another pronoun coming into play: *you, we, our*. Each pronoun reveals more about its speaker than Liz has ever realized before, although '*our*' isn't entirely accurate. Malawi may have been where Alile was born, but the problems the country is going through have nothing to do with her personally. Liz feels conflicted. Her heart goes out to the brave young nurse. Alile's being kind, giving them an out. The reality is, these artificial designations of country and race hold no bearing other than what people have made of them. Liz feels like a heel taking the easy way out. Her heart sinks.

"There's too much suffering in this country," Alile continues. "You've done all you can, but it's we who must end it. You can go. You *should* go."

Kowalski is silent.

"I'll arrange for the others to go on to Mozambique," Alile says.

"But what about you?" Liz asks, unable to address the hurt in her heart.

"This is my country. If I leave then I am giving up on her. I cannot do that. If all the good people leave, there will be no one left to stand up against evil, and I cannot bear that thought."

Liz is silent.

Kowalski goes to say something, but Alile cuts him off with one, sharp word.

"Go."

Go isn't a request, neither is it a command. Go is a plea.

Tears well up in Alile's eyes.

Kowalski stands, rubbing his hands over his face and working his fingers in the corner of his eyes as though he's clearing out grit.

"Promise me," Liz says. "Promise me you'll leave before it's too late. Promise me you'll make a run for the border when the time comes."

"I promise."

Kowalski hugs Alile, which seems to take the young lady by surprise. She holds her hands away from his body so her bloodied gloves don't stain his clothing. Kowalski doesn't care. His face is set in stone. Liz hugs the two of them, tears running down her cheeks.

After a couple of seconds, Kowalski pulls back.

Liz steps away as Kowalski takes Alile by the shoulders saying, "With people like you, there's hope for Malawi."

Alile nods but her head hangs low. She can't make eye contact, and Liz understands why. Liz can see so much in the body language of this brave, young nurse. Changing the culture of a country demands that its people choose a new future. Freedom must be claimed, not imposed. Alile is just one voice, but change has to start somewhere. Change cannot come from without. It must come from within.

Liz feels her lower lip quivering as she goes to say goodbye. The words never come. She leans in and kisses Alile on each cheek, unable to express what she feels inside.

"It's okay," Alile says. "You've done more than could have been asked of you. Thank you. One day, Malawi will be free, and we'll meet again."

Liz acknowledges her without saying anything. Words feel cheap.

She and Kowalski step out into the twilight as the Hummer pulls up, parking in front of the truck. Walking down the stairs leading out of the station, Liz feels as though she's sinking deeper into despair with each step. She's done all she can for Alile, and the other staff members and patients, but guilt gnaws at her heart, condemning her for leaving them.

"This is shit," Kowalski says, turning to Liz as they walk toward the waiting soldiers. "Some bloody world we live in. Someone comes from another world to visit, and we abandon each other, we panic and abandon our sense of humanity. What did these aliens come to see? Mindless animals? Because that's all there is here, that's all they'll find!"

Liz swallows the lump in her throat.

The diesel engine roars to life.

As the vehicles pull out of the courtyard, Liz sees Alile standing there, her arms limp by her sides. A pang of guilt strikes at her heart. She wants to wave, but she can't. There's no joy in this parting, none for either of them.

The hotel is less than three miles away but the journey takes several hours. As they drive through the darkened streets, sporadic gunfire breaks out, echoing off the buildings. In the distance, up on the hinterland, flashes of light ripple through the jungle canopy. Explosions rock the jungle road they traveled during the day.

The staff at the hotel are pleased to see them pull up, making a fuss of the soldiers, telling them they can stay for free. Jameson comments quietly to Liz that he hadn't even thought about money. He mumbles something about taking an IOU for Uncle Sam.

From the hotel's perspective, having US soldiers on the premises provides a degree of security in a city sliding toward anarchy. The hotel gives the Rangers five rooms at one end of the third floor. Jameson arranges for his soldiers to pull sentry duty, setting Liz and Kowalski in the middle room with strict instructions to stay clear of the windows.

Kowalski's a gentleman, offering Liz the first shower. In the sweltering heat of the early evening, a cool shower is refreshing, while the soap seems to clean more than just the pores in her skin. After drying off and getting dressed, Liz steps out of the bathroom, determined to talk with Kowalski about Alile.

Kowalski sits on the edge of the bed. He hands her a can of Coca-Cola, saying, "There's no ice, so it's a little hot."

"Isn't everything in Malawi?" Liz replies, popping the ring on top of the can. "Mitch, about what happened back there. I—"

"I know what you're going to say," Kowalski counters. "It's a triage decision, isn't it? You can't save everyone, so you choose those you can save. You choose them based on those with the best chance of survival. You've got to be cold, clinical, realistic."

Liz sits down on the edge of the bed beside him. Actually, she wasn't going to say that at all. She isn't too sure what she wants to say. She's struggling to separate selfishness from self-preservation. She feels conflicted. For years, Liz and her right-wing brother in England have argued about the role of altruism in society. He takes the position that self-preservation trumps all other notions—that when it comes down to it, people will do whatever they have to in order to save their own hides. On several occasions, she's disagreed, pointing out that she's given her life in medical service to others, and yet now when it matters most, all her idealistic platitudes have been proven worthless. Does that make her weak? Does that make her evil? Flawed? Or just human?

She's silent, lost in a mixture of Kowalski's words and her own thoughts.

Kowalski breathes deeply. "It just sucks, you know?"

Liz nods and sips from the warm can of Coca-Cola. The soft drink tastes disgusting, but she's past caring. Kowalski stares at her, but his mind's elsewhere. His voice is soft, considerate, but a glazed look sits behind his thin-rimmed glasses.

"When I was an intern in Poland, so very many years ago, we had a football stadium collapse. High winds brought down part of the roof, trapping several of the spectators, but that wasn't the worst of the incident. People panicked. They must've thought the whole place was going to cave in. They were scared. They ran for their lives. They pushed, they shoved, they fought to get out of the stadium. Eighty-four people died, crushed to death in the stampede."

Liz swallows the knot in her throat.

"I was supposed to be working the graveyard shift in the emergency department later that evening, but they called me in early when the casualties started piling up in the ambulance bay.

"My mentor was an old German doctor by the name of Hans Grosen. I turned up, and he gave me a blue whiteboard marker. He told me to start numbering the patients outside, grading them from one to five based on the severity of their injuries, writing my medical opinion on their foreheads in the form of a single number. What he didn't tell me is why."

Kowalski takes his glasses off, wiping a tear from his eye.

"I assumed he'd give the fives priority, but he only ever called for the threes and fours. The ones and twos survived with pain management administered by the paramedics.

"Not one of the fives survived beyond midnight, and he knew that would happen—the bastard. I hated him for that. God, how I hated him, and yet he was right. We treated almost two hundred people that night, and we only lost eleven souls. All but one of them carried a five on their forehead."

Kowalski breathes deeply, composing himself.

"To this day, I can't pick up a blue whiteboard marker without my hands shaking. I'm fine with black, green, or red, but just looking at a blue marker brings me out in a cold sweat."

Liz finds her lips pursed, shut tight in anguish. She doesn't know what to say. Kowalski's been thinking about this in far greater depth than she has.

"This whole goddamn country's a five, Liz."

She nods. Tears run down her cheeks as he continues.

"There's nothing we can do—not a single thing!"

Kowalski pats her shoulder gently as he stands up, saying, "Sometimes the right decision is the hardest decision of all. We came here to make a difference. We can no longer do that. As much as I hate to say it, it's time to leave."

Liz struggles to swallow the lump in her throat.

Kowalski starts walking toward the bathroom.

"I'll sleep on the couch," he says. He walks into the bathroom with his shoulders stooped, the weight of an entire country bearing down upon him.

Liz sits there for a few minutes, listening to the sound of running water falling like rain. She feels empty, but she has to move on.

Kowalski's almost six feet tall—there's no way he'll fit on the couch. While he's in the shower, Liz takes a pillow and sheet from the cupboard and turns off the light. She curls up on the couch with the sheet draped lightly over her.

Liz is still awake when Kowalski comes out of the bathroom but she keeps her eyes shut, pretending she's asleep. She doesn't know what else she can say to him. There are no words that can soothe their grief.

Lying there in the dark, she's acutely aware of each passing second. She doesn't know how long she lies there, but after a while she hears Kowalski softly snoring. Ordinarily, he'd kept her awake, but on this night his gentle rasp brings relief. Time marches on and her body demands its rest even if her mind rebels. Within an hour, she's asleep.

In the morning, Liz wakes to the sound of the soldiers playing in the courtyard below her window. They're boisterous, yelling at each other and throwing a football around. It's late when she rises.

This is becoming a habit, and not a good one.

Deep sleep isn't quite the reaction she expected from the stress she's been under, but she feels rundown and worn out, so it's somewhat understandable.

Five.

That number's seared in her thinking. Is he right? As a physician, it doesn't feel right abandoning anyone, no matter how hopeless the cause. If there's life, there's a chance. That's been her mantra for years, but sometimes it's right to let go. People, even entire countries—at some point everyone has to live or die on their own.

Why did they let her sleep so late, she wonders? Doesn't Jameson want to push on to Lilongwe? She remembers the discussion with the Red Cross. Jameson's probably trying to find out what's happening in Lilongwe, so they don't go from the frying pan into the fire.

After freshening up in the bathroom, Liz dresses and heads downstairs. She finds Jameson and Kowalski sitting in a decrepit restaurant by the pool. The water in the pool is green, but that doesn't worry the soldiers who seem hell-bent on emptying the pool with the biggest possible splashes they can muster. They run and jump into the murky water, sending waves crashing over the edge of the pool, out across the cobblestones. The courtyard must have been quite nice once, but missing tiles and cracked walls betray decades of neglect.

Jameson and Kowalski are talking with another man, someone Liz doesn't recognize.

"James Leopold," the middle aged man says, standing to greet Liz as she walks over. "Reporter for Rolling Stone, and African correspondent for CNN."

Leopold's pale complexion is out of place in Africa. His hair's neatly cropped. As a young man, he could've featured in a glossy catalog selling designer suits. He has a natural, handsome look and an engaging smile, the kind that seems to guarantee a sale. Liz figures he's in his mid to late fifties, perhaps his early sixties, still looking handsome and fit. He has a light dusting of gray on either side of the dark hair on his head, making him look distinguished rather than old.

"Elizabeth Bower. I'm a doctor with *Médecins Sans Frontières*."

"The pleasure's mine," he replies, shaking her hand gently. He has a smooth tongue to match his looks.

"Do you want some breakfast, Liz?" Kowalski asks. "They've got eggs. They're not very tasty, but a bit of protein doused in fat never hurt anyone, right?"

"Sure," Liz replies, a little confused by Kowalski and his surprisingly upbeat mood. Last night was a watershed moment for her, but he appears to have switched off after what seemed like a conversation reserved for a confessional booth. Two Hail Marys and three repetitions of the Lord's Prayer, will that wash away the past? Somehow, Kowalski's shut down his emotions, or perhaps that's the impression he wants to give. Either way, she understands. Being doctors, they both know introversion's professional suicide, leaving only an empty shell. There comes a point where you have to bury the past and move on. For her, though, one night seems too quick. She doubts he's over what happened yesterday at the hospital. She knows she isn't.

Liz sits down as Kowalski gets up and walks behind the bar, disappearing into the kitchen. Jameson picks up on the look of surprise on her face.

"The help here is a bit inconsistent. If you want something, you've got to go get it yourself. Your buddy Kowalski isn't a bad chef."

Liz smiles, pouring herself a glass of water.

"Like kids, aren't they," she says, gesturing toward the soldiers by the pool. Elvis is lying on a deck chair with his shirt off, sunning himself, while Smithy's being chased by several of the other soldiers. They crash tackle her, flying into her and dragging her into the pool. She doesn't seem to mind a bit of wrestling.

Bosco's the only one doing any work. He sits beneath the shade of a poolside umbrella, working on the radio. Beside him, another soldier lies asleep with a towel draped over his face.

"Shouldn't they be soldiering, or whatever it is you normally do?" Liz asks. She isn't being mean, she's curious. Jameson must sense her question's genuine, as he doesn't take her comment as a criticism.

"Yeah. Seems a little out of place, doesn't it? But that's army life for you. These guys have not only been trained to fight, they've been trained to exploit. In the army, you never know what's coming next. So if you don't have to stand, you sit. If you don't have to sit, you lie down. If you don't have to be awake, you sleep. You exploit whatever opportunities you have, as you never know what the next forty-eight hours will demand of you, so it's good for them to let their hair down, and have a little R&R. Although I need Bosco to get that damn radio fixed. We have got to find out what the hell's happening in Lilongwe."

Liz nods.

"So, Dr. Bower," Leopold says, pulling out a small worn pad and pen.

"Liz, please," she replies, wanting Leopold to address her informally. She feels a little uncomfortable with his tone, not sure how she's walked into an impromptu interview.

"Liz, what do you make of all this?"

Leopold's already started jotting notes, but she isn't sure why. How can he write something before she's had the chance to reply? Perhaps he's making general observations, catching the mood of the rundown restaurant, or the frivolous attitude of the soldiers as background material. Besides, Liz doubts she can tell him anything of any significance.

"Me?" she says with surprise, composing her thoughts. "Well, I think it's grossly irresponsible for the international community to pull out of Malawi. I don't see how an alien spaceship changes anything on the ground here in Africa. There are plenty of people within NASA and ESA to deal with UFOs. I think the greatest danger we face is not from alien visitors, so much as from our own paranoid reactions."

Leopold doesn't lift his eyes from his pad. He madly scratches notes. It seems pen and paper will never go out of vogue, especially when electrical power's in short supply.

"What do you think of the imposition of martial law?" Leopold asks.

"We're in the middle of a civil war. There's no room for civil liberties at a time like this."

"Oh, I'm not talking about Malawi. I'm talking about the US and Europe."

Liz feels her blood run cold.

"What?" she exclaims.

"How much do you know?" Leopold asks, looking up from his notepad for a moment.

Jameson steps into the conversation, saying, "Nothing." Liz can see he's as taken back by the concept of martial law in the USA as she is. In that moment, the noises around her fade into the background—the soldiers playing by the pool, the government helicopter flying overhead, the sporadic gunfire she's grown accustomed to in the distance all slip into silence as she focuses on Leopold's words.

"The United States has gone into meltdown, with President Addison under house arrest and the National Guard on the streets. Commerce has ground to a halt. Supermarket shelves have been stripped bare. Gas stations are running dry.

"Congress has issued anti-hoarding laws, while ordering public servants to continue working through the crisis, but the vast majority of those in non-critical roles have stayed away from the office.

"The media hasn't helped. They've whipped the country into a frenzy, with reports of alien spacecraft touching down across the United States."

"They've landed?" Liz asks, almost jumping out of her seat.

"No one knows for sure. There's so much confusion. Several videos of aliens attacking a farmhouse in Iowa have gone viral, but they were later debunked as fakes. Regardless, the panic they generated is real. Now, no one knows what to believe.

"Some aspects of society are still functioning, but not many. Schools are closed. The police are overwhelmed. Hospitals are running low on supplies. It ain't pretty. You think it's bad here? At least here we know who the enemy is. Over there, there's mass hysteria."

As he speaks, Jameson turns his head. Liz follows his gaze. A dark tendril of smoke cuts through the air above the city. The smoke trail of a rocket-propelled grenade lashes out at a government helicopter, sending it spiraling to the ground. The chopper is barely a gnat in the distance. Plumes of black smoke billow from its fuselage as it twists and corkscrews through the air, plunging to the city below.

"Yeah, well," Jameson says, "I doubt they're firing RPGs at each other."

Kowalski walks over, placing a plate of scrambled eggs in front of Liz along with a knife and fork.

"Did you want some orange juice?" Kowalski asks, gesturing toward a glass pitcher sitting on a table in the courtyard. The drink has been set out for the soldiers. Plastic cups lie scattered across the table and over the tiles. The football must have struck early on, barely missing the pitcher, knocking the cups across the dusty ground. The ruddy contents in the glass jug look more like Kool-Aid than juice. Ice floats on top of the drink. Liz looks at Kowalski, somewhat surprised he can be so detached and nonchalant as the smoke from the downed chopper billows into the sky. It's as though he's the construct of some surreal dream. She takes a second to reply.

"Uh, no. Thank you."

Her head's spinning. She tastes the eggs. They're slightly salty, but the burst of flavor brings her back to the moment. It's only then she realizes how hungry she is.

"The Russians, the Chinese, and Germans are all on a war footing," Leopold says. "They're mobilizing their armies, but against who? I'm not sure anyone really knows what they're dealing with."

Liz feels as though she's supposed to provide some profound insight. What difference will her opinion make? She averts her eyes, looking down at her plate as she eats. Leopold shifts the subject back to Malawi.

"What brought you into a war zone?"

Liz is barely aware of Kowalski on the periphery of her vision. He wanders out into the courtyard by the pitcher of orange juice, but he doesn't do anything for the longest time. He just stands silently staring up at the sky.

Leopold's question isn't easy to answer, and Liz is in no mood for the patronizing interest of a journalist killing time. She isn't sure how to describe her mood, whether it's a blend of disappointment with herself, anger at the United Nations, or frustration over the warring factions in Malawi, but playing twenty-questions isn't high in her priorities.

"Look at me," she says, taking Leopold off guard and forcing him to look up from his notepad. "Don't just listen to my voice. Don't be deceived by the sense of civility and culture in my accent, or the air of regal British speech in my pronunciation. Look at me for who I am. Look at the dark color of my skin, the tight, curly texture of my hair."

Liz puts her knife and fork down, and holds out her arms. She's wearing a short-sleeved blouse with the top two buttons undone. Her dark African skin is a stark contrast to the soft, white cotton. Although she washed her face this morning, the heat of the day is already causing her to perspire, giving her skin an oily sheen.

"We're all from Africa, Mr. Leopold. It's just a question of when our ancestors left this continent. For me, that was at some point in the 80s, while for you it was thirty to forty thousand years ago, but make no mistake about it, we are all Africans."

"So you hold to your African heritage?" he says, missing her point, or perhaps picking out only what he wanted to hear.

"What is it that defines us? In the West, we like to think we've moved beyond the color of our skin, but we still define each other by the shitty patch of dirt on which we were born. We're all *Homo sapiens*. Genetically, we're virtually the same. There are no differences between us beyond those we make. Our differences arise only in how and where we were raised—and what a difference that is. Coming from the First World, you have a life expectancy somewhere in the high eighties. These people around us, though, will be lucky if they make forty. And why? It's not just the civil war, it's everything we do to each other—the superstitions, the prejudices, the insatiable lust for power, the weakness that leads to corruption.

"A bunch of little green men appear in orbit, and we'll show them what we want them to see. We'll show them our universities, our operas and arias, our Picassos and Rembrandts, but I hope they see this. I hope they see dry, dusty Malawi. I hope they see the orphans. I hope they see the widows. For then they'll see us for the contradiction that is humanity."

Liz looks deep into Leopold's eyes.

"The question isn't, what brought me to a war zone—it's, why the hell are there still war zones? Why do we treat each other with such disdain? When will we grow up? Perhaps ET will have a few pointers for us, if we don't shoot him out of the sky."

Leopold stops writing. He looks past her, out of the courtyard and up at the sky. Liz is incensed. He's ignoring her.

Kowalski sits down next to her with two glasses of orange juice, putting one in front of her even though she said she doesn't want another drink. She looks at him. His eyes are blank—he's struggling with everything that's happening. The world's changing so fast. Like Leopold, Kowalski's got to be filtering what he's heard her say, substituting what he wants to hear. Liz sips at the juice without saying a word, but clearly the pressure's getting to them all. Rather than orange juice, her drink tastes like watered-down Tang.

Jameson gets up with a start, the steel legs of his chair scraping on the tiles. He walks out into the courtyard by the pool. It's only then Liz realizes the yelling and playing of the soldiers ceased a few minutes ago. She turns and looks at the soldiers. They're standing still, looking up at the sky in silence. To her surprise, the gunfire sporadically erupting throughout the city fades. Something's wrong. Liz walks out behind Jameson.

There, in the cloudless blue sky, sits the alien spacecraft hundreds of miles above Earth's atmosphere. Liz isn't sure what she expected, but the sight before her is like nothing she's ever imagined. At first glance, she assumed she was looking at the moon, with its soft bluish white surface visible in the daylight, its dark side hidden in the bright sky, but this is no thin crescent, no silver arc reflecting sunlight from the depths of space. This is a living organism.

Tentacles ripple around the edge of the alien craft. Fine cilia wave with the light. The alien spaceship reminds her more of a single-celled bacterium than a machine that's traversed the stars. Like a waxing moon, most of the craft is hidden from sight, but those surfaces that catch the sunlight show up in incredible detail, revealing the craft's elongated shape.

The craft pulsates—its cilia move in waves, like the wind rippling across a field of wheat. Shapes form like fingerprints slowly fading away. The very structure of the craft seems to change as though it were not a fixed shape. The alien vessel appears to ooze through space.

"What the—?"

Liz isn't sure who spoke, but she's inclined to agree. There's only one thing she's sure of—humanity has no idea what it's dealing with. There are no parallels. There's no point of comparison, nothing to draw upon. Whatever these aliens are, whatever they represent, however they think, whatever their motives, there's no earthly equivalent.

"We're in uncharted waters," she says. Her mind is awash with doubt. Leopold walks up beside her.

"I take it you guys haven't seen the freak show before?"

Liz turns to him, wondering what stunned look sits on her face. "How the—?"

"Yeah," Leopold continues. "It has that effect on everyone the first time."

"What do you know about it?" Jameson asks, stepping backwards next to them. His eyes never leave the craft as it rises slowly above the uneasy quiet of the city. Liz can see his professionalism kicking in.

Leopold speaks with the precision of a reporter providing a sound bite.

"The mothership is the size of Connecticut. NASA says there's no cause for panic, but you try telling that to a bunch of rednecks crowing about anal probes, a bunch of Arabs that won't let women drive, a Buddhist monk, and a corrupt Russian politician. Don't panic, my ass. Hysteria's seized the world. You think Malawi's all fucked up—you should see Yonkers. "

In any other context, Liz would laugh, but it's apparent Leopold isn't joking.

"They're saying it's the end of the world, but that's not the worst of it."

Liz doesn't say anything, she can't think of anything more disruptive than creatures from another world.

"The worst part of all this is those nutters that are trying to bring about the end of the world. For them, this is a biblical prophesy come true, something about a dragon with seven heads."

There is no grandstanding on Leopold's part, these are raw facts.

"NASA released images of the craft a few days ago, just before the UFO moved in from somewhere near the Moon. The press ran with the scientific opinion that the alien presence is benign, but that doesn't matter—all it took was a few fringe groups to run with worst case scenarios about the aliens being monsters from hell, and fear ran rampant through society. The general population freaked out at the thought of an alien spaceship flying overhead with impunity. It's Sputnik all over again.

"It's not just that the alien spacecraft looks scary, it's that the appearance of this grotesque craft has shattered our illusion of control. The universe no longer revolves around us. We like to think we're masters of our own destiny, but that thing's proven otherwise, showing just how utterly insignificant and powerless we really are."

Leopold stutters, which seem out of character for him, making Liz wonder how deeply this has affected him personally.

"At first, it was just the wackos, you know—the cults, the isolationists shacked up in some barn in the middle of farmland, waiting for the Messiah or some shit. Men, women, children—Jonestown all over again. *Then* they started finding normal folk, people that just snapped. Murder-suicides. Poor bastards never reached out to anyone. They should have. They should've said something. They should have *talked* to someone about what they were feeling. They shouldn't have felt helpless. They shouldn't have felt alone. There were people all around them who cared—they just couldn't see it."

Tears roll down his cheeks. Liz starts to say something, but Leopold cuts her off.

"Life should never end that way. Life is too precious. No matter how dark the night, there's always another dawn. Even if someone's on the other side of the world, they're never more than a phone call away, you know?"

Jameson's head hangs low. Liz feels a lump in her throat.

"I should've been there. Not half a world away, drinking myself silly in some shitty bar in a country on the verge of war. But, no, I had to be someone. I had to prove something. I was driven—driven by what? Driven *to* what? To be the big man, the foreign correspondent for a throw-away thirty second slot in the late edition of the news?"

He pauses for a second, and Liz wonders who he's lost. She can't be sure, but she suspects it's his parents.

"Funny thing, this alien spaceship. Makes you see life in a different light. It's as though someone's lifted the rose-colored glasses and I'm finally seeing reality for what it is."

He wipes his eyes.

"It's not their fault," Leopold says. "The aliens, that is. Hell, they haven't done anything other than to show up at the party. It's us. Self-obsessed. For tens of thousands of years we thought the cosmos revolved around us, the sun and all the stars rising and setting on our egos. Oh, Copernicus might have shifted the bounds, putting the sun at the center of the solar system, but we still thought as though everything revolved around us.

"Look at how stupid we are. They come in peace. We go to pieces. They must think the whole bloody planet's an insane asylum."

"But," Liz pleads, "there must be someone down here that's kept their head about them."

"Oh, there's a bunch of scientists banding together to represent humanity, only they don't. They're the minority—the level heads. Even they're victims of the madness."

"I don't understand," Jameson says.

"Fear spreads like wildfire. We're like a herd of buffalo spooked by lightning. The thunder breaks and we charge headlong off the cliff, blindly following whoever's in front of us. Stampedes trample the weak, they bring out the worst in humanity. There's only so much rational thought when the supermarket shelves are bare. There's only so much restraint when the gas pump runs empty. There's only so long we can hold out against our base survival instincts—then we're just animals fighting to survive. It's trample, or *be* trampled."

Leopold put his hands on his head, pulling at his hair in frustration as he turns to one side, making as though he's going to scream.

Jameson takes charge. He seems to understand what's needed. He barks orders at his soldiers. His gruff voice snaps Leopold back to reality.

"Elvis, take Smithy, Brannigan and Phelps, and see what sense you can get out of any refugees coming up from Lilongwe. We need to know if the UN still holds the airport.

"Bosco, I need that goddamn radio fixed. We need to get in touch with the Navy. Get them to send in a couple of helos for evac."

Elvis struts over with his chest bare, sweat dripping from his muscular frame.

"They ain't gonna send shit with RPGs lighting up the sky," he says in his typical Memphis swagger. He picks up his backpack and his M4 rifle, handling them as though they were weightless.

Jameson considers his words. "Then we get clear of Ksaungu. If we can, we make for Lilongwe and grab the last stagecoach out of Dodge. If we can't make Lilongwe, we find ourselves some clear ground and call in the cavalry."

"What if the radio doesn't work?" Bosco asks.

"Same as usual. We march over the mountains," Jameson says.

"Fucking-A," Elvis replies. He seems to relish the prospect of marching for hundreds of miles through the jungle. He's already heading out through the restaurant with three other soldiers.

Liz appreciates Jameson's resolve. He's breaking them out of a slump, not letting his men lose focus.

"You can join us," Jameson says, reaching out a hand to Leopold. For a second, the older man hesitates, then he shakes the soldier's hand.

"I appreciate the gesture, but I'm here for the duration."

Jameson nods respectfully.

Leopold looks back at the alien craft. Whatever its path, it isn't passing directly overhead; its orbit takes it from the southeast to the northwest, but its passage is further to the west, drifting over Zambia.

"I'll be all right," Leopold adds, looking at Liz. Kowalski walks up grinning as though he's on holiday. Between the two of them, Liz knows exactly what's happening.

Leopold seems to be able to switch off his concerns, but it's a facade. She saw him coming apart at the seams just moments ago. Now, he's calm and collected. Like all of them, he's been in Africa too long. He's learnt to disconnect himself from reality so as to deal with the cruelty of war, but that means suspending the normal feelings of empathy one has for another. He isn't calloused. It's a self-defense mechanism. Liz has to do the same thing whenever she operates in surgery; to do any less would be to jeopardize someone's life. Leopold has extended this front to dealing with the aliens. He's suppressing his feelings about his family as, just moments ago, they threatened to boil over.

As savage as a war zone is, it's a known quantity. The prospect of a world torn apart on contact with a vastly superior alien species represents too many unknowns. Unknowns unsettle even the bravest souls. As much as Liz wants to think of herself as coldly logical, she knows there's a bias at play, skewing her perception as much as his.

Kowalski's too calm, making out as though there's nothing exceptional in the sky. Jameson might not show it, but he too must feel the fractured tension.

Right now, Liz could say, 'I saw a unicorn dancing in a rainbow this morning,' and no one would bat an eyelid. It's shock—not from physical trauma, but from sensory overload. Liz has seen this once before, during her first parachute jump.

Standing there in the sweltering heat of the courtyard, her mind flashes back to her first tandem jump from ten thousand feet. The air was surprisingly cold when the door to the small Cessna opened. With stainless steel carabiners locking her jumpsuit to the instructor behind her, the two of them shuffled awkwardly toward the open door. Her instructor told her it would be just like their rehearsal on the tarmac. All she had to do was to swing her feet around, out of the open door, and rest them on the wheel arch, but her mind shut down. She could hear people talking to her, reassuring her she'd be fine, but her body felt numb.

Liz remembers nodding to the instructor, signaling she was ready to go, when all she wanted was to crawl into the cockpit and hide. Those few seconds felt like a dream. The instructor positioned himself behind her, his legs straddling her back. She remembers the countdown from three, which was a ridiculously small number to start from. Why not five? Or better yet, ten? She knew it was a token gesture, something to provide her with a semblance of sanity when jumping out of a perfectly good aircraft, and then it hit her—sensory overload. The instructor pushed forward, tumbling headlong out of the plane with her hanging from his straps.

Apparently, they had thirty seconds of free fall before the chute opened, but Liz felt her mind shut down. There was too much coming at her. All she remembers is sitting on the edge of the plane, and then the chute opening above her. At the time, she marveled at how far away the plane was when the parachute opened. Her mind was jarred by the plane's apparently instantaneous motion. It was only when she reviewed the video from her helmet cam that she realized she had blanked out. Liz never lost consciousness; her mind simply refused to process a series of events that appeared to lead only to her demise. It wasn't until the chute opened that her subconscious returned control to her.

Here she is now in Africa, looking into the eyes of a perfectly rational reporter trapped in a war zone, a veteran of too many conflicts, struggling with the implications of a vast alien spacecraft looming overhead. Leopold smiles, as does Kowalski. Liz smiles too. They're three lunatics trying to find whoever's in charge of the asylum.

CHAPTER 06: ROAD TO LILONGWE

The next morning, Liz wakes to a sharp rap on the door and a soldier's voice yelling, "Get your shit packed. We roll in fifteen." Liz isn't accustomed to being woken with such a vulgar start, and finds herself bewildered. It's dark outside. An amber glow breaks over the city, marking the coming dawn. Kowalski must be downstairs already as his bag is gone and he's nowhere to be seen. Fifteen minutes! Liz would prefer an hour.

"Barbarians," she mutters as she wanders into the bathroom and splashes water on her face. If she is going to be ready to go in fifteen minutes, she's got to hustle.

Liz makes it downstairs within the allotted fifteen minutes, with her bag slung over one shoulder. She walks outside to find she's the first one to reach the Hummer in the back alley. After standing there for a few minutes, it's clear no one else is in a hurry. Liz feels cheated.

A soldiers on sentry duty watches from the second floor, keeping an eye on the vehicles and the back entrance—this is hardly the early start she expected.

Jameson comes jogging casually down the stairs.

"Good morning," he says cheerfully.

"Morning," Liz can't quite bring herself to add the adjective *good* just yet. She's grumpy.

"There's coffee in the kitchen."

"I'm good."

There, she said it—*good* is out there for all to hear, well, Jameson at least.

"We should be ready to go within—"

"Fifteen minutes," she says, cutting him off.

He smiles. She can see he's a little confused by her abrupt comment. Liz softens her attitude, saying, "Yeah, I thought we'd be ready in around... oh... fifteen minutes." If she can figure out who thumped on her door, she'll throttle them. Oh, lighten up, Liz, she thinks. Jameson seems a little perplexed by her attitude, but he isn't in on the joke. He nods as he puts his pack in the Hummer.

"Wouldn't it make sense to just take the truck?" Liz asks out of curiosity, watching as Jameson rummages around in the back of the Hummer. "It's big enough for all of us. Won't our fuel go further that way?"

"This old thing?" Jameson replies. "Nah. Two is one, one is none."

"Sorry? I didn't catch that."

"It's an old army phrase," Jameson says, grabbing another pack from the rear steps of the hotel. "If you've only got one set of wheels and something breaks, you're screwed. If you've got two, you can pack everyone into the one remaining vehicle. Two is one, one is none. It means, ensure you have redundancy."

"Oh," Liz replies, liking the concept.

"Besides," he adds, "We're a small force. Two vehicles make us appear bigger, a force to be reckoned with. A bit of bluster and bluff goes a long way."

The sun is low, barely creeping over the horizon, casting long shadows down the dusty streets. Above them, the alien craft soars through space. The mothership orbits Earth once every two hours, appearing overhead for roughly thirty minutes as it glides across the sky. During the night, the craft shimmered like a chameleon changing colors. To Liz, its coloration was like oil in a puddle—a greasy rainbow of colors, almost metallic in their appearance. Now day has broken, the alien vessel has resumed its ghostly appearance.

Fine tentacles trail behind the craft, waving as though caught in a breeze. Rather than being a machine, the spaceship looks alive. Liz wonders how big the tentacles are. Size is deceptive given the distances involved. The thin strands looks as fine as the hairs on her arm, but they must be massive—reaching for miles.

The previous night, they'd sat up talking until the early hours of the morning, watching for each passing of the alien spacecraft like kids waiting for Santa, at least that's the way she felt. Across the city, a cry would resound as the inhabitants recognized the unearthly shape drifting smoothly above them. At first, Liz thought it was a cheer, but as the night went on she realized it was a wail like that of mourners at a funeral.

In the early morning light, the craft takes on the purples and pinks of the dawn. The sight is hypnotic.

"Do you mind if I ask you a question?"

"Sure," Jameson replies.

"I don't mean to doubt you, and I do appreciate your," she struggles for the word, "expertise in things military, if that's the right way to phrase it. But why did we wait here so long? Why stay two nights in Ksaungu instead of pushing on to Lilongwe? I mean, I know it isn't because you're afraid or anything like that. I don't think that at all. It's just, I thought there was a plane waiting for us there."

She trips over her words. What started out as a good question has degraded into blather.

Jameson smiles. He seems to understand what she's getting at far better than she does herself.

"Combat isn't about shooting guns madly at bad guys; it's about planning and preparation. Rule number one: Never walk blindly into a new arena."

Liz sits on the dusty steps of a fire exit as he speaks. She finally recognizes Smithy on the second floor balcony, peering out across the city with her machine gun at the ready, having kept watch through at least part of the night. Liz isn't sure how often the sentries rotate, but she knows Jameson had two of his team awake at all times.

"Combat is fluid, never static, always changing. Lilongwe is an unknown. While there was the chance of rest here in Ksaungu, and no good intel on Lilongwe, it was prudent to sit tight."

Liz nods thoughtfully.

"Besides, we needed to get that radio fixed. Now Bosco's got the shortwave circuits working, we'll be able to contact any troops still in Ksaungu. Shortwave won't give us over-the-horizon coms, but we'll have line of sight. The standard operating procedure when someone's MIA is for a high-altitude fly over, listening for MAD chatter."

"Mad Hatter?" Liz asks, surprised by the term. "What? Like Alice in Wonderland?"

"No," Jameson adds, laughing. "MAD *chatter*. MAD is an acronym meaning Military Air Distress. They'll be listening for us on the MAD frequency."

"Oh," Liz says, feeling a little stupid. "How far is line of sight?"

"About fifty to a hundred klicks, depending on our terrain and their altitude. From what we've heard, the road to Lilongwe is littered with burned out army vehicles. The rebels fought hard to break the supply lines between the two cities, but the army's keeping the roads open. I mean to squeeze through before the rebels regroup and try again."

Liz breathes deeply. Jameson makes his plan sound routine.

Kowalski walks out of the fire exit with Leopold.

Jameson says, "We roll in—"

"Fifteen," Liz says, again cutting Jameson off. She grins, showing her teeth in a half smile.

"Actually," he replies, "since everyone's up, I was going to say five."

Jameson disappears inside the rear entrance to the hotel.

Liz screws her face up.

"They're not going to like this," Leopold says, talking more to Kowalski than Liz. "The staff here like having the Rangers around. It's like they've got their own personal security service—mercenaries that don't drink or shoot up the bar. This whole section of town's been quiet since you guys arrived. I don't think anyone wants to upset the Americans. They're hoping you'll stay. No one wants to be abandoned, and seeing US soldiers on the ground's given the Africans hope—false hope for sure—but hope nonetheless."

The two men sit next to Liz.

"Have you changed your mind?" Liz asks, turning to Leopold.

"Nope. Have you? Better the devil you know, and all that crap. Besides, there's an NBC film crew due in here at the end of the week. I'll hook up with them."

"Keep your head down," Liz says.

"You too."

Kowalski sips coffee from a styrofoam cup.

"Hey, why didn't you wake me?" Liz asks.

"I thought you'd prefer a little more sleep," Kowalski replies. Liz knows he means well, but she'd rather he didn't try so hard. Kowalski is always trying too hard to be considerate. As long as she's known him, he's always been like that, always prepared to put himself out for others. For once, she wishes he'd be selfish, and not just so she doesn't feel bad. He needs to be selfish for himself, so he doesn't burn out.

"Well, I don't know about you, but I slept like a log," she replies. It might've been short, but it was deep.

Leopold watches the alien craft drifting effortlessly toward the horizon.

"Gives me chills," he says.

Liz understands why he finds the alien presence unnerving, but now that her initial fear has passed, the mystique of an apparently living interstellar spacecraft orbiting Earth awakens a sense of awe within her. She sees an object of beauty, moving with grace as it glides through the heavens.

Kowalski must see her staring into the sky. "Well," he says. "Seems they're happy enough circling around up there, and that's fine by me."

"I wonder what they're thinking about—what they're planning," Liz says.

"Crop circles and anal probes," Kowalski jokes.

"I'm in no hurry to find out," Leopold adds.

"Don't you think it's beautiful?" Liz asks.

"Maybe," Kowalski says, but his answer is little more than a polite way of disagreeing. "But only in the same way a rattlesnake or a shark could be considered beautiful in the eyes of a biologist."

"I'm serious," she replies. "Just because something's different doesn't mean it can't be beautiful. Perhaps not in the way a butterfly is pretty, with colorful patterns on its wings. Beautiful as in delightful—functional—like a bee, or an octopus. Even the most boring of birds with dull brown feathers have a natural beauty, and I can't help but feel the same way about this. There's a sublime beauty to their spacecraft. It's not a pile of nuts and bolts, like our spaceships. It's not streamlined or aerodynamic, with sleek curves and sharp points. It's not from this world, yet it has an earthy feel to it, as though it were something that could grace the cover of National Geographic."

The two men are silent, so she continues.

"I guess we see what we want to see, right? Beauty's in the eye of the beholder. The more I think about how they've traversed a gazillion miles through empty space, looking for our tiny mote of dust adrift in this vast universe, the less I'm afraid. They came to us. They sought us out. They want to know something about us. Isn't that flattering? Here we are, looking up at them in awe, wondering who they are, what makes them tick, and they're looking down upon us thinking the same thing. That's kind of cool—and certainly nothing to be afraid of."

The alien craft slips over the horizon, disappearing from sight behind the distant buildings.

"Yeah, I guess," Kowalski offers.

Her words must stir the journalist within as Leopold's mood softens. He speaks, and Liz gets the distinct impression he's making mental notes for an upcoming article. Perhaps he's conducting a dress rehearsal for the cameras.

"My father used to tell me, fear is our default response to the unknown. It's a survival mechanism, an instinctive reaction over a reasoned response. Our history's checkered with xenophobia—the fear of something different—different people from different countries, different cultures. We're tribal. We want everyone to be the same."

Leopold divorces himself from his previous comments, straightening his thinking. Liz is fascinated to hear him reason through what she instinctively feels is true. That he's able to suspend his own fears and entertain her hopes is a surprise, but perhaps that's what reporters do best—catch the mood. It seems they're adept at placing themselves in another person's shoes.

"We're conditioned to respond with fear, so it's no surprise we're overreacting. It's as though an alien invasion is the only possibility when there must be dozens of other outcomes that could unfold. When was the last time Hollywood showed someone turning up on our doorstep with anything other than a death ray? Blood and guts, with a splash of acid and some hefty explosions gets asses in movie seats. We can't even accept foreigners from Colombia or

Sudan without an air of suspicion, wondering if they're terrorists or drug runners. What hope does someone from another planet have? Someone wears a turban in a mall, and the Muslims are attacking our way of life."

Kowalski laughs.

"Think of what we'll learn," Liz says, wishing the starship would land. She wants to say more, but words fail her. It's taken some time to acclimatize to the concept, but she's genuinely excited about the future. The prospect of getting out of a country sliding deeper into civil war is the furthest thing from her mind. She assumes that will happen. Survival is a trivial detail, something that pales in comparison to First Contact. Mortality itself seem suspended by the alien spacecraft with its iridescent glow at night, and its rippling white surface in the bright daylight. Life triumphs over death, at least for now. The prospect of new life forms coming from a distant star seems to cause the pain and misery of Africa to fade like the night giving way to dawn.

"This," Kowalski says, having completely lost his initial skepticism, "this really could be a new beginning for the human race." His acceptance of her position, and his readiness to move away from pessimism fills her with hope. Deep down, Liz knows her hopes are unfounded and irrational, but she holds to them regardless. When both hope and fear are equal choices, why choose the negative? With hope, she can pretend Africa will find peace. With hope, she can forget about the hundreds that'll die today in the swollen heat, victims of a futile, cruel war.

Jameson comes jogging down the stairs with Elvis, Bosco and Smithy behind him.

Elvis pauses on the last step. Stretching his arms out wide, he cries, "Elvis has left the building," and he steps down onto the road like royalty.

"You're such an idiot," Bosco says, slapping him on the shoulder.

The other soldiers jog down the corridor and climb into the Hummer, throwing the last of their packs in the truck.

Jameson glances at Liz. Something in his eyes snaps her back to reality. He seems to sense her glassy-eyed enthusiasm. She doesn't dare share her thoughts with him.

Elvis is chewing gum with typical American enthusiasm, giving his jaw a serious workout. He's standing beside the Hummer talking with Smithy. Jameson climbs up into the truck as Elvis calls out, "Y'all still want me to come wit-cha?"

"You pulled the short straw," Jameson replies. "You're on babysitting duty again."

Elvis spits his gum out, and climbs into the driver's side of the truck.

Leopold stands by the gate, waving goodbye as Bosco drives the Hummer out of the dusty courtyard, followed by Elvis, Jameson and Liz in the truck. Kowalski is in the Hummer with the other Rangers. Smithy stands in the turret of the Hummer with the lightweight SAW machine gun mounted on rails. She swivels the gun around, scanning the street as they emerge onto the road, daring a challenge. With her helmet, sunglasses, bulletproof vest and camouflage clothing, she looks every bit a US combat soldier. Liz has no doubt about her resolve.

The main street is already crowded, with Africans wanting to conduct their trade before the heat of the day makes the city unbearable. The stench of raw sewage wafts through the air. As the two-vehicle convoy winds its way through the streets, there is a sense of surprise at seeing Americans driving around the city. Some of the Africans wave. Most of them just stare.

Artillery shells rain down on the western suburbs. Clouds of dark smoke rise in thin columns. From what Liz can tell, the team isn't in any immediate danger as they're heading south and the barrage is barely audible over the sound of the diesel engine.

The faces they pass on the street have a look of helplessness. What Liz thought of as exasperation, or perhaps indifference, is neither—these people are resigned to being abandoned. In her mind, Liz finds herself struggling with the identity of the people they drive past so callously. A woman with a young child in her arms stares at Liz with wide eyes longing for pity. Liz feels as though the woman can see right through her.

There are boys playing in the street, kicking a can around between them, oblivious to the murderous thunder creeping over the city. Old men sit in the doorways chewing khat, and spitting on the concrete. Young girls hang washing out of the windows, draping wet clothing over rusting poles and steel wires stretched out between the buildings. What do they make of a visitor from another world? They must have seen the mothership orbiting Earth. They must know change is coming, but for them change has only ever meant oppression.

What do the Africans think of First Contact? From what Liz can see, they're more interested in keeping their heads down to survive another day. What difference will there be for them? Probably none. If anything, life will continue to get worse before it gets better. Without UN troops on the ground, life in Malawi is survival of the cruelest.

    Jameson is quiet. Liz would feel better if he spoke, but he's focused on the road ahead, occasionally talking on the radio with Bosco in the lead vehicle.

    Liz can't look at the crowds anymore. She keeps her eyes forward, watching the road, trying to avoid eye contact with anyone on the pavement. Donkeys, horse drawn carts, and rusted old cars meander down the road, slowing the convoy's progress. Liz finds her eyes settling on a makeshift flatbed truck coming toward them. With no hood, the fan cooling the radiator whirls around dangerously, as does the fan belt leading back to the engine block. Black smoke seeps out from around the engine. As the truck passes by, Liz can hear the rhythmic thumping of an engine seemingly cobbled together with fencing wire. At any point, the truck could shake itself apart.

    As they wind their way out of the city and into the thick jungle hills rising above Ksaungu, the contrast of deep greens becomes a welcome break from the dusty, muddy browns of the open plains. The temperature drops as they climb higher. A cool breeze blows from the east.

    Within a few miles, the concrete road gives way to rough stones and pebbles lining an old dirt track. Landslides narrow the track at points, slowing them to a crawl as they merge with other vehicles making the treacherous journey through the mountains. Government soldiers trudge through the sludge on the side of the track, their boots caked in mud. With rifles slung over their shoulders and their heads hung low, they look like an army in retreat.

Once they are clear of the city, Elvis lightens up. Jameson's looking at the map, double-checking their location and direction.

"Hey," Elvis says with a grin on his face as he peers over at Liz. "Look in the bag." His voice has a conspiratorial tone, as though he is letting her in on the secrets of the universe.

Jameson looks up briefly, watching as Liz opens the canvas rucksack at her feet. He's too concerned with their progress to care, and buries himself in surveying in the map. Jameson picks up a handheld walkie-talkie and speaks with Bosco in the lead vehicle.

"Top of this rise, you should see a T junction, we're gonna head right, veering to the southeast, and head up onto the tableland."

"Roger that," comes the reply from Bosco.

Liz rummages around in the rucksack, bouncing slightly as the truck hits a pothole.

"Does Bosco know you took that?" Jameson asks as Liz pulls out the small, blue, civilian band radio.

"No," Elvis replies, unable to wipe the smile off his face.

"He's gonna kick your ass."

Elvis laughs.

Sitting there holding the radio, Liz is again reminded of the alien spaceship. She leans forward, looking to see if she can catch a glimpse of the UFO flying through space, but the jungle obscures her view of the sky. Dark green trees and vines hang down on either side of the road. Occasionally, pockets of blue break through the canopy, but never enough to see more than a fleeting glimpse of the sky.

"Turn it on," Elvis says. Liz is mesmerized by the radio. What if the aliens are malicious? Does she really want to know before she has to? What good will knowing do? The advocate within her pleads for reason, telling her there's nothing to fear. Learn. This is an opportunity to understand what she's dealing with. What *she's* dealing with? Now, *there's* a thought. So self-centered, so singular in focus, so all-consumed. Perhaps that's the problem with humanity at large, she thinks—most days, we can barely see past the end of our nose.

Liz winds the crank on the side of the radio, giving it a good turn for a minute or so to charge the batteries, then she turns it on. After slowly twisting the dial to move between channels, she picks up a signal.

" ...As Roosevelt said, there's nothing to fear but fear itself... "

She keeps turning. Music ekes through the static—a distinctly African beat—drums with an electric guitar and a female singer.

" ...love will keep us strong, forever moving on, never leaving us alone... "

Ordinarily, this is the kind of station she'd listen to on a Sunday afternoon, regardless of whether she's heard the artist before. The tune is catchy, but on she goes, surfing the various radio channels, listening for commentary about the alien craft.

" ...highs of a hundred and five, with storms in the late afternoon, early evening..."

Three stations down and Liz is strangely relieved not to have found anyone talking about the gigantic alien spacecraft circling

Earth. If anything, that seems to suggest that life moves on, that not everyone is consumed by the alien presence. Then she finds it.

" … Georgia, where residents have responded to the disruption surrounding the arrival of aliens by banding together as a community, pooling not only food and water, but medical supplies."

Another voice speaks in a Southern drawl.

"We've been through a dozen hurricanes. We know what it takes to keep things moving when the economy stops. The sky might be clear, but we understand what it takes to get through a crisis like this, what it takes to kickstart a community and get back on our feet."

The reporter continues.

"Across the United States, from Maine to Florida, from New York to Los Angeles, we're seeing a groundswell of citizen action in place of government programs. Here in Atlanta, Georgia, the residents know the government is largely consigned to the role of historian. As well-meaning as FEMA officials are, the size and scale of an entire country in turmoil means they're largely ineffective."

Another resident speaks, only this time there is a distinct Mexican twinge in the accent, and Liz gets the impression this man is nowhere near Georgia.

"The police, they're too busy. They're running around trying to help everyone, but in the end they can't help anyone, you know? They tell me, don't take the law into your own hands. I say, I'm not taking the law, but I'm not standing by either. There are thugs—people who'll take the shirt off your back. When the wolves come, you need to be strong, show them you're not afraid, you're no sheep. You're not gonna let them take your stuff.

"If you're strong, they go away, but that makes the problem worse. They know they can't take nothing from me, but my neighbor, they think they can take her food. So we stand up for each other. We stand up for those that can't stand up for themselves."

The reporter speaks again.

"Although officials have refused to sanction local activists like Jesus San Lopez, the reality is, with the US economy struggling to find focus, and civil unrest continuing to grow, such community groups have taken pressure off the police, fire departments, and hospitals. With large portions of the workforce refusing to return to work in factories and farms around the nation, the National Guard's stepped in, filling a vital hole in the supply chain. Estimates of the flow of essential goods such as fresh food and processed meats are at eighty percent of normal supply, and yet the shelves are still bare."

A deep voice comes through on the radio as the broadcast switches to another anecdotal testimony from what's intended to be the average businessman.

"For the past decade, I've been flying from Miami to Dallas on business at least once a month, but I've never seen anything like this, even during the hurricane season. Yesterday, there were three of us. Three people on a plane designed for three hundred. Hell, there were more stewards and stewardesses than there were passengers. We joked around that we should serve them the drinks. It's crazy, man. Ever since this thing turned up, the whole country's been spooked."

"We can't get our grain to market," another voice says, a woman talking over the sound of heavy machinery whirring in the background. "We've had a few trucks through, but those drivers are pulling eighteen hour shifts, working through all the farms in this region. The rest of the drivers haven't been seen for dust. I tried to call my distributor, but the phone just rings out. I've been talking to the factory. They say they've got surplus for a week or so in the silos, so they're not too worried, but they can't get enough hands on the factory floor. They're getting stuff out the door, but even just a small drop in supply causes demand to skyrocket. The whole supply chain is out of balance."

The reporter speaks in somber tones.

"US officials are understandably cagey when discussing possible military tactics in the wake of alien contact, and the presence of US fighters conducting daily flights over major US cities is intended more for human attention than as a show of force for the extraterrestrials. NASA officials have confirmed what is being described as a 'close working relationship' and 'cooperation' with the Army, Air Force, Marines and the Navy, but what that means in practice is yet to be seen. Speculation is rife."

A stern voice breaks into the discussion, saying, "Then there's the nuclear option."

Liz gets the impression that whoever is talking is ex-military. From the background noise, it sounds as though he's being interviewed on a street corner.

"While that thing was out by the Moon, she was untouchable, but now that she's in orbit, we can reach her. All we need to do is weaponize our existing rocket fleet, just like the President suggested. He's our Commander-in-Chief. We voted him in. We need to follow him. I believe in President Addison. He's a good man. The Supreme Court has no right to suspend democracy because a bunch of left-wing liberals don't have the balls to make the hard decisions. We will rue the day we let Congress impeach the man for defending our liberty. Nukes are all we've got against these alien critters. If we don't shoot first, we won't be able to shoot at all."

"Others, though, disagree," the reporter says. "They point out that the use of nuclear weapons in space is likely to be counterproductive."

"Nuclear weapons," another male voice says in sober, measured tones, "liberate massive amounts of energy. They're spectacular on Earth. A blinding flash of light, a hail of radioactive particles, and a massive blast wave—a wall of superheated wind and debris, but space is already saturated with radiation. It's a hostile environment. In space, thermonuclear detonations are nothing more than a blip—the appearance of miniature star shining but for a second. Nukes are largely ineffective because there's nothing to compress. If we were to detonate a nuke on the alien craft the electromagnetic pulse would take out any of our own nearby satellites, and we could end up losing valuable communication channels or GPS capabilities for our military here on Earth. Whether we would cause any damage to the alien craft is debatable. From what NASA has observed, their shielding is capable of dissipating nuclear fusion, so it's unlikely anything we could throw at them would even be able to scratch the surface, let alone deliver a mortal wound. Nukes just aren't the silver bullet everyone thinks they are."

Another voice cuts in, a woman's voice.

"This isn't the movie *Independence Day*. There's no hero to save us by shooting Coke cans off the side of a UFO. If it comes to a fight, it's probably going to be over very quickly, and the outcome will be one-sided. The aliens have adopted a polar orbit instead of circling above the equator. By doing this, they're able to cover every square inch of Earth in roughly a day and a half. If we turn this into a nuclear exchange, there's not a place on Earth they can't bomb from orbit. They could obliterate human life over the weekend, so lets keep our pride in check for a bit. There's no war—let's not start one. Now's the time for cool heads."

The reporter cuts in, giving another perspective.

"And US concerns aren't just confined to a potential space war. In the Deep South, the proliferation of small arms such as handguns and shotguns has stretched local police as well as state troopers to breaking point, with reports coming through of murders being undertaken to settle long-standing scores, and petty crime escalating into manslaughter. In one, as yet unconfirmed case, a neighbor was shot and killed in a dispute over stealing water from a well while building up stockpiles against a possible invasion. Reports have come through of people being murdered over the possession of basic ingredients such as flour, sugar, and powdered milk.

"There's no doubt the emergency laws passed by the government have stemmed the initial lawlessness and panic that gripped the US, but rebuilding the trust of a nation in shock will take some time. And as yet, there's been no direct contact with the alien craft. One has to wonder what will happen then."

The speaker changes to that of an angry woman.

"Don't tell me there's been no contact. You don't have someone turn up on your doorstep from the other side of the country without hearing from them first. You want me to think these aliens could come from a million miles away without someone knowing? Without someone inviting them? I don't know what happened at Roswell, but it wasn't a military weather balloon.

"The military's been lying to us for decades. They've been lying to the American people, lying to the government, lying to everyone. They're the only ones who could've kept this secret for so long. The government could never do it, they could never keep their mouths shut, but the military thrives on secrecy. I'm telling you, this is what Eisenhower warned us about—the military-industrial complex. All this, it's been in the plans since then, since the late 50s. Look at the federal budget. Look at what we spend on the military. Forget about the Democrats and Republicans, it's the military that runs this country. Always has. Always will."

"Such sentiments " the reporter says, cutting in, "are not isolated."

A Texas accent comes across the airwaves.

"It's been easy to laugh at abductees. It's been easy to laugh at those that saw a UFO and say they were drunk or delusional, but who's laughing now? The grays are here in force. They mean business. Does anyone take NASA seriously anymore? And NASA's still maintaining the party line, saying, 'There's been no contact.' Who are they kidding? We heard those little green men speak on the radio. I'm telling you, NASA sold us out. They've been planning our enslavement for decades.

"The government's been trying to disarm the population for the past fifty years, trying to take away our rights, trying to get to our guns, and now we know why—so Earth would capitulate without a fight. Well, I don't know about you, but I'm fighting. No alien's gonna take my guns. Washington might surrender, but any goddamn alien sets foot in Texas, he's gonna be eating lead."

"Damn," Elvis says, leaning forward on the broad steering wheel as he turns a corner. "Now that's what I'm talking about."

"You can't be serious?" Liz is aghast, talking over the radio. "You actually want to shoot first and ask questions later?"

"If we don't shoot first, there won't be a later," Elvis replies with a cocky tone that conveys surety. He is chewing on gum as he speaks. "You ever think of that, doc? I mean, seriously, sure, we all wanna get along, but these are aliens. We've got to show them they can't mess with us. Peace through strength. It's the only way, doc."

"What about peace through understanding?" Liz replies, turning the radio down.

"You're talking to a grunt," Jameson says, intervening in the discussion. "Army life is all about peace through hierarchy—peace enforced by authority."

"Please tell me there are cooler heads in Washington?" Liz says. Elvis doesn't seem fazed, so she says, "Peace should be the default, not war. After a hundred thousand years, you'd have thought we'd have figured that one out by now."

"It's all about agendas, doc," Elvis replies. "See, Sarge is right. We have peace by adhering to a chain of command. For us, peace is something to be enforced with the threat of violence. Peace ain't no picnic by the lake in summer. So you gotta ask yourself, Doc. Why are they here? What's their agenda?"

"We'll know soon enough," she says. "We don't have to assume hostile intent."

"We do if we want to stay alive," Elvis replies.

"If they are hostile," she asks, "honestly, what could we do about it? This isn't some Hollywood movie where all you've got to do is get their shields down so our planes can fire a bunch of missiles at them."

Elvis says, "Oh, I don't know, Doc. The US has the most effective fighting force in history."

"In *human* history. Compared to them, we're armed with peashooters. Imagine what would happen if a bunch of bushmen tried to attack you Rangers. Even if they got a spear away at you, you'd mow them down. They wouldn't stand a chance. The difference between us and these aliens is going to be orders of magnitude greater than that. Any act of aggressive by us would be suicidal."

"Better dead than red," is all Elvis can say, quoting an old Cold War mantra. Liz is tempted to take things further, but there is no genuine interest in debate on his part. Liz is frustrated by his closed mind. Her words have fallen on deaf ears.

The radio broadcast is still going. The topic grabs her attention so she turns up the radio.

"We actually know quite a lot about them already," a woman says in calm tones. "We know they're bound by the laws of physics. They didn't just materialize in our sky. They approached us over several months—that tells us something important about their technology. Their spaceship is far more advanced than any we've developed, but not by tens of thousands of years, probably just in the order of a few hundred years, perhaps a thousand.

"Bear in mind, given the immense age of the universe, and the almost four billion years during which life has evolved on Earth, a gap of a million years between intelligent species from different planets would not be unrealistic. If anything, a gap of a million years would be quite small. That these aliens are so close to us from the perspective of the physics we see in use is actually quite encouraging.

"If the appearance of their craft is any indication, their technology is based on what we would call biology. But, biology is simply physics applied to chemistry. Their craft appears almost organic, whereas our spacecraft are functional, designed without any regard to aesthetics. Their craft appears to be alive. Now, that could be an illusion, but spectroscopic analysis and radar suggests the spacecraft we see is a living organism rather than a collection of nuts and bolts.

"As for their possible physiology, we can draw some clues from their approach within our solar system. Bear in mind that in slowing down over a period of several months, they could choose to slow themselves at any particular speed they want. If they slowed themselves faster, they would arrive earlier, that's all. But that they slowed at one sixth of the acceleration we feel on Earth, roughly the same rate as gravity on the Moon, suggests that was a comfortable approach for them. If this assumption is correct, then they're probably not going to be too comfortable here on Earth. Our gravity wouldn't crush them, but it wouldn't be pleasant. It would be like carrying your mother-in-law around on your back everywhere you go.

"Now, some people have raised concerns that all we've heard from the craft is a single, repeated message declaring their peaceful intentions. They wonder why we haven't heard anything beyond that, thinking that we should have established some kind of dialogue with this alien species by now. It's been pointed out that the alien message is in every known language, including some that are geographically confined and essentially redundant, so the aliens seem proficient in communicating. But, again, everything we learn about them is revealing. This limited form of communication tells us something important about our alien visitors and their level of technological advancement."

Liz is hooked on every word. She barely notices the bumps in the road or the rattling noise from the truck engine.

"They're capable of communicating broadly and simply, but not in detail. In the same way, we can process whale calls, taking samples and conducting statistical analysis of behavior patterns to construct a message that is easily understood by other whales. We can even construct individual messages for each different species of whale, using their own distinct dialects, but we can't necessarily hold a conversation with a whale. You see, this reinforces the notion that this alien species is hundreds, but not thousands of years ahead of humanity. Whatever means they have of communicating among themselves, it's vastly different from human speech, placing an impediment in their path when communicating with us.

"As for the conspiracy theorists, it is important to note there's been no attack. There have been no ray guns or super-fast spacecraft racing around, strafing the ground and blowing things up. If we look at the timing of their actions, from entering the solar system, to approaching Earth, to waiting at the Lagrange point, to announcing their presence, to moving into a low earth orbit, we can see there's a pattern. They're moving at a slow, deliberate pace. They're giving us time to accept their presence. They're not rushing in. This is much the same way we would approach an animal in the wild."

Liz is fascinated with the scientific press conference. She isn't sure who's talking, but this woman knows her stuff. She's got to be from one of the space agencies. As her accent is American, Liz assumes she's from NASA.

"We have also observed structures on the craft that match Fibonacci sequences. This is important to note, as it's a clue to what we suppose is the organic nature of the alien vessel.

"Fibonacci was the first person to note that the sizes and shapes we see in nature are ruled by a simple numeric principle where numbers in a sequence are added to each other to find the next number. One plus one equals two. Two plus one equals three. Three plus two equals five. Five plus three equals eight, eight plus five equals thirteen, and so on, with the pattern always growing by the same proportion as the numbers become progressively larger.

"This pattern is important because it's natural. We see it everywhere in our world, even if we don't realize it. Look at the swirl of a seashell, or the point at which branches stem from a tree, or the veins in a leaf, or the shape of a hurricane as seen from space—all these shapes fan out using numbers found in a Fibonacci sequence. Pineapples, pinecones, and sunflower seeds all grow in a pattern described by Fibonacci numbers. Look at the length of your upper arm relative to your forearm, or your thigh relative to your lower leg and you'll find the same basic ratio described by Fibonacci.

"In regards to the alien spacecraft, our telescopes can resolve segmentation in the cilia, the fine tentacle-like appendages surrounding the craft. The ridges covering the body of the spacecraft follow the same scaly pattern we see on snakes and lizards, with the length and breadth of each section following the Fibonacci ratio. Toward the rear of the craft, hidden in shadow, there are slits or fins, similar to what we see in the mouth of Baleen whales. Although we've seen no sign of chemical propellants, we suspect that these structures provide propulsion. As a proportion of the overall length of the craft, they too match the Fibonacci ratio."

Liz isn't sure how much of this Elvis understands, but he seems to be listening intently, as is Jameson.

"From this we infer that the alien creatures themselves must have harnessed some kind of biological process to construct their craft with a form of biotechnology native to their world, perhaps using nanotechnology. Certainly, the oily, metallic rainbow sheen seen on the underbelly in low light echoes experiments with nano-materials on Earth. At its current altitude, a thousand miles above the surface of—"

The radio crackles.

"Sarge, I'm getting reports of Marines holding the airport in Lilongwe." Static breaks up Bosco's voice. "They said the fighting is fierce to the north and east, with armed militias in the south. They advise we approach from the west, coming through the city using the supply route from Mozambique."

Jameson's face lights up.

"Tell them we owe them a round of beers, *Semper Fi*."

"Roger that," comes the reply from Bosco. "Hey, could you pass a message to Elvis for me?"

"Sure."

"Tell that fucker if he touches my stuff again, he'll be joining Presley singing Hound Dog at the Pearly Gates."

Jameson laughs, looking over at Elvis with a grin on his face. "Roger that. Over."

He unfolds his map, allowing it to sit slightly on Liz and up against the dashboard. His finger runs over the lines and curves.

"Okay, we're here, about eighty klicks north of Lilongwe. We need to get off this road, cut inland, then southwest, as though we were heading for the border, before turning back to the capital."

Liz doesn't say anything, but the thought of spending more time bouncing around in their antiquated old truck, with its tired seat springs and stiff suspension, doesn't exactly fill her with joy.

CHAPTER 07: SEEDS

    As evening approaches, the Rangers drive into the exodus fleeing Lilongwe. Refugees march into the setting sun. Thousands of grim faces pass by silently on either side of the truck as the Rangers drive through the tide of human misery. There must be some noise. People must be talking, but the diesel engine is the only sound breaking the tension. Thousands of Africans walk on in a trance, barely acknowledging the US Rangers as they drive past. The swell of men, women and children spread out beyond the dusty track, into the surrounding plains. They shuffle on with their handcarts, goats and cows in tow.

    Liz sits there feeling numb at the heartache unfolding before her. The truck follows the Hummer east toward Lilongwe, slowly weaving its way through the crowds of refugees fleeing the capital.

    Her heart goes out to those staggering on toward what they think of as freedom in Mozambique. They cannot know the misery that awaits them in the overcrowded camps. There is nothing she can do, nothing any of them can do. Without a concerted effort from the international community, there is no way to prevent Malawi from imploding. On they drive, kicking up dust, but the refugees don't seem to notice.

    With the sun sitting low behind them, darkness stretches across the land. Acacia trees and thorn bushes cast ominous shadows. To the north, the alien mothership soars high in the sky, a thousand miles above Earth. In the light of the setting sun, the craft is radiant in pink and yellow hues. Fine specks of dust fall from the back of the alien craft, trailing behind it.

Liz feels a chill run down her spine. Any sense of majesty the craft once held in her mind is replaced with dread as she realizes some kind of debris is peeling away from the spacecraft. Tiny pricks of light appear to drift behind the spaceship, flaring as thousands of smaller alien vessels enter the atmosphere like embers from a campfire.

Elvis sees it too. "What the..."

Jameson looks up from his map. He grabs the radio.

"Bosco. Are you seeing this?"

"Affirmative. What the hell is that?"

"I don't know," Jameson replies.

"If it's the alien equivalent of cluster bombs, we're fucked."

Jameson says a reluctant, "Yep."

Liz leans forward, looking up at the sky, trying to estimate how close the craft will pass overhead.

The alien spaceship appears to be moving diagonally across the sky, but the dust trail spreads out like the wake of a ship. The trail of sparks appears to dissipate somewhere high in the atmosphere. In reality, Liz suspects they've simply lost sight of the smaller component parts. Several larger clumps falling from the rear of the craft cut through the atmosphere like meteors, leaving vapor trails in the stratosphere.

"Maybe it's disintegrating," Liz says. "Maybe this is good. Maybe their ship is falling apart."

Elvis and Jameson both look at her with a glare that makes her feel stupid.

"How big do you think those things are?" she asks.

"Big," Jameson replies.

"That's some serious shit," Elvis says in a matter-of-fact tone of voice. "Hey, maybe they're sowing seeds, like a farmer."

"You think they're seeding Earth?" Liz asks.

"With what?" Jameson adds. No one answers. No one wants an answer.

Liz winds the crank on the radio, giving the batteries a bit of charge before turning it on. Dark pinpricks appear in the sky, peppering the majestic blue atmosphere as they descend to Earth. Everything's changing. Is this her last day on this sunbaked continent that has nurtured life on Earth for billions of years? Liz twists the radio handle, lost in thought.

Africa isn't beautiful, it's stark and desolate. She has no illusions of being swept in some pseudo-romantic sense of awe and majesty. Africa is barren—a dry husk. Vultures clean the bones of a dead wildebeest, putting life in perspective. Nature is cruel. Yet the harsh reality of life and death in Africa still provides some relief from the unknown, the impending dread of alien contact. Now, it seems their fears have been realized. Liz feels Jameson and Elvis silently willing her to hurry as she cranks the handle on the side of the radio.

" ... contact first in Iowa, with umbrella seeds spreading up through Canada and the Arctic, across Siberia, Mongolia, China and Western Australia before crossing Antarctica, and into Africa. Reports have also come in of floaters, gigantic alien creatures resembling what can only be described as jellyfish."

The voice changes to that of a woman.

"At this point, the State Department is refusing to consider this an attack or to classify the phenomenon being witnessed across the world as an invasion, saying they are waiting on NASA to provide more information on the nature of the alien artifacts intruding into our atmosphere.

"The US Air force has circled and followed several of the so-called floaters in a variety of military aircraft, from helicopters to a C130 Hercules. These intercepts have been undertaken for the purpose of photographing and observing the alien craft, relaying information to NASA. There have been no hostile acts undertaken by either side."

There is stunned silence within the cab of the truck. Liz wants to grab the reporter and shake her; how can they not see this as an all-out invasion? For all her posturing with Elvis, she secretly shares his fears. Somehow, in siding with him mentally she feels safer, as though she's aligning with someone stronger, someone better able to defend her. It's a fleeting thought, but in those few seconds the notion is overwhelming, and yet Elvis is silent. His bravado has run its course.

"A spokesperson for the United Nations has noted that the alien mother ship is showing no consideration for international boundaries or geographical land masses, either as we recognize them, or as they exist in the form of continents. The seeding, as it is being called, is following an orbital pattern that bisects rather than comprehensively covers various countries. Congress has issued a statement calling for calm, urging citizens not to panic. And—just a moment—we're crossing live to Capitol Hill where senior NASA scientist, Dr. Frederick Enrado is addressing the House."

Dr. Enrado has a slight twang in his voice, indicating English isn't his native tongue. Liz can't place his Spanish-like pronunciation, but she doesn't think he is from Mexico. She isn't sure why, but she gets the feeling he originates from one of the countries in Central America.

"I appreciate that there is an overwhelming amount of interest in the activities of the alien spacecraft and what the media has labeled *'the seedlings,'* but I must stress that guesswork will only inflame fear. At this time it is important that we remain composed and do not react. We are in a time of transition, a time of initial contact. It is important that we maintain a sense of order until the situation becomes clearer.

"We have established a coarse form of dialogue with the alien entity. As you can appreciate, like any two people from different cultures, with different languages, and without any common ground, communication is limited but the basics of communication are an extension of those already broadcast—*We come in peace.*

"In an attempt to quell the uncertainty and fear being experienced by the population at large, NASA, ESA and SETI are providing transcripts and the raw feed relating to our communication through the various member agency websites. Please remember, the point of this transparency is to counteract the conspiracy theories circulating on the Internet and in the media. At this point, we caution the general public not to read anything into the discussion beyond what is officially stated by NASA.

"We have to take our extraterrestrial visitors at face value when they say they come in peace, even if we don't understand their methods. To react with hostility is to act without reason.

"At this point, our dialogue is limited to simple concepts, the exchange of fundamental identifiers such as Earth, stars, moon, spaceship, etc. If you've seen the transcripts, you'll know it's very much like talking to a preschooler. In that regard, NASA is developing a primer, a means of exchange that will grow in complexity.

"Reading from one of the transcripts, an example of an exchange is: *We come in peace. We come from a star. We come in peace. We come from afar.*"

Elvis can't help himself, blurting out, "It's Dr. *fucking* Seuss! The goddamn *Cat in the Hat* is back."

As funny as his observation is, Liz is irritated by his intrusion. She wants to hear what's being said by a scientist, and not the wisecracks of a grunt.

The radio broadcast continues.

"As you can appreciate, the constant theme in these early messages is to reinforce peaceful intentions. For us to assume anything else would be foolish."

"I am asked what we know about the seedlings that have landed. Unfortunately, we do not know much more than you. Until we can establish field research efforts, media reports offer the best information. NASA is working with several news crews on location to document the alien phenomena so we can begin to draw scientific conclusions. So what do we know?"

He pauses. Paper shuffles in the background.

"I am reading to you directly from field reports. These have been subject only to initial oversight by our contact science team, so any points made here this afternoon are subject to revision as more information comes to hand."

Elvis snaps, "For fuck's sake, man. Spit it out."

As if in reply, Dr. Enrado continues. "The pods, or 'seeds' as they're called, do not pose an immediate threat. Although we don't know their exact composition, or their purpose, they appear to be made out of some kind of biodegradable resin. They don't pose a physical threat, such as being poisonous, however NASA recommends you avoid contact with the pods. Leave them wherever they landed. Remain well away from them until we can determine a course of action.

"The umbrella-like parachutes the pods descend on are flimsy and fragile, deteriorating rapidly with what appears to be some form of oxidation. We have retrieved samples for analysis, but it will take time to investigate this phenomenon properly at a microscopic level, so we ask for patience."

From the background noise on the radio, Liz gets the distinct impression that no one in Washington DC watching the briefing live is any more patient than Elvis.

"The floating entities that have been described as jellyfish are related to the appearance of the pods."

"No shit!" Elvis yells, thumping the steering wheel in frustration.

"Their frequency is far less than that of the pods, appearing only once every couple of hundred square miles, while the pods are spread with a frequency of anywhere from a few hundred feet to a couple of miles.

"The floaters appear to be living organisms resembling squid or jellyfish. The large dark purple bladder structure at the head of the creature appears to provide buoyancy in much the same way as an airship, or blimp. The trailing tentacles have not been observed making contact with the ground. I must repeat that there have been no confirmed cases of floaters touching the ground. Also, from what we can determine, the tentacles are not involved in propulsion. They have been observed streaming in front of floaters moving with the prevailing winds, and drifting behind them when these alien creatures are heading into the wind.

"As I mentioned earlier, the Air Force has approached these creatures on several occasions, circling within a couple of hundred meters of them in fighter craft—the floaters have remained oblivious, ignoring their presence.

"At this point, the prevailing wisdom is not to provoke a military conflict, but rather to pursue peaceful means of communication, opening dialogue instead of entering into hostilities. I'm aware there is considerable opposition to this approach, but I must emphasize, any potential conflict is likely to be one-sided and very much against humanity."

"NO WAY!" Elvis yells. "What the hell is everyone so goddamn afraid of—show them a little muscle. Earn some respect."

Mentally, Liz shifts sides again, moving away from Elvis.

"Please," Dr. Enrado continues, "do not shoot at, or collect either the pods or the floaters. We've had reports of one downed floater in Michigan, apparently in a suicide attack using a light plane. There have also been reports of people gathering seeds, sometimes with the intent of destroying them in a bonfire, at other times with the intent of collecting them. The last thing we need is for this situation to escalate out of hand."

"Out of hand?" Elvis yells. "Has he taken a look out the goddamn window?" He points ahead of the truck at the parachute-like descent of hundreds of resin pods drifting on the breeze. Rather than one per square mile, they are coming down no more than fifty feet apart, catching in bushes and trees, landing on the road among the refugees, and disappearing in the long grass.

One of the pods drifts in front of the truck and Liz gets a good look at it. The seed, if it could be called that, is oblong and somewhat transparent. Like thick glass, there's a smoky, golden color to the resin, and it seems hollow, but with the sun setting behind them she can't be sure.

"FUCK." Elvis swears, staring at something on the road. He pulls hard on the steering wheel, causing the truck to swerve out of a sandy rut in the track and onto the hard shoulder.

The first thing that runs through her mind is the possibility they've hit someone. As the truck bounces up over the rocks, she has a mental picture of one of the refugees being crushed beneath the wheels of either the Hummer or the truck. Elvis slams on the brakes and the truck lurches to a halt. Liz is already thinking about what she can and cannot do medically on the roadside. Ahead of them, the Hummer pulls to one side as well.

"What the—" Jameson cries.

"Bosco ran over one of those fucking things," Elvis says, pulling on the handbrake. Liz finds her heart ease a little. She can see a crushed seed in the tire tracks of the Hummer. A dark amber liquid oozes out onto the sand.

Elvis and Jameson drop down out of the truck and onto the dusty ground. Liz follows a little less gracefully.

"Smithy," Jameson calls out. "Stay vigilant on the approaches."

Smithy hasn't moved from where she's perched in the gun turret of the Hummer. She turns slightly, scanning the road ahead with the machine gun mounted on the vehicle. Refugees wander past, ignoring them.

Jameson is more concerned with the Hummer than the crushed alien pod. He looks at the tires, trying to see if there's any damage.

"Damn," Elvis says, crouching down and looking at the crushed amber pod. He picks up a stick and pokes at the torn umbrella-shaped parachute attached to the pod. The webbing in the chute is no more than a foot in diameter, and disintegrates as he pokes at it. Fine flecks of material trail into the air like ash.

"Leave that alone, you dumb fuck," Bosco says, walking around the side of the Hummer.

"Nice driving," Elvis says, dropping the stick as he stands up. "So, were you stupid enough to aim for this thing, or were you asleep at the wheel?"

Bosco laughs. "I was too busy trying not to leave your sorry ass behind."

Liz ignores them. She crouches to look at the viscous fluid seeping out of the shattered resin casing.

"What are you thinking?" Jameson asks her. "Ever see anything like this before?"

"No."

"So, is it a seed?" Elvis asks. "Are they planting alien marijuana?"

Liz isn't sure if Elvis is trying to be funny or just showing off, but his joke falls flat.

"I have no idea what this is," she replies. "It's certainly not a machine, at least not as we would understand one. There are no moving parts, no sections, no joints, screws, or pins. To understand what this is, you'd probably have to look at it under an electron microscope."

Liz picks up the stick Elvis was holding. Carefully, she positions the stick so it slides inside the shattered remains of the resin pod.

"Oh, man," Bosco says. "Don't touch that shit. Haven't you ever seen one of these movies? You never touch anything gooey. That stuff will turn you into a zombie."

Liz looks up at him without saying anything. The disapproval in her stare should be enough.

"This is what always happens," Bosco continues. "People go sticking their nose where it doesn't belong instead of leaving well enough alone. It starts out all innocent, and then some badass alien explodes out of your chest."

"Give it a rest," Jameson says. Liz appreciates his level head.

Slowly, she uses the stick to pick up the broken, hollow seed.

"I'm telling you," Bosco says. "This can only end badly. Damn thing is probably toxic."

"I hate to tell you this," Liz replies, unable to suppress a tiny smirk. "but if this thing contained any kind of microbial pathogen, we've already been exposed."

"Oh, great," Bosco replies. "That's just fucking great."

"You shouldn't have run over it, you dumb shit," Elvis says, slapping Bosco on the chest.

"Hey, cut it out," Jameson says, finishing their banter.

Although the pod looks like a glass cylinder, on inspection Liz can see it's an elongated hexagon, similar to the inside of a honeycomb.

"What do you make of it, Doc?" Jameson asks.

"Well," she says, very much aware she's anything but an expert, hoping she can shed some light on what they're dealing with, "bees and wasps use hexagonal shapes like this, but not by deliberate design. Hexagons are an emergent shape—the byproduct of maximizing every possible space. Pack regular cylinders together and there is a massive amount of wasted space in the gaps between them. Flex the walls of the cylinders a little and they naturally form a hexagon, filling up all the available room. Hexagons are nature's little space savers."

"So this thing?"

"Dunno, but it's shape is practical—efficient... and look at it. It's disintegrating. Whatever it's purpose was, it's done. Finished. Over."

The light from the setting sun catches the smoky resin, reminding her of the old dark brown medical bottles her mom used when she was growing up. They were tinted to prevent sunlight from breaking down the complex chemical molecules within the medicine, and Liz wonders if the same principle holds true here. She doubts any of the attributes she's noticed are coincidental.

"So we're infected," Bosco says. "Great. That's fucking great."

"I didn't say that," Liz replies.

Goo drips from the resin casing, running down the stick before dropping to the dusty ground. Broken sections of the casing slide with the thick fluid. Both the texture and consistency remind Liz of honey, or perhaps something less viscous, like treacle. There are fine grains mixed within the fluid.

Someone taps her on the shoulder. Suddenly, Liz is acutely aware they've been tapping her shoulder for some time, but she's been too absorbed by what she's looking at and the sensation has only just registered. The tapping is annoying. If Bosco or Jameson want her for something, why don't they just say so—why do they have to touch her? Touch is personal. Touch is privileged. Liz pulls away, deliberately ignoring them as she examines the remains. Get the message, damn it.

The hand tapping follows her as she shifts sideways. Liz rests the broken resin casing in the dirt.

"What?" she says impatiently, wondering what could be so important.

A shadow drifts over her, blotting out the setting sun. As she turns she can see all heads facing in one direction. The refugees stand still, their eyes looking up into the sky. The soldiers stand silently facing the same way. As Liz stands, her line of sight clears the frame of the truck and she gets her first glimpse of a floater. The creature is hundreds of feet up in the air.

Three floaters stretch out in the sky, spaced several hundred yards apart. One of the floaters cast a shadow over the truck, drifting north against the breeze. Sunlight flickers through the tentacles trailing behind the massive beast.

Liz is mesmerized by the sight. Whereas humanity flies into space in what amounts to a tin can, these living creatures are capable of spanning the depths of interstellar space, enduring a bitter cold vacuum, and then making the transition to flying within a planet's atmosphere with ease. What *are* these things?

Each floater is several hundred feet in height, like a blimp, only with a giant, semi-transparent purple bladder keeping it buoyant in the same way a bluebottle jellyfish floats on the waves of the sea.

Beneath the inflated bladder sits a mass of organic pulp. Despite her years of medical study and her interest in biology, Liz isn't prepared for what she's seeing. The mass beneath the presumably gas-filled bladder doesn't appear to have any differentiation. Liz is used to seeing biology as functional, practical, with insects and animals having segmentation, being divided into limbs and organs. The base of the floater, though, looks more like the raw wound of a gunshot. Behind the creature, a series of tentacles stretch out for thousands of feet, floating on the breeze, drifting lazily to one side then another.

Another floater appears from over the forest of acacia trees to the south of them. The massive beast appears as though it is no more than a few feet above the treetops, causing panic among the refugees, but Liz quickly realizes this is an illusion of size. The floaters are at several hundred feet above the road. Given that their tentacles trail below and behind them, remaining well clear of the ground, she figures they must be somewhere around five to six hundred feet up.

The floater passing overhead is majestic—strangely beautiful. The refugees cower, taking cover, as do the soldiers, leaving Liz standing alone on the road, staring up at the creature as though she were watching a whale moving through the ocean.

"Liz," Jameson whispers, sheltering beside the truck.

"They're ignoring us," Liz says, not bothering to lower her voice. "They're not here for us." Although she has no answer to the corresponding question racing through her mind—then why are they here?

Smithy crouches in the turret of the Hummer, making herself as small as possible as she swivels her machine gun around, tracking the beast through the sky.

Liz breathes deeply, taking in the awe of the moment. Within a minute or so, the creatures have passed, leaving long strands whipping slowly back and forth in their wake. The tentacles remind Liz of the elongated tails of sauropods, slowly tapering to a tip so fine she can't be sure quite where they end.

With the floaters drifting north, the refugees double their pace to the west, trying to ignore what just happened. Are they making up for lost time? Liz doubts that, thinking it's simply the single-minded focus of *Homo sapiens*—the characteristic goal-driven instinct kicking in, pushing them on to what they perceive as safety, and not just from the rebels, but from these alien intruders.

"What do you think they want?" Liz asks absentmindedly. "There has to be a reason they're flying through our atmosphere. And these pods, what's their purpose?"

Kowalski comes up beside her. "Well, I'm just glad they aren't after us. Whatever they want, I'm happy so long as they stay away from me."

Jameson joins the rest of the soldiers standing beside the back of the Hummer.

"Threat assessment?" he asks.

"Scary," Smithy replies from up in the turret. "But no imminent threat. Not yet, anyway. They didn't even seem to notice us."

"My money is on a squadron of F22 Raptors," Elvis says. "As nasty as these floaters are, they're not war machines. Couple of missiles and they're beached whales."

Bosco asks, "You really think we're going to catch an evac flight out of here with those things in the air? CENTCOM is going to ground flights, regardless. I think we're alone on this one. All bets are off."

Elvis grins, looking up at Smithy as he says, "Ten days of sweaty men in the jungle. Lucky you." Smithy throws some trash at him, but she's smiling.

"Game plan?" Jameson asks, but Liz gets the distinct impression he already knows what he's going to do—he's inviting discussion.

"Stick with the plan," Smithy says.

"Yeah, we're fucked if we don't hook up with someone else," Elvis says. "We're too big to hide, too damn small to fight. So long as we're around government troops, there's a degree of safety, but I'd feel a whole lot better if we had US soldiers to call on. If we run into rebels, or if any of these flying fuckers turns nasty, it's going to be *Game Over, Player One.*"

"Elvis is right," Bosco says. "For once, the Southern Belle has a point. We need to hook up with those Marines in Lilongwe. Safety in numbers. Uncle Sam's not coming back to Malawi, not with those things floating overhead back home."

"Somewhere someone's got to be taking the fight to them," Elvis says. "Please don't tell me the US of A is letting these things drift through Texas airspace?"

"There's no fight," Liz says, but she's wasting her breath. She shakes her head at his stubborn attitude. No one else offers a reply, not even Smithy. It seems no one is sure what to think.

"Lilongwe raises the issue of the chain of command," Jameson says, looking for a response from his soldiers. Liz steps closer. She and Kowalski might not be soldiers, but they deserve a say in their future. Jameson must pick up on that, as he clarifies his point, opening the huddle to include them. "We're autonomous at the moment. If we hook up with a larger force we'll probably lose flexibility in decision-making. Regardless of the service, anyone ranking beyond sergeant will assume seniority in the chain of command."

"What he's saying," Elvis says, butting in, "is some panicked dweeb could get us killed with a stupid order."

"The more senior the officer—the bigger the asshole," Smithy calls out from the turret.

Jameson softens the point by adding, "Officers can be idealistic, sometimes lacking common sense."

"Oh," Liz says, not used to the idea of handing the responsibility of her life, and possible death, to someone she doesn't know. "So what you're saying is, once we hook up, we're stuck with whoever we get?"

"Luck of the draw," Bosco adds.

Jameson nods, turning back to the soldiers. "We're good for one, maybe two engagements, but Elvis is right. We're too big to hide, too small to fight. Besides, the Marines will be in contact with CENTCOM—we'll be able to report in and get some clarification on what's happening elsewhere."

Elvis spits. "I'm in."

"Yeah, not a lot of choice," Bosco says with a hint of reluctance.

Liz admires the way Jameson works with his soldiers. He knows they have no choice. They're less than twenty miles from Lilongwe, yet it's important to him to maintain a sense of unity even this far along.

"Okay, let's roll," he says, walking back to the truck.

As they get underway, Liz looks out at the alien pods. The strange, organic devices lie scattered in the distance, spread out hundreds of feet apart on the grass, or caught in acacia trees. She doesn't say anything, as no one else seems to notice and she doesn't want to be an alarmist, but they're all broken. They're all leaking. The further the squad drives into Malawi, the more sure she is, noting that not only have the fragile, white umbrella-shaped parachutes dissolved in the wind, leaving a brittle skeleton, but the resin casings have ruptured on most, if not all of the pods. They're breaking down, their dark walls giving way and spewing thick, black sludge over the ground.

What does it mean? If the pods contain some kind of biological agent, what could she do about it? Nothing. Is she being paranoid? Is she reading too much into some unknown alien process?

Sitting there, bouncing with the worn suspension of the truck, Liz knows she's helpless, and that scares her more than any gigantic alien jellyfish floating through the sky. For the first time, she realizes she could die, and not just as some general, vague, far off, abstract notion—right here in Africa, within the next twenty-four hours. The events unfolding around her may lead to her death. Her life is out of control. But death is something that happens to other people, not her, and yet now that delusion is being stripped bare. The alien presence has shaken her confidence in all outcomes bar one. She's going to die. Try as she may, she can't shake that thought from her mind. Liz shifts in her seat, fighting her nerves.

The floaters have gone, disappearing over the horizon to the north, drifting roughly parallel with each other. Liz wonders if they're moving in a flock? In some ways, she prefers having them around. As jarring as the floaters were, they held a sense of awe without being a threat, but with their passing, Liz is left with a sense of fear for the unknown.

What's next?

As the sun sets, and Africa descends into night, Liz can't shake her fear of the dark.

CHAPTER 08: LILONGWE

Jameson climbs back in the cab of the truck, saying, "From what these government troops are saying, it seems the Marines are holed up at the airport to the east of the city. There's also a squad of Pakistani soldiers in the old UN compound in the city center."

Even though the city is in flames, Liz is relieved to see government soldiers manning a roadblock on the outskirts of Lilongwe. A red glow rises over the horizon, highlighting the buildings of the capitol in silhouette. Sporadic gunfire erupts. Liz has no idea of the distances involved from the sound, but the soldiers don't seem concerned. Can't high-powered bullets travel for a mile or more? It's a question she doesn't want answered.

"The captain reckons it's six miles," Jameson adds. "Bosco hasn't been able to raise the Pakistanis on the shortwave, so we're going to hunker down here for the night and move in with the dawn. Pull the truck up over behind the command post."

"Roger that," Elvis replies, putting the truck in gear and driving around the side of a war-torn building. Bullet holes trace a line along the concrete. There's no glass in any of the windows, and no light from inside, but Liz is tired. It looks pretty bad inside, but bad has become a relative term. With the advent of aliens drifting through the sky, it seems the worst a civil war has to offer is nothing compared to the threat of the unknown. The building is actually inviting, providing shelter from prying eyes in the sky.

Liz realizes she's a victim of the illusion of importance. The world revolves around her. Although she knows it doesn't, it's easy to become consumed with her own point of view. Somehow the alien presence is a personal threat. She's torn. She's intrigued by the arrival of an alien intelligence, but scared about what may unfold. The doctor within her has so many questions, but her human side worries. Her instinct is to fear all that is to come. The future seems dark. She wants to unwind time, to go back to simpler days, to return to her village hospital. Certainty—that's what's been lost. There's a bitter irony in finding certainty in a civil war.

As she walks across the dusty ground she notices a government soldier pissing into the remains of an alien pod. She wants to scold him, but what is there to say? For her, it's typical of humanity's approach to just about everything. A few people care. Most don't.

Jameson leads her and Kowalski into a small storage room with a single window. Jagged shards of glass stick out of the frame. There's no privacy, but at least no one will try climbing in.

"We're going to have you bed down here. Try to get some sleep. In addition to the government sentries, we'll post a watch through the night."

Liz nods. Kowalski drops his pack onto the ground. Liz is surprised by how tired she is. She unfolds her sleeping mat and crawls into a thin sheet sack designed to keep mosquitos at bay.

Within seconds, she's asleep, then just as quickly as the darkness descended, she's woken by Kowalski rummaging through his backpack. It's morning, but it doesn't feel like it. Liz could do with more rest.

Light breaks over the city. For a moment, Liz thought she caught a glimpse of the alien mothership through the window, but it's a cloud lit up in soft pink hues high in the stratosphere. A hot wind blows in from the west. The humidity is already oppressive.

"Rise and shine," Bosco says, sticking his head in the door. Kowalski has already repacked his bag. He offers her some water, which she accepts.

"I need to—"

"Latrine's behind the guardhouse," Bosco replies. "Unisex."

Liz fakes a smile. As she walks past Jameson, he hands her a bulletproof vest saying something she misses in the sound of gunfire nearby.

She points at the latrine, saying, "I'll just be a..." There's no need to say any more. Jameson knows. He continues rummaging around in the back of the Hummer. Elvis and Bosco joke around with each other, laughing about something. Smithy checks the magazine on the lightweight machine gun. Liz gets the distinct impression she shouldn't dawdle as the troop is ready to leave.

The smell from the toilet is overwhelming. One of the young Rangers follows her over and stands guard outside the latrine with his M4 rifle in hand. He looks outward, away from the toilet, back toward at the checkpoint. He must have followed her on Jameson's orders, even though she's only thirty feet away.

"Thanks," she says as she comes out. The young man simply smiles in reply and follows her back to the Rangers. His helmet is too big for his head. Liz can't suppress the realization she's being protected by a kid with a machine gun, barely out of high school.

She slips the bulletproof vest over her head. The vest is uncomfortable, designed for men. Liz fiddles with the webbing on the shoulders, trying to let out the breastplate a little as she walks back over to join the soldiers.

"Here, let me help you with that."

Liz looks up to see Smithy with her helmet off. Although her blonde hair is cropped short and is quite messy, she's pretty. Her petite face has natural beauty. It's no wonder Elvis jokes about her being Combat Barbie. Smithy really does look out of place among the Rangers. She belongs in the middle of Vogue magazine, not a civil war.

Smithy loosens the waist strap for Liz.

"Feels like you're carrying lead weights over your shoulders, huh?"

"Yeah," Liz replies sheepishly.

"Not the most fashionable of outfits," Smithy continues, adjusting the shoulder straps for her. "But out here you don't want any attention."

"How do you do it?" Liz asks. She hopes Smithy understands what she means by 'it.' Everything associated with Army life seems so contrary to a pretty young girl like Smithy, but that's the thing about stereotypes—they never really fit.

Smithy shrugs. She's shy, which surprises Liz. From what Liz has seen of the young woman, Smithy's more than capable of holding her own with the male troops, but deep down she really isn't some tough-as-nails butch woman. If anything, she seems more feminine than Liz, which is perplexing.

Smithy tugs on a strap, lengthening it and checking how square the vest is on Liz's chest.

"I'm the youngest of five, four of them boys, so I'm used to the banter."

"But to shoot someone?" Liz asks, not able to bring herself to use the word kill.

"Yeah, that's not easy. I don't think anyone really likes it, but it's one of those things you've got to do, you know, like washing out an old garbage can, or picking up dog shit. You don't want to touch it, but you know what's right so you just get on with the job."

Smithy smiles. "Sounds crazy, but I know what we're doing here in Malawi is important. We're making a difference—you with a scalpel, me with a gun. We're helping people in different ways."

"We are," Liz concedes.

"There you go," Smithy says, finishing up with the straps. She gives the vest one last tug, "You're now officially a badass."

Liz laughs.

"Hey, I've got something," Bosco says, holding the handset for the shortwave radio. The portable military radio has been propped up on the hood of the Hummer with a three-foot long aerial extended. Bosco keeps talking into the radio as the others gather around. Jameson points at something on a map, talking with Elvis about routes through the city. Kowalski leans over, taking a good look, although Liz doubts he knows what he's looking at. Liz strains to understand the words being spoken over the haze of static.

" ... *avoid northern routes... main avenue is clear... sporadic rebel attacks on Dupoint Road...*"

The mood among the soldiers is upbeat.

Jameson turns to her, "We can't get hold of the Marines, but the Pakistanis have a convoy heading for the airfield this afternoon.

There's a military flight from Nairobi, going on to Pretoria. It's due to touch down to pick up stragglers at 1500 hours. That's our ticket out of here."

He smiles, grabbing Liz by the shoulders. For a moment, she thinks he's going to hug her, but he says, "You're going home. Twenty-four hours from now, all this is going to be a memory, just a wild story to share with your family."

She smiles, saying, "And what about you?"

"We need to get in contact with regional command in Dar es Salaam, but it makes no sense for us to stay in-country. We've been separated from our unit. More than likely, they'll have us fly out with you to South Africa, and from there, stateside."

Liz forces a smile. She isn't sure what she feels inside. She's grateful, but it seems too good to be true. Everything has fallen in place.

Elvis shouts, "The US Air Force, baby!" Even though it's still dark, his eyes are hidden behind his gold-rimmed sunglasses. "Ain't no one keeping the US of A out of the skies."

Dawn breaks. Light spills over the city. One of the Rangers comes running over from the checkpoint after talking with several of the African guards. "We're good to go."

"Okay," Jameson says, grabbing his M4 from where it leans against the side of the Hummer. "Let's roll."

Elvis and Smithy high-five each other. He's so big, she has to jump to slap his hand. As the troops climb into their vehicles, Liz watches the two of them with intense interest. They're good kids.

"You be careful," Elvis says to Smithy. "Keep your eyes open, and your head down, and we'll get through this."

"Look out for yourself, big guy," Smithy replies, being cheeky. "You're the target, fat man."

He laughs, slapping her on the back. She pokes him up under his body armor, and he flinches, being ticklish. She clearly loves getting at him.

Smithy climbs inside the Hummer and then appears in the turret. She connects her machine gun to the guide rails and swivels around, surveying the area from on high. Her gun is mounted between a set of thick steel plates providing forward-facing armor, but she's exposed from every other angle.

Elvis climbs into the driver's seat of the truck. They pull out onto the dusty road, and the African soldiers manning the checkpoint wave them on, their yellow teeth showing as they smile cheerfully. Several of them call out, but Liz can't make out what they're saying.

Elvis leans out the window of the truck, yelling, "YEE-haw."

The Hummer pulls ahead of the truck and begins driving down the broad boulevard leading into the city. Tall palms line the road. Ragged, single-story buildings dominate either side of the street. For the most part, they're made from large blocks of sandstone, but beyond them tall concrete buildings loom in the background, stark and impersonal. It's as though Lilongwe has no soul. Black soot mars the walls, curling out above empty window frames, marking where flames have licked the stone. Burnt-out ruins speak of heartache and misery.

Those few people on the street quickly disappear at the sound of approaching vehicles. Wary eyes peer through broken windows. Ahead, smoke rises from the shattered frame of an overturned truck blocking a side road. Smoldering tires form a barricade blocking the entrance to a narrow alley barely wide enough for a soldier to walk down. A bloodied arm hangs from the scarred rooftop.

"You thinking what I'm thinking?" Bosco asks over the radio.

"Guerrilla warfare," Jameson replies, speaking into the mic. "If this is the first mile, I suspect the army is being over-optimistic. I doubt they've got control of the city. Pick up the pace."

"Copy that," Bosco replies.

"If we drive into trouble, keep going. There won't be much depth these improvised fortifications, so we should be able to get clear if we can keep rolling. Keep an eye on those rooftops."

"Roger that."

Rifle barrels stick out of either side of the Hummer, ready to return any incoming fire. Liz is in the middle of the truck's bench seat. Jameson turns toward her, saying, "If we come under fire, we're going to keep moving, okay?"

"Okay," Liz replies, not sure what she's agreeing to.

"Regardless of what happens, our best option is to keep moving. If the Hummer takes a direct hit from an RPG it could disable the vehicle. If that happens, we won't stop. If we stop, we're all concentrated in one spot. The best thing we can do is to keep going, and get out of the kill zone. Only then can we try to render assistance. If we both get caught in the kill box, it's all over."

Liz is silent. For Jameson, *'disable the vehicle'* is a euphemism for seeing his men maimed and possibly killed in an instant. These are people he's served with for years. As a doctor, Liz knows what it means to divorce herself in life or death situations. To disconnect her feelings isn't easy. Compassion isn't something she can ignore, and yet once her head is in that space, a sense of detachment allows her to make swift, decisive, clinical decisions. She understands the necessity of this kind of thinking, but it isn't like switching off a light. It comes with a cost.

"Likewise, if *we* take a hit, *they'll* keep going. They won't leave us, but they'll move away from us so they can outflank any incoming attack."

She nods.

"If that happens, we'll need to take cover until they can assist. We may have to move out on foot."

Jameson is looking deep into her eyes, maintaining an uncomfortable level of eye contact.

"If anyone's wounded, there's not much we can do for them in the short term. This isn't the movies. There are no heroics that can defy the physics of a bullet moving faster than the speed of sound."

Liz knows what he's doing. She's a doctor. Her first reaction is to render assistance, but that could be a mistake in combat. The first priority has to be securing the area so it's safe to provide help. There's no sense in ending up with a wounded surgeon.

"Left two hundred meters," is the call over the radio.

Elvis speeds up, keeping pace with the Hummer, and moving uncomfortably close to the lead vehicle. They race around the corner. Africans, caught unawares, dart off the road and into side alleys. Several of them are carrying AK-47s, either slung over their shoulder or in a casual grip, but they seem more interested in getting away from the Rangers than starting trouble. In the midst of a war, an AK-47 is more of an everyday accessory than a threat.

In the distance, the blackened remains of a bus lies on its side, blocking the road.

"Right one hundred meters."

They turn down an alleyway, reacting to the roadblock. The buildings reach three to four stories as they move deeper into the city. The alley narrows as they bounce out of potholes. Liz feels as though the walls are closing in. A cluster of power lines winds its way between poles dotted along the alley. Clothes hang out to dry, slung between the buildings on wires, providing a splash of color against the otherwise sandy browns of the city.

"Left fifty meters."

They turn into a broad street. An overturned truck forces them onto the other side of the road.

"Looks an awful lot like a coordinated system of barricades," Bosco says over the radio.

"You think they're corralling us?" Jameson asks. "Setting up a chokepoint?"

"They were corralling someone," is the reply, "but I doubt they're targeting us. I doubt they want to tangle with US soldiers."

"Let's get out of here before they realize we're not an effective fighting force."

"Roger that."

The sweep of the road curves to the left and the Rangers find themselves bearing down on a battle a quarter of a mile in the distance. The sound of gunfire echoes off the buildings around them. Government forces spread out along either side of the street, firing on rebels further down the road.

"Get us the *hell out of here!*" Jameson yells over the radio.

"Already on it," comes the reply. "Right twenty meters."

One, two, and then three bullets strike silently on the windshield, high and to the left above Elvis. Cracks splinter through the glass. Elvis hits the brakes hard as he turns to follow the Hummer. Has he been hit? Liz is surprised by how suddenly and quietly the bullet holes appeared. She isn't sure what she expected, but a lethal blow landing without warning doesn't seem right. She turns to him, looking for any sign of injury.

"I'm okay," he snaps as her fingers reach for his shoulder. Liz backs away. Elvis doesn't take his eyes off the alley. There are holes behind him in the cab of the truck, revealing where the incoming rounds punched through the sheet metal and into the rear. There's probably another three holes in the loose canvas flaps by the tailgate. Liz is horrified. Elvis shakes his head slightly and she notices the canvas lining on the outside of his helmet—it's been torn in a sharp horizontal line, marking where one of the bullets grazed the Kevlar.

"I'm fine," he growls, not wanting any more of her attention.

The realization of how close he came to being killed is terrifying.

"Indirect fire," Elvis barks. "Unlucky stray. Goddamn it. What a stupid, fucked up way to go—not even on the end of accurate fire. Shit."

He seems to be angry with himself, which confuses Liz.

"Easy, big guy," Jameson says. "We're clear. We're good."

"Copy that," Elvis replies even though they're sitting across from each other, and not talking on a radio. Elvis pulls on the steering wheel as they round a corner at speed. Liz feels the wheels lift. Jameson is on the radio to Bosco.

She bounces uncomfortably as they dart down yet another alleyway. Women hold their children back as the Hummer and the truck race by inches from their doorways. Dogs scamper for cover. They cross a main road and continue on down the opposite alley. They're traveling too fast. The truck wheels slam into the curb leading back into the alley and Liz finds herself propelled into the air. She has to reach up to avoid hitting the roof.

"Can the Pakistanis render support?" Jameson barks into the radio.

"Negative," Bosco replies. "They're holed up. They're not going to risk troops before the push to the airfield. We're on our own."

"*Fuck.*" Jameson's knuckles are white as he grips the radio handset.

"Left fifty meters. We're no more than two miles out."

Bosco turns onto a dual highway with a concrete median strip. Elvis follows hard behind him. Refugees push handcarts holding the last of their meager possessions. They meander with no particular sense of urgency, staring in wonder as the soldiers speed by.

Liz is relieved to hear their small convoy is heading in the right direction, cutting down the distance to their destination. For a moment there, it felt as though they were going in circles. All the buildings look the same—drab sandy brown facades, torn by war, stained by the desert. Crushed bricks flick up beneath the truck wheels, pummeling the underside of the vehicle like hail. At the frantic pace they're traveling, her body feels as rattled as her confidence.

The two vehicles drive past a park. There are no trees. Dead grass covers a small hill. Heat waves shimmer in the distance. A set of swings and a slide sit to one side on the dusty ground. Beyond the swings there's a burnt-out tank with its right track blown off. Kids crawl under and around the tank, having no interest in the swings. They're pointing their fingers at each other, firing imaginary guns.

There are black smudges throughout the park. It's as though someone has spilled oil on the dead grass, but Liz knows better. The odd skeletal frame of an alien pod's umbrella lies baking in the scorching sun. The pods themselves are gone, having melted like snow in summer.

Further along, they race past a hospital. Bullet holes scar the five story building. There's no movement inside. Most of the windows are broken.

Liz feels a pang of guilt. She knows what's happening inside those walls. The lack of regular power, along with poor hygiene, limited supplies, and an absurd workload will have rendered the hospital no better than those of the American civil war. Surgery will be little more than butchery. So much misery—so little that can be done. That hospital represents everything that is wrong with Africa: good intentions overwhelmed by the cruelty of the moment. She's seen it before, countless times throughout Africa. Anyone with injuries that warrant hospitalization will fare no better than a condemned man on death row.

"Coming up on the markets," Bosco says over the radio, and the vehicles back off, slowing as they turn into a broad, open square. A sea of heads spreads out before them, marking thousands of people in what amounts to little more than a dusty field. Makeshift stalls shade buyers and sellers. Horses, cows, goats and pigs are penned up in small enclosures, looking languid in the heat. Leafy green vegetables wilt in the sun. Flies swarm around stalls selling raw fish and freshly slaughtered meat.

The Hummer slows to a crawl as a sea of Africans swarms around them, trying to sell them produce. They call out, holding up live chickens by the feet, pointing at melons, pumpkins, and gourds for sale.

Elvis is busy turning people away from his door while trying not to run down anyone foolish enough to scoot between the vehicles. Kids call out for American candy. Women hold up ornate garments and golden jewelry hoping for a quick sale.

Bosco is on the radio. "Smithy wants to know if you want her to fire a burst over their heads to clear them out."

"Negative," Jameson replies. "We'd cause a stampede. Just keep rolling slowly forward. She can return fire, but she shouldn't initiate contact. Over."

"Understood." Bosco hits his horn, honking at the throng and yelling for people to get out of the way. A couple of kids climb up on the sidesteps of the truck. They're harmless. Liz can see they're showing off, putting on an exhibition for their friends. They smile, revealing a contrast of crooked, yellow teeth and unrelenting joy. They aren't wearing shirts. Their skinny arms looks anemic, but that doesn't bother them—they've found the Americans.

"Come on, kid," Elvis says. "Let someone else ride."

Liz can't believe him. Elvis is encouraging them. Sure enough, the kid hops down, only to be replaced by another. The teen hollers with delight, holding onto the window frame as he stands on the running board. He pumps his free arm in the air. Elvis jokes around with him, and he too hops down, only to be replaced by a teenaged girl wearing an ornate headdress. She cheers and waves to the crowd.

It takes almost ten minutes to clear the market. As they approach the far side of the square, the crowd peels away, allowing them to leave.

"Can you believe that?" Liz asks.

"That's the thing about Africa," Jameson replies. "The people here are not that different from us. We just think they are. They love, they hate, they cry, they make mistakes. They're human, just like us."

Liz is genuinely surprised by Jameson's attitude. She's only ever seen soldiers as hired muscle, mindless thugs that happen to be on her side rather than the other guy's, but she couldn't have been more wrong about him. Her few days with the Rangers have shown her a different side to the army. They're doing a job, a nasty job—one no man would ever wish on another—but a job that needs to be done regardless.

The Hummer weaves around the edge of the market and onto the quiet streets, followed by the truck.

"Is it just me?" Elvis asks. "Or was that surreal? It's like everyone in the whole goddamn city is back there. Out here, it's a ghost town."

"I don't like ghosts," Jameson replies. "Stay sharp."

A few minutes later Bosco cuts in. "Left in a hundred fifty meters. The UN compound should be in the next block."

Kids run down one of the alleys, playing. They're wearing sky-blue Kevlar helmets with the white UN logo painted on the side. Liz doubts that's a good sign.

The two vehicles turn into a broad avenue running straight for several miles through the deadpan eastern side of the city. In the distance, colored fabric billows out from the rooftops, sweeping down across the road in streamers.

"What is that?" Elvis asks. "A parachute?"

"Too many colors. A hot-air balloon, perhaps?" Liz says, her mind taking her back to the lush green fields of England and early morning rides in wicker baskets hanging from sedate balloons.

The fabric has a purple tinge with hints of scarlet, emerald and a golden yellow hue depending on the way sunlight plays on the windswept material. Sections billow up on the rooftops, catching a breeze that never quite makes it to the ground.

"Too big," Jameson says.

What has initially looked like power lines crisscrossing the street suddenly resolve into a vast network of tentacles strewn on the rooftops lining the avenue.

Jameson says, "Looks like they brought one of those things down." Liz breathes deeply.

"Uh-oh," Elvis says.

A burnt-out armored personnel carrier sits to one side, its tires reduced to melted piles of black rubber. Dark stains mark the dirt—dried blood from bodies long since dragged away. In a couple of places the blood looks fresh. The smell of cordite hangs in the air.

Heartache strikes Liz. There is a sense of disdain for humanity in war-torn Africa, where the price of a life is less than the bullets that tear through them.

At the end of the block, a torn UN flag flies above a battle-scarred, walled compound. Alien skin flutters in the breeze no more than quarter of a mile away.

"Hi, honey, I'm home," Elvis says in his distinct Southern drawl. No one laughs.

"No troops," Jameson says, looking at the factory walls and the rooftops across the road. "Why aren't there any sentries?"

"Look at that thing," Liz says, pointing at the massive dead alien creature sagging over the rooftops. "It's a scarecrow. Who's going to attack them with that thing hanging there?"

Jameson ignores her, grabbing the radio as the Hummer turns to enter the courtyard. "Hold there, Bosco. Something's not right."

"I've seen this movie," Elvis says. "Fucking face-huggers and acid-spitting aliens. We go in there, we're fucked."

Jameson ignores him. He leans forward. His eyes dart between the rooftops. Liz gets the impression he's more worried about an all too human ambush, and she feels it too, like static in the air before a storm. The Hummer stops in the entrance to the courtyard. The lightly armored vehicle reverses out, clipping a power pole on the blind side.

"Get us out of here," Jameson says over the radio.

Elvis hits reverse, twisting his body sideways as he peers out the window, looking behind them. The whine of the engine hits fever pitch as the truck races backwards.

"Bus," Elvis yells, hitting the brakes and twisting hard on the wheel, sending the vehicle sliding to one side. The truck collides with a bus behind them. The jolt passes through Liz as a wave, rattling her bones. In the wing mirror, she can see a burning bus blocking the road behind them, having been pushed in place by rebels. Their AK-47s are shouldered as they heave the barricade in place, but they quickly swing their rifles down once the road's blocked.

Smithy opens up with the SAW mounted on top of the Hummer. From the angle she's firing at, it's clear she's shooting at someone on a rooftop to their right. Plastic cartridges dance across the road, skidding through the dust.

"Go forward!" Jameson yells into the radio.

A trail of smoke billows down the road, skimming past their truck and exploding against the bus. Suddenly, the smell in the air is one of soot, burning rubber and oil. Automatic gunfire breaks like thunder.

The hood of the Hummer explodes in a flash of flames. A fireball rises, but the Hummer continues on, swerving wildly as it passes the entrance to the UN compound. A trail of smoke streams from a darkened window on the first floor of an abandoned store, out across the street and down toward the Hummer.

Liz watches in horror as the Hummer lifts off the ground with the force of the explosion. The vehicle flips, skidding to a halt, and barring their path.

Elvis swerves, making as though he's going to ram the Hummer to push it out of the way, but he rides over the curb, driving half on the sidewalk as Jameson fires his M4 out the open window. Whereas before she thought the gunfire was loud, now it's deafening. The shockwave from each round reverberates through the cabin. Liz can't hear what Elvis is saying. He's yelling, but his words are indistinct. Smoke trails cut through the air followed by explosions tearing up the sidewalk.

Liz feels the rear of the truck slide out from beneath her before she registers the sound of the explosion and the wave of heat emanating from the rocket blast. The truck slides toward the intersection in front of the UN compound.

Jameson is out of the truck. How he moved so fast, Liz isn't sure, but his door is open and he's standing on the road with his legs spread slightly apart, firing short bursts. Jameson swivels, never taking his eyes away from the sights on his rifle.

Liz scrambles toward him when a hand grabs the collar of her vest and drags her backwards. She struggles not to fall, grabbing at the truck door with her hands as she slides out onto the street. Elvis has his M4 cradled so the butt of the rifle sits in the crook of his arm. Like Jameson, he's firing short bursts, three rounds every few seconds. With his other hand he keep a firm grip on her collar, holding her down so she can't see what's going on. He's shielding her, protecting her, keeping her low, but with a ruthless amount of force. The stiff panels of her Kevlar vest make it awkward to move, digging into her hips as she tries to find her footing. Bullets slam into the truck, thumping into the sheet metal inches from her head.

Elvis herds her toward the back of the truck where black smoke billows into the air. She has no choice. He's far too strong.

Jameson comes around the front. There's yelling, but it's not panicked. The Rangers are coordinating their fire.

Jameson shoots in one direction, while Elvis targets rebels in a second floor window.

Elvis shoves Liz down behind the back of the burning truck, pushing her beneath the tailgate, using what little cover he has to protect her. The radiant heat from the flames lashes at her cheeks. Bullets whip past, leaving brief trails through the pungent smoke.

Dark shapes appear in the doorways. Faceless rebels peer out of broken windows. Liz can see the upturned Hummer behind them. Oil and diesel seep onto the street.

Smithy stands defiant in front of the wreckage, firing the SAW on full automatic at rebel soldiers charging at them from further down the street. Rebels drop under the deadly hail she unleashes. Hot shell casings skid across the road away from her. Smithy eases up, turning her attention back to the rooftops with short bursts. Her tiny frame shakes with the recoil of bullets streaming out of the smoking barrel of her machine gun. She's fearless—Liz is terrified. Smithy's standing in the open with no regard for her own safety—Liz wants to run.

"Get her out of here!" Jameson yells over the noise and carnage, pointing at Liz, and signaling for Elvis to keep moving.

Bosco runs toward a storefront with a wounded soldier draped over his shoulder. Bullets kick at his feet. Where's Kowalski?

There are soldiers still trapped inside the Hummer, but they aren't moving. Blood drips from the inside of the shattered windscreen. Smoke billows from the stricken vehicle. Liz gets up, wanting to run over to the Hummer to help the wounded.

A rocket propelled grenade explodes nearby, pelting them with dirt and pebbles, forcing them away from the truck. Liz looks down at a smoldering scrap of twisted metal embedded in the center of her Kevlar vest, knowing how close she came to dying. She staggers backwards, shocked by the blast.

Elvis catches her by the scruff of the neck, grabbing her vest, and dragging her away. He's unbelievably strong. Dust kicks up as bullets thump into the street. Elvis jerks Liz to one side, changing direction, and running for the sunlit side of the street. Liz feels like a rag doll blown about in a storm. Her legs swing wildly, trying to touch the ground as Elvis sprints, carrying her in front of him.

She finds herself slammed up against the wall next to a burnt-out car outside the abandoned UN compound. The rest of the Rangers are on the far side of the intersection.

Another rocket-propelled grenade slams into the cab of the truck, tearing the metal to shreds. Flames leap from the doors. Although Liz is thirty feet away, the concussion wave shakes her body. Blood drips from her lip.

Elvis is saying something to her, but whether it's the shock, or the ringing in her ears, she can't hear him. She can see his lips moving but his words sound distant. The two of them hunker down behind the burnt-out car as bullets cut through the air, coming in waves.

Liz forces herself to listen, willing herself to amplify the sound of his voice. Elvis still has his gold-rimmed dark sunglasses on. His hair is slicked back. The smile on his face is surreal. Even his uniform seems clean. All around her, dirt and grime stain the world, but Elvis looks pristine.

"Don't you worry about a thing, doc. We'll get you out of here."

She can't believe him. In the midst of gunfire and the sound of bullets striking the metal frame of the car, he's grinning like a child. He leans over the hood and returns fire at the growing number of rebel soldiers pouring into the area.

Smithy fires from the far corner of the intersection, providing Jameson with cover as he drags a wounded Ranger to safety.

Liz slumps to the ground, her back pressing against the rusted metal door. She pulls the scrap of shrapnel from her vest. Her ribs hurt. Maybe it's the exhaustion of breathing at an anaerobic rate, or maybe it's the adrenaline wearing off, but her body aches. Her hand runs over her breastplate—her fingers linger in four tiny holes, barely big enough for her fingertips to fit within. The crumpled slugs lodged in her chestplate are still warm.

Tears run down her cheeks. A wave of anguish sweeps over her. Why? How could anyone be so cruel? She struggles to understand how such anger and hatred could be directed at her, when all she ever wanted was to help. The attack is impersonal, though. The rebels know nothing about them—nothing beyond the flag under which they shelter. They know nothing beyond their own blind ideological hatred, and that's something she can't fathom.

Bosco scares her. He comes sliding in beside her like he's stealing bases in the World Series, having crossed between the overturned Hummer and the burning wreckage of the truck.

"It's about *fucking* time!" Elvis says, grinning at his friend.

Bosco says, "Well, someone's got to bail out your ass, pretty boy."

"What's the plan?" Elvis asks, peering out over the hood before dropping back behind cover.

"Sarge doesn't want to risk the doc in the open. We break left, try to find some clear air. He's going to provide cover fire before breaking right. Smithy found a stash of RPGs in that storefront, so she's going to give these bastards a taste of their own medicine."

"That's my girl," Elvis says.

Bosco adds, "Plan is we regroup at the markets."

"W—who?" Liz asks. She can't bring herself to say any more.

"We're down three. Two Rangers and a civilian." Liz swallows the lump in her throat. Again, there's clinical detachment in the Ranger's terminology, although Liz realizes Bosco's comment is as much for Elvis as it is for her—Bosco doesn't name those that have died.

"I'm sorry," he adds, his eyes unable to hold hers as he speaks. "He didn't feel a thing."

Those words—they're lies, and they all know it. The indifference with which Bosco deals with death is all too familiar. Liz has seen this before—the facile comfort of an apparently quick death. No one dies in an instant. As a doctor, Liz understands that all too well. She may not have lost a patient on an operating table, but she's seen a lot of people die.

Sorrow is meaningless to the dead. Even for the living, it's misplaced, however well intended. *Kowalski didn't feel a thing*—it's a statement no one can ever verify. With those few words, Liz feels as though a bullet has torn through her vest, plunging deep into her own heart.

She feels sick. Bile washes up the back of her throat. She looks at the Hummer, but she can't see any movement through the darkened, shattered windscreen.

How would Bosco know? Did he check for a pulse? Without a stethoscope, even that's fraught with difficulty in such a hostile, confusing environment. Perhaps Kowalski's simply unconscious. Would Bosco lie to keep her safe? Maybe he's softening the truth to keep her from being reckless? No. She can see it in his eyes. He hates himself for telling her.

She has to see him for herself. Liz tenses her muscles, preparing to spring out into the maelstrom of gunfire and dart over to the Hummer, when a rocket-propelled grenade soars above them, striking the wall less than ten meters away. A wave of heat washes over her. Fragments of rock and stone rain down, leaving her wondering how long it'll be before she joins Kowalski in the cold, dark silence.

Bosco scrambles out from behind cover, over to the stone wall dominating the street corner. He has his back to her, marching forward with the barrel of his M4 leading the way. His rifle is pressed hard into his shoulder, becoming almost an extension of his body. He fires a couple of rounds, seemingly oblivious to the gunfire directed at him. From the other corner, Jameson and Smithy open up, laying down suppressing fire.

"Time to go," Elvis says, grabbing Liz by the collar.

"No."

She's safe here. The rebels can't shoot her as she hides behind the car. As if in defiance of her thoughts, high-velocity rounds rain down around her, punching holes through the wreckage. If any of these bullets hit outside the small square that marks her vest, they'll pass clean through her. Her only measure of safety comes in not being seen, but it's only a matter of time before an AK-47 round finds its mark.

Elvis drags her to her feet, his fingers locked around the collar of her vest.

"Let me go," she yells, panicking at the thought of returning to the firestorm in the street and pulling away from him. "You have no right."

Elvis crouches beside the rusted engine bay of the vehicle.

"We'll debate freewill in combat situations later, doc. For now, we have to move or we're dead."

Bullets whistle past her head. Elvis pushes her on, firing at rebels across the road. Her feet stumble. Bosco crosses the intersection. His eyes never leave the sight on his M4. He leans forward, moving at a jog, his rifle pointing down the street as he fires.

"We've got snipers at two o'clock," Elvis yells. "Launchers on the rooftops."

Bosco is focused on only one thing—getting clear of the intersection. He drops an empty magazine out of his rifle and slams another in place in a fraction of a second. All the while, his rifle never leaves his shoulder, and his eyes never leave the gunsight.

Jameson and his team fire rocket launchers of their own. Bricks and mortar fly through the air, exploding from the rooftops. Smithy has abandoned her SAW and is using a regular M4, firing short bursts at someone in the building ahead of them. Whereas the other soldiers stay behind cover, Smithy is oblivious to self-preservation. She stays on the move, her combat boots kicking up dust as she runs in short sprints away from the intersection, moving in the opposite direction from Elvis and Bosco. She's constantly turning, identifying another threat, and firing. Jameson has a man draped over his shoulder, running hard after her as the other soldiers follow, darting between storefronts. Bullets whiz and zing as they whip down the street.

Elvis pushes Liz across the road behind Bosco. It isn't that she's resisting Elvis, she simply can't keep up. Her feet feel like lead. Her legs are clumsy.

The intersection is covered by rebels on the flat rooftops. Liz spots a rebel opposite Jameson lining her and Elvis up with a rocket launcher mounted over his shoulder.

"Won't feel anything," she mumbles under her breath. "Not a thing."

There is no comfort in that thought, but it's all she can hold to in the moment.

Elvis must see the rebel as well as he quickens his pace, throwing Liz against a wall on the far side of the intersection. He slaps his arm across her chest, flattening her against the crumbling brickwork as the RPG strikes the corner. Liz never hears the blast.

The sudden compression of air around her seems to crush her fragile body, and she finds her ears ringing with an eerie high-pitched whine. Clouds of dust envelop them. She's confused, disoriented. Her ears ring but there's silence at all other frequencies. It's as though someone has pulled the plug on a stereo.

Dirt, dust, rocks, and bricks billow across the street, hurled outward by the explosion. Elvis staggers forward, walking away from what's left of the wall. She felt the blast travel through the air, through the wall, even through Elvis as his arm held her pinned against the brickwork. She's stunned, desperately wanting to catch up with reality, unsure what has happened. There's blood everywhere, but she feels no pain. Shock?

Elvis falters, his boots catch on the debris scattered across the road. His glasses are gone. His helmet has been blown off his head. Blood has been splashed over his face and neck.

He staggers forward, oblivious to the carnage around him. Bullets kick at the dust by his feet. He falls to his knees. His back is straight but his head is bowed as though he's kneeling in prayer. It's only then Liz notices a dismembered, bloodied arm lying some fifteen feet away in the middle of the road. Blood stains the ground, turning the dust black.

Liz feels a hand on her shoulder.

"We've got to go."

Bosco's words are muted even though he is shouting just inches from her ear. His words leak slowly into her silent world.

"Nooo."

"There's nothing you can do for him," Bosco yells above the battle. "If you die, then his death has been for nothing."

Liz looks at Bosco through tear-stained eyes. She's already pulling the belt from her waist. The sound of explosions, bullets flying, and men screaming rises in a crescendo, but none of that matters. She can't leave Elvis.

"He's not dead," she cries.

Liz pulls away from Bosco, surprising herself with her own strength.

She shuts out her fears, moving into overdrive. Liz grabs Elvis by the shoulder and wraps her belt around the shattered remains of his upper arm, pulling it tight and stemming the flow of blood. The blast has left his bicep in tatters, a white bone protruding from a mangled mess of bloody flesh. His arm has been severed above the elbow. By strapping her belt across the muscle leading from his shoulder, she hopes to contain the arterial bleeding.

A bullet rips across her shoulder, skimming her skin, and tearing at her flesh. It feels as though someone has branded her with an iron.

"*Fuck. Fuck. Fuck.*" Bosco is manic. He fires erratically, turning one way, then the other. He drops another empty magazine, sliding another in place seamlessly. "What a shitty way to die. Jesus, Mary and Joseph—this is a complete clusterfuck."

Liz ignores him. She slaps Elvis on the side of his face, staring deep into his eyes as she speaks. "Elvis, look at me. Come on, I need you to be here—now. Look at me. Remember me? I'm Doctor Elizabeth Bower. You're in Malawi. You're in a firefight. I need you to focus. I need you to come with me. Do you understand?"

The distant glassy look in his eyes gives way to a lethargic nod. Liz helps the giant of a man to his feet, struggling to support his weight. Two sharp stabs of pain cut into her back—she's been hit. Her bulletproof vest took the brunt of the impact, but the pain surging through her is like being struck by a baseball bat. Liz staggers forward, almost dropping Elvis.

"We're *fucked*," Bosco cries. "We are so *fucked*."

Jameson and his team are gone. She remembers how he described the different sounds of gunfire back in the village, the violent snap of the M4 compared to the throaty roar of the rebel AK-47s. There is only one M4 firing—Bosco's.

Liz tries to run, but Elvis is too heavy. It's all she can do to keep him from collapsing in the street. She sways under his weight, driving hard with her legs and pushing on, doing all she can to keep going.

Bosco moves behind the cover of a storefront further down the side road, moving as though he can somehow will Liz and Elvis to run faster.

To her surprise, the AK-47s stop firing. For a moment she holds out hope they've escaped, but mentally she knows they're barely twenty feet from the intersection. Something else has happened, but what? The lonely crack of the M4 continues, but the dynamics of the ambush have changed.

Bosco is hit first in the leg, and then in his right arm. He staggers forward but can't bring his M4 to bear. Whoever's shooting at him is toying with him, disabling but not killing him. Out of desperation, he uses rifle as a crutch, holding onto the stock as he pushes the barrel of the rifle against the ground, desperately trying to stay on his feet.

Ahead, a crowd of African rebels run in toward them yelling and screaming, but they aren't shooting. They want them alive. They reach Bosco and begin clubbing him with the butts of their rifles. They knock Elvis to the ground as well, but they leave Liz standing there covered in his blood.

Liz watches in horror as one of the rebels slips a black sack over Bosco's head, pulling a drawstring tight around his throat. She cries out in horror as her hands are pulled behind her back and bound tightly with rope. Her world goes black as a sack is jerked over her head. The rope around her throat restricts her breathing, causing her to panic. Liz is pushed forward and falls awkwardly to the ground, unable to break her fall with her arms.

One last thought goes through her mind as the butt of a rifle slams into her head.

They want us alive.

CHAPTER 09: COLOSSEUM

"Wake up," a gruff voice demands. The steel cap of a boot kicks at her arm as she lies on a rough concrete floor.

Liz is groggy. Her eyes struggle to focus. The back of her head throbs. Her hands are unbound so she reaches up, gingerly touching her bloodied, matted hair. The sunlight streaming in at a low angle tells her several hours have passed. Night is approaching. Slowly, she sits up, her back pressed against a brick wall.

Liz looks around, expecting to find herself in prison, but she's on the upper floor of an abandoned factory. Broken skylights dot the ceiling. The roof has collapsed further along the vast, desolate factory. There's a gaping hole in the concrete floor directly below the crumpled corrugated iron peeling in from the roof. The damage must have been caused by an artillery shell, or perhaps a bomb dropped from a plane. Reinforced steel bars protrude from the shattered concrete. The concrete slab was punctured long ago as the floor is clean, with debris swept to one side. This must be a warehouse, a staging area, as there's no manufacturing equipment.

Elvis leans up against the wall beside her. His head hangs low, but he's conscious. He must be in excruciating pain, but he doesn't show it. He mumbles under his breath. Fluids ooze from the bloody stump that was once his arm. His head rolls softly to one side, and Liz doubts he's coherent. The physical and mental shock he's suffered would've killed most men.

Beyond him, Bosco sits with his legs splayed out in front of him. A bandage has been wrapped around one of them, stemming the flow of blood from a bullet wound. From the rushed, careless manner in which it's bound, she figures he's tended to his own injuries using the combat trauma kit on his belt.

Rebel soldiers gather around. "I am General Alad Humar Adan," one of them declares, stepping forward in front of them. "You are terrorists, mercenaries, taken into custody by the People's Liberation Army of Malawi."

The general, if he really *is* a general, looks no more than twenty years old, although it's never easy to tell the age of African men. He's tall and thin. His dark skin glistens with natural oils, while his curly hair is shaved on the sides, rising a few inches above his head, accentuating his height.

He smiles, gloating over his captives. There are at least fifty other rebels milling around. Some of them have their AK-47s shouldered, others hold their rifles casually, waving them about as though they're toys, joking with each other. They're smoking, but Liz doubts it's tobacco. There is a glazed look to their bloodshot eyes.

"Do you not know me?" the general demands, putting on a theatrical pose in response to their lack of acknowledgement. "To you, I am Will Smith, and this is my *Independence Day*." The soldiers behind him laugh.

"You see, for me, this alien invasion is no fantasy, no movie full of special effects. I have faced the demon and defeated him. I have brought *down* the alien. He has bowed before my feet. Soon, all nations will come to me, to learn how to defeat this terror."

Adan struts before them. His accent is clipped, betraying his local pedigree. "To you, I am a hero. I am Laurence Fishburne. I am Denzel Washington. To you, I am Samuel L. Jackson, and do not forget the L., it is very important: L. is for Leroy. You see, I am Jamie Foxx. I am all your heroes rolled into one."

Adan marches back and forth with a small white cane hooked under his arm. He's wearing riding boots like those Liz once wore while conducting dressage in England, only her boots were scuffed and worn. Adan's knee-height boots are polished to a brilliant black shine. The medals on his chest look as though they're made from plastic, not that she's going to point that out.

"I am Augustus Caesar. I am Alexander the Great. I am Napoleon. I have defeated the United Nations. I have defeated the United States. Now I have defeated monsters from another world—I am invincible!" Liz averts her gaze, looking down at his boots as he turns before her.

"What?" Adan snaps. She looks up. Adan is facing Bosco. "What ARE you looking at?" Adan pulls the white cane from under his arm and points it at Bosco. It's a riding crop. Adan flicks the whip through the air. It flexes. From her short stint assisting vets as a teen, Liz knows the kind of injury riding whips can cause a horse. In the wrong hands, they're instruments of cruelty.

Blood sprays across the wall as Bosco's head reels to one side.

"I asked you what you were looking at?" Adan demands.

Liz tries to make herself as small as possible, her head bows, her shoulders hunch. She can hear Bosco choking on his own blood.

"Do you think you can disrespect me?" Adan shouts, enraged. "Do you think you Americans can come here and kill our people with impunity? Do you think you can get away with these crimes? You murder our women. You kill our children.

"Ah, but you no longer hold a gun. No longer can you bully us, push us around. Now, *we* hold the guns."

Adan turns back to his troops, holding his hands out wide as he speaks to them.

"You see, there is no land of the free. There is no land of the brave. The only bravery these men know is when they are holding a gun. They are cowards. The only justice they know is the justice that comes out of the end of a barrel. But there is no justice in Africa, there is Just-Us." He laughs, turning back to Bosco.

Adan uses his riding whip to raise Bosco's chin. "We will have our justice. You will pay for what you've done to our land. You will pay with your blood for what you've done to our women and children. You will—"

"Stop it," Liz cries, knowing it's a mistake as the words leave her mouth, but she can't help herself. She has to say something.

"What have we here?" Adan asks, his theatrical anger subsiding for a moment.

"I am Doctor Elizabeth Jane Bower, with *Médecins Sans Frontières*. These soldiers were escorting me to the UN compound when we were ambushed."

Adan crouches down in front of her, moving her face around with his bloodied whip. "Look at you. Look at your skin," he says. "Why do you side with these white devils? Why do you betray your own people?"

Liz doesn't reply. She knows anything she says will only play further into his hands.

"I have rescued you," Adan says. "I am your general, your liberator, your hero."

Liz can't help herself. "You're an asshole."

Adan laughs, "Is it only your women that can speak? Are you not men who can speak for yourselves? Has the US Army been castrated?"

The African rebel soldiers laugh at the Rangers.

"Leave her alone," Bosco says, and Adan wheels to face him again.

"So we have an American hero here after all. Who are you? Are you Bruce Willis or Sylvester Stallone? Or are you an old-fashioned hero? From the days when everything was black and white? Are you John Wayne? Or perhaps, Ronald Ray-Gun?" Again, the soldiers laugh on cue.

"Get them up."

Soldiers grab them, pulling them to their feet and gripping them by the arms and shoulders. Elvis grimaces as he's pushed forward. He staggers, his feet barely able to carry his weight, his boots dragging on the ground with each step.

Adan leads them over to the edge of the gaping hole in the concrete floor. Chunks of concrete hang from reinforced steel bars around the shattered edge of the dark hole. On the ground floor, a series of double bed mattresses have been piled haphazardly on top of each other.

"This is the colosseum," Adan proclaims as Liz, Bosco, and Elvis are pushed toward the edge.

The rebels are excited. They talk rapidly with each other as they spread out around the edge of the broad hole, vying for the best vantage points.

Liz doesn't understand. Adan explains. "They are taking bets on how long you will last. So far, no one has survived more than five minutes against *the beast*."

Looking down into the devastated lower floor, dark stains stretch out across the concrete. Blood splatter soaks several mattresses. Most of the blood on the concrete appears dry, but at least one patch looks wet.

"You who are condemned to death—you will fight this day for your lives. As Caesar, I hold the power of life and death in my hand. You are my gladiators. You will wage war against the beast—and if you win, I will grant you your freedom."

Elvis slips and almost topples forward into the hole. Liz grabs him, pulling him back, putting his one good arm over her shoulder.

Liz still doesn't understand what Adan is asking of them. What beast? Does he have a lion down there? Or are they to fight each other to the death? If so, they simply won't fight. She wouldn't, Elvis can't, and she doubts Bosco will buy into Adan's madness.

"Where are you, my beauty?" Adan calls out. "Where is my monster? My beast?"

One of the soldiers leans over the hole. He strikes the butt of his rifle on a loose clump of concrete dangling from a reinforced steel rod. A whip lashes out from the darkness below, cracking in the air just inches below the shattered concrete. The motion is smooth, and surprisingly quick.

"What the—?" Bosco cries.

Several more blood red, whip-like tentacles strike out, trying to reach the edge of the crumbling floor.

"Ha, ha, ha!" Adan yells. His voice is theatrical, although he has no need to inflate her fear—the creature is terrifying. From the shadows, there is a rumbling, seething sound, like rolling storm clouds before thunder breaks.

"You see. You are not the first ones to be caught by the great General Alad Humar Adan."

Her legs shake. Bosco looks pale. Elvis groans, mumbling, "No, no, no."

Troops jostle for the best positions around the vast hole, peering into it from all angles. They point and call out, yelling with excitement. Money changes hands in fistfuls as several impromptu bookies move among the troops, collecting loose notes in a helmet.

"But I am magnanimous," Adan announces, handing his riding whip to one of the soldiers standing next to him. Liz gets the feeling the general has given this speech before. "I will not send a man to his death unarmed. No, that wouldn't do for sport. I am fair. I am just."

Adan pulls a revolver from his holster. He flips the gun to one side, opening the cylinder block and exposing six chambers.

"Do you see this?" he asks, emptying the bullets into his hand. "This is a .44 Magnum, the most powerful handgun in the world. This gun could blow your head clean off your shoulders. So, you've got to ask yourself one question. 'Do I feel lucky?' *Well, do ya, punk?*"

The soldiers laugh at his Clint Eastwood impression. Adan makes as though he's going to hand the empty gun to Bosco, but instead he tosses it carelessly into the gaping hole. The gun clatters across the concrete, coming to rest in a pool of fresh blood.

The soldiers roar with delight.

"I give you a chance—a fair chance. If you can kill the beast, you can go free."

Adan holds up a single bullet. He drops the bullet in Bosco's outstretched hand as the rebels cheer. Liz can see Bosco weighing the bullet, tossing it slightly in his hand.

"No," Elvis says, pushing down on Liz as he straightens to face Adan. "This is crazy."

Bosco touches him gently on his good shoulder.

"Don't worry, big guy," he says, smiling as he clutches the bullet. "I'll see you in hell."

One of the soldiers steps up behind Bosco, nudging him with his AK-47. Liz can see Bosco weighing his options, lining up the soldiers training their rifles on him. He has no choice. It's jump, or be pushed.

He turns, winks at Liz, and then launches himself out across the massive hole in the floor. Bosco leaps as far as he can. He falls heavily on the mattresses some twenty feet below, catching the pile on one side and rolling onto the concrete floor.

Liz is horrified. She watches as Bosco scrambles to his feet. He limps to where the gun lies. Beneath her, the alien creature screams like a wild animal, thrashing and striking at the concrete. Dark red tentacles flicker in the shadows. The rebels yell, chanting something in their native tongue.

Bosco grabs the gun. He loads the pistol, slipping his lone bullet into an empty chamber and moving the block in place. He cocks the gun, pointing it into the darkness. He looks calm. Liz is terrified. She can feel her left leg lifting off the ground as it shakes within her boot. An intense fear seizes her mind as the worst of her nightmares unfolds before her.

Bosco backs away from the shadows, staying in what little natural light falls through from the upper floor, keeping his back to the mattresses. He spins one way, then another, pointing the gun out straight before him. Liz can't hear the monster over the noise of the rebel troops yelling around her, but Bosco turns at sounds, spinning as he hobbles on his wounded leg. Whatever that thing is, it's fast.

Bosco points his gun down, as though he's aiming at something low to the ground on the other side of the mattresses, and then spins around with the gun thrust out at chest height.

The creature is stalking him, looking for an opening. Like a lion moving through long grass, or a shark circling in murky waters, the alien seems to be weighing up its options, using the shattered crates and concrete supports for cover as it lurks in the shadows. The monster is trying to disorient him, wanting to confuse him.

Bosco slips in a pool of fresh blood, loosing his footing for a second, and the alien seizes the opportunity to strike. Tentacles reach for him. He scrambles to get away, but stumbles on debris.

Liz sees the shot before she hears it. The revolver recoils as a flash appears at the muzzle as the crack of gunfire echoes through the empty factory. As the gun recoils, the creature strikes, lunging at him from the darkness.

Hundreds of tentacles reach for him, engulfing him, slashing at his clothing and tearing him apart. His body is flung around like a rag doll. Whips flay his skin, breaking his bones, and shredding his torso. His Kevlar vest is sliced into ribbons, while his boots are torn in half, still holding the crushed remains of his feet. Within seconds, there's nothing but bloody gristle where once a man stood. A dismembered hand lies to one side still holding the revolver. Liz struggles not to vomit.

The rebel soldiers cheer. "Two minutes ten seconds," someone yells. Another roar rises from the soldiers.

Liz finds herself shaken by the violence of Bosco's death. Is that all life amounts to? She barely knew him, but there had to be so much more to his life. Liz can't switch off at the sight of death. Although she's been surrounded by an appalling loss of life since she first arrived in Malawi, she can't ignore what happened to Bosco. He's not a statistic. Just moments before, he was a living, breathing human being, and the stark finality of his death hits her hard.

Bosco has parents. Everyone does. He probably has brothers and sisters as well. Are they older or younger? Have they gone into the army as well? Or did they escape this fate, becoming accountants or nurses, mechanics or shopkeepers. From his Midwestern accent, it's clear Bosco grew up somewhere in Ohio, or perhaps Indiana, bouncing on the knee of proud grandparents. He attended school, probably fell in love a couple of times, and one fateful day, decided to join the army. What was that day been like? Did the sun shine brightly, or was it dark and grey, with sullen clouds brooding overhead?

Money changes hands as the winnings are distributed. Liz is in shock. Life unfolds in slow motion as she stares at a pair of US army boots still standing in place on the blood-soaked concrete.

What drew Bosco to army life? Was it a sense of adventure? A desire to escape the mundane routines of life? Had his father, or perhaps mother served with distinction, inspiring him as a boy? Did Bosco sign up for patriotism, or pay? What about all the soldiers he met along the way, what will they hear of this? Will they ever learn about what happened here today, or will they simply hear that Bosco is MIA presumed KIA? Will anyone hear of his courage?

Liz feels an ache in her chest. Life shouldn't be snuffed out like a candle. Tears run down her cheeks.

"You are next," Adan says, looking at Elvis.

"No," Liz cries. "This is wrong. You can't do this."

Adan laughs. "Oh, but I can."

"Look at him," Liz pleads. "He can barely stand."

Adan smiles at her. There's wickedness in his eyes. He holds two bullets in his hand, holding them up high so the soldiers understand what he's proposing.

Adan yells, "What do I hear for a double? How long can two of them last against the beast? Do I hear four minutes? Is anyone going to take four minutes for the two of them? Do I hear five? Will anyone brave six?" The rebels cheer, calling out in response as the gambling begins. Money rapidly changes hands.

"You sick bastard," Elvis says, struggling to hold himself upright. Liz can feel him trembling. Even with his shattered arm lost below the elbow, his bulk makes him look formidable, especially as his bulletproof vest bulks out his chest. His gruff voice sounds resolute, but Liz knows —like her, he's as afraid of dying. There's no way they're getting out of here alive.

Adan holds out the bullets for Elvis, but with a tourniquet around his torn bicep, and his other arm slung over her shoulder, he can't take them. Liz holds out her hand, but Adan plays up the incident.

"Your movie hero Arnold Schwarzenegger was so tough he didn't need bullets to kill the predator. Are you our Arnold? Can you kill this monster with your bare hands?" The soldiers laugh, jeering at them. "Should you change your mind," Adan says. "You will have to find your bullets."

"No," Liz cries as Adan tosses the bullets carelessly out over the vast hole. Liz watches as they sail through the air, bouncing on the mattresses. One falls to the left, the other bounces on further, rolling to the right.

"*Fuck*," Elvis says under his breath.

Liz feels the butt of a rifle thrust hard into her back, forcing her toward the jagged hole in the floor. Below her, the alien monster seethes with anger, lashing out with its razor-sharp tentacles. "No," she screams. "This isn't fair."

"Fair?" Adan cries in reply. "This is not fair? You bomb us with your Raptors, you occupy our country, you force your systems and beliefs upon us, you destroy our traditions, and you want to talk to *me* about what is fair? Hah. I say, you have as much chance down there as we do against your bombers."

Another shove in the back brings her to the edge of the abyss. Concrete crumbles beneath her boots. Elvis jumps out before her, clearing the torn strands of reinforced steel bars protruding from the shattered concrete. He lands on a mattress, rolling on his good shoulder.

Liz jumps. She has to. If she waits to be shoved, she'll fall awkwardly and miss the mattresses. Breaking a leg on the concrete floor doesn't seem like such a smart idea, so she jumps. Jumping is her only option, and yet it feels like suicide.

Liz doesn't make it as far as Elvis, and she has no idea about rolling to soften the impact. She lands on a single mattress off to one side, and is shocked to feel the jarring blow resonate up through her ankles, knees, hips, and spine. She collapses in a heap, with pain tearing through her body.

In the darkness, the monster screams. Elvis leans up against the crushed remains of a wooden crate, using it to help him stand. Liz gets to her feet. Her ankles ache. The soles of her feet feel as though someone has been pounded on them with a sledgehammer.

"Bullets," Elvis says. "Get the bullets." Liz looks around. From the ground, the layout of the floor looks entirely different. She swings around, looking at the pile of mattresses, trying to get her bearings. Above her, the soldiers roar with excitement. Adan stands defiant—laughing, gloating. From his position on the edge of the hole, she's able to orient herself. She has to be within a few feet of the bullet that fell by the crates.

Elvis staggers over to where the revolver lies in a pool of fresh blood, crushed bone, and shredded body tissue. He's in excruciating pain. His movements are coarse. His shattered arm hangs limp by his side, nothing more than a bloody mess of pulp and bone.

Liz runs her hands through her short, dark hair, which helps her concentrate as her eyes scan the ground, looking for the bullets. Small rocks and splinters of wood lie scattered over the rough concrete. Patches of blood stain the ground. Her eyes dart back and forth, manic to find the bullet. Streaks of blood mark the concrete. Splatter patterns wrap around the support pillars.

Something moves in the shadows. Thousands of blades slash at the air, cutting through the darkness. Liz looks up. She can't help herself. Her heart races. Although she knows she should keep searching for the bullet, she has to see this alien monster. Her desire is irrational, driven by fear. There, in the darkness, she catches the faint outline of the monster, just a glimpse of spikes and tentacles writhing in anger as the creature moves along the far wall of the factory. Above her, the rebels are chanting, willing the creature to attack.

Elvis falls to his knees, and then to the concrete—exhausted and in excruciating pain. He uses his one good hand to pull himself on, slowly creeping across the floor. He grabs the gun, peeling Bosco's fingers from the pistol grip. He leans up against a concrete support pillar. The physical toll of his injuries has sapped his strength. He struggles, fighting against fatigue and shock. His gloved fingers grip the revolver, and he wipes the gun against his clothing, trying to clean it.

"Doc, I need those bullets," he yells.

Liz is down on her hands and knees. She's sure this is where she's saw one of the bullets come to rest. Her hands sift through the debris, her fingers desperate to clutch at metal, and not wood or stone.

The alien roars. Within the darkened room, there's a sound like the rush of a storm in a forest. The monster closes in on Elvis.

"Where's that goddamn bullet?" Elvis cries. He points the gun into the shadows, bluffing.

Liz scrambles back to where she landed, searching frantically for the first bullet. The mattress she fell on has slipped off the pile and twisted to one side. She's almost directly below Adan. She can't see the general, but she can hear him gloating, calling out with delight.

"Get me that *fucking* bullet," Elvis yells.

He staggers away from the monster, but his legs can't carry him. He falls awkwardly, crying out in pain as he sprawls out on the concrete.

Liz is frantic, searching on her hands and knees for the bullet among the fragments of broken wood and bits of rock scattered across the ground. Above them, the rebel soldiers laugh. Elvis rolls on his back, pushing frantically away from the alien creature as it slowly advances on him, venturing out of the shadows. His boots slip in the blood of his fallen comrade. Adan and his troops cheer for the alien.

The creature rears up above Elvis, its tentacles slashing at the air. As the alien moves into the light, Liz gets her first good look at the monster. Mentally, she struggles to process what she's seeing. Rather than a single creature, such as a lion or a tiger, the alien appears to be a chimera, a hybrid, a combination of creatures.

What she'd thought of as tentacles are flexible blades. Liz is tempted to think of the alien as a giant sea urchin, or a western tumbleweed, with an inner core like that of a basketball. Spikes protrude in all directions, but the heart of the creature is a seething mass, constantly moving, rippling, and changing shape. She can't articulate why, but in her mind the two concepts don't mesh, they're incongruous.

Rigid spikes rest on the ground like pikes or poles, while the upper spikes flex like whips, giving the top half of the creature the appearance of an octopus thrashing around with its tentacles. As the alien moves, these soft, flexible limbs become stiff, changing their function from what was presumably analogous to arms transforming into legs. As the creature rocks, the dark, seething mass at its heart compensates for the motion, swarming and staying still relative to the rotation of the legs.

"BULLETS," Elvis yells. "I need those bullets NOW." He's on his back, kicking at the concrete with his legs, trying to push himself away from the alien.

Liz can't take her eyes off the creature. She's terrified. Her hands continue to run over the debris, but she doesn't look down. Then, under the fingers of her left hand, she feels the smooth cylindrical shape of a cartridge. She picks up the shell and feels for the bullet at its tip, wanting to ensure this isn't an empty brass casing.

"Got it," she yells, as though merely finding the bullet has solved their dilemma. Elvis backs up next to her, sweat dripping from his brow.

The creature is wary of leaving the cover of darkness. Could it be that the alien is light sensitive? Probably not. More than likely, its behavior is a deliberate strategy to avoid the potshots from the rebels.

Elvis opens the revolver with one hand, flicking the main cylinder so it swings out to the side. He pushes the ejection rod against his knee, knocking a single spent brass casing out of the gun. His hand is shaking. He holds the revolver so Liz can feed the lone bullet into one of the empty chambers in the cylinder block, but she struggles to get the bullet in. Although it only takes a moment, she's trembling. It feels as though she's fumbling for upwards of a minute.

Elvis has his back against one of the mattresses. His head lolls to the side as he flicks the chamber back into the Magnum. He rests the gun on his chest and moves the cylinder so the bullet is in place, ready to fire. Liz hadn't thought about it, but only now she realizes she should've placed the bullet in the upper chamber. She's horrified to think she's slowed the process even further.

While they're preoccupied with the gun, the monster retreats into the shadows, apparently sensing the weapon is loaded. Liz can see the alien understands the danger represented by this gun, even with only a single bullet.

"Three minutes," one of the rebels yells, although to Liz it feels as if three hours have passed. Sweat drips from her forehead, running down her neck. Her hands are shaking, but she knows what she has to do. She scrambles up the pile of mattresses as Elvis calls out, "Find the other bullet." She's already on it.

From the spongy mattress top, Liz watches as the creature moves around behind Elvis, forcing him to turn. Elvis has no strength left. He struggles to twist around as the alien outmaneuvers him. With only one good arm, he's forced to put the revolver down so he can use his hand to turn his body. His boots slip on the bloodied concrete. He's exhausted. He can't turn to face the alien as it means rolling on his severed arm.

Above them, General Adan laughs and cries out with glee, enjoying the spectacle. The creature is almost directly below Adan, but the general is safe, standing back from the edge, with just his upper torso visible from the ground floor.

Liz has to force herself not to stare at the alien. Her eyes scan the floor for the second bullet. It's impossible. There's too much debris. She can see several spent shell casings, any one of them could be the second bullet, but from where she is, she can't tell for sure. She goes to jump down on the other side of the mattresses and start searching, but she's aware the creature is moving in for the kill. Elvis is helpless. She can't leave him.

Elvis rolls over onto his stomach. He has both arms out in front of him, even though one is little more than a bloody stump. He's trying to bring the gun to bear on this creature from another world, but he can't lift his aim.

This isn't right. Ever since the aliens arrived in orbit, Liz has had visions of a peaceful encounter, a sharing of knowledge, culture, art and music. Is she wrong? Naive? How has humanity's first encounter with another intelligent sentient being descended into open warfare? Reason should rule, not base survival instincts. Her heart sinks at the bitter reality confronting her—kill or be killed. Is this the message of life from beyond the solar system? Or is it Earth's primitive mantra being blindly repeated?

She slides down a mattress, landing beside Elvis. The gun is shaking so violently in his hand he couldn't hit the far wall, let alone this creature. Liz pulls the gun from his feeble fingers and his arm collapses, falling limp to the concrete. The hammer on the Magnum is cocked, ready to fire.

Liz has one shot. She has to make it count, but how? She has no idea how many people Adan has sentenced to death in his so-called colosseum, but none of them stood a chance against this monster.

The alien braces itself, drawing its tentacles in, protecting its central core. Although Liz didn't see what the creature did to protect itself when Bosco fired, she saw what happened next. One bullet won't make a difference. She knows what's coming. Her hand trembles, shaking as she tries to gain composure. Sweat drips from her forehead, stinging her eyes. Her fingers shake. The gun feels so heavy, as though it has a will of its own and wants to fall back to the floor.

Adan laughs. His white teeth gleam in the low light. Liz raises the gun.

Gripping the butt with both hands, she breathes deeply, calming her nerves. Her finger squeezes the trigger. The sudden crack surprises her, while the recoil from the Magnum throws her hands up over her head, and she loses her grip on the revolver. The gun clatters across the concrete somewhere behind her.

Whip-like tentacles lash out before her, a blaze of blood red knives slashing at the air. Liz sinks to her knees, grimacing, waiting for the inevitable.

Above them, Adan reels to one side, struck in the chest by the bullet. Liz catches sight of blood spraying through the air as he falls from sight. She and Elvis may die down here, but at least their murderer won't walk away. He was almost exactly above and behind the creature when she fired, making it easy to adjust her aim and take him out. For someone that dedicated her career to saving lives, killing Adan felt strangely satisfying.

She closes her eyes, not wanting to see what happens next. The yelling and cheering stops. Those voices she can hear sound muted and distant. Silence follows her thunderclap of violence.

She couldn't kill the alien and she knew it, but then, she never wanted to. Perhaps it's misplaced idealism, but she desperately wants to believe that two intelligent species from different parts of the universe could meet as equals, regardless of their technology or biological background.

Her bullet struck Adan in the chest, of that she is sure, but quite where is difficult to tell. She must have caught one of the lungs, but she doubts she's hit his heart. If anything, she's surprised she hit him at all. Does Adan have a medical team skilled enough to save him from major trauma to the torso? She doubts it.

Liz can hear the alien moving toward her. She grimaces, keeping her eyelids pressed shut, not wanting to watch the horror unfold. Loose stones and debris crunch under the creature's tentacles as it edges forward. Liz huddles, making herself as small as possible. Warm tentacles run over her face, through her hair, across her shoulders and down her body. She's shaking violently with fear, resigned to her fate. Slowly, the alien withdraws, leaving her kneeling in a pool of her own urine.

After what seems like an age, Liz opens her eyes. The alien is gone. She looks up at the shattered concrete lining the hole. No one's there. Elvis is unconscious. Liz feels as though she's the only person left in the world, but something is watching her from the shadows.

CHAPTER 10: WATER

Night falls. Dark shadows creep across the floor. Moonlight shines through the gaping hole in the roof above the shattered upper floor.

Liz hasn't heard anyone walking around or talking since the shooting, at least no one human. The alien scuttles around sporadically, but it seems to be giving her a wide berth. That's fine with her.

Elvis is the focus of her concern. He hasn't regained consciousness, and she's worried. There is no way of knowing just how much blood he's lost. The shock of a major amputation like this would've killed most people, but Elvis is a fighter. Her medical training kicks in, and she sets about caring for him.

Hah, what a joke. Caring for a severe trauma case with no medical equipment while locked in a cellar with a murderous alien. Only this isn't a cellar. The windows have been sealed from the outside with steel plates. Thin cracks between the sheets of armor plating allow her to peer into the moonlit street—and it isn't a murderous alien, at least not in her case, not yet.

Liz feels she has to stake out her territory. She doesn't feel comfortable remaining in plain sight beneath the gaping hole in the upper floor, but she doesn't want to chance upon the alien either. She pulls a mattress from the pile in the center of the floor, dragging it across beneath one of the steel plates blocking the windows. A thin strand of light pierces the darkness. Somehow, having a faint glimpse of the outside world gives her hope.

Two of the mattresses near the bottom of the pile are still in their original plastic wrapping. Liz realizes this is the closest she'll come to anything sterile, so she drags those over as well, leaving the rest of the mattresses where they lie.

She tears the protective sheeting off one of the mattresses and reverses the plastic, exposing the inside as she tears away long strips. Using the edge of her belt buckle, she cuts through the fabric on the clean mattress, and tears strips of cloth, reasoning that these bits of plastic and cotton cloth are the closest thing she'll get to fresh bandages and dressings.

Elvis is more difficult to shift than the mattresses. Liz pulls him over to the darkened window by grabbing under his armpits and dragging his legs along the floor. She lays him on a sheet of plastic she turned inside out, hoping to reduce his exposure to bacteria, and then positions him on a mattress, all the while aware she's being watched by otherworldly eyes. The creature moves slowly, but she can see it feasting in the gloomy darkness, drawing up the blood where Bosco fell and Elvis lay wounded.

In the half-light, she gets her first good look at his arm. The tourniquet is tight, much tighter than she remembers, but that's good. Not only will the tourniquet stem the flow of blood and compress the nerve channels, it will stop the spread of microbes back into his body. Looking at him, there isn't much that can be done outside of arranging a medical evacuation, and that isn't going to happen.

Even if she could get a medevac to Lilongwe, there isn't much that can be done for Elvis in-country. In any other circumstance, he'd be airlifted to a specialist US military hospital, either stateside or in Germany. He needs skilled surgeons working on him. The severed nerves and arteries will require microsurgery to close off properly. Liz figures an experienced surgeon would probably amputate the remains of his arm just above where the tourniquet is set. It wouldn't leave much of an arm, but he'd live.

Tiny bits of metal stick out of his vest. His body armor protected his torso, otherwise the blast would've killed him outright. Liz counts five scraps of shrapnel larger than a silver dollar. Any one of them would have been fatal had they hit his exposed neck, or one of the arteries in his thigh.

"Hang in there," she whispers, but in reality, she's surprised he isn't dead already.

She remembers that US soldiers carry some kind of combat morphine. No, it's fentanyl they carry these days—much stronger than morphine, and it isn't in a syringe, it's like candy, something to suck on. From memory, it looks like an elongated lollypop, only without the stick. Liz rummages through his pockets and the packs lining his belt. Nothing. As Elvis lies there, she inserts her finger gently into his mouth and feels around on the inside of his cheeks. She can feel a sticky substance inside his left cheek. He's self-administered, rightly so—that's how he was able to endure the pain.

Liz tries to clean and treat his wound as best she can with her impromptu bandages, but it's pointless. Deep down, she knows there's nothing she can do for him. He'll probably linger on for a few hours, perhaps a day, but then he'll die. She has no way of replacing the fluids he's lost, and no way of providing him with antibiotics or an intravenous drip, no painkillers, no antiseptics. She's staying busy while he dies regardless, and that realization breaks her heart.

She sobs. "Don't you die on me, Elvis. Don't you dare—You're a soldier, damn it. Fight for your life." He can't hear her, but still she speaks.

"Come on, Elvis, you old hound dog—Come on—Vegas, remember? You're going to take us all to Las Vegas, and show off those blue suede shoes—*Love me tender,* Elvis. *Don't—be—cruel.*"

Liz pushes her fingers up against his jugular, searching for his pulse. It's there, but it's weak and erratic. "I'm sorry," she says softly. "I'm so sorry I got you into this. Oh, God, I'm so sorry."

Is there anything she can do for him? Sitting there on the side of the mattress, Liz hears a soft, steady drip in the darkness. Somewhere nearby, water's leaking from a tap. It's just the distraction she needs. She could wet his lips. Even just a few drops of water in his mouth every minute or so will be absorbed by his body. Her efforts are pathetic, but she doesn't want to admit that to herself. She has to get Elvis some water. She has to do something, anything. In some ways, Elvis becomes a proxy for her own life. If she can keep him alive, it gives her hope for herself.

Liz takes several of the torn strips of cloth and follows the wall, listening for the drip. Rats scurry away as she approaches. What about the alien? In her concern for Elvis, she's forgotten about the terror waiting in the dark.

Liz steps lightly, inching forward slowly with one hand running along the wall, as much for comfort as for guidance. Her heart is racing. Her ears prick at the slightest sound. She's never known such oppressive darkness. Humidity hangs in the air.

Further along the floor, moonlight drifts through cracks in the sealed windows, teasing her with the promise of light. Liz creeps on with one hand tracing the wall and the other feeling at the air, wanting to avoid bumping into anything in the dark warehouse.

Suddenly, her outstretched hand touches something unearthly. The soft flesh of her palm rests against dozens of stiff spikes, each one as sharp as the tip of a needle. She freezes. Slowly, she pulls her hand away, only on breaking contact, she has no idea where the alien is, or what it's doing, and that terrifies her even more. When she touched the spikes, the creature was still. In the darkness, she can hear the alien moving—she only hopes it is moving away from her. Gingerly, she reaches out again, feeling at the air. Nothing.

Why would it do that? Why would it deliberately block her path? Or is the alien as blind as she is in the darkness? What does it think of her approach? Does it think she's trying to find it? Her mind races with the possibilities as fear wells up inside her.

"Water," she says. Saying it is irrational, that much is obvious, but Liz feels she has to declare her intentions, even if there's no hope of the creature understanding. "I need water. We need water or we'll die." There's silence. "Water—Two hydrogen atoms sharing electrons with a single oxygen atom, forming a simple molecule via a covalent bond."

She's babbling, but there's reassurance in speech—it's passive, non-threatening. Nothing she's said will make any sense to a creature from another world, but communication is an attempt at reason over violence. She's speaking to soothe her own nerves, hoping her words give the creature the opportunity to realize she means it no harm. By talking, she's making her presence known—she isn't sneaking around in the dark. She hopes the alien understands why she spoke, even if it doesn't understand the meaning behind her words.

"We need water to survive."

There's been no attack. This is progress. She's communicating, even if it's only one-way and poorly understood. She figures the alien will hear that one word repeated, and at least understand that water is important.

"Water, that's all I want. Just a little water."

Do aliens even have ears? And what are ears? Technically, they're exceptionally sensitive sensory organs capable of differentiating between pressure waves oscillating in a diffuse mix of gases. On Earth, senses like hearing are fundamental to life. Every multicellular organism without exception responds in some way to touch—even plants. The evolutionary path from touch to hearing is well established, and some species, like bats, take that further, using sonics instead of sight to view the world around them. Could the sense of hearing be universal? Will a creature from another world understand spoken communication?

"Water is important for our biology." She could kick herself. Hell, most people on Earth don't understand biology, let alone an alien intelligence from another planet. Just keep repeating that word—water. Let the creature figure it out.

"We're almost seventy percent water. All our chemistry takes place in water. Without water, we'll die."

The alien has shown sensitivity to touch, reaching out to feel her face after she fired at Adan. Hearing is simply the sensitivity of touch applied to vibrations in the air. The creature must be able to hear something.

But what chance is there the alien will even register her speech as deliberate? Even on Earth, speech takes multiple forms. Cuttlefish speak with light. Spiders speak to each other through vibrations in a web. Cats speak more through pheromones—the chemical signatures in their urine, than with either a growl or a snarl. If humanity can't converse with other species on Earth, what hope is there of talking to an alien? Even intelligent mammals, like apes and dolphins, are limited to the most rudimentary of human concepts.

"Water."

Water continues to drip nearby, urging her on.

Moonlight drifts through the cracks. The alien is fifteen feet away, close enough to strike if it chose to. The creature backs up, crossing into a thin stream of light slipping through between the steel shutters. Its tentacles, fronds, whips, spikes, or whatever they are, wave in the soft breeze cutting through the stifling heat. The alien positions itself beside one of the steel panels covering the next window, drawing on whatever draft circulates within their dark tomb.

"All I want is the water. I'll take some water and leave you alone. Do you understand? Water, and I leave."

The creature remains where it is. Its thin arms wave softly like wheat in a field. If the alien has heard her, it doesn't show any kind of acknowledgement. Liz feels as though she's creeping up on a lion in the undergrowth.

Her fingers run along the wall and over the distinct shape of a steel pipe running vertically to the floor above. She follows the pipe down to a dripping tap. There's probably another tap directly above this one on the upper floor.

Beside her, there's a thin crack between the steel panel and the wooden window frame. Liz spots a splinter of loose wood. It's no more than an inch wide, but it's almost two feet in length. If she can pull that away, she'll get a better look outside—not only that, she'll let in more light. What will the creature make of such an act? Will it feel threatened?

"Water," she says, hoping to reinforce that she wants nothing more. With her eyes locked on the alien fronds, Liz grips the splinter and pulls, hoping it will give way easily. The shard of wood is still firmly attached at its base, but she's able to twist it sideways, widening the gap. Moonlight creeps in.

The creature continues to watch her impassively, or is she imagining it watching her? Does the alien view her with curiosity, or malice? Does it recognize either notion? Does it even have eyes? Somehow, the creature saw them wielding the gun, so it must have a sense similar to sight.

Water drips with regular monotony from the tap into a puddle next to the drain. To her surprise, insects swarm about the small pool on the floor. She crouches, examining a trail of insect-like creatures leading back to the alien. For a moment, she loses her fear. A sense of wonder and curiosity takes hold

"Water," she says. "You need water."

The alien doesn't respond.

On one level, Liz is repulsed by what look like cockroaches. On another, she's fascinated by the reality of life arising on some other planet around a distant star. The tiny creatures have segmented bodies with an exoskeleton much like an insect on Earth, yet they appear almost spherical, not just round in two dimensions. They're able to swivel beneath their shell segments, so there's no way of telling which way they're facing other than from the direction in which they travel.

The insects vary in size from that of a small bead, to a pea, to a marble, with the largest being no bigger than a Ping Pong ball with crab-like legs. There has to be more to these creatures, but in the half-light, this is all Liz can distinguish. There's no way she's going to pick one up for a closer look. Somehow, they're gathering water, moving in a living stream as they scuttle between the puddle and the imposing alien.

Liz turns the rusty tap, allowing water to flow softly. She cups her hands and drinks deeply. The water is as fresh as can be expected in Africa. Liz soaks her makeshift bandages. She goes to turn off the tap but thinks better of it. Perhaps the alien creature will understand this as a gesture of friendship. The insects are excited by the additional water flow, even though the water simply runs out of the puddle and into the drain.

"Water," she says, backing away and leaving the tap running. She can't bring herself to turn her back on the creature, so she retraces her steps, creeping backwards along the wall. When she's two shuttered windows away, a distance of twenty feet, the creature moves forward into the moonlight by the tap.

"Water," she says again, as a means of bidding the creature farewell. Finally, she turns and heads back to Elvis.

Sitting on the mattress, Liz cradles the wounded soldier's head, squeezing the cloths one by one into his mouth. Water dribbles from his lips, but in a reflex reaction, he swallows.

"You're doing great, Elvis," she says, lying to a dying man.

After fussing with him, doing what little she can to make him comfortable, Liz rests on one of the other mattresses. She decides to go back to the tap with some plastic, and use it to carry some of water back to him, as she wants to continue hydrating Elvis, but she's exhausted. She wants to stay awake. She feels an obligation to stay alert and look out for Elvis, even though she knows there is nothing she can do for him. Try as she might, sleep overtakes her, and she slumps on the mattress.

CHAPTER 11: MORNING

Morning breaks with birds singing outside the darkened warehouse.

For a moment, Liz forgets where she is. In the soft light, her eyes deceive her. The air on the ground floor has cooled overnight, providing relief from the day before. Already, the heat is starting to build, but for now it is almost a summer's day in England.

It's the smell that shocks her awake. Having lived in Africa for almost two years, Liz is used to the rancid smell of overpopulated cities, but this is different, it's like the stench of rotten meat burning in a fire.

Beside her, there's the soft clatter of insects swarming over each other. Liz turns, horrified to see Elvis being buried alive by a swarm of alien insects. The tiny bugs crawl all over him, covering his arms and legs, running through his hair, over his face. Beyond them, the blood-red alien stands like a sentinel. Liz is repulsed by the realization it's devouring his body.

"No," she yells, scrambling to her feet.

She crouches, ready to jump at the swarm and pull him to safety, but there are thousands of the insects swamping him.

"Don't eat him. Leave him. Let him go."

Her movement startles the spiky alien looming over Elvis. Its fronds stiffen. The alien flexes, almost doubling in size. Its tentacles, previously limp and waving like the branches of a tree in the wind, strike out like spears. This is the best view she's had of the animal. The spiky alien is on the other side of the mattress, directly opposite her, with Elvis lying beneath the beetles, or bugs, or whatever they are, scattered between them. The central mass of the creature is awash with insects. They swarm around its body like ants, moving in waves, pulsating like bees in a hive. Streams of tiny creatures scurry down the alien's stiff, spiky legs, running back and forth to Elvis.

"No," she yells again, losing her fear and stepping forward. "Get off him."

Liz begins pulling handfuls of insects from his body, sweeping them away, trying to clear them from his chest. The insects become highly agitated. They hiss and snap what seem to be mandibles, threatening to turn on her and devour her.

She has to save him. She can't let Elvis die, not like this. Yet for all she knows, he's already dead. Liz grabs at his shoulder, trying to pull him away from the alien and the swarm of insects.

Hundreds of the tiny creatures begin climbing up her arms, tearing at her sleeves, scaling her legs and biting at her trousers, but she won't give up on Elvis, even if it means she dies. Liz staggers backwards as the insects clamber up to her face, forcing her to drop him as she fights desperately to brush them away.

The alien doesn't move, which surprises her. It's content to let these miniature assassins overpower her. Insects clamber over the mattress.

"No," she cries again. "Don't you understand?" She has Elvis by the collar, and tries to drag him across the mattress. "Don't you know? Life is too important. Life is too precious."

Elvis is heavy. She can't move him more than a few inches at a time. She's crying, sobbing. "Please. Leave him alone." The dark insect-like creatures clamber up into her hair, crawling across her neck and face. She shakes herself, swatting them and knocking them from her.

With all the energy she can muster, she lifts Elvis. She drives with her legs, using her thighs to push away from the horde covering the ground, and exposes his upper torso. The swarm of insects spreads out around her, encircling her. It's then she sees his arm, and she freezes in place.

Whereas before, Elvis had his left arm severed just above the elbow, the humerus bone now extends down to a bare joint, connecting to the ulna and radius bones of the forearm, and on to the wrist bones, metacarpals and skeletal fingers. The bones are wrapped in a transparent coating, a membrane of some sort. It is as though someone has attached the skeleton to his body and wrapped it in plastic, or molded in jelly. Blood pumps through the membrane. Lymph fluids surge in response to thin contracting muscles. Tendons, nerves and veins, they're all there in an stunted, anemic form, as though his arm is that of a malnourished child. The tourniquet is gone. The ragged flesh from his upper arm has been knitted back into muscle and sinew, although his bicep and triceps are perilously thin. They're attached to tendons on the lower humerus.

"Please, leave him alone." Liz breaks out in a cold sweat. These are her words, but she hasn't spoken them. Words echo around her. "Don't you understand? Life is too important. Life is too precious." Even though she's looking at the alien, the words repeated back at her come from no particular direction.

Liz releases her grip on Elvis, allowing him to sink back into the swarm of alien beetles. As she does so, the insects climbing over her drop to the floor, scurrying away. Stunned, she staggers backwards, tripping on the soft mattress, but keeping her footing.

Liz watches as the alien creature empties of the tiny bugs. To her surprise, there's no central mass. The scarlet spikes extend all the way to the heart of the structure without forming any discernible bulge at all. With all of the insects swarming over Elvis, the alien is motionless. It's then Liz realizes what she's looking at: an empty frame. What she and everyone else has assumed was the alien is nothing more than an empty vessel—a vehicle.

What is this thing? An alien? Or aliens? What she'd thought of as inconsequential insects, mere worker bees gathering food, is actually the heart of what she assumes to be a single entity. When she, Elvis, and Bosco turned the gun on the creature, the spiky framework protected the insects that made up the central core. Now they're swarming over Elvis, repairing his arm. It's the core that's alive.

As best she understands what she is seeing, these insects *are* the alien intelligence. Watching them at work, she understands how vulnerable they are, and yet they've committed themselves wholly to helping Elvis, rebuilding his arm. They've left their protective weaponry lying idle beside them.

Liz crouches, watching them carefully. The tiny creatures are in the process of consuming the spare mattress, ingesting the cotton cover, the padding and the springs. To one side, a line of alien insects weaves its way back and forth to a nearby wooden crate. She could be watching ants advancing on a picnic hamper, only these creatures are devouring the wood. Somehow, they're gathering the material they need to fabricate a new arm. To build a functioning arm, they have to be operating at a microscopic level, applying some kind of nanotechnology that allows them to cultivate cell growth at a radical pace. Liz was asleep for six or seven hours, and the results of their efforts are spectacular.

Are they reading his DNA and fabricating his arm in the same way humans would build a car? Or are they accelerating and extending the natural regenerative processes of human cells in some way? They have to be stimulating some kind of pluripotent process, like stem cells. How are they controlling and directing the growth? How are they orchestrating the biological process for building arteries in one area, bone in another? Get those mixed up, and the results could be fatal.

Liz is fascinated by the vague outline of Elvis lying beneath the swarm. Thousands of insects scurry over him. There's harmony to their motion. Those creatures sitting on his good arm remain unusually still. While most of the creatures are moving around rapidly, these are stationary. They must be using bilateral symmetry to guide them. Somehow they've sensed the structure of his right arm, and are forming a mirror image on the left. Most people have arms and hands of differing sizes, with the right usually bigger than the left. Liz wants to check his new arm once it's fully formed to see if that notion still applies, or if his new arm is an exact mirror of the right.

Hunger pangs gnaw at her stomach. She tries to ignore them, but she's ravenous. In the soft light, she leaves the creatures to continue their work, and returns to the tap for a drink. On her way, she creeps up behind one of the crates near the central pile of mattresses. She sits there for a few minutes listening, hidden from sight beneath the open hole. There's no one on the upper floor. She can hear movement out on the street, but not upstairs.

After having a drink, Liz peers through the gap in the wooden frame. She tries pulling on the wood again, and manages to enlarge her view. Looking down the road, she sees steel beams propped up against the shutters. Adan, it seems, was determined to keep the alien from escaping.

The street beside the factory is quiet. Occasionally, a soldier walks casually down what seems to be more of an alley than a road. The building at the far end is important, and must open onto a main road, as trucks and bicycles stop there for supplies. From what she can tell, she's nowhere near where they were captured. The buildings look different.

After checking on Elvis and seeing him still buried in the swarm of tiny creatures, Liz decides to explore the rest of the lower floor. The spiked alien sits motionless to one side, confirming her suspicions that it is a vessel rather than a living, intelligent being on its own.

"I'm just going to look around to see what I can find," she says, not sure who she's talking to—and certainly not expecting an answer. It just seems polite. The creatures crawling over Elvis ignore her so she wanders off. Liz is careful not to step on the streams of creatures disappearing into the darkness as they go out across the floor, presumably hunting down more raw materials for the reconstruction effort.

At a guess, the lower floor is sixty yards long by thirty yards wide. There are offices at either end, which have been boarded up with wood instead of steel plates. She tries to break through one of the doors with her shoulder, but that only works in Hollywood, and she ends up with a sore arm after barging into it a couple of times. There's a kitchenette. The tap works. She finds soap and a couple of sponges, not that she needs them. There's a butter knife and a couple of forks in one of the drawers, along with a small plastic jug, so she takes them. There's no food, which is a bit disheartening. She goes through the cupboards a couple of times to make sure she hasn't missed anything.

A steel door at the end of the corridor leads to the road outside, but it's locked. As this is at the far end of the building, away from the main road, she thinks this could be a good place to escape. Liz lies on her stomach and tries to peer beneath the door. Using the knife, she lifts the weather strip on the other side.

There's no noise outside. After a few minutes, a car drives past. People laughing in the vehicle, but other than that, the back road is deserted. Liz wonders if there's a guard standing watch. Surely, they have someone watching their alien enclosure. A soldier could be standing beside the door and she'd never know. Patiently, she waits, realizing the more she can learn, the more options they'll have once Elvis is back to full strength.

After an hour, she's satisfied there isn't a guard on the back door. At one point, a soldier matches past, but he doesn't slow his pace and doesn't talk to anyone, which strengthens her suspicion that there's no guard posted outside.

She gets up and looks carefully at the door. The hinges are on the inside. She tries lifting one with the dull blade of the knife, but she can't get it to budge. It might be something Elvis could manage, though. For the first time, she feels as though they're going to get out of this mess alive.

Liz returns to Elvis and sits watching as the alien insects work. She'd love to see the progress in more detail, but has to accept that something remarkable is occurring at a cellular level beneath this swarm of intelligent creatures. Hours pass like years.

At times, the black sheen on what appears to be the outer shell of the alien insects takes on different hues, but these seem to be coordinated. In addition to that, the motion of the creatures attending to Elvis undulates with a kind of rhythm. It seems to confirm what she suspects, that these creatures are working in unison, as though they're a single organism. As strange as that seems, the human body is nothing more than a collection of cooperating, specialized cells, albeit with only the brain having sentience. The alien insects have more autonomy than human cells, but the concept of collective cooperation to form a single whole is not that different to life on Earth. She might like to think of lions, and bears, and dolphins as separate animals, but in reality, at a cellular level, they're convenient conglomerations of astonishingly similar biological processes, not that dissimilar to this creature.

She goes back to the tap and cleans the knife and forks in running water before collecting water in the jug.

Shortly before sunset, Liz hears someone walking on the upper floor. She creeps behind a broken wooden crate, careful to remain hidden. Two soldiers appear on the edge of the vast hole. From the number of voices she can hear, there are more soldiers standing just out of sight, or it could be that the others are positioned further around the hole, outside her field of vision.

"There's the gun," one of the rebels says.

"But did you see them die? Did you see the monster kill them?"

A soldier shines a light into the darkness. "They're dead," he says, moving the light across the carnage. "Do you think anyone could survive down there? Look at the insects, look at how they feed on the blood."

Liz hadn't noticed before now, but the rebel soldier is right. A stream of tiny alien creatures feeds on the blood, gristle, and sinew from Bosco's remains. The alien must be using this to rebuild Elvis' arm.

"There's been a fight," another soldier says. "They're dead. There's no way they could've defeated the monster with just one bullet."

"General Adan wants to be sure."

"I am sure," another soldier says from somewhere out of sight above her. "What? Don't you believe me? Why don't you go down there and check?"

"I'm not going down there."

"Hah," the first soldier replies. "There's no way *I'm* going in there with the beast. They're dead. That's all Adan needs to know."

"But there are no bodies."

"There are never any bodies."

For a moment, the spotlight rests on the crate Liz is hiding behind, and she panics, thinking she's been spotted, but the light moves on, flickering around the edges of the mattresses.

"There's so much blood—fresh blood."

"Yeah," another soldier agrees, talking himself into the same conclusion. "The blood is fresh. They're dead. They've beaten Adan to the grave."

Liz is relieved when they leave. That the soldiers think they're dead means no one will be looking for them when they make their escape. She returns and sits beside Elvis.

Night falls. The tiny creatures continue their work. A cool breeze fights its way through the cracks in the steel plates. Liz stands beside the narrow slit for a while, willing the breeze to blow harder. The alien ignores her. She likes that. Given the alternative she faced when they were shoved in the hole, being ignored is a gift.

Can this alien creature really save his life? As doctor, Liz understands modern surgery is only a few steps removed from medieval butchery. Anesthetics, x-rays, and razor-sharp scalpels have all made a massive difference, as has the knowledge of the function and purpose of various organs, but the approach is still coarse. But being able to operate at a microscopic level—to manipulate cellular biology like this alien does—that would be an astonishing advance. She only hopes Elvis hasn't deteriorated too far. He still hasn't regained consciousness, and she wonders about the stress on his internal organs. If he were in hospital, she'd have him on a drip to keep him hydrated while his body stabilizes.

Liz wonders about the creature, or creatures. She's curious about their biology, how they function as a unit, where their intelligence arises, how their metabolism works, what they consume for fuel, if they respire, or need water. On Earth, all life requires homeostasis—the ability to metabolize food for energy so as to maintain the biological steady state that allows life to continue.

Hearts beat every second. Oxygen circulates with each breath. Trillions of finely balanced chemical reactions synchronize to give us the privilege of being alive, and all without any conscious thought. Does alien life operate the same way?

The alien seems to be utilizing the water from the tap, but she's not sure whether that's to support cellular processes. They could use water in a steam engine for all she knows.

For Liz, that the same basic set of atoms, forming the same molecules, can result in life on another planet is astonishing. On some other planet, the same laws of physics and chemistry gave rise to at least one other intelligent species, one capable of traversing the stars to seek out more life forms. Looking at the dark walls that surrounded them, though, this probably isn't what they had in mind when they signed on for this particular mission.

Liz sits on the mattress and watches the insects busying themselves. There's something hypnotic in their tireless rhythm. She finds her eyelids growing heavy. In the end, she falls asleep more through boredom than anything else.

When she wakes with the dawn, the alien(s) is/are gone.

Elvis lies alone on the shredded remains of the mattress next to her. She creeps over, looking at his arm in wonder. He'll need some physiotherapy to build muscle mass, as his forearm looks withered, but apart from that, his new arm appears normal. The skin is pale, and there's no hair or fingernails.

Liz runs her hand down his arm, gently feeling the texture of the muscles and bones. As much as she hates to draw on a cliché, the skin on his hand is as smooth as a baby's bottom. That brings a smile.

Elvis groans, responding to her touch. His eyes flicker. Her eyes widen. She's excited at him waking. Does he know what just happened? Was he in any way conscious during the repair? Or is he experiencing something akin to waking from a general anesthetic? Elvis tries to speak, but his voice is croaky.

Liz helps him sit up, propping him against the wall. Coarse stubble covers his cheeks, his upper lip and chin, marring his usually impeccable image. His sideburns look shabby. Liz gives him a sip of water.

"What the hell happened?" Elvis whispers. Liz smiles. Something in her eyes seems to trigger the realization and his hands shoot out in front of him. "Wh—how?"

Elvis turns both hands over. The look on his face is one of awe. He's clearly fascinated by his new left arm and hand. Gently, he runs his right hand over the fingers of his left hand, around his wrist, and then works slowly up toward his elbow, before moving around to his upper arm and bicep.

"How do you feel?"

"I feel—fine, just a little weak."

"No pain?"

"None."

Liz has tears in her eyes.

"How did you do this?" he asks.

"Not me," Liz replies. "The creature. The alien. Somehow, it rebuilt your arm."

"But why? What happened?"

"I shot Adan," Liz replies in a matter-of-fact tone. "I guess the alien approved."

Elvis laughs. He tries to get up, but falls back against the wall. His head rolls to one side. He looks exhausted.

"Easy, big guy."

Elvis shifts his weight, using his arms to assist, and moving with a surprising amount of dexterity, given what he's been through.

"Does it feel any different?" she asks.

Elvis thinks about the question for a moment before replying, "No. It just looks—childlike."

Liz smiles, saying, "I suspect that with time, and a bit of exercise, you'll be fine."

"But if it—why kill Bosco?"

"I don't know. The creature must have felt threatened, perhaps scared. If I were stranded on an alien planet, and they'd corralled me into some dark, musty prison, spoiling for a fight, I'd be terrified."

"You think it's scared?" Elvis is perplexed by the idea that an alien can feel fear.

"We've seen too many movies," Liz continues. "Too many films with badass aliens that know nothing of mercy. In Hollywood, aliens have acid for blood, or they fly spaceships with ray guns we can't hope to match. Or they transform themselves into huge, terrifying beasts that can only be beaten by some downcast reject of a hero, but reality, it seems, begs to differ."

"That—that thing tore him apart."

"I've been thinking about that," Liz replies. "I've watched the alien on a number of different occasions now, and I think we've got our wires crossed. What we think of as the '*alien*' is probably nothing more than a Hummer, or a tank, from its perspective. The alien itself seems more like a hive of bees. I guess there's a queen in there somewhere, but those thrashing tentacles are a diversion. The real creature is in swarm, or perhaps it's the swarm itself." Elvis is silent. "It spoke to me."

"It did?" Elvis asks, surprised.

"Yes, but with simple repetition. It wasn't a spontaneous, natural sentence, as such, just my own words repeated back at me, but they were used appropriately, they made sense. I'm not sure how, but it spoke, probably not using anything even remotely like vocal cords. Perhaps using something akin to an amplifier and a speaker—it was mimicry, but it spoke... but it never said anything I hadn't said first."

Elvis stretches his new arm, working the muscles. "Damn, it's never felt so good to be alive."

"There's one thing I don't understand," Liz says.

"What?" Elvis replies, surprising her with how coherent he is given all he's been through since the ambush. Liz looks back at the shattered hole in the ceiling, not more than thirty feet away.

"Why didn't they shoot us?"

"The rebels?" he asks.

"Yeah. I mean, I'd just shot Adan. They had me dead to rights. There were so many of them—they all had rifles. Why didn't they shoot? They could've shot us like fish in a barrel. Why didn't they kill us?"

"You have to remember who you're dealing with," Elvis replies. "These aren't professional soldiers. They're thugs, and General Adan ain't no general. He's an egomaniac. Our closest equivalent would be a mobster, someone like Al Capone. Only Adan is worse.

"Warlords surround themselves with legends. Up on the tableland, we had one of the outlying chiefs tell his troops he was bulletproof. To them, he was a god. In the same way, Adan would have spent years cultivating a loyal following, building a cult around his personality. Those rebel soldiers were never trained to think for themselves. They were trained to blindly follow orders."

"So no one told them to shoot?" Liz asks.

"Maybe. Who knows? The shock of seeing their glorious, invincible leader struck down would've shattered their world, perhaps only for an instant, but it was enough for them to leave us to the alien.

"It's the African big man syndrome. The big man demands loyalty. He talks big. There's a strict hierarchy. Once you shot Adan, there was no one in a position to say '*Fire.*' Remember, most of these so-called soldiers were kids or teens when they were recruited into this mafia. There's no honor, no dedication, not in the way we think of it. The top brass are motivated by ideology, but the rank and file follow whoever feeds them."

Liz sips at the water in the jug. She offers some to Elvis. He gulps it down, emptying the jug.

"Where is it?" he asks, wiping his mouth. "The alien, where did it go?"

"I don't know," Liz replies.

"I bet that alien wants to get out of here as badly as we do—I think it helped us so we could help it escape."

Elvis is stiff as he moves, swinging his legs around slowly so he can stand.

"Whoa there, cowboy. You're not going anywhere," Liz says, putting her hands out to keep him seated on the mattress. "As for your theory about the alien, I'm not sure we should be striking up an alliance just yet. We know nothing about this creature or its motives."

"It's trapped," Elvis replies. "Just like us. We both need to escape."

"We need to be careful, Elvis. We can't read our own emotions into those of an alien intelligence."

"I've got to see it," he says. "That thing saved my life. It didn't have to, but it did—that means something. Please, help me stand up."

Liz helps him to his feet. His knees are weak. It takes all his strength not to fall back to the mattress. Liz puts his right arm over her shoulder, taking some of his weight.

Thin strands of light seep through the cracks in the barricaded windows. Dark shadows spread across the floor. There's no movement. Together, they struggle forward. Elvis shuffles as he walks.

Liz hears a noise from the far end of the floor. They hobble on to find the alien in the kitchenette. The creature is examining the drawers Liz went through the day before.

The alien stops what it's doing as they approach. Its tentacles freeze, and for the first time, Liz sees some recognition of their presence in its actions. The core of the hybrid creature pulsates with a rhythm that reminds her of a cardiovascular system, but she understands that what looks like a rippling, undulating surface is actually a swarm of individual creatures.

"It's retracing my steps," Liz whispers.

"It wants to escape," Elvis replies.

The tentacles continue sweeping over drawers, and cupboards, touching the counter and the kitchen sink.

Sunlight creeps around the steel door at the end of the hallway. Fine lines crisscross the dust. The creature has tracked her motion. It must have been curious to know what she was looking at beneath the door.

Elvis urges Liz on, edging closer to the creature despite her wanting to pull back.

The tentacles closest to them stiffen into razor-sharp spikes. Although Liz flinches, Elvis holds no fear of this strange creature. Even though it rebuilt his arm, Liz can't shake the image of Bosco being shredded seconds. In the army, tank crews have soldiers trained as medics, but that doesn't make them an ambulance. If cornered, the creature could lash out with unbridled violence.

The pulsating mass of insects is probably three to four feet in diameter. In the soft light, color flickers across the surface. Thousands of tiny shells appear to bristle as the two of them approach.

Although Liz has interacted with the alien on several occasions, this is the first opportunity Elvis has had to see the creature as anything other than a killing machine. He's relaxed, even though his only memory would be of the alien tearing Bosco apart. He was unconscious while the alien operated on him, and yet Liz senses an affinity between them.

Elvis reaches out with his feeble left arm, leaning across the bench. The alien responds. Its blade-like fronds wrap around his hand. A stream of tiny creatures races back and forth, clambering over his fingertips.

Liz is fascinated. Awe overwhelms her desire for caution.

Elvis breathes deeply. He pulls his hand back, and the tiny creatures return to the core of the thorny alien structure. The spiky creature rolls out of the kitchenette, moving slowly around toward them. Liz backs up, but Elvis doesn't move, limiting her ability to step away.

"Wait," he whispers. The massive creature moves toward them, squeezing through the doorway, the tips of its fronds touching lightly against the ceiling. The alien transportation device rolls up to them. Liz pulls away, but Elvis stands his ground.

"Relax," he says. "It's okay."

Dark red fronds wave before her. Liz is in two minds. The framework seems to be alive. Looking at the fluid motion with which it sways, it appears to be sampling the air, but she's seen these blades standing idle, like an abandoned car. Perhaps this is the alien equivalent of a packhorse, while the rider is the swarm of minuscule creatures at its core.

Elvis resists her attempt to keep some distance between them and the alien. He clearly wants to see what the creature will do. "It won't hurt you," he whispers. Liz isn't so sure.

She swallows the lump in her throat, and stiffening as a clutch of fine tentacles touches at her face and neck. Liz suppresses her revulsion, struggling not to turn away. Tiny insect-like creatures clamber along the outstretched tentacles, racing up toward her face.

She shuts her eyes. The fronds are gentle, as soft as suede, passing lightly over her cheeks, across the bridge of her nose, over her eyebrows and around her lips, but Liz can't stop shaking.

"Easy," Elvis whispers. "Just go with it."

The tentacles withdraw. Liz opens her eyes. Several insects sit on the tips of the alien fronds, inches from her face, apparently taking a good look at her.

"Need to be careful."

Liz goes rigid. Those are her words, but she hasn't spoken. Those were the words she spoke to Elvis a few minutes ago, when they first began searching for the creature.

Elvis looks at Liz. These are her words, spoken back to her using her own voice.

"Retracing my steps." Again, it's her voice coming from the creature.

"Yes," she says softly in reply, her heart racing at the realization that she's conversing with a creature from another world. "We're looking to escape." Elvis has his arm over her shoulder, but he's no longer leaning on her. She turns to one side, allowing the spiny creature to twist and turn on its spikes and roll out onto the darkened factory floor.

This is the first opportunity she's has to observe the alien's means of locomotion in detail. Although the tips of the spikes appear rigid when the alien rolls forward, they flex as they brush the concrete, almost slapping the ground for grip. The creature can move in any direction it chooses without appearing to change its orientation. It could probably turn on the proverbial dime.

"Escape," the creature says, using her voice as it weaves its way around a crate and out of sight. Somehow, even in the sweltering African heat, Liz feels a chill at her own voice being adopted by this bizarre creature.

The alien disappears into the shadows. Her heart is racing, her palms are sweaty. She's not sure, but it seems the creature wants to keep its distance, and is staying away from them. From her perspective, that's mutual.

"Magnificent," Elvis says. "Did you hear that? It can talk."

Liz is silent, struggling with what this creature actually is, and the daunting prospect of communicating with a being from another world. The alien appears to be just as flustered with the communication gap. Although the creature has used human words appropriately, it has to learn them first. Somehow, the alien has a grasp of the fundamentals of speech. Perhaps not speech as she or Elvis understand it, but the alien knows how to associate human sounds with distinct concepts, and to her surprise, the creature gets those concepts right.

They walk away from the kitchenette.

Liz is overwhelmed by a desire to articulate what has just happened, to make sense of the encounter for herself, if for no one else. "This is incredible," she begins, barely able to contain herself. "It understands the mechanics of language.

"My mother is from Germany, and I used to spend my holidays in Berlin with my grandmother. I speak four languages, but I'm only fluent in English. Several of my friends are truly multilingual, but although I can speak fragments of French and German, I struggle to make the mental switch between thinking in

English and thinking in another language." Elvis listens as they make their way back to the mattresses. He seems to appreciate that she's working through what just happened.

"I can translate with ease. Occasionally, I think in German, but English is home, so I think I understand how this creature feels. I used to be so envious of those that could make the switch effortlessly. Perhaps this alien creature feels the same way about us. Language must be a universal constant, differing only in how it is communicated."

In her mind's eye, Liz is back in Germany—young, wide-eyed, and on summer break. She can remember the sights and smells, the humidity, the lush farmlands, the fresh fruits. She remembers how difficult it is to order coffee, or to find her way around the city, as she stumbles over the German language like a klutz.

Her grandmother worked at the Helen Keller Institute in Berlin. She was a teacher, and introduced Liz to several blind students. Liz was impressed by their agility of mind, their ability to compensate for the loss of sight. Now, in the gloomy shell of an abandoned factory, the pieces of the puzzle fall into place.

"Think about how remarkable language is," she says. "Here on Earth, there are several ways of sharing concepts. As closely related as speech appears to be to writing, the two are really worlds apart. We've settled on dark marks on a page to represent speech, but raised dots on a page work equally as well for the blind, while hand gestures and facial inflections convey the same versatility, using nothing more than sight to speak to the deaf. For this alien creature, human speech probably feels a little like sign language would to you or me."

"Huh," Elvis replies.

Liz is working herself into a manic state, a kind of euphoria. If she didn't know better, she'd swear someone had just slipped her a batch of freshly baked hash cookies.

"Whether it's words spoken in the air, letters on a page, or fingers curled and tapped on the opposing hand, language is about taking abstract grunts, markings, and gestures, and using them to express thoughts." Liz marvels at the implications of what has just transpired with the alien.

"Instinct requires no conscious thought. Instinct is reactionary, but even the most instinctive creatures need some versatility beyond reacting—that's how intelligence first arose.

"I used to volunteer in the dolphinarium in Berlin as a teenager. We could see dolphins were intelligent, but communicating with them was frustratingly difficult and very limited. There's no doubt dolphins are smart, but in an entirely different manner than we are.

"Over the last century, we've studied tens of thousands of dolphins in a variety of settings, from marine biology labs to theme parks. We've observed their physiology, their habits, their interactions with fishermen and children, and their culture, but we can't speak with them. They're intelligent mammals just like us, and yet we can't converse with them. They can learn from us and communicate on our terms, but we've yet to learn anything about their language, if their communication could even be called speech. Perhaps we'll have the same difficulties talking with these creatures." Liz laughs at the thought, adding, "That alien probably thinks it's dealing with the galactic equivalent of dolphins."

"Eek, eek," Elvis replies.

Liz laughs. She hopes the alien can't hear them. What will this astonishingly intelligent interstellar being make of a joke? Humor works only if you are in on the twist. Humor is all about the irony of understanding conflicting ideas.

"And music," she says. "If you ignore song lyrics, and only consider instrumental music, it's still fair to say music is a language. It can be written down, but it communicates aesthetics instead of words, emotions rather than ideas." Her mind is buzzing with these concepts as they approach the mattresses by the steel shutters.

Elvis says, "If we're going to get out of this hellhole, we need to work together, and that means being able to communicate with this creature." He slumps on the one remaining good mattress.

"How are you feeling?" she asks.

"Exhausted."

"I'll get you some more water."

Liz takes the plastic jug and works her way along the wall, looking for the leaking tap. A couple of soldiers walk past, talking. Liz is quiet. She takes her time filling the jug, trying not to make any noise.

With the sun high in the sky, the heat is oppressive. Sweat drips from her brow. She takes a drink, and returns with a full jug.

"Adan is dead," Elvis whispers as she hands him the water jug. "I heard a couple of soldiers talking while you were gone. They're trying to figure out what to do with the creature."

"What are they thinking?" Liz asks, her eyes widening with fear.

"They weren't in earshot for long, so I only picked up on a fraction of their conversation, but they're going to burn down the factory. From what I could tell, it sounds like they're having trouble coming up with enough fuel to flood the floor. They don't want it to escape from the fire. I suspect they've got plenty of diesel, but they need some gasoline to get the party started. Diesel won't burn by itself. It needs an accelerant."

"We've got to get out of here," they both say in unison. Liz smiles, and gestures for Elvis to continue.

"We've got to make a move tonight."

Liz holds up the butter knife, saying, "The steel door at the far end of the floor—the hinges are on the inside. I tried to budge them, but they're stiff."

Elvis scratches the stubble on his chin, saying, "Okay, that's good. We can work with that. Try to find a large stone, something you could hold in your hand, preferably with a flat surface, and I'll use that as a hammer. The hinges may have seized, but a few sharp taps should get them moving."

"Then what?" Liz asks, trying to be realistic about their escape. Getting outside the building is one thing, but that doesn't mean they're free. They could go from the frying pan to the fire.

"We're going to need a truck."

"A truck?"

"For our friend. Besides, we'll have a much better chance mobile than on foot."

"We're taking the alien with us?" Liz asks, surprised by the notion. They loosely discussed freeing the creature, but she hadn't considered taking the alien with them. "Why?"

"Because it doesn't stand a chance alone."

"But it can tear people apart," Liz reasons, not understanding his concern.

"Do you know how you hunt lions or tigers?" Liz is silent. "In packs. A lion is more than a match for a lone hunter, but not against a group of men working together. No, our buddy wouldn't last more than an hour out there alone. He'll attract too much attention."

"He?" Liz asks, objecting to his arbitrary assignment of gender.

Elvis smiles, looking very much like the rock star he did when she first met him, albeit one that has been partying hard for several days.

"It," Elvis replies, "It'll attract too much attention."

"So where are we going to take her?" Liz asks, being deliberately provocative. She suspects the whole notion of gender is irrelevant—it certainly looks that way—but she likes stirring Elvis—it's good for his morale. He grins at her choice of pronoun.

"We take her with us," Elvis replies. "Jameson's out there somewhere. We need to hook up with him, and get the hell out of Dodge."

"With a creature from another world in the back of a truck?"

"Why not?"

"Why not indeed," Liz replies. "Best idea I've heard all day."

CHAPTER 12: NIGHTFALL

The sound of trucks driving down the alleyway beside the factory wakes Liz from her slumber. Elvis is standing by a crack in the steel shutters, peering outside. It's good to see him on his feet.

"Tankers," he says softly. "They're getting ready for the party."

Liz gets to her feet and peers out through another crack. She watches as a soldier climbs down from the cab of a truck and slams the door. The sign on the side of the tanker reads "WATER," which confuses her.

"Water?" she asks.

"It wouldn't go down too well if they torched the entire neighborhood," Elvis replies. He points further down the alley. "I got a glimpse of a gas tanker as well. It's going to be quite a show."

"We've got to get out of here."

"Not so fast," Elvis replies. "We don't do nothin' 'til all's quiet and everyone's asleep. Patience, doc. It's a fundamental of good military strategy."

Liz knows he's right, but she doesn't like waiting. She's stir crazy. She feels as though she has to get out of this prison now. She no longer fears the darkness—she's hungry, her back aches, she has a headache, and her muscles are sore. None of that makes being patient easy.

"Moonrise happened less than ninety minutes after sunset. When the Moon's directly overhead, it'll be around two in the morning. That's when we'll make our move."

"How will you know," Liz asks, straining to see the sky through the thin cracks in the windows. She can't see the Moon.

"Shadows. When the shadows are at their shortest, the moon's at its zenith. When the shadows stop shrinking, and start growing again, changing direction—when that happens, the Moon has begun to descend. That's when we'll make our move."

Liz grits her teeth.

"You could never wait for Christmas, could you?" Elvis asks.

"Nope."

Liz sits on the edge of the mattress. She's feeling weak from a lack of food and the stress of running on adrenaline. Her legs are shaking from fatigue.

"So," Elvis begins. "What about Stella? How do we get her to come with us?"

"Stella?" Liz asks, surprised by his choice of name.

"She needs a name."

"And that name is Stella?"

"It means star."

"I know what it means," Liz says gently. She shakes her head. In a serious tone, she adds, "Just remember, cute and cuddly Stella can rip your arms out of their sockets. She can flay your flesh quicker than a Great White Shark. Were she to come up against a full-grown African lion, or a thirty-foot crocodile, my money would be on her walking away without a scratch."

"But she didn't hurt me," he points out. "She saved my life."

"You've seen her in action. Remember, she no more identifies with you than you do with a wild Bengal tiger, or an Arctic polar bear."

"This is different. She's intelligent," Elvis protests. "You saw the way she treated us in the kitchenette."

Oh, what a turn of events! During the drive from Ksaungu, it was Liz appealing for reason. Elvis was the skeptic. Now, the roles have reversed. Although, having an arm rebuilt at a molecular level would probably melt *her* heart as well.

"Look, I think she's intelligent too, but we need to be careful we don't read our own thoughts and feelings into her actions—the consequences could be disastrous."

Elvis purses his lips. "She could have left me to die, but she didn't. I think we owe her the benefit of doubt. We can't leave her here to die... I owe her my life."

"I know," Liz replies. "We're all in this lifeboat together, fighting against the storm, but when that door opens, our world will change. She may come with us, then again, she may not. She may not trust us. She might choose to strike out on her own. When that door opens, all bets are off. Like you, I'd like her to come with us, but honestly, I doubt she'll go for it. You can lead a horse to water, you can't make it drink." Elvis looks hurt. For all his rough, tough exterior, he seems fragile.

"There's a gulf between us," Liz says. "It's void as big as the distance that separates our planets. It's all too easy for us to assume she's just like us, to interpret her actions like those of a human, but they're not. I want her to be one of us, to be a good guy or whatever, but she's not, she never will be. When she speaks, she uses my voice, but there's no conversation. She's mimicking me, that's all—copying me like a parrot." Tears roll down his cheeks.

"She's smarter than a parrot," Elvis replies.

"I know. But just like a parrot, her physiology reinforces the differences between us. There's a chasm separating us. She can no more understand what it means to be human than we can understand what it means to be alien."

His voice stiffens. "You're wrong, Doc. Maybe I can't describe what I'm feeling in scientific terms, maybe I'm projecting my own feelings on her, but I never asked her to save my life. She did that herself. She chose to do good. I've got to believe there's more to her than some wild animal. You said it yourself back in the truck—there's intelligence there. That's more than having the smarts to know two plus two is four, or to fly between stars. She cares."

Liz breathes deeply, unsure how to respond to his plea. As if on cue, the creature rolls softly into view. Liz wonders what the alien heard, and how much she understood from their conversation.

Elvis walks fearlessly toward the creature. There's a connection between them. They reach for each other. Liz watches as his fingers touch the fronds. His hand skims across the tips as though he were running his fingers over a field of wheat.

The pulsating core of the creature hums like an electrical substation. Liz is of two minds as to the alien's composition. Stella moves so fluidly, it's as though she were an individual, and yet the tiny creatures at her heart suggest otherwise. Liz can't figure out what she is, but then, she realizes, perhaps both models are wrong. Perhaps some other alien rationale holds true, and the creature's more of a symbiotic whole.

The alien dwarfs Elvis, but that doesn't appear to bother him. They both relish the soft touch. The strength latent in the fronds is apparent. Being spherical, there are fronds drifting through the air above and beside him, but he's not intimidated by her size.

"We're going to help her, right?"

At this point, Liz doesn't have any choice, regardless of how uneasy Stella makes her feel. She's alarmed by the relationship between Elvis and Stella. As docile as tigers may seem in captivity, there's always the danger of them turning on their trainers, regardless of how long a pair has worked together. Liz feels his disregard for prudence is reckless. The possibility of a reactionary temperament hasn't occurred to him. Stella dismembered Bosco. She could turn on either of them without any humanly discernible reason. She could be using them, playing them. They could be a novelty—no more than pets in Stella's mind.

Every instinct within Liz cries out, no, but she says, "Yes— We'll help her get home."

The creature pulls Elvis closer. Her dark tentacles wrap around his arm, enveloping him, but he isn't afraid. He's receptive, enjoying the encounter. The alien towers several feet above him. Fronds flicker over his shoulder, slowly reaching up to his neck and face, but he shows no fear.

"Home?" Elvis says. "Do you understand? Home? Come with us. We'll help you get home."

"Home," the creature replies, but it hasn't mimicked his voice. The alien has retained Liz's distinct tone, duplicating both her soft pronunciation and her British accent. Liz finds that perplexing. As long as she was the only one communicating with the creature it made sense for Stella to duplicate her voice. But now, when she's clearly more comfortable with Elvis, she still chooses to retain the vocal persona associated with Liz. Liz doesn't understand why, and that frightens her.

Liz recalls the term 'home' being used three times in his sentence, four if she counts her initial use of the concept. Perhaps the alien has simply repeated the most commonly used word in mimicry. There's an assumption at play. How can they know what the creature actually understands? Words are only ever meaningful in their context.

When Europeans first encountered other cultures, translating languages was a painfully slow exercise, relying heavily on visual clues and comparisons. Translation efforts would go on for years. None of that has happened with the alien. This could all be nothing more than guesswork on the creature's part, as if it's playing along with curious chimps. When the factory door opens, Liz thinks the alien will bolt. The creature releases Elvis. Who initiated the separation? Did Elvis pull away, or did the alien let go?

"Home, Stella," he says as the alien moves back into the shadows, just on the edge of their vision. "We're going to get you home."

Liz doesn't want to ask how. For now, it's enough to escape their dungeon.

Time passes slowly.

Elvis stands watch, peering through a thin crack between the steel panels welded over the window. Liz watches the alien as she appears to preen herself. Tiny insects scoot up and down the fronds, pausing on occasion to focus on a particular part of a certain strand in much the same way cats licks their fur, and then pause to rid themselves of a parasite.

After a while, Liz decides to try talking with the alien. If they can converse, they can reason, there will be nothing to fear—she hopes. "How much do you understand?" she asks.

She sits on the edge of the mattress, looking at the seething mass of insect-like creatures pulsating in the core of the alien. Supple fronds sway with the breeze. Liz is out of her depth. She has been ever since the Osprey lifted off, abandoning them in the village. Somehow she's bluffed her way through until now, but she feels as though she's sinking in quicksand—one wrong move and she's dead.

"Do you know what I'm saying?" she asks. "Can you grasp how our speech works?"

The alien remains silent.

What intelligence lies in that vast, seemingly contradictory nest of creatures? Is she one entity or thousands? Does her intelligence arise from a hive mind? Does she think? Does she feel? Certainly, Liz has seen fear in her actions, but that could be her own interpretation of the creature's survival instinct.

What senses does the alien, or aliens have? How has she survived on Earth, in an environment that's surely hostile to her either in terms of chemistry, or atmospheric pressure differences, or the strength of gravity—there must be significant differences between their two worlds. Does the spiny carriage offer anything more than transport and weapons? Is it analogous to an astronaut's spacesuit? Why haven't any of the other aliens come looking for her? Why haven't they mounted a rescue mission? Perhaps they assume she's dead? Or is it that they don't care?

"Just because someone's mute doesn't mean they don't understand," Elvis says.

"Understand," the creature says, again repeating the most common word in a series of sentences, recognizing the topic, if not the content. Liz could kick Elvis. If he'd remained silent, if the creature had replied with *'understand,'* having only heard the word once, that would've been progress. As it is, Liz has no way of knowing whether Stella's still simply parroting concepts back at them using some kind of advance analytical algorithm as a substitute for effective communication, or whether she really does understand. Everything they've heard could simply be the bluff of an intelligent creature trying desperately to bridge the chasm. Interstellar poker.

"There has to be intelligence here," Elvis says. "We've seen too much to think otherwise. She's like a foreigner, like an American in Paris that can't speak French."

Liz catches a slight change in the throbbing hum of the insects, and she raises her hand, signaling for Elvis to be quiet.

"Intelligence," she says, addressing the creature. "We're talking about your intelligence." The creature's quiet. Liz repeated the word intelligence on purpose, wanting to see if the alien would mindlessly mimic yet another common word, or perhaps even a phrase. That Stella doesn't is perplexing, challenging her assumptions.

Elvis says, "Well, there are a few things we need Stella to understand if we're going to get her out of here. We need her to understand the basics of movement. We need her to respond to instructions. Let's see if we can get her to associate sounds with actions, kind of like the kids' game, *Red Light, Green Light.*"

Elvis beckons for Liz to stand. She gets to her feet, feeling a little silly. Elvis moves back about ten feet and says to Liz, "Green light—Red light—Green light—Red light." With each phrase, Liz either walks forward, or stands still. When she reaches him, he turns to the creature and asks a simple question with a single word, "Understand?" The alien's silent.

"Again," he says, and Liz returns to the mattress. Elvis says, "Green light—Red light—Green light—Red light—Understand?"

"Understand," the alien replies, still retaining Liz's voice.

"Okay," Elvis says, turning to the creature. "Green light."

The spindly alien structure, some nine feet in height, sways as it rocks forward on thin legs, rolling unnaturally toward him.

"Red light."

The words have barely left his lips when the creature freezes in place.

"Green light."

Again the prickly orb moves forward. Elvis stands his ground, waiting until the last second before saying, "Red light." The creature's almost on top of him, her razor sharp fronds wave inches from his face.

"This is good," Elvis says. "We've taught her two key concepts—green and red, go and stop."

On cue, the alien replies, "Understand."

"Can you see how she's doing that?" Liz asks. "How is she speaking?"

"It's the bugs on the upper surface," Elvis replies. "Whenever she talks, they vibrate like one of the old speaker cones."

"Huh!" Liz replies. That explains why there are times when the alien's speech seems to come from all around her. Unlike human speech, the alien's words aren't directional, at least, not horizontally. The creature's words bounce off the ceiling at her, and so seem to come from everywhere.

"We've got a couple of hours before we make our move," Elvis says. "We need to get that gun, and work on loosening those hinges."

As the two of them get up, the alien swivels in place, apparently asking for permission to join them.

"Green light," Elvis says softly. The creature follows behind them. For Liz, it's unnerving to hear the alien creeping up quietly behind her. Unlike her own footsteps that fall with a soft, steady, rhythmic crunch, the motion of the alien is more akin to the sound of the wind rustling in the trees.

"Just like a puppy dog," Elvis says.

"A giant puppy dog" Liz replies, "*with tentacles.*" Elvis doesn't respond. In the dim light, she can see him grinning.

They reach the mattresses beneath the shattered remains of the upper floor. Elvis picks up the gun from where it lies in the dust. "We need to find that bullet."

"Is one bullet going to make any difference?" Liz asks, crouching down, and searching with her hands in the low light. It's hopeless. She's clutching at shadows in the darkness.

"One bullet won't hold off an army, but could make the difference between life and death. It might buy us some time."

The alien seems agitated. Liz worries the creature is upset seeing Elvis brandishing the revolver. She looks up, and amidst the swarm of tentacles flicking back and forth, one remains still, outstretched toward Elvis. The fine tip of a single frond wraps around a bloodstained bullet.

Elvis reaches out cautiously, saying, "Nice work, Stella." His voice is anything but confident. Like Liz, he's at least a little nervous when the possibility of violence arises. There was no way for either of them to know how the creature would react to seeing the gun again, or the thought of being shot at, but Stella seems relaxed. Elvis takes the bullet from her and slips it into the revolver. Slowly, he tucks the revolver into the small of his back. No sudden moves is a smart idea.

On reaching the door, Elvis uses his fingers to carefully examine the hinges before setting to work with the butter knife and a rock. The hallway's pitch black. The only light comes from behind them—a faint glimmer seeping in through the cracks in the sealed windows on the factory floor. The alien stands beside one of the windows, casting an eerie shadow. Liz finds her heart racing at the sight of tentacles waving in the darkness.

"Yeah, that's going to come loose real easy," Elvis whispers, turning to one side and sitting back against the wall. Liz leans against the other wall, facing him. She slides down, sitting on the rough concrete.

"Now we wait," he says.

Liz wants to press him to move sooner, but Elvis is patient. This must be an ingrained military discipline. She has no doubt that when the moment arises, he'll act with surprising speed and aggression. In the past twelve hours, he's gone from being almost an invalid to his old self. His left arm doesn't look any different than this morning—it's still anemic, but that doesn't bother him. He has what appears to be a normal range of dexterity.

The alien waits outside the narrow hallway. Liz wonders what she's thinking. The spiny structure spans a sphere nine feet in diameter, with the swarming heart of the creature centered at chest height. By retracting her tentacles, the alien can squeeze into the hallway, but her motion in a confined space is restricted.

Elvis takes out the revolver and places it on the ground between them. Liz can barely see the outline of the chrome plated cylinder and the elongated barrel. The pistol grip fades into the indistinct darkness.

They sit there listening for any sounds beyond the door, but the night is quiet. The concrete floor is hard. Liz feels sore. She shifts from one butt cheek to another every few minutes, unable to get comfortable. Elvis probably thinks she has ants in her pants.

A cool breeze slips beneath the door and Liz feels upbeat, but then she doesn't have to worry about stealing a truck. She's content to think it'll be easy for Elvis.

Every half-hour or so, Elvis gets up and checks the angle of the moon shining in through one of the cracks in the steel shutters. Finally, he comes back and says the two words she's been waiting to hear, "It's time."

Stella speaks from the darkness, "Understand."

CHAPTER 13: RUSH

Quietly, Elvis taps at the hinges on the inside of the door, removing them and placing them neatly to one side.

He whispers. "There are a couple of dangers here—points at which our escape could be compromised. The first is when I remove this door."

Liz has become so accustomed to the darkness that her eyes easily pick out the soft gleam of polished steel as Elvis slips the gun behind his back again.

"I'm going to move the door, but once I do, it's important you stay put. I need to assess the situation on the other side. If there are any guards outside, things are going to go hot. I won't shoot unless I have to. I'll use the knife to incapacitate them."

"The butter knife?" Liz whispers.

"You'd be surprised how effective any length of metal is when used with sufficient force in a vulnerable spot."

Liz doesn't say anything. *Vulnerable, effective, incapacitate*—these are military euphemisms. The army uses indirect terms for killing people. As for the butter knife, he's right. Working in ER, Liz has seen people accidentally impaled by some of the most unlikely objects: loose fencing, upturned chair legs, screwdrivers. During her time in the accident and emergency ward at the St. Albans hospital in London, she had a father turn up with a child's toy airplane embedded in his abdomen. Soft tissue punctures are nasty.

Elvis says, "At this point, our greatest ally is stealth—being thought of as dead has its advantages. If bullets start flying, even just one shot, the gig's up. It'll be like hitting a wasp nest with a baseball bat."

Elvis rests his hand on her shoulder. All she can see is the outline of his head in silhouette.

"If that happens, run. Understand?"

Liz nods, not that he'd know in the dark.

"You don't look back. You don't wait for me. You don't stop and hide. Run as fast and as far as your legs will carry you. Distance is your friend. Got it? Treat that first shot like a starter's gun at the Olympics. You don't wait for any kind of confirmation from me. If there's gunfire, you're running a *goddamn* marathon. Yeah?"

"Yeah," she says.

"Moving targets are hard to hit, especially at night. You need to run like the hounds of hell are snapping at your heels. If you can, run *behind* cover, but don't stop. The further you get, the better."

Liz breathes deeply, steeling herself for what's to come.

"In the initial rush of adrenaline, you'll find you're good to sprint out to about a hundred yards, then your lungs will start to burn and your legs will feel like they're dragging lead weights. Back things off, pace yourself, but don't stop. Slow to a jog if you have to, but keep running. If these bastards catch you, they'll kill you. The only thing you can do is to outdistance them. If they lose sight of you, even for a moment, they're going to be forced to slow down and search for you in case you've gone into hiding, so use that to your advantage and keep moving. Don't. Stop. For. Anything."

He removes his hand from her shoulder, saying, "Government troops hold the western side of the city, so if you head away from the rising sun you're running towards them."

Elvis pauses before adding, "With any luck, I'll be running alongside you, okay?"

"Okay."

"Ready?"

"Yes," Liz replies, feeling the adrenaline already pulsating through her veins.

"Good. I need you to help me with the door."

Elvis uses the knife to jimmy the steel door out of the metal doorframe. Moonlight seeps in through the cracks widening around the edges. Liz finds herself holding her breath as she braces her hands against the door, helping him move it slowly, trying to avoid the slightest noise. Elvis positions himself by the hinged side of the frame, peering out into the street.

"A little more," he whispers, and Liz edges back, struggling under the weight. Elvis looks through the widening gap. He lifts the door, pulling at it while turning sideways and squeezing through the narrow gap.

Liz takes the weight of the door, preventing it from falling inward. Elvis looks angry. His lips clench. His body is coiled, ready to spring into action. He holds the revolver in his right hand, keeping it high against the inside of the doorframe. Once the gap's wide enough, he steps through with the gun leading the way. Liz starts to follow, moving toward the gap only to see him hold his hand up, signaling for her to wait.

"There's a crate on the left, hiding us from view, but it's also blocking my view. Wait here while I look around." Elvis creeps forward in the shadows.

Liz peers through the gap. She can see down the desolate street to her right. The surrounding buildings lack windows. There are roller doors and fading signs, but few windows in the front facades, confirming her suspicion that they were dragged into some kind of commercial district.

In that instant, Liz suddenly realizes her arms are the only thing holding the metal door. As she steps to one side, the door starts to fall inward—its weight seems to grow as the center of gravity shifts. Liz braces herself, spreading her legs and pushing hard until the metal slab is vertical again. Sweat drips from her brow.

A steel door crashing to the ground would attract as much attention as a gunshot. Liz shakes in panic. She pushes the door past the vertical, allowing it to lean up against the doorframe, jammed on an angle. Her fingers are clammy.

Elvis creeps back over. "We're clear. There's a light at the far end of the alley beside us, but nothing at either end of this street. I can see down the alley beside the factory; there are a couple of guards down by the tankers, but they're pretty lax."

"Help me with the door," Liz says, starting to lift.

"Not just yet. I've got to get a truck first, remember."

"You're going to leave me?" Liz is horrified.

"Hey, you keep the gun," Elvis says, pushing the revolver into her hand.

"What?" Liz whispers, taken back by the notion.

"If anyone jumps you, pull back on the hammer and fire. Aim for the center of the chest. Squeeze with certainty. Don't jerk at the trigger."

"You can't leave me," Liz protests, struggling to keep her voice down. She leans against the wall inside the hallway. Her head pokes through the gap while the rest of her body remains in the darkness.

"Listen. I need you to think straight. You, me, and Stella creeping through the streets at night wouldn't end well. We'll attract too much attention. One man alone can move unseen. You've got to trust me on this—I'm coming back."

"But the gun? Don't you need the gun?"

"If I get to the point where I need to open fire on someone, a single bullet won't be enough."

Elvis points. "If everything goes according to plan, you should see a truck pull up down there. No headlights, and you know it's me. I need you to sit tight until then, okay?"

"Okay."

"Remember, if you hear gunfire, you run. Okay?"

"Okay."

"If I'm not back within two hours, move out on foot. Okay?"

"Okay."

"If you see the horizon lightening and sunrise approaching, get the hell out of Dodge. Okay?"

"Okay."

"Stay in the shadows. Move away from the rising sun."

"Okay."

"Everything's going to be fine."

"Okay," Liz replies yet again, although she's anything but convinced. Her face must betray her doubts.

Elvis smiles, saying, "Hang in there, sugar pie." Sugar pie? Liz has never been called sugar pie before, and doubts she ever will again. As patronizing as the phrase is, it's disarming in a way only Elvis can manage.

Elvis keeps to the shadows, working his way down the road before disappearing around the corner, never looking back. Liz would feel better if he had. She leans the door against the doorframe and slumps against the wall. The revolver feels ridiculously heavy. It's as though the gun knows it doesn't belong in her fingers and is trying to escape.

In the half-light, she can just make out the alien at the end of the hallway behind her. With all that's transpired in the past few minutes, she'd forgotten about her interstellar friend. Tentacles flicker in the darkness. That's when it strikes her—the door's open. This is what the creature's been waiting for. What will Stella do, now that freedom's so close?

"Red light," Liz says. "We need to wait here. We have to wait for Elvis."

"*Green light.*"

Liz feels the hairs on the back of her neck stand.

"No. No. No," she whispers. "Red light. It's not safe. Not yet. Red light."

The alien advances on her, pulling in its whip-like tentacles as it moves down the narrow hallway. Liz stands, facing the creature in the darkness.

"No, please. Don't."

"*Green light.*"

"You don't understand. If you go out there, they'll find you. They'll kill you."

"*Green light*," the creature repeats. Liz feels as though she's talking to herself. As her voice firms, so does the alien's mimicry.

"Red—"

"*Green light*," the creature insists, cutting her off mid-sentence.

Tentacles begin striking the walls in anger, threatening violence. The seething, writhing mass of fronds closes in on her, blocking the hallway. The central mass of the creature hums, pulsating like a hive.

Liz holds out one hand, signaling for the creature to stop.

"You've got to trust me. I want to get out of here as much as you do, but I can't. It's a red light for me too. You have to wait. I'm here with you. I won't leave you. Red light, please understand. Red light."

"*Green light*," the creature replies, raising her own voice against her, almost on the verge of yelling. Thrashing tentacles break through the particleboard lining the hallway. Before her, a mesh of razor-sharp whips cut through the air barely a foot from her face.

Liz feels the grip of the revolver in her hands. Her fingers tighten on the handle. With her thumb, she pulls back on the hammer, cocking the gun.

"*Green light*," the alien screams. Liz expects rebel soldiers to come bursting through the door behind her. She trembles. She considers raising the gun and threatening to shoot. That worked in their initial confrontation, when Adan first cast them into his colosseum. The alien responded by retreating and protecting her core. Will she respond the same way again? Or will the threat of violence destroy the trust they've established? Did any such trust ever exist? Or is it simply a construct of her imagination?

Liz suspects a threat would work, but she can't bring herself to offer what would only ever be a hollow bluff. There has to be another way. Violence is cowardice—the petty refuge of a dull mind. She has to let the creature go. If the alien wants to chance itself alone on the run, Liz has to respect that.

Her thumb grips the hammer, slowly lowering it back in place against the firing pin of a bullet already set in the chamber of the revolver. As she does so, the creature freezes. Not one of the hundreds of tentacles threatening to strike her move. The various blades seize in midair, regardless of the contorted shape in which they're held. For a moment, it's as though Liz is looking at a modern art sculpture.

Her is heart pounding. Perspiration breaks out on her forehead. Her fingers are shaking. Try as she might, she can't stand still. She's too scared—the creature has only just realized she's holding a loaded gun.

Liz crouches slowly, placing the gun on the ground while keeping her eyes on the pulsating mass at the heart of the convoluted creature. The tentacles remain stationary, locked in place, and she wonders what this intelligent being from another world could possibly be thinking.

"Green light," Liz says softly, stepping to one side, hoping the alien can squeeze past. She has no doubt the alien's tentacles can manipulate the door to move it out of the way. She only hopes the door doesn't crash to the concrete floor.

There's silence for the best part of a minute. Sweat runs from her forehead, stinging her eyes, but she fights the urge to wipe it away. Sudden movements don't seem wise. Liz presses her back against the wall, trying to give the alien as much room as possible, but she refuses to step outside the door. She's stubborn. Elvis told her to stay put and she will. She believes in him. She's convinced he knows what he's doing, and this is the only way she can conceivably communicate that belief to this strange alien intelligence.

The alien remains motionless, less than a foot from the gun. Liz finds herself wondering how much Stella understands about what's transpired between her and Elvis. Is the alien looking at the gun? Is she looking at her? Perhaps seeing her in far more than the visible spectrum, so woefully inadequate in the dark? Can Stella sense her heartbeat? Can she measure her body temperature, or detect the rush of adrenaline signaling a flight or fight response? Does this creature understand how unbearable it is for her to neither run nor fight? Outwardly, the creature may seem inert, but Liz doubts that's true of her inner reasoning. Liz feels as though Stella can read her mind.

Finally, the creature replies, saying, "*Red light.*"

Liz breathes deeply. Her body, so tense just moments before, relaxes, and she slides down the wall. At the same time, the fronds and blades of the creature flex and sag. Liz is surprised by the parallels between them, and the sense of relief they both share.

What point of logic convinced the alien to wait? It had to have been that Liz surrendered the gun without threatening her.

In that instance, Liz gets a glimpse into Stella's thinking. Like her, the creature must be subject to a raft of emotions. Just like her, the alien has to choose whether to blindly follow its own instincts, or to think critically. This otherworldly mind has had to rise above its own fears and doubts.

Liz doesn't stop to consider what the alien's going to do next. It's enough for her to realize Stella isn't going to proceed. Liz assumes the creature will back away again, keep her distance, but she doesn't. She feels tentacles touching her shoulder, only they aren't probing or glancing over her shirt, they're resting limply on her arm and thigh as she sits there in the darkness. Liz reaches out with her other hand, resting her fingers on the thick, leathery appendages. Tiny insects stream back and forth, barely touching her skin before retreating again. It's as though they're timid, shrinking at the thought of being touched but wanting to touch her nonetheless.

"I know," she says. "Oh, how I know, but we have to be brave. For now, it's a red light. Elvis will come back for us—I know he will—then we'll have a green light."

The alien's silent. Sitting there, Liz can feel a pulse running through the limp fronds resting on her leg. Unlike a human heart, the alien creature pulsates with the stutter of a water pipe with air in the line.

She sits by the edge of the doorway, peering down the road, hoping, almost willing Elvis to appear, while dreading the awful implications of a violent gunshot breaking the stillness.

What will the alien do if she hears the crack of gunfire close by? Liz has already picked out her escape route—a dark alley leading away from the factory on the other side of the back road. She isn't sure if it's heading west, but if they're found, she needs to get some distance between her and the soldiers around the factory. Anywhere that leads away from the guardhouse on the main street seems like a good idea. Once she gets well away from the building, she'll turn west. What will this interstellar creature do if she sees Liz running from the factory? Will she follow her? Does Liz want her to? Minutes pass like hours.

After an age, Liz notices the sky beginning to lighten. With the Moon low on the far horizon, the skyline had been as dark as coal, but now it warms with the promise of a rising sun. Stars begin to fade. The sky reveals growing color pushing back the night. There's still an hour or more before dawn, but her heart sinks.

"Where are you?" she whispers, longing for Elvis to return. As much as she wants to fight the realization, it's time to go. Turning to the creature, she reluctantly says, "Green light."

To her surprise, the alien's lethargic. The creature registers her words, but it takes time for it to respond and stiffen its spiky tentacle-like legs. Could Stella have been asleep? Every animal on Earth sleeps. Even single-celled amoeba follow a day/night circadian rhythm. Do these aliens have a similar biological process? Perhaps she's reading her own exhaustion into the creature's behavior. Maybe the alien's lost in thought. As for her, there's nothing Liz would love more than to curl up in a soft bed. The thought of running madly for her life through the war-torn streets of Lilongwe is daunting, but Elvis was right—it has to be done.

She gets to her feet, leaving the gun behind, and begins heaving the door to one side. When she turns to pick up the revolver, it's gone. She looks up. The creature holds the gun by the barrel, with a tentacle wrapped around the shiny steel. Liz reaches out and takes it cautiously from her.

"Thanks," she says, checking the bullet is chambered. "Green light," she repeats softly. Liz knows this is the command the creature has been waiting for, but Stella seems reluctant to escape, as though she too is longing for Elvis to return.

What will happen to them on the run? How far will she get through this decimated city? Once people start moving around in the daylight, how far can she go with an alien following close behind? Her natural impulse is to hide, but Elvis said not to hide. Liz knows it'll be difficult to fight the desire to crawl into some dark hole and hope for the best. Who should she trust? Her judgment or his?

What about Stella? The alien trusts her, but what has Liz done to earn that trust? Nothing. In hindsight, with Elvis failing to return, they would've been better off being on the move several hours ago, putting more distance between them and the rebels. Does Stella realize that? Will the creature feel betrayed when that becomes obvious?

Elvis hasn't returned. Liz has to strike out on her own with Stella, with just one bullet to protect them, one bullet to attract hordes of rebel soldiers. Liz wants to say she's sorry. She feels she should apologize in advance, but the creature won't have any idea what she's talking about.

As Liz moves out of the doorway, into the shadow of the crate, she sees a covered truck pull up at the end of the road with its lights off. Her heart leaps. Elvis climbs out of the cab, and opens the back of the truck.

"Green light," she says softly, beckoning Stella outside.

Multiple alien fronds pick up the door, manipulating it as the creature passes through the doorway, leaving the door in place behind it. At a glance, to a casual observer it looks like the door's still closed. Clever.

Liz peers around the side of the crate, looking to see if anyone's further along the road. Once she's sure no one's watching, she darts across the rough gravel road. Stella keeps pace beside her, rolling forward on her spindle-like legs. The alien creature moves swiftly and silently. Liz gets the impression Stella could easily outpace her, but the alien remains at her side over the hundred yards or so it takes to reach the truck.

Elvis stands in the open back, waving with his hands, urging them on. The alien springs up, landing in the cargo deck. Elvis begins pulling down the canvas cover to hide her from view when Liz climbs up as well.

"Don't you want to ride up front?"

"No," she replies, struggling to catch her breath. "I need to be with her. To let her know everything's going to be okay. As scared as we are of her, I suspect she's terrified of us. She needs someone with her."

Elvis nods. "Hey, I got through to a government checkpoint on the shortwave radio in the truck. They said there are Americans are holed up at the US embassy. I think they mean the Rangers, so that's where we'll head."

Liz reaches out, touching at the blood seeping through his shirt, running from his shoulder down his front.

"You're bleeding."

"It's not my blood," Elvis replies with a grin.

How can he respond like that? For her, there's nothing laudable in the violence of war, and yet she's glad he can disconnect himself like this. His casual disregard has to be some kind of psychological defense mechanism, insulating his mind from the horrors he has to inflict on others to survive. One day, this will catch up with him. One day these memories will haunt him. Although his acts are justifiable, they're odious nonetheless. Post-traumatic stress isn't cowardice. There's only so long a sane person can maintain the illusion of detachment necessary to survive in a war zone. When his fall comes, she hopes it isn't from a great height. She hopes there'll be someone there to catch him.

CHAPTER 14: EMBASSY

The alien creature wraps its tentacles around the wooden slats in the back corner of the truck, holding on as Elvis speeds through the darkened streets. Liz sits to one side, bracing herself as the vehicle careens one way, then another. Elvis has a lead foot, both when accelerating and braking.

The canvas cover at the back of the truck flaps in the breeze, allowing the growing dawn to seep through. The sky's dark. Streaks of scarlet light up the clouds high above, slowly transforming the night into a ruddy pink morning. With just a few clouds in the stratosphere, it's going to be another scorching hot day.

Liz sits across from Stella wondering what this magnificent creature's thinking. As for her, she's regretting not sitting in the cab with Elvis. Her heart pounds. There are times when the truck feels like it's out of control, flying around corners, bouncing out of potholes, accelerating madly. Her *life's* out of control. She wants to yell out to Elvis and ask him to stop—let her out, but she knows her feelings are misplaced. Getting out won't solve anything. She has to be strong, and endure. She knows she shouldn't read her own emotions into Stella's character, but she can't help but wonder if the alien feels the same way. The pulsating mass of tiny creatures at the heart of the creature appears to grimace the same way she does with each erratic turn.

Elvis stops the truck on several occasions, and Liz can hear him talking to Africans. As he drives away, she gets a glimpse of the roadblocks they're negotiating.

Liz is going to be sick. Fumes leak into the back of the truck. The unrelenting motion of the loose canvas flap seems to pound inside her head. In the growing heat, the sides of the truck seem to close in on her, causing her to feel claustrophobic, nauseous. Her world narrows as she fights not to vomit.

Finally, the truck slows and turns sharply, as though they're entering a property, rather than turning onto yet another road. Liz can hear voices calling out, American voices. The truck rides up over the lip of a curb, with the engine whining. Smithy and Jameson call out to Elvis. Her heart jumps. They've made it.

"Goddamn," Jameson cries.

"You sorry son of a hound dog," Smithy yells with affection in her voice.

The cab of the truck rocks as someone jumps up onto the running board below the driver's door.

"Hey, babe," Elvis says in his best Barry White voice. "Did ya miss me?"

"Don't you *hey babe* me," Smithy replies, trying not to laugh. "Scare me like that again, and I'll hunt you down and kill you myself."

Elvis laughs.

Liz wonders how much Stella understands of their speech. Certainly, a figurative, idiomatic phrase like that must be confusing. She isn't sure, but she thinks she can hear Smithy kissing Elvis as he drives slowly forward. Liz figures it's good that Stella can't see Smithy and Elvis, as their contradictory banter would be confusing.

Liz creeps toward the rear of the truck, wanting to get out of the stinking, hot, claustrophobic space. For a moment, she forgets about Stella, thinking only of her relief to be safe with the Rangers again.

"Where's Bosco and the doc?" Jameson calls out.

"Bosco didn't make it," Elvis replies, his voice breaking. "Doc's in the back."

The truck turns in a semi-circle before coming to a halt. Pebbles crunch beneath the tires. Liz sits by the tailgate, ready to climb down.

"What the hell happened to your arm?" Jameson asks as he and Smithy walk with Elvis toward the rear of the truck. Liz tries somewhat awkwardly to climb over the tailgate.

"Oh, you think that's wild, wait until you get a load of our guest!"

Jameson comes around the back of the truck and, to Liz's surprise, grabs her as if she weighs next to nothing. He swings her down from the truck, giving her a bear hug.

"Liz," he cries. "Damn, it's good to see you."

Liz was never one for being touchy-feely, but she's relieved to see him too. She stands there blinded by the bright sunlight.

"You made it!" Jameson says, still holding her by the shoulders and squeezing her arms affectionately. "I can't believe you made it out of there, but damn, here you are."

"Here I am," Liz replies, still somewhat overwhelmed.

She squints to adjust to the light. Colors rush at her from all sides. An American flag flies on a flagpole positioned in the center of the courtyard. The truck has driven around a circular driveway, passing beside an oval with green grass growing in a carefully manicured lawn—green grass! Outside of the jungle, there's no green to be seen, and after the last few days of darkness within the warehouse, the vibrant, spring green of something as simple and commonplace as grass on a lawn is utterly astonishing.

Small sprinkler heads have been set recessed every ten feet around the curb, ready to spray water over the lawn. There are flowers around the base of the flagpole. Are there any other flowers in Lilongwe? Liz feels as though she's hopped out of the truck and into North America.

She glances around, and reality undermines her perception. To one side, over against the high outer walls of the embassy, palm trees and shrubs mark the start of a tropical garden. It would be aesthetically pleasing were it not for the black soot staining the cream wall, the scattered bullet holes, and the spray of dried blood. Like everything she's seen in Africa, the US embassy is a violent contradiction of life and death.

Smithy is glowing. Her smile reveals her beautiful, straight white teeth. She punches Elvis gently on the chest.

"You had us worried, you big, dumb, hick redneck," she says, unable to wipe the grin off her face.

"Rock god, remember," Elvis replies, winking at her. Smithy pushes him playfully, clearly wanting to reassure herself he's real and actually standing before her again.

"What happened to you guys back there in the intersection?" Jameson asks. He clarifies what happened to the rest of the squad. "We had tangos all over us. We fought a rolling action to the east, and made it out of the kill zone through a back alley, carrying our wounded with us.

"We've been sending daily recons out to the market, hoping you'd drag your sorry ass back there. We talked with the locals, but no one would even acknowledge the attack happened. If they knew anything, they weren't talking."

Elvis climbs up on the back of the truck. As he rolls the canvas to one side he says, "We were captured by a warlord, some egomaniac by the name of General Adan. He—"

Jameson peers into the back of the truck, cutting Elvis off before he can finish. "What the—?" he cries, stepping backwards. "What the hell is that?"

Smithy backs away.

"Sarge," Elvis begins. "I'd like to introduce you to a friend of ours, Stella."

Stella stays away from the light streaming in through the open canvas. Her tentacles wave in the air. The alien moves across the back of the truck, seeking the shadows.

Elvis stands in the opening, beckoning the creature to come to him, coaxing her forward like a horse trainer.

"Jesus, Mary and Joseph," Smithy breathes. "Elvis, what have you done?"

Elvis laughs. "Green light, Stella. It's okay. Green light."

Slowly, the seething mass of tentacles and whips moves forward. As the alien approaches the back of the truck, Liz expects Elvis to jump down to get out of the way, but he doesn't. Elvis has no fear of the strange-looking creature.

Jameson backs across the grass, moving away from the truck. "Mother of God," he whispers. His hand rests on his sidearm.

"Don't," Liz says, resting her hand on his. "That *really* wouldn't be a good idea."

Looking back at the truck, Liz gets her first good look at the creature in the sunlight. The brilliant reds and scarlets of the alien's tentacles are shocking to behold. They shine like polished glass, reflecting the light. As the alien fronds wave in the breeze they seem to sample the air. Stella's trying to assess how safe it is outside the truck.

"Green light," Liz says, reinforcing what Elvis has said.

Liz watches as dozens of slick red blades wrap around Elvis. He's completely unfazed. Jameson is shocked. Smithy holds her hand over her mouth.

The swarm of insects at the heart of the alien have an iridescent pearly sheen to their black shells. Although Liz knows they're a mass of individual insect-like creatures, in the sunlight they look like the folds and crevasses of the cerebral cortex, a brain in motion, vulnerable and exposed to the elements.

Up until this point, Liz thought of the brilliant red appendages reaching out from the core as tentacles, but in the light of day they look more like brightly-colored blades of flax, only that analogy's too organic, perhaps flexible blades of colored steel or fiberglass would be better. As they flex, they change not only their length, but their width and thickness, adapting themselves from fine, feeler-like structures to blades that sway like ribbons in the breeze. Stiff spikes support the creature's weight, stabbing back and forth like crab's feet.

Elvis steps down, helping the alien out of the truck. Soft red blades envelop the right side of his body, wrapping around him as though the creature were clinging to him more for security than anything else. As nervous as Jameson is, Liz suspects the alien's even more apprehensive.

Having been harassed, corralled, fired upon, injured and threatened during her brief time on Earth, Stella must feel as though Elvis is the only native she can trust, the only one for whom trust is mutual. Even Liz can't completely let down her guard around the alien creature, but Elvis has no such reservations.

Liz finds their relationship fascinating. She hopes Elvis remembers her warning, not to read too much from his own emotional responses into the reactions of the alien, and yet he clearly feels the need to protect Stella. Perhaps it's the change of environment. In their dark, gloomy dungeon, the factory floor felt like her domain. Out here, she's on his turf.

An eerie silence falls over the courtyard. Smithy crouches, her hand still over her mouth. Like the others, she's in shock.

"Green light," Elvis says.

"Green light," the creature replies, still using Liz's voice. Is that deliberate to include her, Liz wonders, or is the creature simply being consistent? Regardless, Liz walks over beside the alien as naturally as she can. Despite her reservations, she wants to show the soldiers there's nothing to fear.

Jameson looks at Liz as the alien's voice registers. The shock on his face is palpable. Liz raises her hands in a gesture of acceptance, as though it's all her fault, trying to indicate she has no more idea than he does. Jameson shakes his head, but he's smiling.

The various US soldiers around the courtyard nervously check their surroundings, clearly thinking about any possible hostile move.

For all they know, this creature's some invincible, acid-dripping monster from another planet—and that isn't too far from the truth.

Jameson, though, ever the professional, seizes the moment and calls out to the soldiers. "All right, enough standing around. What's the matter? Haven't you seen an alien before? Smithy, get that gate shut. Jones, Marshall and Davies, since you're on the wall pulling guard duty, you need to face the other way. Elvis—stop showing off, and take our guest inside."

Elvis grins. "Yes, sir."

Smithy doesn't move. Jameson taps her on the shoulder. Slowly, she gets up and goes over to the gate.

Elvis walks toward the main building. Stella follows. She's never more than a few feet from him. It's clear she isn't going to let him out of her sight until she feels safe. Liz follows them.

"You three," Jameson says, coming up behind them, "You have some explaining to do."

Jameson took that quite well, all things considered. She loves his use of '*You three*,' as though somehow she and the alien owe him an explanation. In reality, it's only Elvis that's answerable to Jameson, but that doesn't bother him in the slightest. She turns back, expecting a grumpy look on his face, but he's grinning as he comes up beside her.

Jameson shakes his head, speaking to Elvis as he says, "If it was going to be anyone, it'd be you." Elvis smiles. Liz laughs. He's right. Is there anyone better suited to introduce Earth's culture to an alien species?

As they climb the broad marble steps leading up to the portico in front of the embassy, Liz watches to see how Stella negotiates this obstacle. Her spindly feet, so reminiscent of a sea urchin, make a smooth transition from sharp, pointed spears to curved blades with some flex in them. They slap the ground softly, wrapping themselves over the uneven surfaces, providing Stella with a spring in her step.

Bullet holes pepper the walls. Burns and scorch marks speak of a violent struggle. Patches of dried blood on one of the low walls indicate where the wounded took cover during a vicious firefight.

Jameson catches up with Elvis, directing him to one side. He's surprisingly relaxed given their unusual company.

"Why couldn't you have brought home a cat? Or a dog, like everyone else?"

Elvis laughs.

"What am I supposed to do with an alien, Elvis? Honestly, do you think about these things before you do them? Can you imagine the paperwork?" They both laugh.

Liz isn't too familiar with the various branches within the US military, but she can tell several of the soldiers staring nervously at them are either navy or air force from their blue uniforms.

"At ease, gentlemen," Jameson says. It takes Liz a second to realize he's joking. It's Elvis and his cocky smile that gives it away.

They enter the reception area, and walk down a long corridor. The formerly white walls have fresh gouges and bloodstains. Jameson leads the way, with Elvis following. Stella is immediately behind him, while Liz brings up the rear with two rather awkward soldiers providing security. They're carrying M4 rifles slung over their shoulders and aren't in any way threatening.

Jameson leads them into a cafeteria. The tables and chairs have been used to barricade one end of the room overlooking the courtyard. A couple of the tables have been put back on the linoleum, but most of them still lie in a tangle by the windows. Jameson gestures to a table and a few chairs.

"Lieutenant McAllister's on his way," one of the trailing soldiers says, standing guard by the door.

"Well, he's going to love this," Jameson replies.

Stella wheels around the room as Elvis and Liz sit at the table. She's inquisitive. The alien probes overturned chairs, the shattered remains of a vending machine, with cans of coke and candy bars strewn across the ground. She's most interested in the serving benches with their stainless steel tops.

There are two jugs full of water on the table, along with a bunch of paper cups.

"No coffee, I'm afraid," Jameson says, pouring water into the cups and handing them to Elvis and Liz. "Are you hungry? Can we get you some food?"

Liz nods, drinking the water quickly, and getting a refill.

One of the soldiers by the door slips carefully along the wall, and into the kitchen to get them something to eat.

"What about our friend?" Jameson asks. Liz notes that Jameson keeps the table between him and Stella as the creature moves around the room. Liz and Elvis are content to sit there comfortably, with the alien rummaging around the cafeteria, Jameson's still unnerved by her and doesn't sit down until Stella settles.

"She likes water," Liz says, trying to be helpful.

Elvis takes the glass jug over to the creature. He places it on the stainless steel bench, asking, "Are you thirsty?"

The creature stops and begins examining the pitcher. Liz watches as a stream of bugs race up and down the blades touching briefly at the jug. Before her eyes, the glass appears to dissolve as the creature assimilates both the jug and the water at once.

"Well, she likes that," Elvis says, laughing as he sits. He turns to a soldier standing by the kitchen and says, "Same again, bartender." Elvis turns his chair around and leans on the seat back as he watches Stella.

A young lieutenant walks in and freezes in the doorway. Instantly, the alien bristles, all its appendages stiffen like swords.

"Easy, girl," Elvis says in a soft voice. "It's okay. We're safe. We're among friends."

Liz isn't sure whether Stella understands his words, or just the tone of his voice, but she relaxes and goes back to examining the serving line. She opens drawers and cupboards, just as she had in the kitchenette within the factory.

"It's okay, Frank. Just don't make any sudden moves," Jameson says.

"Is that—?"

"Yep," Jameson replies. "Apparently it is."

Jameson seems to accept Stella, but the young lieutenant is nervous. He never takes his eyes off her.

"Are you sure this is safe?" he asks quietly.

Elvis smiles, saying, "If you don't shoot at her, she won't tear your arms out of their sockets." Liz isn't sure that helps.

"We've got to call this through," the lieutenant says. "Command's not going to believe this."

"What happened back there?" Jameson asks. Liz notes he's looking intently at Elvis and his withered arm.

"We were overrun," Elvis begins. "I lost my arm while sheltering from an RPG. Stella gave me a new one."

"What?" Jameson asks. "She just carries spares?"

Elvis laughs, gesturing to his elbow as he says, "It was a bloody mess. Somehow, she rebuilt my arm. I don't know how." Jameson looks to Liz.

"I saw it, but I can't explain it," she says.

"From there," Elvis continues. "I hotwired a truck and we came here."

Jameson scratches the side of his head. He looks bewildered. Elvis is compressing an inordinate amount of detail into just a few words, but Jameson lets that slide, clearly impressed. Having an alien before them is just too fantastic. There will be time for a proper debrief at some point, but not now.

"And Bosco?" Jameson asks.

"They killed him," Elvis replies, cutting in before Liz can say anything that might incriminate the alien.

On one level, it's a lie, and yet Elvis is right to blame the warlord. It may have been Stella that carried out the sentence, but it was passed by Adan and his men. Elvis isn't being strictly honest about what happened, and Liz understands why. He's protecting Stella. Given the creature's menacing appearance, the last thing anyone needs to hear is that she shredded a Ranger. Liz, though, can't leave the details so scant. She's determined to say more while being careful not to implicate Stella.

"Adan captured us," she says. Elvis shoots her a fierce look, clearly wanting her to shut up. "He murdered Bosco in front of us."

"And the alien?" Jameson asks.

The lieutenant sits down next to Jameson. Liz notices the glazed look in his eyes. He's in shock, and not up to resolving this puzzle, but Jameson is.

"They threw us in with Stella. We don't know where she came from, or how they captured her, but she was there before we arrived, trapped on the ground floor of an abandoned factory."

"Adan captured her?" Jameson asks, pulling at the threads of the story. "You're sure of that?"

"Yes," Liz replies.

"So you saw Adan alive?"

"Yes."

Elvis has his lips clenched tight. He looks angry.

"Do you know how or when Adan died?"

Liz shakes her head.

"We heard he was killed by a woman—a foreigner."

Liz looks down, avoiding eye contact with Jameson. She's afraid if she explains her part in Adan's death, she'll give away Stella's part in Bosco's.

Jameson isn't satisfied, but the lieutenant is. The young man smiles, saying, "Well, what you've accomplished is extraordinary. You've escaped in the confusion surrounding the general's death, and you've freed an alien. God only knows what we're going to do with—her, but you did the right thing."

The soldier returns from the kitchen carrying a plate with several packages of food wrapped in foil. Like the lieutenant, he approaches the table from the opposite side of the alien, keeping it between him and Stella. Liz notes they have no idea how fast Stella can move, but she doesn't want to spook them so she remains silent. If they feel safe, all well and good.

"Is there anything I can get for—?" the soldier asks.

"Another jug of water," Elvis replies.

In reality, they have no way of knowing what Stella needs. Another jug of water's a good guess, but it's only a guess. It could be the equivalent of a Mars Bar to the alien—hardly something that will provide any real nourishment. Liz doubts Stella can make use of terrestrial proteins. Perhaps raw materials are best.

"Okay," Jameson says. "Well, it's damn good to have the two of you back, even if you have brought home a stray. McAllister and I are going to have to call this through.

"I'd like to ask you to stay here. You're not under arrest, but I'd rather the three of you didn't go wandering around. There are toilets over there, and we'll get you anything you need, but for now, just stay put while we figure out what to do from here."

"Roger, that," Elvis replies.

"Okay," Liz says, feeling it's important to respond for herself.

Jameson and McAllister get up cautiously, taking pains not to scrape their chairs on the linoleum, or make any excess noise. Stella appears to ignore them. As they leave, Liz can hear them talking excitedly in the hallway.

For her part, Stella has found an indoor palm two feet high. Extraterrestrial bugs run along her outstretched arms, examining the leaves, trunk, soil, the pot itself. She's particularly interested in the soil.

Liz pokes at the food packets on the table.

"What's this?"

"They're MREs," Elvis replies. "Meals Ready to Eat."

As unappealing as they look, Liz is past caring. She tears one open and begins eating something that tastes vaguely like corned beef and sweet corn mixed with a limp, leafy vegetable that has long since lost its green. Whether it's spinach or okra, it tastes precisely how it appears—disgusting. Liz can't see this pre-cooked meal as desirable for anything other than the raw consumption of calories.

Elvis tosses one of the MREs across the floor toward Stella. The package slides over next to the palm. The alien probes the foil packaging, tearing it open and examining the contents for a few seconds, before turning back to the palm.

"Well, what do you know?" Elvis says to Liz. "MREs are now MRAs, Meals-Rejected-by-Aliens."

He laughs, taking a bite out of something that looks distinctly like cardboard.

CHAPTER 15: EVAC

Time drags. Elvis falls asleep. Liz isn't sure quite how he can sleep so soundly while sitting on a chair, but he rests his head on his elbows as he leans on the table, and starts snoring.

Liz watches Stella. The alien finds a spider web in the corner of the cafeteria. With a deft touch, she examines the silk threads, observing how the spider responds to various vibrations. Flies buzz around, Stella catches one with her lightning reflexes, snaring it between two pincer-like ends of her scarlet-red fronds. She holds the fly gently, so that the insect continues to beat its wings, trying to pull away. From her core, extraterrestrial insects stream upward toward the fly, examining it in detail.

After a few minutes, Stella places the fly in the spider's web and watches as the arachnoid scurries over to envelope it in silk. At least, '*watches*' is the best verb Liz can think of to describe the six or seven blades poised around the web, each with an extraterrestrial beetle at its tip, somehow observing what's going on.

There's a newspaper rack by the door. Liz picks up a glossy magazine adorned with images of the latest celebrities gaining fifteen minutes of fame.

"Forgive me," she says, placing the open magazine on the floor next to Stella. "Don't look too closely at the content, but this is how we communicate in written form, with words and pictures."

For the first time, Liz realizes the creature's multitasking, but not in the swiftly switching manner as a human would, giving only fleeting attention to several different activities in rapid succession.

The vast swirling arms on the creature continue their observation of the palm at one level, the spider on another, while several thin blades begin examining the magazine.

Liz steps back, wanting to observe how curious the alien is about the contents of the magazine with its two-dimensional images of three-dimensional people and scenes from nature. The creature picks up the magazine with the tips of her fronds, making Liz wonder how she achieves such a gecko-like grip.

Stella examines the magazine, more interested in the physical medium than the content. She probes the thickness of the paper, the binding on the spine, the dimensions of the page, the way pages rub together, but she only flicks through a couple of pages before putting it down.

"I know how you feel," Liz says, sitting back down.

Stella splits open several palm leaves—not vertically, as Liz would cut through a leaf with scissors. She splits them sideways, separating the upper and lower face of the leaf with surgical precision.

A swarm of insects at her heart moves in a stream out to her extremities, whether they're simply all taking a look, or retrieving samples for some kind of analysis back at the core, she's not sure. The alien's examining a level of biology most humans would walk past without a second thought.

Liz is tired. She rests her arms on the table, crossing them like Elvis, resting her head on the soft muscle of her forearm. For a few minutes, she stares lazily at the astonishing creature with its fronds reflecting the light around it, and its inner core a hive of activity. Slowly, she drifts off to sleep.

When she wakes, she wakes with a rush. Liz recognizes the roar immediately. Fighter jets are blazing past somewhere overhead.

"Hey," Elvis says, seeing she's awake.

Liz sits up. Her neck's sore, but she's surprised to find her head has been resting on a pillow. Someone must have seen her sleeping, and slipped a pillow beneath her head. Liz wipes saliva away from the corner of her lips. She's been dribbling in her sleep, making her feel a little embarrassed. There's a slight damp mark on the pillow, but Elvis doesn't seem to notice, or perhaps he doesn't care.

The position of the sun has changed. The shadows that had been so long in the early morning now cut back at a sharp angle. The day is hot. Fans turn on the ceiling, circulating the air, bringing no relief. It has to be about one in the afternoon.

"Sleep well?" Elvis asks.

"Like a rock," Liz replies. "Hard and uncomfortable."

Elvis smiles. He's changed into a white singlet, leaving his blood-encrusted jungle shirt hanging over one of the chair backs. A nice, neatly ironed shirt lies next to him, but in the heat of the day he hasn't put it on.

Although Elvis doesn't have sunglasses, he's slicked back his hair, having shaved to give his face a clean-cut look with sharply defined sideburns. The King is back. Sure, his arm still looks anemic and stunted, but he's as cocky as the day she met him. She wonders if he's used water, or perhaps vegetable oil from the kitchen in his neatly combed hair. A little oil would last longer, but would attract dust. He must've used water, she thinks. Either way, the rock god's ready to run out on stage.

Several rows of plants line one of the walls and the bench-top. They weren't there when Liz fell asleep. There are palms, ferns, flowering daisies and orchids—every plant that speaks of somewhere other than Africa.

"They must figured she likes botany," Liz says.

"I guess so. I was asleep. Stella seems to like flowers. They keep her amused."

Dirt has been tipped out on the floor and piled up neatly, like sand run through an hourglass. Several of the plants are lying on the ground, their roots exposed to the air. Stella seems enthralled by their diversity.

"Looks like she's been having fun," Liz says, trying to suppress a yawn.

"They brought you a change of clothes," Elvis says, gesturing to a set of Army fatigues and a towel sitting on the table. The clothes aren't just clean, they've been ironed. Liz picks them up; a shirt, pants, a nice new leather belt, a pair of white socks and some underwear. No bra, though, but that's no surprise as sizing isn't generic. The underwear isn't flattering, but it's clean.

Liz goes to the bathroom. She's stiff and sore. She uses a hand towel to wash at the basin. After changing, she takes some time to splash water over her face and through her hair. When she comes out, Elvis is eating a candy bar. He offers her one.

"The chocolate's melted, but if you're looking for a sugar hit, they're not bad."

Liz takes the candy bar, saying, "Thanks." She doesn't recognize the brand, but she's sure it isn't supposed to be so limp and mushy. Peeling back the wrapper, she struggles not to make a mess as she eats. Liz ends up licking her fingers, and places the grotesque-looking wrapper in one of the paper cups.

The sound of helicopters grows louder.

Liz stands and moves over by the broken windows. As she stares out across the city, a flight of four F-22s banks hard to one side. Their engines roar as they cruise low over the city. Explosions rumble. Smoke drifts above the distant buildings. A few seconds later the ground shakes to the rhythm of a distant explosion.

Jameson walks in. The sound of helicopters passing overhead rattles the building. The alien bristles.

"Easy, girl," Elvis says. Stella relaxes. Whatever connection the creature holds with Elvis, its trust is resolute. Although the thump of rotor blades continues to beat at the air, the creature goes back to comparing flowers. Troops slide down fast ropes thrown out of the helicopters, dropping onto rooftops surrounding the embassy.

Elvis walks over and stands by Liz near the window. "What's going on, Sarge? Those aren't US choppers. Those planes don't have US markings."

"South African Defense Force," Jameson replies.

"I thought the UN had pulled out of Malawi," Liz says.

"They had. That is, until they realized that the only alien left on the planet's sheltering in the US embassy."

"I don't understand," Liz replies. "What's happened?"

"The mothership has returned to its original position near the Moon. From what we can tell, they're preparing to leave. From what I've heard, this whole thing has been a clusterfuck from the start. Everyone's been so goddamn paranoid.

"People fear that which they don't understand, and fear leads to lousy decisions. The Russians and the Chinese were convinced the US was behind the floaters, that the floaters represent some kind of alien-human alliance led by the West. No one could believe NASA wasn't on top of communication with an alien fleet moving through our atmosphere. Truth's a bitch. The reality was, we were as surprised as everyone else.

"The Russians brought down any floater that crossed into their airspace, while the Chinese used tactical nukes against a bunch of floaters that entered the atmosphere over Mongolia. There was no way they were going to allow a bunch of aliens to drift over Beijing or Shanghai.

"The US was more tolerant. At least, it wasn't our official position to bring down the atmospheric craft, but there were plenty of rednecks willing to try. Once the floaters were down, the hunting began. There's been news footage showing US civilians parading the carcasses of dead aliens through the streets of Dallas-Fort Worth, Des Moines, Iowa, Oklahoma City, you name it.

"A couple of trigger happy pilots in the National Guard brought down a floater outside of DC. That the alien craft was passing almost fifty miles inland from the Capitol didn't matter. They complained about lost comms, and said they had to take the initiative. The media treated them like heroes. As far as the press was concerned, they were repelling the invasion. NASA pleaded for reason, but no one listened. They were too busy celebrating our independence from an alien war that never actually happened."

Liz is speechless.

"Apparently, your buddy with the red, wavy fronds can be pretty darn vicious when cornered, but these aliens are still no match for a gang of armed men motivated by sixty years of Hollywood hyperbole. It didn't take too long for word to get out that the alien's core is vulnerable. No armor. Can you imagine that? Going into battle without any armor?"

"They didn't think they were going into battle," Liz says, feeling indignant.

"Yeah, well, we fucked this up. We were pumped. Too many movies or ghost stories, I guess, but we were ready for them. Problem is, they weren't ready for us."

"So what's going to happen to Stella?" Elvis asks.

"I don't know," Jameson replies.

Liz doesn't believe him. There was a slight hesitation in his reply, just enough to cause her to doubt him.

Jameson must catch the look on her face, as he continues. "As soon as I confirmed we had a live alien in custody, control got passed from CENTCOM to NASA. There are a whole bunch of guys stateside dying to talk to you two—well, to you three."

"I won't let anything happen to her, Sarge." Elvis grits his teeth. He looks as though he could take on the entire US Army singlehanded.

"Easy, big guy. No one's going to hurt her. In fact, that's what all this is about. The South Africans have orders not to let anyone come within a mile of the embassy. They're going house to house, driving everyone out, pushing them back beyond the cordon. That fly-by, that's purely for show. Those birds don't need to come in that low. They're flexing muscle, sending a signal to the rebels that the gloves are off. There's two AC-130U Spooky gunships en route with orders to flatten anyone that so much as sticks their head out of a window with a weapon. Malawi's center stage. Lilongwe is going into lockdown."

"And your orders?" Liz asks.

"To keep you safe—all of you."

"Next steps?" Elvis asks.

Jameson smiles. He's been concealing something, but Elvis has called his bluff. Jameson would be lousy at poker.

"Look, don't worry. There's no conspiracy here. The UN's going into overdrive to protect your friend. No one's going to let anything happen to her."

"Where are they taking her?" Elvis asks coldly. Liz gets the impression Elvis knows what's happening, perhaps not the specifics, but he understands the military mindset. NASA might have executive control, but operational control has to lie with a military general somewhere, and Liz doesn't even want to think about the political machinations of the United Nations complicating things further.

Jameson says, "There's no secret base at Area 51 or anything like that. The powers that be simply want to get the alien into a secure environment."

"*Where?*" Elvis demands.

"The USS William Lawrence is steaming down from Dar El Salam into the straits between Mozambique and Madagascar, while the Ronald Reagan has turned back from Diego Garcia, and is heading toward Dar El Salam to provide air support."

Liz cries out, saying. "You're going to put her on a goddamn warship? Are you mad?" She can't help herself.

"Think about it," Jameson replies. "She's in the middle of a war zone. It's the safest option."

Liz shakes her head.

"They're sending in an Osprey to take you to the USS William Lawrence."

"What if we don't want to go?" Liz demands, her hands resting defiantly on her hips. The lieutenant stands behind Jameson. He's quiet, letting Jameson do the talking.

"No one's going to force you to do anything," Jameson replies, his hands out in a gesture of friendship. "Look, Liz. It's me. You know me. Remember back in the village? There's nothing I wouldn't do to keep you out of harm's way. I'm not going to do anything that would hurt you, or Elvis, or this creature. Sure, I've got orders but, honestly, if I thought they were in any way belligerent I wouldn't hesitate to fight back."

He breathes deeply.

"Listen, they're flying in a NASA specialist from India. He should get to the Lawrence around the same time you guys arrive on deck—at least, that's the plan."

"The plan?" Liz asks, raising an eyebrow.

"Liz, we've got to get you out of this country."

Liz doesn't like plans being made without her input. Elvis might be used to that kind of authoritarian treatment, but she isn't.

"So you decided to throw us on a helicopter?"

Jameson throws his hands wide in mock surrender. "What would you do, Liz? Where could you go? Everyone knows you killed

Adan. You think the rebels will allow you and your friend safe passage? What about government troops? They'll sell you out in a heartbeat with the price that's on your head. Even if you could get Stella out of the city, where would you go? Where on Earth would she be safe?"

"So what's your plan?" she asks.

"Liz," Jameson replies, "the plan is to get you safely into NASA's hands. The William Lawrence is simply a meeting point. Trust me."

"I trust you," Liz replies. "The problem is, I don't trust anyone beyond you."

"You have to. You and Elvis have done something remarkable, something incredible. You've saved the life of one of these creatures at a time when everyone else has been shortsighted and acted out of fear. Now, the world's rallying around you. You've got to trust those that can help you."

Liz sighs, looking deep into his eyes.

"Do you trust them?"

Jameson nods.

Liz wants to believe him, but with each step the situation slips further out of her control. What control has she ever really had? None. What can she and Elvis do with a creature from another world? Where could they go? Where would be safe? There's nowhere left to run. They've escaped Adan's men, now they have to trust someone. They can't run forever.

"Stella ain't going nowhere without me," Elvis growls. It's a double negative, but Liz appreciates the emphasis.

Jameson nods, providing his consent. He looks at Liz.

"We've got to get her home," she says.

Again, Jameson nods.

Liz glances at the creature with her twisting fronds. She suspects Stella knows some of the terms they've used in their discussion, at least those she and Elvis have taught her, but Liz doubts the alien understands what's been said. If the creature understands, it doesn't let on as it continues to examine the plants.

Elvis walks over toward the alien, saying, "Home, Stella. We're going to take you home."

"Home," the creature says, still using Liz's voice. It's only then Liz notices the soldier holding a small camera as he stands in the doorway, capturing their conversation and the creature's reactions on video. This will make for interesting viewing.

"Yes. Home," Elvis replies, running his hand over the alien's glassy fronds as though they were sheaves of wheat. The creature towers over him, reaching to within a foot of the ceiling. The edge of its tentacles appear sharp. If Liz didn't know better, she'd expect to see Elvis withdraw a bleeding hand.

Someone whispers in Jameson's ear. He turns to the two of them, saying "We've got a Ac-130 Spectre on station, with the Osprey on approach. We need to get to the rooftop helipad. I don't want to hang around. Even with all this firepower bearing down on the city, I don't want to tempt a fool with an RPG."

"Green light, Stella. It's time to take you home," Elvis says as he grabs his starched shirt from the table, carrying it like a jacket over his shoulder. He follows Jameson through the doorway, out into the hallway. The alien doesn't hesitate. Liz follows behind the creature. The cameraman beside her leans down to get a long shot.

As they cross the reception area, Liz is aware of eyes watching from all sides. No one on Earth has ever seen an alien like this, at least not in a natural, unthreatening situation. There's an understandable level of curiosity. This is the stuff of legends.

Jameson leads them up a broad staircase, along a first floor corridor, then waits behind a metal fire door overlooking a rooftop helipad.

"How do you think she's going to take the noise of a helicopter?" Liz asks. "And what about the disorienting motion associated with flight?"

"How did she take the truck ride?" Jameson asks in reply.

Liz shrugs. There's a world of difference, though he doesn't seem to think so.

Looking through the small glass panel in the door, Liz sees the Osprey come in hard. The pilot wastes no time putting the craft down. The rear ramp lowers and a single soldier jogs out—the loadmaster.

Jameson opens the door. The noise in the corridor jumps from that of a library to a heavy metal rock concert. Unlike the pilot of the Osprey that touched down in the village of Chikangawa, this guy isn't powering down its engines—they sound like a freight train roaring past.

The alien bristles and begins moving back toward Liz, away from the door.

"You're scaring her," Liz yells.

"We have to go," Jameson yells back.

"Green light, Stella. Green light," Elvis pleads, but the creature ignores him.

Liz knows she has to do something, but the prospect of being skewered by glistening blades terrifies her. She drops to one knee, making herself small. Fronds lash out in front of her. She has visions of being shredded like Bosco, but something similar transpired when the factory door was opened. Stella responded to her back then, not more than twelve hours ago. Liz closes her eyes.

"I know," she says softly, unable to hear her own voice over the rush of noise, but she knows Stella can hear her. Liz has long suspected Stella understands far more than she lets on. "I know you're afraid. I'm afraid too."

In the factory, using the same terms in different ways helped Liz communicate basic concepts. She hopes that same approach will work now.

"We're all afraid, but we need to get you home. We need to get you away from here." She opens her eyes. Several of the insects sit on the end of the fronds closest to her face, swaying gently before her, examining her. "I know you've been hurt. We all have, but don't be afraid. You need to trust us—we're taking you home. It's a green light, Stella. Green light."

"Stella," Elvis calls out over the howling wind. "Green light, baby. We're taking you home."

"Home," the creature replies.

Slowly, the alien moves back toward Elvis.

Liz watches as the tiny creatures nearest to her remain on the trailing fronds. They leap from one swaying, spindly appendage to another as the spiky alien apparatus rolls away from her, keeping their focus on Liz, ensuring she continues to follow them.

Elvis stands on the tailgate of the Osprey, calling out over the noise of the engines. Stella stays beside Liz, following her onboard. No sooner are they in the cargo bay than the Osprey lifts off. The loadmaster closes the ramp as the embassy disappears beneath them. The last people she sees beyond the ramp are Jameson and Smithy, waving.

Elvis moves up through the empty belly of the craft, taking a seat near one of the few windows in the fuselage. Stella moves to his side. Liz is perplexed by the unpredictable behavior of this complex alien creature. She staggers through the aircraft as it rises, holding on to webbing hanging from the sidewalls, struggling to keep her balance. These are clearly combat pilots. Comfort isn't a concern. Although they need to be safe, it isn't as if anyone on the ground knows they're carrying an alien. Her stomach's queasy. She wonders whether she should ask the loadmaster for a barf bag. Moving hand over hand through the cargo hold, she sits opposite Elvis. There are airsick bags in a pocket on the wall. She grabs a bunch, shoving them in her pockets.

The loadmaster stays down by the ramp, and Liz understands why. The alien half-envelops Elvis. Stella anchors herself, wrapping her scarlet fronds around one of the seats, and some webbing high on the side of the craft, but Stella's so close to Elvis that she covers most of his chest. Elvis isn't bothered by the swirl of blades drifting past him. Bugs swarm over his chest, around his neck, and down his anemic left arm. Liz is fascinated. She wants to get up close, to watch what they're doing, but their magic, for lack of a better word, probably isn't visible beyond the microscopic level, perhaps even at a molecular level.

Elvis points at his head. He slips on a pair of headphones with a small microphone attached. Liz looks around and grabs a pair from the wall. There's a knob on the side. She twists it and the whine of the engines vanishes.

"They're noise canceling," Elvis says. Although she sees his lips move, the sound of his voice comes through the headphones as though he was standing behind her. "You've got three channels. Cargo hold, cockpit, and air traffic control, although we can only talk on the cargo loop."

"Aha," Liz replies, rapidly becoming accustomed to the tinny sound of her own voice echoing back to her. "This is cool. I could get used to this." Normally, as an NGO, all she ever got were earplugs.

"How does it feel?" she asks, gesturing toward his arm, which is now a seething mass of tiny creatures.

"Like a massage, a real deep one."

"Huh."

"Flight time's three hours, twenty minutes," the loadmaster says. Liz gets the impression he's just letting them know he's on the cargo loop more than anything else. Privacy's rare in the military.

The door to the cockpit opens slightly. Someone begins to step through into the cargo hold, but they get a good look at the huge alien apparently devouring a soldier, and change their mind. The door slams shut. A few seconds later, another voice speaks over the cargo loop.

"Is everything okay back there?"

"We're good," Elvis replies, winking at Liz.

"Roger that, will relay to command."

There's a pause for a moment before the pilot adds, "We'll monitor the cargo channel. If an emergency arises and you need us to put down, let me know."

"We'll be fine," Elvis says.

Liz is doing her best not to laugh. What for them has become commonplace must seem like something out of a horror movie. *The poor pilots. They're probably half-expecting the alien to come tearing through the cockpit door to smear their brains all over the windshield.* All those crazy alien movies haven't helped.

Elvis sees her trying to suppress her laughter. He holds his finger up to his lips. She mouths, "I'm sorry."

Liz has to say something, not just to keep from laughing, but to help the pilots understand. To remain quiet would be cruel. She tries not to laugh as she speaks, but it's difficult to convey a sense of seriousness.

"Ah, please don't be alarmed. It must look awfully disconcerting, seeing our interstellar guest for the first time, but she's as gentle as a lamb."

It's a lie, but what harm will yet one more white lie do? Hearing it from both a woman and a doctor should soothe their nerves a little.

"Roger that."

Liz is curious. "So," she says. "Did you guys draw the short straw for this mission?"

"No ma'am. This is voluntary."

"That's brave of you."

"Or stupid," the unseen officer replies. Liz likes him already, and laughs somewhat politely in reply, just enough to sound civil.

The flight levels out, so she stands, looking out of the small porthole on the side of the craft. She has to pull on the curled audio cord leading to her headset to move over enough to get a good look.

"How high are we?"

"Twelve thousand feet."

Although the window's small, if Liz moves around she can see a wider field of view. Above them, several fighter jets sit off in the distance, heading in the same direction. There's another helicopter to one side, slightly ahead of them. She catches a faint glimpse of another craft from the edge of the window.

"They're not taking any chances, are they?"

"No, ma'am."

The jungle canopy rolls over the hills, smothering the land in a sea of green. A large lake passes beneath the Osprey—its blue waters look serene. In the distance, the ocean looms large, an abrupt end to Africa. Liz stands there for a while, watching as the shoreline approaches. She wants to talk, but for the pilots and the loadmaster any conversation's limited, while she gets the feeling Elvis doesn't want to talk openly. He seems happy to freak everyone out.

She sits down again, slouching. Before long the rhythmic pulse through the fuselage causes her to drift off to sleep. It feels as though no sooner has she closed her eyes than someone's saying, "We're five minutes out." Several hours have passed.

The headphones hurt her ears. Like everything military, they're designed to be functional, not comfortable. She lifts them away from her ears for a moment, wanting to free her head from their vice-like grip, but the deafening sound of the engines overrules her discomfort so she puts them back on. Five minutes can't come soon enough.

Liz is tempted to get up and watch the landing out the window, but that isn't the smartest move, and besides, what would she see? Nothing but the ocean. Looking sideways, she won't even see the ship until they touch down.

A couple of minutes later, the pilot says, "Fifty meters."

The Osprey slows its descent, hovering as it picks its spot for landing. The wheels touch down gently, and Liz breathes a sigh of relief as the engines power down.

Stella has been quiet throughout the trip, but during the descent the alien must realize they've arrived, as the tiny insects swarming over Elvis return to the bulbous heart of the spindly creature. Elvis looks at his arm. It appears entirely normal, as though nothing had ever happened to him. Liz shakes her head in admiration. There's a lot she could learn from Stella.

The engines drop to a whine, and Liz removes her headphones. The rear ramp lowers. Liz can already feel the gentle sway of the ship beneath them as it rolls through the swell of the open ocean. The smell of sea spray fills the air.

Several officers stand on the deck well beyond the Osprey's open tailgate, but Liz's eyes are drawn to the film crew. There are three camera operators.

"Green light," Elvis says, getting up and putting his shirt on.

Liz and Elvis walk side by side down the ramp, shielding Stella, but it's a token gesture. Out of the corner of her eye, Liz watches Stella edging forward behind them, wary of a new environment. Can she swim? This could be terrifying for her.

The flight deck's mostly empty, but further along the ship, sailors work with a crane, wrapping chains around some piece of heavy equipment.

The welcoming committee gives them plenty of room to step down onto the deck.

"I'm Captain Helen Lovell," one of the officers says over the sound of the dying engines. "This is my XO, James Davidson."

Liz is pleasantly surprised to meet the female captain of a warship. Both she and Elvis introduce themselves. Liz shakes hands with Captain Lovell, while Elvis salutes.

Stella keeps her distance on the deck of the ship with its rough, painted-grit surface designed to keep sailors from slipping in the wet. Stella looks magnificent against the drab, battleship grays surrounding her. Her fronds glisten in the sunlight.

Liz hopes the pleasantries put the alien at ease. In shaking Davidson's hand, she can feel his fingers trembling. It must be nerve-wracking to put on an air of civility with a massive alien creature looming blood red behind them.

The film crew are wearing NASA polo shirts.

"Dr. Anish Ambar," says an older man, speaking with an Indian accent. His face is kind, his skin a soft shade of brown. He's impeccably groomed, with a neatly trimmed mustache and short black hair. Soft grey highlights pepper his mustache, but his hair still retains its youthful hue. "Director of Astrobiology with SETI, based out of Mumbai."

"It's a pleasure," Liz replies. She starts to introduce herself, but Dr. Ambar continues speaking.

"Dr. Bower, we're deeply indebted to you and your colleague for preserving the life of this remarkable creature."

Liz turns, "Dr. Ambar, this is Stella. Stella, Dr. Ambar." There's a nice inversion in a formal introduction. Liz hopes Stella picks up on that, with the repetition making it clear these are names.

Over the past day, Liz has observed how the alien alters its height by flexing or softening the blades that carry it onward. Here, on the deck of a US warship, the creature raises up on the tips of its blades, giving it a height of ten feet. Its Medusa-like head of scarlet fronds sways with the motion of the ship.

The cameras are rolling, catching footage of the majestic red blades and the swarm of creatures at Stella's heart. One of the cameramen steps out to get a clear shot of the alien. Stella reacts, bristling, with her fronds stiffening like sword blades.

"You're going to have to put those away," Elvis says. "She may think they're weapons."

"Of course," Dr. Ambar replies. The cameramen don't have to be told—they take the cameras off their shoulders, holding them next to their thighs, still recording, but without appearing threatening. Lovell and Davidson look nervous.

Stella ambles closer to Elvis and Liz.

"Easy, girl," Elvis says, touching her sharp spear tips. Stella responds, with her fronds wrapping gently around his hand like leather straps. She relaxes her legs as well, allowing the fronds that hold her up to flex and settle on the deck. The NASA film crew catches the interaction on video. Dr. Ambar's amazed.

Captain Lovell says, "We've been instructed to provide you with anything you need. Food, water, a change of clothing, access to a telephone or the internet. We're at your disposal."

Liz is a little overwhelmed. She says, "We're fine."

"Where's the bathroom?" Elvis asks.

Captain Lovell points to a steel door with a high lip set well above the deck, saying, "You'll find access to the head through there. Second door on the left." Just the mention of a bathroom has Liz suddenly bursting to relieve herself. She berates herself for not being first to ask.

"Stay here, Stella," Elvis says. "I'll be right back."

He has his arm out, gesturing for the alien to remain, but the creature doesn't understand, and moves toward the door, following him.

"It's okay, Stella," Liz says, reaching out and brushing her hands against the slick, red fronds. To her surprise, they wrap around her wrist. Stella seems nervous about losing sight of Elvis, and Liz can feel the fronds tightening as Elvis closes the door behind him. How do you explain going to the bathroom to a creature from another planet? All she can say is, "He's coming back."

Those words seem to register with the alien. The creature must remember her using similar terms when Elvis left the warehouse to get the truck.

"It's fascinating to observe how you two interact with the alien," Dr. Ambar says. "She feels a dependency on you guys, that much is clear."

Liz says, "She gets stressed when she doesn't understand what's going on."

Dr. Ambar says, "Stress, fear, trust. I never thought I'd see such distinctly human emotions in an extraterrestrial intelligence."

"I guess they're universal constants," Liz says.

Elvis returns, so Liz excuses herself to use the bathroom as well. The inside of the ship is utilitarian. Cables run in bundles close to the roof, disappearing into the bulkhead at points. Pipes marked with water, waste, coolant, and fire suppressant run along one wall leading down to a steel door designed to seal the compartment in the event of an emergency. Liz feels lost even though there's a clearly marked sign for the bathrooms.

When she returns to the outside deck, she notices a few of the crew removing a safety rail behind the Osprey. She catches the end of a conversation between Elvis, Dr. Ambar, and Captain Lovell.

"If you'll excuse us," Captain Lovell says. "We need to get this deck cleared and report in to the task force. The alien craft's no more than seventy nautical miles out, and I want to make sure we're not in breach of our obligations."

Both Liz and Elvis start to speak, stunned. Elvis lets Liz continue.

"I'm sorry, could you explain?"

"Dr. Ambar?" Lovell says, stepping back. She and Davidson walk briskly away. They climb a set of stairs leading from the flight deck to the comm tower. From there, they waste no time disappearing inside the bowels of the ship.

"It's okay," Dr. Ambar replies, seeing the concern on Liz's face. "We should be fine here, they just want to dump the Osprey."

"Dump the Osprey?" Liz says, confused.

She looks back. Several sailors dressed in chemical warfare suits are working with a low profile, heavy-duty tractor to push the Osprey toward the stern. The flight crew from the Osprey stand to one side, watching as the squat-looking vehicle with beefy tires pushes on the wheels of their aircraft. One wheel on the Osprey slips, crashing with a thud on the edge of the landing deck, and Stella flexes.

"It's all right," Elvis says, remaining in physical contact with the creature to provide some reassurance.

The tractor repositions itself, pushing on the front wheel of the aircraft. The Osprey plunges overboard, disappearing into the ocean with a splash.

The NASA film crew discreetly records Stella's reaction from several angles, watching as she again bristles defensively at the sharp crack of noise and the motion of the tractor.

Liz looks down the length of the ship as crewmen and women dump various pieces of military hardware over the edge of the USS William Lawrence. Although she doesn't recognize most of the equipment, she does catch sight of a platform-mounted Gatling gun. It's the size of a compact car, with a large steel plate at its base, and some kind of radar dome set near multiple gun barrels. The crew releases a chain, and it plunges into the sea, disappearing beneath the waves in a burst of spray.

"What's going on?" Elvis asks.

"We've been in contact with the mothership," Dr. Ambar says. "They're coming to get her."

Liz doesn't know whether to be excited for Stella or wary.

"You're using her as bait?" Elvis asks, defensive.

"Not as bait," Dr. Ambar replies in his Bombay accent. "She's a peace offering. We are trying to show this interstellar alien species that this was a mistake. Returning Stella is a goodwill gesture, something to let them know we're sorry for what's transpired. We're making amends. This is a repatriation."

"But you've been in contact with them?" Liz asks. "You can talk to them?"

"Not so much talk as make declarations. We think they may understand more than they let on when they speak back."

"They talk back?"

"Yes. However, their replies are often just a bunch of nouns thrown together. There's no grammar or syntax, just blunt nouns and the odd verb. After we made it clear one of their kind had survived, they sent a floater. We observed the craft enter our atmosphere about two hours ago, over water rather than land."

Dr. Ambar points behind the ship. "The airspace around us is clear of any human aircraft for over two hundred nautical miles. We should get our first glimpse of the rescue craft from somewhere over there. In the meantime, the Lawrence is under orders to demilitarize. They're throwing all their weaponry overboard along with anything that could be mistaken for a weapon." He pauses for a moment. His voice sounds introspective, sad. "They're leaving. They're abandoning the petulant children of Earth."

"I don't understand? Why would they leave?" Elvis asks.

"They said they have what they came for."

"What *did* they come for?" Liz asks.

"We don't know. We were hoping you might be able to help us figure that out. I have my own ideas, but nothing concrete. If they came to examine our intelligence, they've surely concluded we're barbarians. We've ruined our first contact with life from beyond this small orb."

"What were the pods?" Liz asks. "Did you get to examine any of them?"

"Yes," Dr. Ambar replies. "But they broke down rapidly in our highly oxygenated atmosphere.

"We were able to examine some of the organic residue. In nature, there are roughly twenty or so amino acids that make up the bulk of the proteins we observe, but we know of over five hundred amino acids in all. These alien creatures and their pods incorporate roughly three hundred of these acids in their biology, making them distinct from any life form on Earth." He adjusts his glasses as he speaks.

"It's no surprise, of course, after all, they're aliens, but it rules out any kind of panspermia relationship between us." Liz nods.

Dr. Ambar continues, saying, "We think the pods were probes. A team of researchers out of MIT detected a faint electromagnetic signal from one of them, and was able to observe the signal change as the pod was exposed to different kinds of organic substances. Even something as simple as the motion of someone entering the room was enough to elicit a unique transmission. The probes appear to have been sampling Earth."

"So they were like sonar buoys?" Elvis asks.

"Yes. They weren't seeding Earth, they were surveying our biology, gathering information on our ecosystems in much the same way as we'd conduct a survey of life in a rainforest. The pods were designed to be passive, non-intrusive, breaking down rapidly once their work was complete. That's only my idea, but I think that's why they're leaving. The survey's complete."

"That makes no sense to me," Elvis says. "They've come all this way—why leave so soon?"

"Look at us," Dr. Ambar says. "We've been acting like spoiled brats. We've been throwing tantrums, carrying on like they owe us something. They owe us nothing. Our focus has been so insular, so egotistical. Earth is all about us—humans. Maybe, just maybe, they disagree.

"We can rage all we want, but they don't owe us anything. As hard as it is to accept, there's a lesson here for humanity: the universe doesn't revolve around us."

Dr. Ambar steps slowly past Elvis, reaching out toward Stella.

"We killed hundreds of them. We're not even sure how in most cases. Once the decay process starts, their bodies are gone within days, leaving nothing but trace elements. Most of them died in the crashes. Those that survived were hunted. Our bullets never so much as scratched their frames. So curious."

Stella allows Dr. Ambar to touch her stiff legs as they spread wide across the deck to keep her stable.

"This specimen's the first one I've heard of that's docile."

"Oh," Elvis replies. "Docile isn't a word I'd use to describe Stella. You don't want to see her when she gets angry."

"It isn't anger," Liz says. "It was fear. When we first met, she was afraid of us."

"Fear?" Dr. Ambar says, somewhat lost in thought at the concept.

Hundreds of tiny creatures stream down the alien's fronds, touching Dr. Ambar's fingers briefly before retreating again.

"Magnificent," he says.

One of the camera crew standing next to Dr. Ambar says, "I'm picking up oscillating shades in both infrared and ultraviolet."

Dr. Ambar and Liz look down at the camera operator's screen as he holds his camera low. The screen's divided into quarters, with false color representing the various spectra. The patterns differ from each other, and from those they're seeing in the visible spectrum.

"Perhaps they speak using light—like cuttlefish?" Ambar suggests.

Liz shrugs, unsure whether any terrestrial comparisons apply.

Elvis points at the horizon. "They're here."

CHAPTER 16: GOODBYE

A floater is visible on the horizon, moving parallel to the USS William Lawrence. Even at twenty miles, the bulbous head is apparent, as are the trailing tentacles.

"I want footage from multiple angles," Ambar says as Captain Lovell steps back out onto the flight deck. "James, get up to the bridge. Stay on the wide-angle as long as you can. Stevens, head to the stern. Campelli, you stay with me."

The camera crew splits up.

Lovell walks over, saying, "We're currently heading due north at 18 knots with a slight headwind. We'll hold this course until the rendezvous' complete. The alien vessel's gaining at a steady rate so I don't see any problem with this bearing. Do we have any idea if, or how the craft will land?"

Dr. Ambar and Liz look at each other bewildered.

"We're 509 feet in length, displacing 6,800 tons light, with a total displacement of 9,000 tons when fully laden. With our current loading we have roughly 1200 tons leeway. Do you have any idea how heavy that floater is, or if it'll touch down in its entirety?"

Liz bites her lip. The prospect of being accidentally sunk by the weight of the alien craft hadn't crossed her mind. She just assumed everything would be okay.

"I'm sure we'll be fine, Captain," Dr. Ambar replies. Liz knows that tone of voice, that's the *'I've no bloody idea, but I'm in charge, so it will be fine!'* pseudo-authoritative tone she's used so many times before as a doctor. It's a bluff, the bravado of a mind confident of tackling whatever may come, only in this circumstance it's misplaced, and they both know it.

Captain Lovell doesn't question Dr. Ambar's vague assessment. In a bland, matter-of-fact tone, she says, "We have an escort of two destroyers, the USS Dewey and the USS Sampson, but they're over the horizon—fifty nautical miles to our north-east, ready to render assistance if needed. My crew's on standby for evacuation. If the order is given to abandon ship, you'll be given life jackets and directed to a life raft."

Dr. Ambar nods, saying, "Understood. Thank you, Captain."

Lovell excuses herself.

Stella has spotted the floater. Her core lights up with rolling patterns, glistening in the sun.

"Green light," the creature says, and Dr. Ambar has a double take, looking at both the alien, and Liz, recognizing Liz's voice. She smiles. Dr. Ambar seems to want some kind of explanation. Liz shrugs her shoulders.

"Yes," Elvis replies. "Green light. You're going home, Stella. Home."

"Home."

The alien's fronds no longer wave with the breeze, they stiffen momentarily, but not in a manner that's hostile. It's as though the creature's stretching, then relaxing. The core of the alien continues to display an astonishing variety of patterns, moving in a manner reminiscent of a kaleidoscope.

Liz, Elvis and Dr. Ambar stand with the camera operator, watching Stella as she scurries around the deck of the warship in excitement.

Stella can't stay still. Liz is surprised to see her childlike excitement. Perhaps they're more alike than she thought. Could it be that intelligent life everywhere experiences the same basic emotions? Fear, excitement, joy, sorrow and satisfaction? These are primal parts of animal intelligence. As much as she likes to think of herself as coldly logical, she knows that's a myth of her own choosing—the Mr. Spock persona is as fictitious as the Starship Enterprise. Those that consider themselves logical are blind to the emotions that drive them. Here, she can see the same sense of effervescence she knows she'll feel setting foot in England again, or upon seeing her mom and dad. It's the thrill of being alive.

Stella's fronds slap at the deck. She races from one side to another, back and forth, zigging and zagging. For the first time, her fronds change color, pulsing from red to blue, passing through every hue in the rainbow.

"She's as excited as a puppy dog," Elvis says.

"We've got so much to learn," Dr. Ambar says.

The camera operator moves to one side, getting a shot of them, with Stella racing around on the deck as the floater looms in the distance. Liz finds herself wondering who's watching—human and alien. Dozens of faces line the portholes behind them, each vying for a clear view, with camera phones held up to capture this extraordinary moment. Is this encounter being broadcast live? Liz feels as if she should be doing something other than just standing there.

"Isn't she beautiful?" Dr. Ambar asks.

"Yes, she is," Liz replies, not having thought of Stella in such terms before. Dr. Ambar awakens the sense of awe she feels when she first saw the alien spacecraft in orbit above the atmosphere.

They watch Stella as the floater drifts to within a mile, slowly moving closer to the William Lawrence. Liz marvels at the brilliant plumage displayed by the alien vessel. The extended bladder keeps the floater buoyant in Earth's atmosphere. The rich purples, yellows, and reds stretching across the alien bladder are accentuated by the sun as it sits low on the horizon.

The organic craft paces itself so as to reach the warship without overshooting. By the time the floater's overhead, it matches both their speed and direction. As the floater reaches the Lawrence, it descends, coming down from several hundred feet. This is a larger craft than those Liz saw in Africa, dwarfing the warship.

The wind howls. Sea spray hangs in the air. The warship rolls slightly with the swell. All eyes are on the tubular proboscis descending from beneath the floater.

To Liz, the proboscis looks like a human trachea. There are dozens of what appear to be cartilage rings, evenly spaced, providing the proboscis with structure, allowing it to form a tunnel large enough to drive a car inside. There's no differentiation between the base, sides, or roof of this windpipe-like structure. It looks the same from any orientation. Liz wonders about its function when it isn't rescuing stranded aliens.

"Here we go," Dr. Ambar says.

The underside of the floater rests on the mast extending above the bridge of the USS William Lawrence. If the captain wasn't already freaked out, she will be now. Liz watches as the radar domes on either side of the mast disappear into a thick mat of blood red organic matter. As the proboscis extends down to the lower flight deck, the sound of metal groaning under the weight of the floater fills the air. Liz feels the warship shift beneath her feet, slewing slightly in the ocean.

The proboscis reaches within a few feet of the deck of the warship. Stella races up to it, clambering onboard. Within a second, she's gone. The proboscis rests on the deck, oozing a sticky, transparent saliva. There's no goodbye, no acknowledgment of all they've been through, no emotional parting. Stella's gone.

Dr. Ambar steps back. Elvis and Liz remain where they are, ten feet from the fleshy appendage. Liz isn't sure what the alien craft is waiting for, but the seconds pass, slowly turning into minutes. Elvis looks at her but doesn't speak. Words fail both of them. Looking down the empty alien trachea, Liz sees what seems to be mucus lining the inside of the fleshy tube.

Over the howl of the whirling wind, she hears two words, "Green light."

Stella rolls down the inside of the proboscis. She moves around the tunnel, racing through the trachea in a corkscrew motion that takes her over the ceiling several times.

"Green light. Understand? Green light."

"What do you—" Elvis never completes his sentence. Like Liz, he knows what she means. The alien creature wheels before the two of them, its gooey fronds gently slapping at her arms, and raking across his chest. Again, Stella cries, "Understand. Green light. Understand."

Liz hesitates. Stella rocks around behind her, gently urging her on with her fronds softly tapping her back and shoulders.

"Understand," the creature says again.

From behind her, Dr. Ambar says, "Go."

Elvis is already walking forward. He reaches out with one hand and steps inside the proboscis, saying, "It smells like dirty socks." Looking at the slimy substance sticking to his hand, he adds, "This is going to get messy." Liz swallows. "Come on," Elvis yells, already clambering inside the organic alien structure. "What are you afraid of?"

"How about—everything?" Liz says, to which Elvis laughs.

"What's the worst that could happen?" he asks as she walks forward to stand in front of the proboscis. Mucus oozes around her boots.

"We could die."

"We could," he agrees.

Why did he have to agree? He's not helping. He's supposed to say something encouraging.

Liz stands before the alien structure, realizing that with one step, she'll move from her world to another—from the coarse, gritty, battleship-grey flight deck of the USS William Lawrence into a living creature that has traversed the stars. She takes a step forward, feeling the spongy inside of an alien trachea. The soft squish beneath her boots is a stark contrast to the firm deck of the warship.

Liz reaches out, leaning to one side so she can use the proboscis for balance, and steps into the creature. It doesn't feel right, to be standing on soft tissue. Everything about what she's doing screams, "No!" This is the stuff of nightmares. She wants to turn and run, but Elvis is right. There's nothing to fear. There's no other way to know anything about these exquisite creatures than to venture onto their spaceship. This is an honor Dr. Ambar would relish.

No sooner has Liz's other foot left the deck of the warship than Stella rushes past, twirling across the side, then the roof of the floater's windpipe-like tubular structure.

The proboscis lifts off from the Lawrence. Liz looks back. She watches as the warship drops away. Dr. Ambar waves farewell as naturally as he might to a relative leaving on a plane. Liz has never been one for heights and has to fight a sense of panic. It's the loss of control, the loss of any certainty that upsets her. Within seconds, the Lawrence looks like a toy boat rocking in the vast blue ocean. The Lawrence recedes until all that's visible is the wake spreading out in a V-shape across the water.

"Come on," Elvis says, calling to her.

The opening of the proboscis begins to close like a sphincter, forcing her to move on. The cartilage-like rings are twenty feet apart, with a gooey sludge in between. Liz struggles in the soft tissue. It's hard to keep her footing, and she falls to her knees. Thick mucus covers her pants.

"Well," she says, accepting a sticky hand from Elvis to help her stand. "Things could be worse."

"That's the spirit," Elvis replies.

For all her bravado, she's trembling. The distance between the fleshy rings in the tube shorten, contracting as the proboscis is withdrawn into the alien floater, reducing the distance they have to travel to reach the underside of the creature.

"We're not being eaten alive or anything like that—are we?" Liz asks, trying to laugh at herself.

"Just like Jonah and the whale," Elvis says, not helping.

The proboscis shakes, but not as a building would in an earthquake. The floater seems to be choking, perhaps dry heaving. The rings contract to the point they're touching, allowing the two of them to step over the sludge as they make their way into the bowels of the alien floater. Another fleshy, sphincter-like opening allows them to step out of the proboscis and into the body of the creature.

"Oh, wow," Liz says, looking at the vast open bladder above them. In some ways, it's like looking up into a hot air balloon, only the skin of the creature is semitransparent. The enormous bladder is colored in soft blues, pinks, yellows and ruddy hues. "It's like being inside a soap bubble."

Tiny insects swarm around them, dominating the lower walls, racing back and forth in what seem to be impromptu highways darting in different directions. Fluid pulses through looks like massive arteries.

Stella says, "Understand." It's neither an admonition nor a question, rather a statement—almost a greeting the way she uses it.

"Understand," Elvis replies.

Stella leads them through the inside of the massive creature. For Liz, it's like walking on a trampoline. The ground beneath her is spongy and irregular. Elvis follows the spindly alien as it moves toward the front of the craft. Several other 'Stellas' wheel past moving in the other direction. Liz can't tell them apart.

The floater begins to pulsate, surging up into the stratosphere. The bladder contracts in much the same way a high-altitude balloon would, becoming almost shriveled in appearance as they climb. Each pulse drives them on toward outer space. The strength and frequency of each pulse increases, and Liz has to time her steps to avoid falling.

The front of the craft is transparent, providing a view over the ocean. Already, the curvature of Earth is visible. The sky darkens, even though it's still daylight. The sun, though, is close to setting. Clouds dot the sky below them, casting long shadows across the ocean.

As they stand there in awe of an entire planet receding beneath their feet, bugs begin swarming around them. At first, Liz ignores the tiny creatures, but after a few seconds it becomes apparent she's their focus.

"You okay?" Elvis asks, seeing the concern on her face.

"Yeah, fine." Liar.

Thousands of aliens begin clambering over their boots and up the outside of their trousers. Insects claw at her skin. Liz shudders, overcome by an impulsive desire to rid herself of these creatures.

"Easy," Elvis says, taking her hand. "It's okay. Go with it."

"Understand?" Stella says, but this time her inflection makes it a question.

"Understand," Liz replies, determined to overcome her reservations.

"I understand," Elvis replies, being far more relaxed than her. Liz swallows the lump in her throat. He's experienced this before, when Stella rebuilt his arm, but for her, the prospect of being devoured by what seems to be millions of cockroaches is utterly repulsive. Elvis squeezes her hand, saying, "It's going to be okay. Just relax."

Relax? The horde of insects clambers up to her waist, burying her legs in a mountain of tiny creatures. She breathes deeply, holding her hands out, dreading the approaching swarm.

"Is this—normal?"

"I've been through this before," Elvis says. "We're going to be fine. Deep breaths."

"Deep breaths," she says, pursing her lips and exhaling.

"Look into the distance," he says. "Try to think of something else. It's like a trip to the dentist—a little discomfort, a few sharp pricks, and it'll be over before you know it."

Liz says, "Over? What will be over? No. I don't think I want to know."

"It's going to be all right," Elvis says, but he doesn't know that. He's guessing.

The craft surges higher, pushing harder as it strives to escape Earth's atmosphere. The bladder recedes, being drawn into the canopy overhead.

Bugs swarm around her waist, slipping beneath her shirt and clawing at her stomach. Rather than tickling, they're scratching. Liz holds her arms out straight, rising up on tiptoes, trying to reach above the swell, hoping they'll stop, but on they come, clambering over her chest and running along her shoulders.

"Don't fight it," Elvis says as bugs run up and down his neck, climbing in his hair.

The sea of insects around her reaches up to chest height. Liz couldn't shake them loose if she tried, and she struggles with the thought she's drowning in a sea of alien creatures. They race over her arms, and cling to her hair. At first, she tries to shake them off, hoping they'll read her body language, but they won't be deterred. Liz closes her eyes, squeezing her eyelids tight, and breathes through her nose as cockroach-like feet scale her face, climbing up on her cheeks. She's panicking, fighting a feeling of claustrophobia, of being buried alive—eaten alive!

Elvis lets go of her hand. She'd rather he didn't, and she reaches for him, but can't find his fingers amid the swarm of insects.

She barely notices the intense pulsing of the craft, which has gone from once a minute to a shudder several times a second. Insects cling to her eyebrows. Tiny legs scratch at her eyelids. She tries to move, to shake one of the insects away from her nostrils, but she can't.

On the craft goes, pushing them higher and faster.

She can't breathe. The weight of insects pressing down on her is intense. Her body convulses. Thousands of needles prick at her skin, sending waves of pain rushing through her. She wants to scream, but she can't.

Suddenly she's falling, plummeting, plunging. It's as though she's racing down the far side of a rollercoaster, going faster and faster. Her body shakes. As her eyes are still tightly shut, it takes a few seconds to realize the insects are gone. They left—all of them—but how? One moment, they were swarming all over her, crawling under her clothes and scratching at her skin, the next they've disappeared.

Liz opens her eyes and she's in space. The sun has set, and Earth is shrouded in darkness. She can't shake the feeling she's plunging headlong down an elevator shaft, but there's no rush of wind. Elvis is floating beside her, and contrary to the sensation of her stomach rising and her heart pounding madly in her throat, he's not moving.

"Are you okay?" he asks.

She swallows, forcing back the bile rising up in her throat, and nods. He reaches out, taking her hand, and it's then she realizes they're alone. For a moment, she panics, turning, and looking for the alien floater. Nothing. No thin transparent skin, no iridescent bladder, no Stella, no mass of swarming insects—no alien spacecraft at all.

The two of them are floating freely in space.

CHAPTER 17: ORBIT

"Wh—how is this possible?" Liz asks, gripping his hand. Just the slightest squeeze propels them together, and they bump into each other in slow motion, before rebounding awkwardly. Neither dares let go. "I don't understand."

"You got me, doc."

Elvis stares down at his boots. Hundreds of miles below, clouds mask a dark ocean.

"This is impossible," Liz says, looking around them, reaching out with her hand and trying to touch at the seemingly invisible alien spacecraft. "How is this real?"

"I—I don't know," is all Elvis can say, not taking his eyes off his boots.

"Are you?" Before Liz can finish her sentence, Elvis heaves. Vomit projects from his mouth, while his body is propelled backwards, pulling her with him. The motion is subtle, but there's enough of a reaction for her to be drawn to him. She collides with his chest, and rebounds softly. They both flex, trying to control their motion. Drops of vomit float in space before them.

Elvis wipes his mouth with the back of his hand. "Sorry."

"It's okay," she says, holding on to his shoulder, and using his larger frame to steady herself. The vomit sails into the distance without hitting anything. By her reckoning, she loses sight of it after about forty yards.

"Where are they? Where did they go?" he asks.

"I don't know," she replies. "But we should be dead."

"They did something to us, doc. Them critters. Just like they did to my arm. They gave us some kind of immunity to space."

"Maybe," Liz replies, astonished at the vast empty expanse before her. Eternity unfolds in slow motion. Space seems infinite in its depth. Even with Elvis beside her, she feels alone, exposed, vulnerable.

"Stella?" Elvis calls out. He waits a few seconds for a response, before yelling, "STELLA?"

They've been abandoned. Floating freely in space without any visible means of life support.

The two of them are tumbling slightly. Their combined motion is miniscule, but slowly accumulates so they're rotating once every four or five minutes, moving on all three axis rather than simply turning around. The effect is such the vista before them is constantly changing. There's no up, no down. At times, the horizon is before them, with Earth spinning by beneath their feet. A few minutes later, it's as though they're lying upside down, or leaning drunk against a bar, and Earth seems to slide away into the distance. Liz finds herself drawn to their direction of motion, often looking over her shoulder or past her legs, trying to keep her eyes on a fixed point to keep from being sick. She feels helpless.

"I don't feel so good," she says, trying not to vomit.

As they come around again, Elvis lashes out with one of his arms, kicking with his legs and trying to stabilize them, but it's pointless and has no effect.

"Goddamn it."

Liz says, "Without something to push off, there's nothing we can do to stop tumbling."

As Elvis kicks with his feet, their motion surges, but always returns to the same rate.

"My boots," he says, reaching down and undoing the laces. "I can feel them shifting."

"What are you going to do?"

"Throw them."

"That just might work," she says, taking her boots off as well, and holding them in one hand. "Equal and opposite reaction, right? Throw them one way, and we'll move the other. But we need to line this up carefully."

"So how exactly do we make this work?" he asks.

"With great difficulty," she replies. "You want to throw from the center of your chest or you risk imparting some spin to your motion. We should probably be as close as possible to avoid twisting."

"Climb on my back, doc."

Earth drifts lazily overhead, slipping sideways. Reality is topsy-turvy. Elvis readies himself. He's impatient. They twist around so they're facing backwards.

"Wait for it," she says. Elvis gives her one of the boots, holding the other in front of him like a basketball.

"Be careful. Throw too hard, and we'll tumble the other way."

"I've got this, doc. I can feel the rhythm."

As they come around, with the Moon at their back and an entire planet beneath them, Elvis launches one of his boots away from his chest, giving it a smooth but firm shove and sending it hurtling into the distance. Liz can feel the precision in his motion, the push of his muscles and the flex of his hands. He seems to be able to sense the balance needed. If anything, they drift slightly back the other way.

"Sweet," he says. Turning on the spot takes a little practice, but he flexes like a cat, working with his stomach muscles and twisting around. Liz leans over his shoulder, tying the remaining three boots together, and lashing the laces around the soles so they move as one.

"Use this to position us."

She places the boots in front of them and Elvis grabs them, jostling with them to stabilize their motion. She lets go of him and drifts to one side, still holding onto his sleeve.

"Easy," he says, pushing off the boots and getting one last micro adjustment in before they drift out of reach.

"That's better. Much better," she says.

The view is breathtaking, with the Moon rising rapidly before them. Its soft light reflects off the vast, lonely Indian Ocean. To the north, the subcontinent is visible, a jagged coastline curving over the horizon. Cities appear as specks of yellow light fighting off the darkness. Clouds drift lazily, swirling with the currents.

"What the hell are we doing up here?" Elvis asks.

"I don't know. I don't understand," she whispers, remembering the last words spoken by Stella. The alien had been emphatic—*Understand?* Liz isn't sure what she's supposed to glean from this experience beyond the majesty of seeing their home world from orbit. Perhaps that's it. Maybe the aliens want them to understand how precious Earth is. Every astronaut to ever escape the chains of gravity has been humbled to see Earth from space. From the ground, the planet seems impossibly big, dominating every aspect of life, but from orbit it's a fragile orb, a tiny lifeboat adrift on an endless sea. The faint glow wrapping around the horizon highlights how perilously thin the atmosphere is. Liz would feel a little more comfortable if her view was from behind a porthole rather than drifting freely through space in some invisible cocoon.

"Look," Elvis says. "A shooting star."

Several tiny streaks cut through the darkness, blazing across the sky as they enter Earth's atmosphere, only they're below them. It's unnerving to look down at a meteor lighting up the night.

"That's beautiful," Liz says, in awe of what she's witnessing.

A shadow falls over them, blocking out the moonlight and plunging them into darkness. Instinctively, they both look to see the jagged outline of a massive asteroid tumbling slowly overhead. Fractures appear in the vast rock as it splits in two, breaking up, and separating into what are sheer mountains adrift in space. Even in the low light, the detail is astonishing. Craters, cliffs, mounds, and craggy rocks litter the surface.

"I—ah," Liz says, unsure what to make of the sight. She expected to see the alien mothership, but this is no organic spacecraft—it's a behemoth tumbling on a parabola toward Earth, breaking up on approach. Although the fractured asteroid appears to be traveling slowly, Liz is aware her perspective is deceiving. They may appear to be stationary, but to be in orbit they must be traveling at tens of thousands of miles an hour.

"Stella?" Liz asks the darkness, unsure what's happening. "I don't understand."

The asteroid lumbers on, curving through space as it overtakes them, plummeting toward Earth. A trail of debris stretches out behind it, falling in toward the dark planet.

Streaks of light cut through the night as dozens of meteorites blaze through the atmosphere below them. Instead of petering out and disappearing, they burst, showering the planet with glowing fragments. Plumes of white vapor erupt out from the various points of impact scattered across the sea. Although the rings look small at a distance, each of them would easily span ten miles.

"What's happening?" Elvis asks as more meteors rain down on the planet.

Dozens of fiery streaks curve through the atmosphere before thumping into the ocean. Concussion waves ripple through the sea, forming tsunamis.

Indonesia passes beneath them—a dark elongated landmass, followed by an archipelago of hundreds of tiny islands. Liz doesn't reply to Elvis. She can barely fathom what's she's seeing as an entire mountain tumbles into the atmosphere. Fire seems to form around the leading edge. Chunks are torn off by the violent entry. The meteor vanishes on impact, disappearing in a blinding flash. As their eyes adjust to the darkness, a wall of compressed air ripples out from the newly formed crater. Molten ejecta sprays into the atmosphere, glowing as it rains down on the surrounding islands and crashing into the sea.

"No, no, no," Elvis says. "What is she doing?"

Liz mumbles. Her heart sinks. A single word escapes from her lips. "Revenge."

Islands disappear beneath their feet, swamped by walls of water racing across the ocean, and still more meteorites fall. The tempo increases. Red streaks scar the sky, raging with anger, pounding the planet in their fury.

"STELLA," Elvis yells, arching his back and flexing every muscle in his body as he bellows, "STELLLLLLAAAAAAA!"

He looks around, trying to find something, someone to direct his anguish at, but the two of them are entirely alone, lost in orbit.

Dark clouds choke the planet.

As dawn breaks, a comet approaches. Its body is easily visible in the bright light, with jets streaming from the surface like geysers, spraying vapor into space and forming a coma easily twice the size of the twisted lump of rock and ice. Were it not so deadly, it would be beautiful to behold. Like the massive asteroid, it appears to move slowly.

"This is madness," Elvis says.

Liz fights the lump in her throat. "It is."

They've gravitated together, holding loosely to each other. Remaining stationary is impossible, and Liz finds she has to adjust her position with micro-movements every few seconds to prevent drifting apart or twisting around. Her clothes float on her frame, drifting slightly away from her skin, giving the impression of being detached. Even such mundane, familiar feelings, like that of being touched by cotton, have been stolen from her.

In the daylight, the devastation on Earth is apparent. Dark black clouds swirl in violent eddies. Flashes of light mark a succession of impacts as a string of broken meteors fall in a cluster.

Tens of thousands of miles away, the comet continues its approach, heading toward the far side of the planet.

"We should be down there," Elvis says, choking up. "If this is to be our end, we should all die together." His eyes are glazed. His bottom lip quivers. "Why would she do this to us? Why force us to watch?"

"I—I don't know."

Out beyond the horizon, somewhere over the Atlantic or perhaps in the Mediterranean, a comet the size of Mt Everest slams into Earth. Although they can't see the point of impact, the flash of light is unmistakable. It seems wrong to witness the destruction of humanity in utter silence. With each blow, hundreds of thousands, millions, perhaps billions of people perish, and the two of them are powerless to do anything other than watch. Liz is overcome by grief.

The planet drifts by serenely beneath them, seemingly oblivious to the orbital bombardment, but life on Earth is being driven to extinction. It takes half an hour before the comet impact is visible to Liz and Elvis. A massive pressure wave moves through the atmosphere, following the curvature of Earth, spreading like a ripple on a pond, briefly pushing away the dark clouds blanketing the planet.

"Why?" Elvis asks, but the answer is apparent. From what Jameson told her, humans slaughtered dozens, if not hundreds of creatures like Stella. From the perspective of these aliens, justice is being served. Liz feels she has to reply on behalf of humanity, hoping some alien intelligence is watching—listening.

"We made a mistake," she says, pleading with the void. "We killed your people, but this—this is wrong. An entire species—no, an entire planet full of millions of different species is dying down there. Should all of life pay for the folly and stupidity of one?"

The silence that follows her words seems to condemn her. She wants there to be an answer—a solution. Liz desperately wants to believe there's some way humanity can escape their fate, but this is no movie. The heroes can't steal a UFO and blow up the alien mothership. This is no Hollywood script. A bunch of fighter planes can't take on spacecraft tens of thousands of years more advanced, and somehow miraculously come up with a win. This is reality. The aliens haven't used death rays, or even nuclear weapons—there's no need for such extravagance. Gravity is far more effective with just a few lumps of rock wreaking a level of destruction never before witnessed on Earth. The dinosaurs were wiped out by a single asteroid roughly six miles across. Liz has seen at least three that size, not counting the comet.

As if in response to her pleas, dozens of asteroids burst through the cloudbanks below them, leaving vapor trails that span hundreds of miles. Molten rock billows into the atmosphere. There will be no reprieve. Earth is covered in a seething mass of turbulent clouds. Ash billows into the stratosphere, being swept away by the high-speed winds, marking where volcanoes have ruptured from the fractured mantle, and still they come. Asteroids pepper Earth, striking with the ferocity of a shotgun blast. The devastation is without mercy.

"It was a mistake… a mistake" she says over and over, her words trailing into silence. Tears form in her eyes, only instead of running down her cheeks, they well up, creating blobs in the corner by the bridge of her nose, forcing her to wipe them away. Tiny droplets float before her, dancing in the weightlessness, reflecting the light around her.

Night falls in an instant. The abrupt change is unsettling. Vast lava fields glow hundreds of miles beneath them, sporadically breaking through the thick clouds. Hell has risen from the depths and consumed the planet.

"Is there no end to your anger?" Liz asks. Elvis holds her close, wrapping his arms around her. "Is it not enough to destroy us? Do you need to wipe out every trace of life on Earth?" She sobs, burying her head in his shoulder, but in the weightlessness of space, it's impossible to rest against him. As soon as either of them relaxes, they begin to drift apart.

"It's gone," Elvis says. "All of it. Everyone." Like her, he's deep in shock. The bitter reality that confronts her is like a knife being plunged into her chest.

Liz says, "They've sterilized Earth. Everything's been destroyed. Every book ever written, every work of art, every sheet of music—gone. Every plant. Every flower. Every animal. Every insect. Even microbes."

A string of volcanoes erupts. Rivers of lava cover the land, glowing in the darkness.

"Nothing can survive that," she says. "Earth is now as barren and lifeless as the Moon, or Mars."

"What about us?" Elvis asks. "We're alive."

"For now... but even with whatever magic they have sustaining us here in orbit, we'll be dead within a few days."

"How?"

Liz speaks with detached, clinical precision. "Dehydration leading to organ failure."

"I don't understand?" Elvis asks. "Why were we spared?"

Liz doesn't have an answer for him.

Elvis asks the question plaguing her mind. "Why make us witness the destruction of our own world?"

"I don't know."

Elvis slips the belt from his waist, saying, "We've got to do something."

"What?" Liz asks with disbelief. There's nothing to be done. For her, the idea of doing *something* borders on comical, but for Elvis, action carries meaning. He seems to find solace in being resourceful.

"Give me your belt."

Liz slips her belt from her waist. Even such a simple act imparts some torque to her body and she finds herself twisting sideways, drifting away from him. Elvis links the belts together, and fixes one of the buckles to a loop of his pants, tying the other end to her. At first, their impromptu tether is erratic, and they bounce a little as it flexes, but slowly their motion becomes more stable. Being busy is good. She welcomes the distraction.

Liz feels sick. She finds it helps if she keeps her eyes on the horizon rather than looking at Earth. Watching clouds pass by below her feet is nauseating, but the soft glow on the horizon is soothing. Clouds smother the planet. Occasionally, a ruddy smudge spreading out below them reveals massive plains flooded with molten lava, but the clouds give no hint of either land or sea.

"What's that?" Elvis asks, pointing above and behind them. Liz turns slowly, not wanting to send herself into a tumble. A thin strand of white material weaves an erratic path forward through space, passing just above them. "Is that... alive?"

"I don't know," Liz replies, watching as the leading edge splits, branching in different directions. Several fine twigs grow out from the main trunk. Some of them come to an abrupt halt, while others continue to grow and divide. "It might be."

"It looks like bone," Elvis says.

"Or coral," Liz says, observing how, unlike a tree, the structure only appears alive at its tip. A small glow marks the leading branches. Most of the wispy twigs have come to a halt, no longer glowing, or expanding. "Coral grows like this, all kinds of different varieties piled on top of each other—staghorn, brain, and fan corals... Ossification, is the term," she says, losing herself in a moment. "It's alive only at the leading edge."

Occasionally, the tortured shape compresses, on the verge of dying, with only a thin strand continuing forward. Then suddenly, several filaments ignite and race ahead, dividing into different branches. To her, it's little more than the drunken sketch of a madman. There's no discernible pattern to the twisted, gnarled shapes. In some places, the branches build upon other branches, fanning out before leading to a dead end. In other regions, there are thousands of thin filaments, almost like those of a 60s fiber-optics lamp. The strands are tightly clustered, reaching in all directions, but they too seem to die. Only a few sections continue to grow.

"What do you think it is?" Elvis asks.

"Up here? Out in space? No idea. Something alien."

"Ya think," Elvis replies sarcastically. Liz gives him a playful punch, but her punch propels her slightly backwards. She spins, instinctively reaching out for something to steady herself. Her hand grabs at the structure. A shock runs through her body, like that of electricity being grounded, but once the initial pulse has passed, she's fine. Holding onto something, however bizarre, is comforting. Hurtling headlong through space without any visible means of support is unnerving. The alien structure provides an illusion of substance. Already, it's fifteen feet long, and branching in two distinctly different directions—almost as though it has been cleaved in two.

"It has to mean something, right?" Elvis says.

"I guess."

Day breaks yet again, barely an hour after night fell. The speed with which a night and day pass in orbit is bewildering. One complete orbit must take around two hours, with half of that time spent in the sunlight, the other half in Earth's shadow. To her surprise, the clouds have largely cleared. The land below is dark. Craters pockmark entire continents, with ejecta scarring the land— long thin trails radiate from the point of impact, reaching for hundreds of miles, following the curvature of the planet.

Earth is unrecognizable. It was dusk when they departed the USS Lawrence, which would put dawn somewhere over the Pacific, or perhaps America. They should be coming up on the Atlantic, but there's nothing beyond an endless scorched plain. Even the atmosphere looks different. What should be white clouds look sickly—a blend of yellow and green. A few lakes are visible, but the water is dark, almost black.

Elvis pulls himself up next to Liz. He tries to sit on the structure, but in microgravity he simply floats over one of the branches.

Liz feels the tingle of electricity beneath her fingers. The point at which she's holding the stem pulsates. As she moves her hand, the structure responds to her motion. A molten blob appears before her, not unlike those that undulate within lava lamps. It takes Liz a moment to realize she's controlling a hologram. The soft image floats just above the branch. Following a hunch, she lets go, and grabs at the ethereal edges of the soft glowing blob. It responds, resizing as she moves her fingers. With a twist of her wrists, what appears to be a pocket of gel rotates through the air in front of her.

"What the hell is that?" Elvis asks.

Liz zooms in. "I think it's a microbe—but it's like no cell I've ever seen."

She turns it over, looking at the squishy innards.

"If this was a terrestrial cell, these bits of glitter would be ribosomes, and that dark smudge in there would be the nucleus."

"Something survived?" Elvis asks.

"I don't think so," Liz replies. "This is too primitive. The cell wall is barely defined, and would rupture easily. There's no flagella—no means of propulsion."

She works with her hands, zooming in on what appears to be the nucleus.

"That must be the alien equivalent of DNA," she says, gesturing to a tumbled mess of string that looks more like a pile of discarded shoelaces than something that's alive. "But it's small—far too small... It's junk. There's RNA and DNA in there, which is all wrong.

"The smallest viable genome on Earth is, I don't know, a hundred thousand base pairs... two hundred thousand maybe... humans have three billion. I doubt there's more than a couple of thousand in here. This thing is tiny."

"What does it mean?" Elvis asks.

"I don't know. Maybe they're seeding Earth." Liz is clinical in her analysis, which is her way of dealing with the immensity of all that's happened. "I mean, it's an entire planet—and it's empty. From their perspective, Earth is prime real estate."

Elvis is quiet. This isn't what he wanted to hear.

Night falls again. Neither of them talk much. Below them, lightning storms rage across the planet. At times, there are thousands of flashes in just a few minutes. Whatever's happening down there, it's violent in the extreme.

"But where are they?" Elvis asks as dawn approaches. A thin blue strand curls around the edge of the planet, marking the first rays of a new day, and then within seconds, the sun has risen and the day is upon them.

Liz looks around. "I don't know. I mean, their mothership is big—so big it was easily visible from Earth, but space is stupidly big. They could be sitting off somewhere by the Moon and we'd never know it. They'd be just another star in the sky."

During this particular orbit, her eyes struggle to adjust to the light. Her body revolts against the brilliant sunshine catching the ruddy clouds swirling to form a hurricane. The dense cloud cover blots out most of the planet. The sky has a pinkish hue.

Liz is tired. Her mind's lethargic, fighting against rational thought, wanting only to sleep. This orbit seems longer than the last, and she finds her self longing for the darkness. Elvis must feel the creeping fatigue as well. Neither of them slept the night before, and caught only a catnap in the embassy. It's been thirty, maybe forty hours since she last slept soundly, and as night falls yet again in orbit, she closes her eyes and drifts off to sleep.

A blinding light breaks her slumber after less than an hour. The sun is relentless.

Elvis is asleep, but he's looped the belt around one of the thin, scraggly dead branches so they don't drift away. He's snoring. He's taken off his shirt and wrapped it around his head, using it as a blindfold.

"What the hell," Liz mumbles, undoing the buttons on her shirt. She instinctively feels self-conscious—as though the whole world is watching—but the world is dead, and Elvis is asleep. What place does modesty hold when you're waiting to die? Besides, she's wearing a bra. She wraps the arms of her shirt around her head, tucking the loose portions in as she tries to block out the light, and closes her eyes. Somehow, light still seeps through—blood red inside her eyelids. Liz turns her back to the Sun, but any unanchored motion is seemingly perpetual, and she simply rotates until she's facing the Sun again. She positions herself beside the branch, facing backwards, and tries to go back to sleep. Liz is tired, but her mind is racing at tens of thousands of miles an hour—just like her body.

Finally, she begins to drift off to sleep, only to be woken by the sensation of falling. The problem is, it's no dream. She *is* falling. She's in free fall around a planet. Sleep eventually overwhelms her but it's fitful rather than restful. Liz wakes dozens of times for the craziest of reasons, and gets angry at herself. Sleep should be a refuge, not a place of torment.

A hand rests on her shoulder, and she wakes. After wrestling with her shirt, she slips it back on.

"Sleep well?"

"No."

"Me neither," Elvis says. Liz is grumpy. She'd rather have slept a little longer, but she quickly realizes why Elvis woke her.

Earth looks like Mars. Craters still pockmark the surface, but their sharp edges have softened with erosion. The land, though, is red. Fault lines are visible from space. Like the seams on a baseball, they wind around the planet. A handful of brilliant azure lakes dot the plain. They're almost iridescent in the sunlight. Volcanoes spew ash high into the air where it's carried by the prevailing winds. There's no ocean. Only a handful of wispy clouds sit high in the stratosphere.

"Wow." For a moment, her sense of loss is replaced with wonder. There's a rugged, natural beauty to the landscape. As the terminator approaches and they're plunged back into darkness, Liz gets a glimpse of a black ocean hundreds of miles beneath them.

"I can't believe they've just abandoned us," Elvis says as the shadow of Earth passes over the massive coral structure floating above them. The bleached white, seemingly dead tree curves through space ahead of them, branching out for hundreds of yards. It's impossible to tell if it's still growing, and Liz is past caring. The cryptic nature of such an impossible device is lost on her.

Elvis looks dejected. "We helped her," he says. "We rescued her from Adan and his men. Why would she do this to us?"

This is the first time their conversation has come back to Stella. Up until now, their focus has been on the destruction of life on Earth, but being alone in orbit feels like being locked up in a prison cell. It's difficult not to take this punishment personally.

"They've got to be out there," Elvis says. "I just can't believe Stella would abandon us. Not after all we went through together. Not now that we're all that remains of life on Earth."

Liz likes his reasoning, but reality begs to differ.

"Maybe they're doing something," Elvis says, not realizing how absurd his statement sounds. "Maybe they'll come back."

"Maybe," is all Liz can say in reply. She doesn't want to crush his dreams. Hope, however misplaced, is all Elvis has left. Liz can't take that from him.

The rapid pace of a night and day in orbit becomes overwhelming. All sense of time is lost. The physical notion of being disoriented while weightless blends seamlessly into being disengaged from any awareness of real time. Occasionally they drift off to sleep, only to be woken by the strobe like effect of a night and day being compressed into just a few hours. The impact of this rapid cycle is to heighten the fatigue and heartache they feel.

How long have they been up here? How many orbits have they completed? Earth seems sedate. Occasionally, they catch a glimpse of the alien structure still growing ahead of them—at a guess, it stretches out well over a mile, perhaps two. It fans out sideways, curving with them in orbit.

Another dawn breaks and Earth is a snowball.

"I did not see that coming," Liz says.

"It's frozen. The whole planet," Elvis says.

Pack ice dominates the sea. Sheets of ice blanket the land, stretching from the polar regions to the equator. Glaciers leave a jagged path as they carve their way across the mountains. A few thin strips of ocean are visible between the ice flows. A volcano spews ash into the air as lava cascades down the ice, sending steam billowing into the atmosphere.

"I don't understand," Liz says. "This is all happening too fast."

"What is?"

"They're terraforming Earth, but the pace is insane. This is a hundred million years worth of glaciation in just an hour. How is that possible?"

"Look at us, doc," Elvis says. "We're drifting through space without spacesuits, without a spaceship, and you're worried about a little ice?"

"Not a little ice. These climate changes—all of them—they're on a scale that defies physics."

"That defies *our* physics," Elvis says. He's got a point.

Night falls, but Liz is unsettled by what she's seen. Nothing adds up. Over the next hour, the ice begins receding in the darkness, exposing the barren, lifeless land, but such rapid action makes no sense—not over the course of centuries, let alone hours. Geological activity like this is the domain of millions to hundreds of millions of years. What's driving this physical phenomenon?

Thunderstorms dominate the equatorial regions. Lightning crackles through thick cloudbanks. Occasionally, meteors streak through the sky, but unlike those from a few days ago, they burn up harmlessly in the upper atmosphere. Dawn breaks, and the jagged outline of a continent is visible on the horizon. Glaciers still dominate the land, but they've largely receded to the poles. Liz is confused. She feels as though she's solving a jigsaw puzzle without seeing the picture on the box. The land below her is unrecognizable, but a green tinge along the shoreline catches her attention.

"That," she says, pointing and getting Elvis' attention. "That's life."

"What? Like plants and stuff?"

"Yes," she replies. "And those patches in the sea, they look like algae blooms. While the green inland must be plant life—photosynthesis."

"Stuff like chloroform?" Elvis asks, correcting himself with, "Chlorophyl, right?"

"Yes."

"So plants are growing back? Life's returning to Earth?"

"Maybe," Liz says.

Elvis scratches at his cheeks, and Liz realizes his stubble is the best timepiece they have in orbit, as he shaved back at the embassy.

"How long does it take?" she asks, gesturing to his cheeks. "Your stubble?"

"Oh, this?" he replies, grabbing at his chin. "Two, maybe three days."

"Are you hungry?" she asks.

"No."

"Thirsty?"

"No... why?"

"You should be. We both should be."

"But we're not," he says.

"Why?"

"Hey, come on, doc. I asked you first."

Night rushes upon them. The day plunges into darkness as they swing through the shadow of the massive planet. Snow and ice blanket the northern hemisphere, but the rocky interior of the various island continents are covered in lush foliage. The stark deserts that dominated Earth are all but gone, being banished to a handful of equatorial regions.

"Astonishing," Liz says, in awe of the transformation she's witnessing. What was once a lifeless rock is again teeming with plant life, at least.

"Do you think they're down there somewhere?" Elvis asks. "The floaters, I mean."

"I don't know."

"Are they like—doing all this?"

"Could be." Liz has no idea. Regardless of how crazy it might seem, she's open to all possibilities. Reason is at work down there, even if they don't understand the logic. The aliens have cast their design over Earth and are applying their vast biotech resources to terraform the planet.

Like every other orbit, Earth passes by hundreds of miles beneath them. Islands, oceans, entire continents drift by revealing an ever-changing variety of habitats. Another massive asteroid slams into the land, striking a peninsula near the equator, and sending out a wall of devastation. Where there was once greenery, now dark clouds blanket the planet, choking it.

"Why would they do that?" Elvis asks. "Why destroy what they've created?"

"I don't know."

As night falls, the turbulent clouds part. Already, there's greenery again. The resilience of this alien world is incredible to behold. Lightning crackles from a string of active volcanoes forming a mountain range on some unknown continent. Ash clouds leave dark smudges stretching across the sky.

Shortly before dawn, Liz spots what she thinks is another meteor, only instead of skimming the atmosphere in a blaze of light it's blinking—flashing.

"What's that?" she asks, pointing behind and below them. Whatever it is, it's keeping pace with them, slowly advancing on them.

"Stella?" Elvis asks.

"I don't think so."

Dawn breaks and they lose sight of the light, but Liz positions herself so she's facing in that general direction, watching as the planet whizzes past beneath her, curling away over the horizon. She's determined to keep an eye out for something—anything. The prospect of not being alone in orbit is tantalizing. Whatever that was, it wasn't alien. The light seemed more like a navigation aid, the kind used by boats at sea. Could someone else have survived the devastation? Perhaps the International Space Station was spared. Have they seen her and Elvis? Are they coming to get them?

"Hey, look at that," Elvis says, pointing at a faint dot passing above the immense blue ocean rolling beneath them. "Is that?"

"I think so," she says. Elvis grabs her, squeezing her shoulder.

"You mean, someone else made it?"

"I—Maybe. I hope so."

Slowly, a space capsule drifts closer, moving on an angle, gliding toward them. The shape is unmistakable—a cone with a flattened nose, similar to the Apollo command modules of old.

"It is... It is," Liz says. She waves, wanting to attract their attention.

"Hot dog," Elvis yells.

Liz says, "They must have been in orbit when the asteroids hit. They're coming for us."

"But where will we go? We can't go back to Earth," Elvis says. It's a good point. Given the rapid changes they've witnessed, and particularly early on with all the out-gassing caused by hundreds of volcanoes, there's no way of knowing if Earth's atmosphere is breathable. Just because plants can flourish doesn't mean humans can. Over the course of life on Earth, the oxygen levels have varied from almost non-existent to over twenty-five percent. Where does it sit now?

The capsule turns to face them. Sunlight reflects off a polished chrome hatch. Shadows move behind the windows. There's a NASA logo on the side of the module, along with the distinct red, white and blue of a US flag. Liz has never been so thankful to see the Stars and Stripes.

Tiny bursts of gas allow the capsule to position itself with precision. The craft inches closer. The hatch opens outward. An astronaut conducts egress in a slow, methodical manner.

"This is real, right?" Elvis asks. "I mean, you're seeing this too? It's not just me."

"It's not just you," Liz replies. Life is surreal. Three days in orbit have left them both in a daze. Liz has wondered more than once if everything that's happened to them is just a dream, only she's never experienced a dream so real, so all-encompassing, and so extended. No, this isn't a dream.

White gloved hands reach for a rail beside the hatch, anchoring a tether. The astronaut's suit is stiff, his life support backpack is bulky, while his movements are slow. His legs barely flex as he positions himself outside the craft.

"What about that?" Elvis asks, pointing at Earth. "Are you seeing what I'm seeing?"

"Is that—Florida?" Liz asks in astonishment. The vast peninsula reaching down from the Continental US is lush, bursting with plant life. Cities appear as grey smudges on the land. Dark seas dominate the gulf, while Key West is surrounded by azure waters. Various sandbanks are visible from space, stretching for hundreds of miles just beneath the surface of the ocean. There are dozens of islands beneath them. Spotted cloud cover sits over the Bahamas, but they too are surrounded by bright, clear, azure waters. A hurricane is forming out over the Atlantic. Large clouds swirl in toward the eye wall.

"How can that be Florida?" Elvis asks.

"I don't know."

The astronaut has his visor down, reflecting the distorted shape of the alien structure back at them. He beckons, waving with his hand, signaling for them to launch themselves out across the void.

"There's only one way we're going to find out," Liz says, pushing off the structure and propelling herself toward the Orion spacecraft. Her skin tingles with anticipation, while her heart is in her throat. The capsule is further away than she realizes. What seemed like just a few feet is closer to thirty, but she drifts effortlessly toward the Orion.

The astronaut reaches for her, grabbing her and pulling her in. Liz slips inside the hatch, noting that the other astronauts are suited up, but in lightweight spacesuits. Their helmets are clear domes, and they're wearing what appears to be flight suits, or perhaps the kind of pressure suits worn by high-altitude military aviators.

They look alarmed—horrified. It's her lack of a spacesuit. They're shocked, surprised to see she's alive, looking at her as though she's an alien. Elvis follows behind her, working hand over hand as he clambers inside the tiny craft. The main astronaut closes the hatch behind them. There's no sound as the hatch clips shut and the locking wheel is spun in place. The lead astronaut raises his outer reflective visor, and Liz realizes he's a she. She smiles from behind an clear glass dome, mouthing something, and pointing to a gauge on the control panel. The patch on her suit reads, *Sam Ellison, Commander*.

Slowly, the pressure within the capsule builds. Liz feels her ears begin to ache. She opens her jaw, wanting to equalize with the changing pressure.

Like her, Elvis is in awe of being inside a spacecraft. He holds onto a rail beside her, saying, "Look," as he points out the window. The alien mothership sits high above the white tree-like structure, but Liz is convinced it wasn't there before.

The commander releases her gloves and then twists her helmet, while one of the other astronauts helps her with her backpack. A pair of gloves floats freely in front of her, bouncing off each other and summersaulting before being grabbed by one of the other astronauts, and being stowed.

"Copy that, Houston," she says. "Switching from PPT to VOX. You're on speaker."

"Dr. Bower?" a familiar voice asks.

"Anish?"

"Yes. Yes, it's me, Dr. Ambar. How are you? How is Elvis? Are you guys okay? Do you require any medical treatment? Food? Water?"

Elvis and Liz look at each other with bewilderment.

"Ah, we're fine," she says. Elvis raises an eyebrow, and she feels as though she can read his mind. She knows the question he wants to ask. "How are you?"

There's silence for a moment before Dr. Ambar says, "I'm fine... Why do I get the feeling yours is a loaded question?"

"It's just—" Liz begins, but she doesn't know where to start.

One of the astronauts hands her a drink in a sealed foil bag, with a small straw protruding from the top. She sips at the orange juice. It's slightly warm, and tastes bland, but she's not complaining. Elvis sucks his dry in a matter of seconds.

Commander Ellison says, "We're going to need to get you strapped in. Our orbit has residual motion relative to the structure, so we need to pull away. We don't want to get tangled in those branches."

"Oh, right. Of course," Liz says.

"Yeah, damn," Elvis says. "You do *not* want to be stuck up here, believe me."

The other astronauts help buckle them into the flight seats. Commander Ellison is already working with the controls, edging the craft back.

"Switching to PPT," she says.

One of the other astronauts speaks softly, saying, "PPT is Push-To-Talk, while VOX is Voice Operated—effectively always on."

Liz nods, staying silent, not wanting to distract the commander.

With the crew strapped in, Commander Ellison eases the craft backwards, increasing their distance to several hundred yards, all the while talking with Houston. There's some discussion about radar readings and altitude. Commander Ellison and her pilot talk about changing orbits.

The commander turns to them, saying, "We're pulling back roughly a mile, but we need to wait until we swing in to perigee—our closest approach to Earth—before we can undertake a full burn. We're currently in a lower, faster orbit, so we'll overtake the structure within a few minutes."

Liz nods.

"Hold on, I'm going to bring us around so you can get a good look at her."

The Orion rotates until the leading edges of the tree become visible.

"Beautiful, huh?" the commander says.

Neither Liz nor Elvis reply.

The pilot says, "I'm getting some great visuals on the HD camera."

"Where to from here?" Liz asks, feeling a little anxious about getting back to Earth.

"Orbits are strange," the commander says. "Burn when we're closest to Earth and we'll lower our apogee when we're furthest away, which is currently right on the cusp of that structure. So we need to conduct a burn in about half an hour to ensure we stay well clear of it next time around. We've got three orbits before we'll be in position to de-orbit and splash down in the Pacific. By this time tomorrow, you'll be sunbathing in Hawaii."

"Sounds good to me," Elvis says, rather emphatically.

"I've got Houston on the channel. Switching back to VOX so you can talk."

Elvis leans toward the control panel, unsure where the microphone is, but wanting to be heard as he asks, "Is there any news about my squad?"

There's talking in the background as his question is discussed within Mission Control. "I'm told your team is in South Africa," Dr. Ambar replies.

"Good. Good," Elvis says. Liz can hear the relief in his voice. For the past few days, they thought *everyone* was dead. They're both still in shock, and struggling to catch up with reality.

"Liz, I can't wait to get you back for a debrief. We're all very excited. You must be thrilled."

Elvis cuts her off, saying, "You have no idea."

"What can you tell us about *the gift*?"

"Gift?" she asks, noting that all three astronauts are staring at her.

"It's all we've heard from them. They told us to collect you from the gift. Like their original message, it was broadcast in multiple languages, but without any further explanation."

Liz and Elvis look at each other, at a loss to explain what's happened to them.

"How big is it?" Liz asks.

"Seventeen miles long, with a circumference of twenty two miles," Dr. Ambar replies. Liz stares out the window at the strange, contorted shape twisting through space. She's lost in thought, trying to make sense of their shared experience over the past few days.

Dr. Ambar says, "Given its size, there was media speculation about the threat it might pose as its orbit decays. But it's orbiting in the exosphere above 700 miles, so that won't be a concern for the best part of a century. Tidal forces should be tearing it apart, so its material strength must be insane. We've got a whole bunch of people down here itching to talk to you about the gift."

"Gift?" Elvis mutters, staring at her. She shrugs.

"What can you tell us?" Dr. Ambar asks. "What is this gift?"

Liz thinks about it for a moment before replying, "It's a book."

"*A book?* I don't understand."

"It's the book of life," she says. "A chronicle of how life evolved on Earth—from the Late Heavy Bombardment through four billion years until now."

Elvis looks at her with surprise. He's stunned.

"It's interactive. You get to see everything. Every catastrophic event to ever strike the planet, and the response of various organisms as they struggled to adapt and survive. Ah, we saw the Great Oxygenation Event, the Snowball Earth, the Cambrian Explosion. Even the impact that wiped out the dinosaurs. It's all there—the evolution of life on Earth."

"Oh, wow," Dr. Ambar replies. "Wow. Wow. Wow... So how does it work?"

"You pick a spot on the structure, and a hologram reveals the composition of that particular life form at that point in time. From there, you can zoom in on the nucleus, examine chemical reactions, look at the DNA."

"Amazing... Did you find us? *Homo sapiens*?"

"No... We're just one tiny leaf on this vast, mighty tree. It's mostly microbes."

"And we can visit it?" Commander Ellison asks.

"Yes. This is their gift to humanity. I get the feeling we'll be studying this for decades to come."

"And that's it?" Dr. Ambar asks. "They didn't say anything else to you?"

"No."

"We had hoped they'd change their minds."

"About leaving?"

"Yes," he says. "Do you think anything's changed for them?"

Liz doesn't know for sure, but her mouth speaks what her heart intuitively feels. "No."

There's silence as that sinks in. Liz has no idea who's listening, but she suspects it's probably everyone. Having heard a variety of radio broadcasts back in Africa, she's well aware of the effort NASA has put into transparency. She imagines her voice is bouncing around homes all across the planet, and she understands their fears, their frustrations. She has to give them something else to hold on to.

"We've been living in a dream for so long—imagining aliens attacking us, enslaving us, and plundering our resources—we simply weren't ready for reality. We read our own fears into their arrival. We projected our own prejudices upon them. But they're not like us. They're alien in every possible way. Even when they try to give us something wonderful, our reaction is to be afraid—to misunderstand their intentions. It's—It's sad. Tragic, really."

Liz peers out the window, watching as the alien mothership recedes into the distance. "There's a lesson here for us. We value gold and diamonds. We obsess over money. But we've never really realized the magnitude of the treasures around us. Our world is an oasis in the vast empty desert of space. Life is worth so much more than we ever imagined. For them, it was worth the time and effort to cross the immense expanse between the stars just to visit our world for a few days."

Commander Ellison says, "But there's so much more we could learn from them."

"And we will," Liz replies. "From their gift—an entire library of the history of life on Earth."

"We've got a lot to learn," Elvis says. With his distinct southern drawl, and sounding very much like his namesake, Elvis Presley, he adds, "O man, take care! What does this deep midnight declare?"

Commander Ellison and Liz exchange curious glances, unsure where that phrase came from. Elvis stares out the window at the vast, lonely, dark emptiness of space. He speaks with an almost hypnotic rhythm.

"I was asleep—

"From a deep dream I woke and swear:—

"The world is deep,

"Deeper than the day has been aware."

Liz jokes with him, saying, "*Who* are you, and *what* have you done with my friend?"

Elvis laughs, turning to her and smiling. "We're better than this, doc. We need only look at the stars each night and wonder. They keep life in perspective, yah know?"

"So what was that?" she asks, curious. "Poetry, or song lyrics?"

"Nietzsche, baby." Only Elvis could pull off those two words in the same sentence.

Liz shakes her head in disbelief. He's completely disarmed her. "And how do *you* know Nietzsche?"

"It's from *Thus Spoke Zarathustra*," Elvis replies, leaving Liz even more befuddled. He gestures with his hands, making as though it should be obvious. "The King opened all his concerts with it."

Liz is taken back. She's incredulous. "Elvis Presley opened his concerts quoting Nietzsche?"

For a moment, Liz and Elvis are the only people in the entire universe. The Orion module, the astronauts, Dr. Ambar in Mission Control, and billions of people listening in all cease to exist in her mind. It's just her and Elvis again, sitting on an alien branch, floating in space, watching Earth drift by beneath their feet.

"Ha ha. Nah. Strauss. He opened his concerts playing Strauss."

"Strauss?" she asks, still not following his convoluted line of reasoning.

Elvis smiles, winking at her. "*2001: A Space Odyssey*, doc. *Thus Spoke Zarathustra* is the theme music from the opening. Strauss wrote it to capture Nietzsche with music. The King loved it. He had it played by a brass band during his Vegas concerts." In a deep voice, Elvis cries, "Daaaah, Daaaaaaah, Daaaaaaaaaah... Dah, Daaah!"

Liz shakes her head.

"Did he have a chimp hitting rocks with a bone?"

"No, but I'm pretty sure the drummer was a close relative."

Liz says, "And I thought we were being serious here?"

"We are," Elvis replies. "You're right, doc. We were asleep. All of us. But now we're awake. Life is deeper than we've ever imagined. I think we're going to be okay—and Stella, I think she knew we'd figure it out. She knew we'd understand."

Liz smiles, shaking her head in wonder. "And we did."

In the depths of her mind, Liz can almost hear the creature speaking to her one last time, using her own voice as it implores her, "*Understand?*" Perhaps that's what humanity has been missing all this time—understanding—as that's all that ever keeps fear at bay.

The End

AFTERWORD

Thank you for your kind support of independent science fiction.

Xenophobia was originally released in 2013, but at the time I couldn't write the ending I wanted. I tried, but it was technically beyond me, so I developed an alternative ending for the first edition, following a *Star Trek-esque* storyline, with these alien creatures holding court on the folly of humanity. At the time, it worked, but in the back of my mind the original ending nagged at me, and I longed for the opportunity to revise the story as my writing style grew.

Aliens should be alien, and not just in their appearance—in their mannerisms, motivations, and reasoning.

Xenophobia is ultimately a story about how we treat each other, which is highlighted in this novel by a civil war and the intrusion of intelligent aliens. Fear leads to misunderstandings. Our ideology and cognitive biases color the way we see the world. As exciting as it would be to encounter intelligent extraterrestrials, I suspect our penchant for the sensational, for conspiracies and distrust, for hidden agendas and illogical beliefs would grossly distort First Contact. And it's not just those who cling to a flat Earth or creationism that would be at fault, we collectively have a drive to be self-centered and that taints our view of reality. I hope this story has gone some way to exposing that bias. The universe does not revolve around *Homo sapiens*.

I'd like to thank the following people for their support in writing *Xenophobia*. In no particular order, thanks to Commander

Mike Morrissey (USA, Retired) for his assistance in the military aspects of this novel, Brian Wells for his patience, Jae Lee for his sketches, John Walker (Autodesk/Fourmilab) for his keen eye. I've lost track of how many times this novel has been edited by Ellen Campbell and Andrea Reed.

The cover art for *Xenophobia* was designed by Jason Gurley.

The reference to the Elvis Presley song, *Viva Las Vegas*, is deliberately vague, being deliberately crafted to avoid any copyright infringement (with none of the actual song lyrics being used in the story). Copyright for *Viva Las Vegas* is held by *Mort Shuman Songs* and *Pomus Songs Inc*. In the same way, the only reference to any other songs performed by Elvis Presley are their titles, not their lyrics.

The way we treat each other here on Earth will undoubtedly influence how we approach an intelligent alien species. If we can't get it together between ourselves, we're not going to get on well with the neighbors. In the words of Gene Roddenberry, creator of Star Trek.

"If we cannot learn to actually enjoy those small differences between our own kind, here on this planet, then we do not deserve to go out into space and meet the diversity that is almost certainly out there."

There are no easy answers to the dilemma of xenophobia, as is borne out by the social, religious, and cultural clashes that occur in regions like Africa and Central Asia, or in Chicago and London for that matter. After millions of years existing in small tribes, we're hardwired to be accepting of our own clan, and see differences as dangerous/disruptive. These tendencies have been bred into us long before *Homo sapiens* arose as a distinct species on its own, so it's no wonder these attitudes still influence the modern world.

Here in Australia, elections always seem to herald a fresh round of xenophobia as politicians seize on the fear of foreigners, and the bogus concept of "border security" to secure votes (not borders). With 170,000 immigrants arriving each year, a few thousand arriving by boat makes no difference. The only real concern is that migration through unauthorized channels is a dangerous proposition, with people losing their lives on the open sea. But asylum seekers with a genuine case should be accepted regardless of whether they arrive by boat, by plane, or on a sleigh from the North Pole, but fear is seldom rational, and that's the perspective I've tried to capture in *Xenophobia*.

The inspiration for Stella's biology came from the image of a human spinal cord neurosphere.

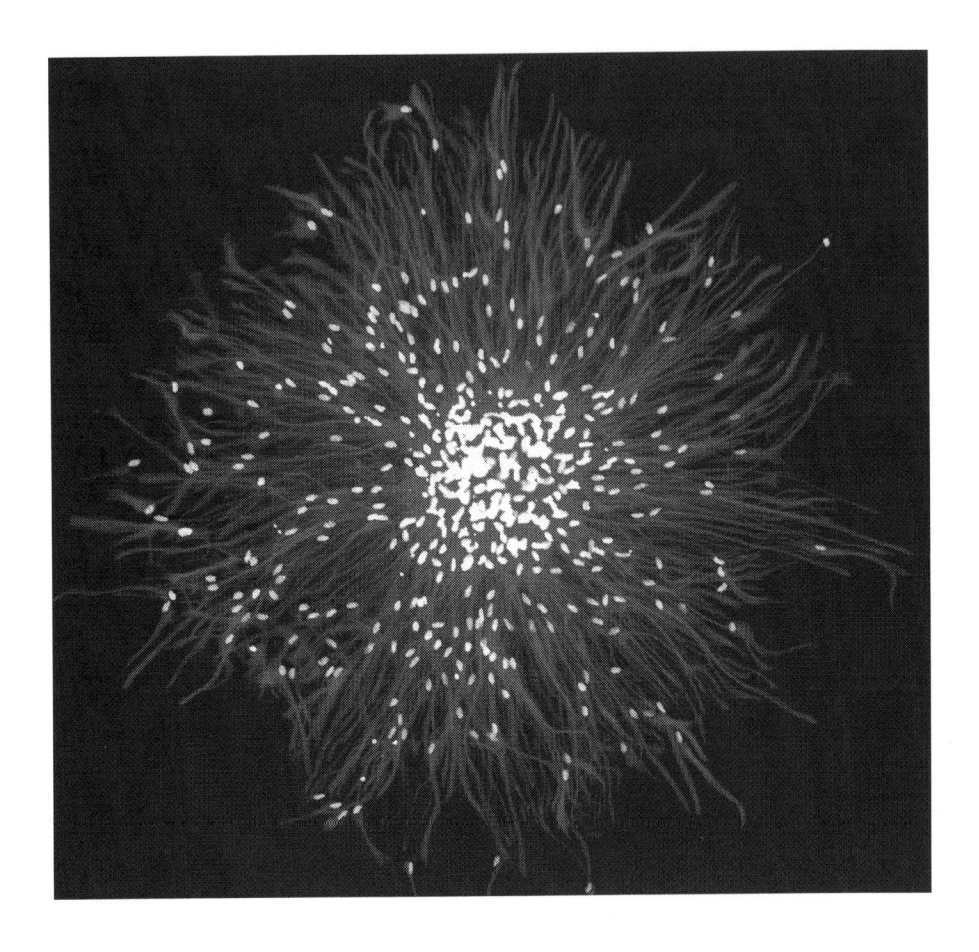

Neurospheres are a culture system composed of free-floating clusters of neural stem cells). We have billions of these in our bodies. This image was taken by Micheal Weible from the Department of Anatomy and Histology, University of Sydney, Australia. (see http://www.cellimagelibrary.org/images/42514)

Any alien visiting our planet would be appalled by how we treat each other. They'd also be shocked by our calloused disregard for life in general. On one hand, they'd be astonished by the interconnectivity of the millions of species alive on Earth, but on the other they'd be saddened by how we've treated the planet. We need to conserve both our dignity and Earth's remarkable diversity.

We live on a unique world. For us, life is commonplace, but as best we understand the universe at large, life is rare—the rarest commodity in thousands of light years. Hollywood has aliens attacking Earth, plundering minerals and sucking water from our oceans, but the reality is, these commodities are found in absurd abundance throughout space. For too long, we've valued gold and silver, diamonds and rubies, but the true riches are found in life itself.

If an intelligent alien species ever does come across Earth, the jewel they will seek is one we can freely share: Life.

From an alien's perspective, it would be fascinating to explore the diversity of life on Earth. They'll want to understand our evolutionary pedigree, and will probably spend far more time in museums and universities than they ever will in the White House. *Take me to your leader? Piffft. Take me to your library!*

Any alien intelligence that reaches Earth is going to be far more interested in our art, music, and literature than they will be in world domination. You won't find them buzzing around in flying saucers, making crop circles, or conducting anal probes, they'll be on archeological excavations, or conducting biodiversity surveys of our jungles and rainforests, or perhaps helping provide drought relief, or assisting us to clean up the plastic that chokes our oceans. You'll find them on paleontological digs and catching butterflies, as life itself is the true treasure of Earth.

Thank you again for supporting independent science fiction.

Feel free to reach out to me on Facebook or Twitter, and join my email list to learn more about my writing. I won't bore you with a list of all my other novels, novellas and short stories, but at last count there's over twenty to choose from if you're interested in reading something else I've written.

Please take the time to leave a review online, as your thoughts on this book are invaluable to other readers.

Peter Cawdron
Brisbane, Australia
March, 2017

OTHER BOOKS BY PETER CAWDRON

Thank you for supporting independent science fiction. You might enjoy the following novels also written by Peter Cawdron.

COLLISION

Tunguska, Roswell, the Bermuda Triangle, the Mary Celeste... For hundreds of years, the danger of collision has been ignored as mere crackpot theories, until now, and now it's too late.

Collision is a short story commission by Vanquish Motion Pictures for development in film and television, and is the first in a series of character-rich, mystery-driven science fiction grounded in science fact.

STARSHIP MINE

James Patterson is a gay accountant living in Keyes, Oklahoma—deep in the Bible Belt—the religious heartland of America. He's also the first person to make contact with an extraterrestrial intelligence seeking to understand our world, and that makes him the most important person on the planet.

FREE FALL

Free Fall first appeared as a short story in The Z Chronicles, and serves as a prequel to What We Left Behind.

Jackson is an astronaut testing a prototype interstellar craft in deep space. When he returns home, there's no one to greet him. Earth has fallen silent. Now he must decide—stay in orbit, watching a dead planet roll slowly by beneath his windows, or land on Earth and fight for life?

WHAT WE LEFT BEHIND & ALL OUR TOMORROWS

Hazel is a regular teenager growing up in an irregular world overrun with zombies. She likes music, perfume, freshly baked muffins, and playing her Xbox—everything that no longer exists in the apocalypse.

Raised in the safety of a commune, Hazel rarely sees Zee anymore, except on those occasions when the soldiers demonstrate the importance of a headshot to the kids.

To her horror, circumstances beyond her control lead her outside the barbed wire fence and into a zombie-infested town.

"Five, Four, Three, Two—count your shots, Haze," she says to herself, firing at the oncoming zombie horde. *"Don't forget to reload."*

ALIEN SPACE TENTACLE PORN

A 1950s hospital. Temporary amnesia. A naked man running through Central Park yelling something about alien space tentacles. Tinfoil, duct tape, and bananas. These are the ingredients for a spectacular romp through a world you never thought possible as aliens reach out and make contact with Earth.

MY SWEET SATAN

The crew of the Copernicus is sent to investigate Bestla, one of the remote moons of Saturn. Bestla has always been an oddball, orbiting Saturn in the wrong direction and at a distance of fifteen million miles, so far away that Saturn appears smaller than Earth's moon in the night sky. Bestla hides a secret. When mapped by an unmanned probe, Bestla awakes and begins transmitting a message, only it's a message no one wants to hear: "*I want to live and die for you, Satan.*"

SILO SAGA: SHADOWS

Shadows is fan fiction set in Hugh Howey's Wool universe as part of the Kindle Worlds Silo Saga.

Life within the silos follows a well-worn pattern passed down through the generations from master to apprentice, caster to shadow. "Don't ask! Don't think! Don't question! Just stay in the shadows." But not everyone is content to follow the past.

THE WORLD OF KURT VONNEGUT: CHILDREN'S CRUSADE

Kurt Vonnegut's masterpiece *Slaughterhouse-Five: The Children's Crusade* explored the fictional life of Billy Pilgrim as he stumbled through the real world devastation of Dresden during World War II. Children's Crusade picks up the story of Billy Pilgrim on the planet of Tralfamadore as Billy and his partner Montana Wildhack struggle to accept life in an alien zoo.

THE MAN WHO REMEMBERED TODAY

The Man Who Remembered Today *is* a novella originally appearing in *From the Indie Side* anthology, highlighting independent science fiction writers from around the world. You can pick up this story as a stand-alone novella or get twelve distinctly unique stories by purchasing *From the Indie Side*.

Kareem wakes with a headache. A bloody bandage wrapped around his head tells him this isn't just another day in the Big Apple. The problem is, he can't remember what happened to him. He can't recall anything from yesterday. The only memories he has are from events that are about to unfold today, and today is no ordinary day.

ANOMALY

Anomaly examines the prospect of an alien intelligence discovering life on Earth.

Humanity's first contact with an alien intelligence is far more radical than anyone has ever dared imagine. The technological gulf between humanity and the alien species is measured in terms of millions of years. The only way to communicate is by using science, but not everyone is so patient with the arrival of an alien spacecraft outside the gates of the United Nations in New York.

THE ROAD TO HELL

The Road to Hell is paved with good intentions.

How do you solve a murder when the victim comes back to life with no memory of recent events?

In the twenty-second century, America struggles to rebuild after the second civil war. Democracy has been suspended while the reconstruction effort lifts the country out of the ruins of conflict. America's fate lies in the hands of a genetically engineered soldier with the ability to move through time.

The Road to Hell deals with a futuristic world and the advent of limited time travel. It explores social issues such as the nature of trust and the conflict between loyalty and honesty.

MONSTERS

Monsters is a dystopian novel exploring the importance of reading. *Monsters* is set against the backdrop of the collapse of civilization.

The fallout from a passing comet contains a biological pathogen, not a virus or a living organism, just a collection of amino acids. But these cause animals to revert to the age of the megafauna, when monsters roamed Earth.

Bruce Dobson is a reader. With the fall of civilization, reading has become outlawed. Superstitions prevail, and readers are persecuted like the witches and wizards of old. Bruce and his son James seek to overturn the prejudices of their day and restore the scientific knowledge central to their survival, but monsters lurk in the dark.

FEEDBACK

Twenty years ago, a UFO crashed into the Yellow Sea off the Korean Peninsula. The only survivor was a young English-speaking child, captured by the North Koreans. Two decades later, a physics student watches his girlfriend disappear before his eyes, abducted from the streets of New York by what appears to be the same UFO.

<u>Feedback</u> will carry you from the desolate, windswept coastline of North Korea to the bustling streets of New York and on into the depths of space as you journey to the outer edge of our solar system looking for answers.

GALACTIC EXPLORATION

<u>Galactic Exploration</u> is a compilation of four closely related science fiction stories following the exploration of the Milky Way by the spaceships Serengeti, Savannah, and The Rift Valley. These three generational starships are piloted by clones and form part of the ongoing search for intelligent extraterrestrial life. With the Serengeti heading out above the plane of the Milky Way, the Savannah exploring the outer reaches of the galaxy, and The Rift Valley investigating possible alien signals within the galactic core, this story examines the Rare Earth Hypothesis from a number of different angles.

This volume contains the novellas *Serengeti*, *Trixie and Me*, *Savannah*, and *War*.

LITTLE GREEN MEN

Little Green Men is a tribute to the works of Philip K. Dick, hailing back to classic science fiction stories of the 1950s.

The crew of the Dei Gratia set down on a frozen planet and are attacked by little green men. Chief Science Officer David Michaels struggles with the impossible situation unfolding around him as the crew members are murdered one by one. With the engines offline and power fading, he races against time to understand this mysterious threat and escape the planet alive.

REVOLUTION

How do you hide state secrets when teenage hacktivists have as much quantum computing power as the government? Alexander Hopkins is about to find out on what should have been an uneventful red-eye flight from Russia. Nothing is what it seems in this heart-pounding short-story from international best selling author Peter Cawdron.

HELLO WORLD

Hello World is a short story set in the same fictional universe as *Alien Space Tentacle Porn*.

Professor Franco Corelli has noticed something unusual. The twitter account @QuestionsLots is harvesting hundreds of millions of tweets each day, but never posting anything. Outwardly, this account only follows one other twitter account—@RealScientists, but in reality it is trawling every post ever made by anyone on this planet. Could it be that @QuestionsLots is not from Earth?

In addition to these stand-alone stories, Peter Cawdron has short stories appearing in:

Legacy Fleet Chronicles

The Telepath Chronicles

The Alien Chronicles

The A.I. Chronicles

The Z Chronicles

Tales of Tinfoil

WELCOME TO THE OCCUPIED STATES OF AMERICA

Seven years after the invasion of the grubs, 110 million Americans have been displaced by the war, with over 50 million dead. Ashley Kelly was crippled by a cluster bomb. While the world crumbled, she spent seven years learning to walk again, and she'll be damned if she's going to lie down for anyone, terrestrial or extra-terrestrial.

Printed in Poland
by Amazon Fulfillment
Poland Sp. z o.o., Wrocław